Praise for *Wink Murder*:

'Jo Nesbo, Stephen King, Patricia Cornwell, Ali Knight'
Independent Books of the Year, 2011

'Knight's promising debut . . . crackles from first page to last . . .
She could be very good indeed.' *Daily Mail*

'A really enjoyable read.' Martina Cole

'A tight-plotted, too-close-for-comfort thriller that races to the
finish . . . pacey and disquieting' *Stylist*

'Knight's knack with plot ensures that everything rattles along
nicely in Nicci French territory.' *Independent on Sunday*

'A fast-paced whodunit.' *Woman and Home*

'A tightly constructed, suspenseful thriller that will have
you turning pages and keep you guessing all the way to the
dramatic conclusion.' *Shotsmag.co.uk*

'A psychological drama that grips from first to last' *Choice*

'A crackling, energetic read, full of action'
Sunday Tasmanian, Australia

'Tightly-plotted, high-pitched psychological thriller . . . what
bright new talent Ali Knight does so successfully, and with a
welcome fresh eye, is broach the great divide between public
and private space.' **** *Daily Mirror*

Also by Ali Knight

Wink Murder

About the author

Ali Knight has worked as a journalist and sub-editor at the BBC, *Guardian* and *Observer* and helped to launch some of the *Daily Mail* and *Evening Standard's* most successful websites. Ali's first novel, *Wink Murder*, was chosen as one of the *Independent*'s Books of the Year 2011. She lives with her family in London.

Visit Ali's website to find out more about her and her psychological thrillers at www.aliknight.co.uk and follow her on Twitter @aliknightauthor

ALI KNIGHT

The First Cut

HODDER

First published in Great Britain in 2012 by Hodder & Stoughton
An Hachette UK company

First published in paperback in 2012

1

A CIP catalogue record for this title is available from the British Library

B format paperback ISBN 978 1 444 72108 9

Printed and bound by CPI Group (UK) Ltd, Croydon, CR0 4YY

Hodder & Stoughton policy is to use papers that are natural, renewable and
recyclable products and made from wood grown in sustainable forests.
The logging and manufacturing processes are expected to conform to the
environmental regulations of the country of origin.

Hodder & Stoughton Ltd
338 Euston Road
London NW1 3BH

www.hodder.co.uk

For Stephen, my partner-in-crime, with all my love

Prologue

Nicky gave a squeal as the lounger by the pool tipped a fraction too far and she landed on her back, feet pointing at the stars.

'Look out, red-wine tummy wash,' Grace giggled from the seat next to her.

Nicky groaned and reached out for a towel to wipe the mess off her T-shirt. 'Urgh, it's everywhere.'

'Where's the bottle opener?' Sam called from the patio behind them. 'Shit!'

They heard vigorous swearing as something smashed on the paving stones.

'We'll never get our deposit back on this place,' Nicky said, staring up at the large house, its stone pale grey against the inky sky beyond.

'Who cares?' Grace murmured. 'We've had such a laugh.'

Nicky smiled to herself. Grace was right, as always. It was one of the most fun holidays any of them could remember. Grace had found the house on the internet and a group of her friends had chipped in to hire it for her thirtieth-birthday celebration. Set in winding roads a short distance from Oxford it had a pool, a pizza oven, a ping-pong table and even a lake. It was much grander than they had expected and their lives seemed shinier and more exciting now they were here. Their August week was also a heatwave, which at times made them think they were in an enchanted foreign land where the sun always shone and evenings were always this balmy.

Grace sighed. 'It's such a shame Greg isn't here. Bloody cameramen.' Nicky caught her friend's eye and they giggled again. Grace was the first one of their crowd to get married. Nicky had resigned herself to the fact that this would mean she would see less of Grace, but Greg's work took him away a lot and if anything she saw Grace more now than when they had been dating.

'God, I'm pissed,' Nicky declared loudly, having to make a big effort to raise her voice as she heard screams from behind the bushes across the lawn. Someone was spraying the hose.

'I need some water,' Grace said, standing and stretching. She strolled to the patio where they had eaten earlier that evening, her black dress billowing out behind her.

'Can you get me my smokes? They're on the table.' Grace turned and smiled, her blonde hair turned almost white from the sun and the chlorine. Greg was lucky to have her, Nicky thought. But then she would think that about any man. Grace was her oldest and closest friend. They were the same age, the same year at school, but Grace had always played the role of older sister, the sensible one, the smarter one. The successful and beautiful one, come to that. Nicky absent-mindedly fluffed her short hair into spikes. She didn't mind. She heard Grace and Sam's low voices. Water. That was Grace all over: a glass of water for every glass of wine. She was cautious and moderate, so unlike herself. She burped and watched a lilo drift in a slow circle in the pool. She'd go for a swim once she'd had her millionth fag of the day—

Her thoughts were obliterated by a shrieking car alarm from the front of the house.

Sam threw her hands in the air in a 'that curse of a bloody car' gesture.

'Whose is that?' Grace shouted.

'Probably mine,' Sam groaned. 'God, where are my keys?' She looked around half-heartedly in the gloom. The noise built in intensity, ricocheting off buildings and walkways. Nicky saw bodies running through the garden in the dark towards the gravel drive on the other side of the house, disconnected shouts and questions almost drowned by the noise. 'My keys, my bloody keys . . .'

'Try the kitchen,' Grace said. 'I think I left my bag on the lawn.' She walked off beyond the pool.

Nicky stayed put. She'd got a lift to the house with Grace so there was nothing she could do. But a few moments later she stood, swaying uncertainly. That damned alarm was bringing on a headache. Another deeper siren joined the first, like a demented electronic chorus. She walked over to the table and found her fags, but there was no lighter. The spilled drink on her T-shirt was sticky; she felt hot and bothered. She looked back at the pool, the underwater lighting making the water glow a sickly green. A much better idea came to her. She walked across the lawn and crouched down by the row of thick bushes between the lake and the house and enjoyed a wee in the great outdoors – well, a wee in the manicured Cotswolds. She carried on to the lake. The alarms faded a little. She stood on the small wooden jetty and stripped down to her bikini, then sat and let her legs swish lazily in the coldness. It was much darker out here; the lights from the house and garden didn't encroach this far. The water slap-slapped against the wood as she lowered herself into the inky water, too deep to feel the bottom, and struck out for the middle.

Nicky loved swimming at night. She liked the feel of water caressing her skin, the way sounds penetrated further and echoed longer. A muddy lake floor didn't make her cringe, like it did to Sam; she enjoyed the squishy sludge between her toes. She dunked her head and swam a few breaststrokes below the surface, then emerged and lay on her back, kicking gently.

The car alarm stopped and silence dropped around her like a heavy curtain. She heard a splash.

'Hello?' she called out instinctively, but no one answered.

It was too dark to see the edge of the lake and it took her a few strokes to swim close enough to make out the blurry jetty and the bank. 'Are you in? It's lovely,' she called.

There was no answer.

Tossers, she muttered to herself, sober now and ready to get out. Damn, she didn't have a towel. Grace would have said that was just like her, starting something without being fully prepared. It would be a cold walk back to the house. She swam for the bank and saw an indistinct, dark shape floating in the water. For an instant she thought it was a tree trunk, and then she smiled. It was the giant plastic crocodile from the pool. Perfect. She reached out to jump on it and wrestle like she was an Aussie adventurer lost in Arnhem Land, taking on the fourteen-footer in a battle of life and death . . .

It was too solid. And it rolled.

Nicky's weight took her and the object under the water. She was caught sharply unawares and scrambled to get back to the surface. She began to struggle as fronds of weed became entangled round her neck, touching her arms and face with tickly, unnerving edges. She broke the surface with a strangled groan as the object pitched this way and that with her splashes. It was so dark she couldn't see the thing that still floated in front of her. A terrible panic took hold. The car alarm started again, wailing with renewed force. She scolded herself for getting the jitters and forced herself to put out her hand and make the shape real, understandable and unthreatening. The fronds brushed her hand again.

This time she knew for sure it was hair.

Nicky screamed as the moon came out from behind a cloud and bathed everything in a pale shimmer. The hair was long; the body floating face down in the lake wore a black dress. She screamed much louder, half sinking with the effort as she was unable to touch the bottom. She grabbed Grace and tried to turn her, shouting incoherently. She knew she was in a desperate race against time, that every second in the water pulled Grace further away from life. With ungainly, struggling strokes she fought for the bank and finally managed to touch the soft lake floor. With the extra traction she dragged Grace, still face down, towards the edge, desperate to get her the right way up, to stop her drowning, but Grace's unconscious body made her too heavy.

Nicky shouted to be saved, hollering for the big boys in the house to come and help her. She flailed in the reeds, the car alarm shrieking unhindered, blocking the sound of her own desperate cries. She got both feet on the bank then put her hands under her best friend's armpits and little by little managed to pull her from the lake, Grace half on top of her like a drunken lover. Nicky dragged her a few feet along the grass to where it was flat and dropped to her knees, turning Grace's body by yanking at her shoulders. Her white hair was a dark halo round her head, the moonlight washing colours black or midnight blue. Only the wedding ring on her lifeless finger glinted dully. Nicky bent down, ready and pumped to give her the kiss of life, but the moon illuminated only the black stain of Grace's blood, spreading relentlessly across her chest. Her neck had been slashed from ear to ear.

Sam had finally found her keys in her upturned bag next to the cooker and had tiptoed in a painful, bare-footed hobble across the spiky gravel of the drive. After much swearing and jabbing at her key fob she had got her car to stop making that insane racket, and had turned to go back to the pool and her bottle of beer. The noise that surrounded her, carrying over the rural silence, almost froze her blood. The screams couldn't be coming from a human being. No one could possibly be suffering that much.

I

Nicky tried to ignore the man poking her in the arse with his bag as she watched the woman in front try to stuff a bag the size of a fridge in the overhead locker. Why were they called lockers anyway? They fell open if you hit turbulence, and – with the pelting rain outside that they were still trying to shake off after the ungainly sprint across the tarmac – their trip home was bound to feature a lot of that. She hoped she wasn't the one to get bonked on the head by the leg of *jamon* bought in a fit of love for all things Spanish at duty-free.

'Move along the aisle and take your seats, please,' said a stewardess with an accent it was impossible to place – Moldova? Latvia? The man behind huffed as Nicky waited for the woman to finish pushing and shoving. They didn't move an inch. The plane was filling up from the back door. She saw passengers surging forward, filling the window seats she wanted for herself. Finally the woman turned and did the squat-lean-hunch manoeuvre to get out of the way and Nicky slid past, eyes locked on the row where she would perform her own personal contortions to get into the doll-sized seats. Budget air travel was a blast.

'You can't sit here,' a stern woman in the Day-Glo uniform of the airline said, her blood-red nails jabbing at the row Nicky had her eyes on.

'Wing exit?' Nicky asked.

'You can't sit here,' was the reply. Nicky wasn't going to argue. She wondered if the stewardess was a robot, programmed with only three sentences: 'You can't sit here', which she'd already heard, 'No', and 'That'll be ten euros' (without a please). She moved down the plane, her case bumping on the headrests, and began to stuff her own bag, the size of a cooker, into the locker.

'Here, let me help.' A broad and hairless hand reached out for the case and gave it a confident shove. The hand and hers managed to squeeze it into the unforgiving space and slam the door shut on it, like it was a tawdry secret they wanted to forget. 'After you,' she heard the man say to her neck. Nicky didn't hesitate. She shuffled towards the window without even looking round. To hell with manners, it was everyone for themselves in here. She heard the squeak of the plastic beneath her thighs.

'Thanks.' She said it to the graphic of a woman crawling along a smoke-filled cabin, which was stuck to the seat back in front of her. They'd taken away the pocket that used to contain a dog-eared magazine, the sick bags and a piece of crinkly orange peel. She glanced over at the man, now sitting in the aisle seat.

'We have a full flight today, so please use all available seats,' the tannoy announced. The man looked over sheepishly and Nicky got her first proper look at him as he moved to the next seat along. She fought the desire to grin stupidly. Life always did that to her: stunned her with its ability to spring surprises when she was least expecting them – not all of them pleasant. The man sliding over the armrest was gorgeous, just peachy. He had dark hair that gleamed like a seal's pelt, a strong profile and brown eyes that with one glance managed to suggest fun and a bit of danger. And he was young. Nicky saw a small knitted braid of something round his wrist. She had a sudden flashback to a holiday in Santorini with Grace – another lifetime ago – and dropped his age to the early twenties.

'Sorry.' He shrugged and fidgeted, glancing at her with one dark eyebrow raised. He seemed absurdly big for the seat, his shoulders pushing over the boundary into her space.

'I think the owner of this airline is a dwarf.'

He turned to her fully now. 'He's keen to punish anyone over five foot six.'

'Too selective. Anyone with a stomach. Have you tried the food?'

'Of course. Cost me ten euros for a burger.'

Nicky tried to remember when she had last seen a smile that good. Probably not since she'd been married. Stop it, she told herself sternly. Naughty Wife was rearing her head. She watched him punching the recline button on his seat.

'They'll be over in a flash to tell you to sit upright.'

He leaned towards her conspiratorially. 'I like breaking the rules.'

She felt a flutter of excitement across her stomach. He was forward and daring and Nicky found herself hoping that a weekend trying to breathe life into a dying friendship could be redeemed with a little flirtation on the home leg. After all, where was the harm?

He shuffled about trying to locate the seatbelt ends. 'I think this bit's yours.' He held up the strap with the metal buckle for her. His gesture felt loaded with possibilities. A grin formed on her face and started to meander across her cheeks.

A forceful gust of rain splattered the plastic window and they both stared out for a moment. 'Typical. I came to Spain in the worst rainstorm for two years.'

He blew air out of his cheeks. 'Have a good time?'

Nicky actually considered this question. 'No.' She gave a little laugh. 'You know, I really didn't have a very good time.' Those eyebrows shot towards his hairline again. 'Sorry, sorry, I—'

He interrupted her. 'Forgive me, I'm Adam.' He held out his hand and she shook it.

'Nicky. What should I forgive you for?'

'Because I'm asking you questions and you don't even know my name.' Adam was distracted by a man slumping down in the aisle seat. They all shifted and rearranged themselves. Adam's elbow slid over to her side of the armrest. 'So, what went wrong in Spain?'

She wondered where he'd acquired his manners and his confidence. Private school, maybe even boarding school? She reminded herself that he wasn't long out of whichever institution it was.

She waved her hand dismissively, thinking: don't complain, don't carp about life. Stay positive. After all, every day is precious. She'd learned that the hardest way possible. She had a running total in her head of the number of days she'd lived without Grace. Weeks would sometimes go by and she wouldn't think about that total, but she could always recall it. When would that internal counter stop marking the death of her best friend?

Nicky fiddled with her shoulder-length hair. 'I guess I realize that I've grown apart from someone I used to be close to.' The flight attendant slammed shut the plane door and pinned an orange strip of material across the window. Nicky was unsure how that tiny piece of material would help in an emergency. She saw Adam was watching her intently with those dark eyes. He seemed to be really interested in what she was saying. Nicky wondered with a jolt of loss whether she used to be like this all those years ago – curious, excited by the new.

'Go on.'

Nicky took a deep breath. 'I went to see an old friend for

the weekend. She's married with two kids and living in Bilbao. We had absolutely nothing in common any more. Her interests were all about her kids; mine lie elsewhere. And that was kind of that.' How simple our complex stories can be made to sound, Nicky thought. Sam. The legendary party girl – until *that* night. Their relationship had not survived Grace's death. That tragedy had changed them all in different ways. Sam had run away to Spain, married a doctor, become teetotal. Nicky envied Sam's ability to escape her past, to create a new identity. She would never be able to do the same. Grace was the sister she never had. Their relationship had withstood the teenage years, separation at university, a string of boyfriends and periods of work overseas, yet had still held strong, through Grace's marriage to Greg and beyond. They had been blessed with an unshakeable bond and they had blithely assumed it would go on like that for ever, right up to the same old people's home when their husbands were long dead and their children grown, still gossiping, still laughing, still friends.

How wrong they were.

Grace had never seen past her thirtieth birthday. Nicky felt the familiar rage build in her chest and pushed her knees against the plastic seat in front. She refocused on Adam, who was looking at her, waiting. 'What were you doing in Spain?'

'Seeing my friend Davide.' He paused. 'So what do you do for a living, Nicky?'

'I write obituaries, for my sins.'

'Wow! That sounds really great!'

Nicky couldn't resist a smile. He was so young! So enthusiastic! So unlike the jaded and cynical person she had become, her heart crusted over with grief and questions that would never be answered. 'I like it, which is a bit of luck since I do it every day. I'd say having done what you liked is pretty high up the list of people's wishes at the end.'

Adam leaned back into his seat. 'It's funny how people only sum up their life at the end of it. How they unburden themselves as it all draws to a close. My aunt is dying, basically.'

'I'm sorry.' She meant it. She knew she didn't have a monopoly on suffering or grief, though it sometimes felt like it.

He waved her sympathy away. 'She's led an interesting life. Maybe that's all we can ask for. But when she's lucid she spends her time looking back and she seems so full of regret. The past haunts her.' He shook his head. 'I think it's important throughout your life to close the chapters as you go.'

Nicky considered this. It would be a mistake to think that just because he was young he was naive. She put her hands in her lap and looked out of the window. *Closure.* Such an American word, but, like a lot of Yank ideas, catching. Her wedding ring was cold against her fingers. A lack of closure on Grace's death was causing big problems in her marriage.

She turned back to him as they taxied to the end of the runway. 'So, what do you do?'

'Oh . . .' He tailed off. 'You know how it is with young people today. Not in education, not in training.' He flashed her a devastating smile. 'I went to circus school for a while. Learned to fly trapeze, juggle, that kind of thing.'

Their conversation was interrupted as the roar began underneath them and they were sucked back against the seats. Nicky found take-off a thrill.

She heard Adam mutter a low 'Christ.'

She saw his hands were white with the effort of gripping the armrests. 'Flying not your thing?'

'No, no, it's not that. I'm claustrophobic. I don't like crowds. Being all thrust up against other people.' He shuddered a little.

The plane eased to horizontal as they left the ground.

'Take-off inevitably makes me think of what it would be like to crash-land with all this lot right around you.' He cocked his head to indicate front and back. He gave an embarrassed laugh.

'At least if you die you know you don't go alone.'

'Shoulder to shoulder with your fellow passengers.' He groaned.

'They say it's the safest form of travel.'

'That doesn't help, I'm afraid. My fear's not rational. Like so much of what we do, it's irrational. I wonder if it's the loss of control I can't stand. Maybe I'm a control freak.'

'Your fate in someone else's hands.'

He cocked the eyebrow at her again. 'Indeed. Someone who's been on a three-day bender with five Thai prostitutes and chooses landing time to catch up on his lost sleep.'

'You know, I once read an article about plane crashes, which claimed that the reason most people die is that they assume they're going to die on impact, and so they don't make the effort to get out. They passively await their fate.' He was nodding, looking at her intently as she spoke. He had dark hair that sat up in a cute tuft at the front and he looked like he was listening to a private joke. 'The ones who fight, survive.'

'Would you be like that?'

'You bet! I think at that moment all my worst character traits would come out. I'd be climbing over people to escape, chewing off limbs.'

Now it was his turn to laugh. She saw more of those perfect teeth and his eyes that crinkled up at the corners. The lines disappeared the moment he stopped, his skin with its lovely texture springing back to its correct shape instantly.

'Remind me not to be in front of you come the first day of the sales.'

Good-looking, and fun too. Life is for living, Nicky thought.

God, would she fight, fight for every day that was afforded her. Had Grace fought? She shuddered. They told her the death was quick, that she was dead before she hit the water, but there was still so much they didn't know. Nicky would be trapped for ever in the purgatory of what ifs and why.

'You can rest assured I'd get to the widescreen TV before you.' She was flirting and she didn't care.

Adam threw his hands out in a gallant gesture of defeat. 'It's all yours, Nicky, all yours.' He paused. 'At least you're honest. I like to think I'd be the hero, running across the tarmac with twin babies under my arms, saving them from the big explosion behind me.' He narrowed his eyes and looked at her and she felt the shards of physical attraction pierce her. 'The gap between our hopes for ourselves and the reality is pretty big. We'd all love to be a hero, but in the end we probably just save ourselves.' Adam leaned towards her. 'Gosh, this is a DMC.'

'A what?'

'A deep and meaningful conversation.' Nicky laughed. 'You know something else? They say that twenty per cent of all couples meet on a plane.'

Nicky gave him a look of mock horror. 'That is *not* true.'

Adam continued. 'Sitting side by side for hours, far from home. You can think about the big things in life – and have a drink.' They both looked towards the galley where an air steward was pulling out the drinks trolley. 'Beer or wine? Plain or salted peanuts?'

When they landed the sun was shining, the robot from Bulgaria was smiling and no one shoved her. She floated down the plane steps on warm good feeling and walked across the tarmac with a swagger. Luton's beautiful, she thought. The customs channel was as far as they could go together, because beyond that she was headed for the car park and he to the train. She kept their goodbye light as they formally shook hands before she continued across the concourse. She couldn't resist turning round and there he was, staring after her as she'd suspected he would be. They smiled at each other and for a glorious moment she saw her younger, carefree self burst through the shell she had erected around herself in the aftermath of Grace's murder. Thank you, Adam, she said to herself.

2

'Why is it always the ugliest clothes that are locked up?' Greg was looking at a leather jacket with long tassels dangling from the arms, and trying to pull it off the hanger. Nicky watched him trace his hand along the white security wire that ran away into the depths of the rail.

She smiled, feeling the ruffles on the front of a blouse. 'You should see the handbag section.'

'No, thanks.' They weaved past some animal-print accessories balanced on a dead-tree display. 'Get off me, you maniac!' Nicky whirled round to see Greg wrestling with a leopard-print scarf.

She started giggling. 'I've missed you.'

He came up behind her and put his arms tightly round her, resting his chin on her neck. 'I've missed you too.' They stayed just so for a long moment, neither of them wanting to move, until Greg stood up straight and looked about. 'Which floor are we on? Haven't we been through this section before?'

She loved days like this with Greg, drifting around town, just the two of them. He'd come back from working in LA two days ago and they were fitting back together after his long absence. In a few days he would be gone again, forging his burgeoning career in the States, but for now he was here and she was enjoying his company.

'Come on, I want to buy you something fabulous. Maybe once we've paid the exit signs will reappear, as if by magic.'

They walked to a section full of dresses and started picking items out.

'Can I be of any help here?' The sales assistant's smile was an invitation to splurge.

'You betcha,' replied Greg, dumping a pile of dresses in her hands. 'She needs the changing room.' Greg was blond, tall and loud. A bit like herself, she knew. He had a strong chin, blue eyes and an imposing physical presence that was hard to ignore for women and men alike. Life just seemed more fun with Greg. She shut the curtain behind her and changed into a blue dress.

She came out onto the shop floor. The sales assistant was laughing at something Greg was saying. He turned towards her, his face expectant. She shook her head, looking down at the dress. It wasn't right; it was too sack-like and came across as sad. She swished away behind the curtain and picked up a red patterned shift.

Six months after Grace's death Nicky started dating Greg. Grief bends and twists relationships into unrecognizable shapes. They were both in mourning and they leaned on each other, then one day that leaning turned into something more physical. A lot more physical. She was at pains to tell people it had not been planned or even ever thought about when Grace was alive. When Nicky first met Greg he was simply the man that Grace loved, a filmmaker who lived half his life in London and half abroad, chasing his dreams. He was full of talent and ambition and such self-belief that no one would bet against him succeeding. Grace already owned and ran a successful gastropub, which she had started with some money from her dad. They fell in love, he proposed and she accepted. They got married and then a few months later, with Grace's thirtieth looming, Nicky had started trying to persuade Grace to celebrate her birthday properly. They would all have a laugh and it would be a great holiday, a way to enjoy herself when Greg was away.

Nicky stared at herself in the changing-room mirror. She didn't see any of those former friends now. The recriminations and the suspicions killed their relationships. The media went mad for the story, but the police couldn't solve it. No one was ever charged; there was no trial. The picture might have been confused, but several clear facts stood out: Grace was killed before she ended up in the water, and a blood trail was found leading away from the lake and the house, probably to a car. The alarm was likely to have been set off by the killer, which meant no one heard it leave.

Nicky told people that their beginning had been easy. She knew that sounded absurd, considering the circumstances, but it was easy to fall in love when they had a tragedy that united them. Life seemed precious, fate was cruel and time felt short. She had fallen in love hard and fast, and so had he. It was as if by being together they could keep Grace alive. And that had worked beautifully for eighteen months – right up until they were married. It was what came afterwards that was the problem. It was then that it had all changed.

Greg poked his head round the curtain and looked her up and down. 'God, you look great in that. Come here.' He pulled her to him across the litter of clothes on the floor and gave her a kiss. 'Let's buy it and go get some lunch. I'm starving.'

They rode the escalator to the ground floor and skirted hats, then Greg paused by the flower shop. 'I'm going to buy a notebook,' Nicky said. 'I'll see you here in a minute.'

Greg nodded as she headed off to the stationery department, where she spent some time deciding between a green and a yellow patterned notebook. She paid and came back to the florist's, but couldn't see Greg. After standing for a while looking through the crowds of people she began to circle out to find him. She went past designer bags then came to the beauty department and saw his broad back at a counter. A woman so young she looked like she'd only just hatched was standing opposite him, behind a glass counter. Nicky hung back for a moment to see if Greg was buying her a surprise. She didn't want to spoil it. The woman leaned across to Greg and touched him on the arm. Nicky watched as her glossy lips shrank from a smile into a look of disquiet.

'Sir, are you OK?'

Nicky started towards her husband as a bunch of flowers slipped from his hand and landed on the floor. The woman had rounded the display now, unsure whether to come closer. Nicky watched Greg slump forward on the counter. She put her hand out to him, wondering if he was going to faint. His face was white, his eyes closed. 'Greg, what's the matter?'

He didn't answer. He looked as if he hadn't heard her, didn't even realize she was there. It took her a moment to see that he held something in his hand which the assistant was trying to take from his grasp. It was a bottle of perfume.

'I was showing him this reissue of an old classic. He smelled it and then he . . . he went like this.' She was Australian, her voice low and concerned.

'Greg?'

He opened his eyes with what looked like a great effort and straightened up. 'I'm fine, I'm fine.'

'You don't look fine.'

The shop assistant smiled. 'Perfume has a very powerful ability to conjure emotion and memories. You know, research shows that once a woman finds a perfume her partner likes, she tends to wear it for years. Maybe this will become your signature scent!' She was in selling mode, trotting out the company guff.

Nicky rubbed Greg across the shoulder. 'It's OK, honey, it's OK,' she said quietly.

Memories. They had both been ambushed at different times by the past, by objects that connected to Grace. Greg didn't look at her but walked off towards the aisles of men's underwear.

Nicky picked up the bottle and felt the cold weight in her palm. She steeled herself, knowing where she would be transported when she put the bottle to her nose. She sniffed the tiny black hole and frowned. A distinct, lemony fragrance hit her, but Grace did not come flooding back. This was not something she had ever worn; it wasn't her perfume. 'Greg?'

She found him holding a display stand, rubbing his forehead.

'What was that all about?'

He smiled, keen to move on. 'Nothing, nothing at all.'

'*That* was nothing?' They stared at each other in silence. 'Let me in, Greg.'

He laughed but it was without humour. 'It's nothing, honestly. Jet lag, that's all.' He strode away, closing off any chance of talking about what had happened.

She was about to follow and have it out with him, when the Australian assistant called out, 'Madam, madam! He's left the flowers.'

Nicky turned back into the beauty section as the woman held out the delicately wrapped bouquet. Nicky took it, but it felt like a consolation prize.

3

The doorbell rang as Nicky was sieving hot tomatoes and swearing. She'd decided to cook a meal for Greg's family and, with hope triumphing over experience, had chosen a complicated recipe that was slowly and painfully turning into a disaster. Everything was taking longer than she'd anticipated, allowing her to drink more and care less about the food.

'Greg, can you get it?'

She was answered by a chorus of voices advancing on the kitchen. She burned her fingers on the tomatoes as Greg's mother, Margaret, loomed in for a kiss and a hug. Arthur came over and pinched her cheek and then proceeded to demand the bottle opener. Greg's sister, Liz, brought up the rear of the party with her son, Dan, who sloped in last. Dan had gelled his hair so that it stood up in stiff peaks. A smell that Nicky assumed was meant to imply mountain freshness but screamed 'awkward teen approaching' wafted towards her. She half began to put her hand out to try to ruffle his hair, and then realized he'd get tomato in those peaks.

'Whatever are you doing?' Liz asked, sniffing with implied disapproval. Nicky gave up sieving and slopped the tomatoes back into the saucepan. How predictable: Liz had begun sniping before she'd even sat down.

'You really don't have to make such an effort, love,' Margaret added, peering unconvinced into a pan. Margaret approached any stove as if it was a deeply untrustworthy foreigner that would rob her sooner than it would boil eggs.

Her only interactions with such an implement over the years had been to open the oven door and slam in the frozen item before retreating across the room, poised for fight or flight. To see Nicky actually leaning against it with gas rings burning was, for Margaret, as wondrous as watching a pagan ritual.

'I like making an effort . . .' she began, but was stopped by Greg's large hand on the back of her neck, massaging.

'You OK, babes?'

She wanted to shout 'No!', but gave a thin smile instead. She wished they had the evening alone, that he hadn't invited them. The Petersons were a herd, moving like wildebeest over the plain, stampeding over to their house whenever Greg put in an appearance. His trip home was far too short; they'd hardly had any time alone and he was going again in two days. She wanted him to herself, and felt guilty about it.

She heard Arthur cheer as he pulled a cork from a bottle of red wine.

She stuck on a smile as Liz eyed them coolly from the corner sofa, taking small slurps of wine. 'How long you back for, Greg?'

'Four days. It's a flying visit.'

'Hope you're not getting too lonely, Nics.' Nicky slid a knife through the cellophane on a packet of cod fillets and didn't answer. Liz leaned back into the cushions, her short hair a defiant grey that she refused to dye, even though Margaret was always nagging her to. Nicky watched her narrow her eyes at the garden, as though the trees and shrubs were an advancing enemy. Their kitchen was large, their house in a grand avenue in north London. Liz the divorcee had to make a tortuous journey from a terrace in south London to see them. She was a social worker whose shift pattern gave her this weekend off. Nicky wished she was saving children today. 'Here in this big fancy house all by yourself.'

'Christ, Liz, give it a rest!' Greg snapped.

Liz smiled knowingly at Nicky as she took another slurp. Nicky picked up the fillets and felt the slime spread across her fingertips. Liz liked to pick at scabs, she liked to play dirty – and, looked at a certain way, there was dirt in abundance.

Nicky thought that having survived Grace's death, she was strong enough to withstand anything, but other people's reactions to her altered relationship with Greg were hard to take. Liz had simply given her that awful, secret smile of hers, like a shark about to attack. Grace's brother had been more straightforward – he came round to the house threatening to hurt Greg and Nicky. Grace's father no longer spoke to them. That cut to the heart, but it was to be expected. Grief killed relationships; it was death's last laugh.

But Nicky never wavered in her belief that Grace would have been happy for them. And Nicky felt it was her duty as Grace's best friend to quell the rumours, the vicious slurs, the insinuations that Greg was responsible.

He was the grieving husband, the widower. He might have been thousands of miles away when it happened but, as the husband, Greg was automatically one of the prime suspects. The police had grilled him, of course, over and over again, about his relationship with Grace and about the money. Grace's death made him a rich man. He'd sold Grace's gastropub – what else could he do? Yes, he said defensively, he'd made a lot of money from the property boom, but Grace was gone and it wasn't his line of work. Nicky wondered to what extent his subsequent success as a director of photography on big-budget films, his drive and ambition, his workaholic tendencies, were based on a need to prove the doubters wrong, to show that he wasn't someone who lived off a dead wife's money.

The twists of fate were cruel, Nicky believed – she had not only lost Grace, she had lost Grace's family too, given them up for Greg. Now, five years down the line, she occasionally wondered if he was worth it. She drummed her fingers on the worktop, the old desire for a calming cigarette nagging at her. She'd quit smoking after Grace's murder in a desire to try to cleanse herself and start anew, but old habits were hard to break.

She watched Liz kick her shoes off and yawn, put her stockinged feet on the ottoman and lounge on the sofa in the house Greg had bought with Grace's fortune.

She suddenly felt a fire of defensiveness for Greg and anger at the doubters, at those who hadn't believed him. She was the one who'd been woken night after night by him thrashing this way and that in the bed, gripped by the night terrors. She was the one who'd wiped away the tears of the grieving widower.

'Don't do any for Dan. He won't touch it,' Liz shouted as Nicky began frying the fish.

Margaret was inviting her out to the house in Essex, telling her she had a new swinging garden seat, perfect for the hot weather. Nicky answered in distracted, half-finished sentences. The cod skin was sticking; it wasn't going to work well.

The fish spat angrily at her from the pan. 'Do you need to turn the heat down?' Greg asked, moving across to the stove. She felt his hand on her bum. Bit busy now, she thought, irritation beginning to bloom inside. Greg was confusing; some moments he loved her with an intensity that seemed uncontrollable, and at other times he was cold and unresponsive, as if she'd done something wrong but she never knew what. This might happen to all couples forced apart for too long, but truth be told, she felt abandoned.

Margaret made a fuss of laying the table while Liz argued with Dan about putting his DS away.

Nicky glanced over at Greg as he started chopping parsley with an ostentatiously large knife.

'Be careful with that knife, Greg,' Margaret counselled. 'It looks ever so sharp.'

Greg speeded up his action and then threw the knife in the air, catching it by the handle on its way back down to the floor. Margaret gave a small scream. 'Oh, in moments like this I ask myself, what would Bruce Willis do?'

Liz rolled her eyes. 'Be serious.'

'Bruce is always deadly serious, fighting for his family.'

'You ever met Bruce Willis?' Dan asked hopefully, attracted to the glamour of his uncle's job.

Greg turned to Dan conspiratorially as he tipped the parsley over the fish fillets and Nicky brought the dish to the table. 'Mr Willis to you. I've met him a couple of times. Know something, Danno? He once said something important to me.' Greg paused and Nicky saw Dan's eyes widen in antici-pation. 'He said: "Yippee-ki-yay, Yippee-ki-yay."'

'Don't you mean "Yippee-ki-yay, motherfucker!"?' Dan shouted. Liz gave her son a stare that would have shrivelled spring bulbs.

'Put it there, Danno!' Greg high-fived his nephew. 'One day you should come to Hollywood with me. We'll have fun.'

Fourteen-year-old Dan turned to his mum. 'Can I really go one day?'

'We'll see.' Liz gave her brother a look that Nicky couldn't decipher. Liz sniped at Greg but she adored him, that much was clear. Nicky tuned back into the conversation.

Margaret was mid-flow as they sat down and began raiding the serving dishes on the table. 'I'm only your mum, dear, and I'm resigned to never seeing you, but with Nicky it's a different story. You need to look after your wife, Greg, work out what's important.' She waved her fork uneasily.

'Mum, with all due respect, that's something for Nics and me to talk about.'

'Those that play together, stay together,' Arthur added.

'Isn't it pray?' said Liz.

'You get my point.'

They were talking about her as if she wasn't there. It was a Peterson family trait.

'If you're away too long it just leads to fights—'

'Bruce Willis is always fighting someone,' Dan interjected as he bit into a huge piece of fish. Nicky hoped with petty pleasure that Liz had noticed.

'No, Danno, he's fighting *for* someone,' added Greg. 'Usually his family.' He glanced at Nicky but looked quickly away. Nicky put her hands in her lap as the Petersons chomped in double-quick time through the meal she had spent ages creating. Greg was slippery. If he was put on the spot he tended to revert to irony and jokes to avoid having to confront what was being asked of him. 'So at this moment I wonder what would Bruce Willis do? In a time of crisis, how would Bruce react?'

'He'd kill someone!' Dan shouted.

Nicky heard Liz drop her fork on the floor.

She put her head in her hands and was hit by a waft of something unpleasant on her fingers. The house would smell of fish for days afterwards as she tried to scrub away the lingering bad smells.

4

Nicky should have taken the day off work. Greg was leaving that evening and he wouldn't be back for ten weeks, but the desk was two down – Bobby was off with stress and Mike had been handed the black bin liner just a week ago – and she needed to show her face. She didn't want to lose her job.

She watched a man in overalls carry a dead yukka out of the editor's office. I should write the obituary for this whole industry, she thought, as Maria plonked a flat white on her desk, from Costa Coffee on the ground floor.

'Good riddance,' muttered Maria as they watched their former boss's boxes being stacked on a trolley.

'Be careful what you wish for,' Nicky replied.

'I've given up wishing for anything,' Maria said. 'That way I can't be constantly disappointed.'

'You'd think in this job we'd gain a sense of perspective on life – and death,' Nicky said.

'Perspective is for fools,' Maria said, leaning forward over the desk. 'Now, how was your shagathon?'

Nicky made a face and she caught Maria looking at her. There was a pause.

'You know, whenever I ask you about Greg, you give me this tragic look.'

'He's leaving tonight.'

'I already know that.'

Maria was a good journalist: persistent and nobody's fool.

Nicky squirmed. She fiddled uselessly with the corner of a piece of paper. 'He's away so much, it pisses me off.'

'So move to LA, go freelance, get knocked up – you've got options.'

Nicky sighed. She loved Maria. She was relentlessly upbeat about other people's options and pessimistic about her own. What she couldn't tell Maria was that she was frozen. She suspected that if she announced to Greg she was moving to California, he would suddenly find an excuse to be working in China. It wasn't the distance, it was the intention. Not for the first time Nicky wondered if theirs was a love that had been born of something that was fundamentally wrong and so wasn't sustainable.

Maria reached over the computers and wiped a Post-it down on her desk. 'This guy's phoned twice already this morning.'

It took Nicky a moment to place the name – it was Adam from the plane. She'd forgotten about him. Sort of. 'Did he say what it was about?'

'No.'

She felt Maria's eyes boring into her as she picked up the phone, but there was no connection to the mobile number.

'Another option is to have an affair,' Maria said slyly.

Nicky didn't answer. She felt a blush creeping across her cheeks.

'Well, well, you are a one,' Maria said quietly to her computer screen and Nicky threw the plastic top of her coffee cup at her.

She looked up to see Bruton, the news editor, advancing across the office towards them. Advancing was the right word, Nicky thought. It applied to glaciers as they travelled down valleys and perfectly described the speed Bruton adopted in the office. She had never seen him rush, not even when the Twin Towers collapsed, but he was sharp and quick and it was a mistake to equate his physical slowness with a lack of mental agility. Bruton's movement petered out when he eventually came alongside them.

'What we got today?' His voice was a truck emptying gravel.

'There's a former chancellor of Durham Univ—'

He interrupted Maria. 'Boring. Don't lead with that.'

Nicky picked up the reins. 'We've got an actress in Ealing comedies who had an affair with a former president—'

'Picture?'

'It's sexy and good enough quality to run big.' He nodded, then pulled a white plastic tube from his trouser pocket and sucked deeply on it. Nicky continued. 'There's a climber who scaled Everest and invented a crampon that—'

'No. The editor's been sacked. We don't have to indulge his interests any more.'

'Bruton, it looks like you're smoking a tampon applicator,' Maria said.

Bruton took the piece of white plastic from his lips and stared at it uselessly. He coughed and a sound like stones rattling in a bag hit them. He stared with disappointment at the substitute cigarette; it wasn't giving him the hit he needed. He pointed the tampon applicator at the empty editor's office. 'Word is we're going downmarket.' Maria gave a sarcastic hurrah. 'That means more affairs, more scandal and more dead women.'

'So it's goodbye to civil servants,' Nicky added. And at that they all cheered before Bruton was ambushed by a fit of coughing so severe Nicky felt concerned enough to get out of her seat and pat him on the back.

Nicky loved her job and had happily done it for years. She knew there were journalists who looked down on obituaries, thought of them as pages to flick through on your way to the sport. There was also no opportunity to have your name attached to what you wrote; an obituary belonged to the deceased and no one else. 'There'll be no promotion into a column from this desk,' Maria sometimes said. Nicky wasn't going to get a colour headshot in the paper any time soon; wasn't going to get the smallest taste of a low-grade kind of celebrity. That suited her just fine. She did wonder, however, being surrounded by death so much, what would be written in her own obituary. Not much. In that she was just like millions of others, living out her small and incon-sequential life. Only a tiny number, Nicky knew, ever made an impact, ever did things important enough to be written about, to have their details stored on electronic files, the story of their lives written before that life was over. For everyone else it was a case of one day you're here, and then you're gone; cancer or an accident or finally old age ends it with hardly a ripple. Good and bad deaths, but still a life to sum up. She took a sip of coffee. And then there was Grace, defined not by her life, but by the way she died; remembered for not having been served by justice.

'You look miles away,' Maria said, twisting a pen around in her hair and poking it into the middle of a makeshift bun.

Nicky smiled. 'I'm thinking about death,' she said.

'Don't spend too long on it. I think of it like flu – catching.'

Nicky spent the morning scanning news wires for sudden announcements, spoke to some freelancers and then, since the sun was shining, went for an early lunch. As she was crossing the lobby she came up short. Adam was sitting on a sofa by the door.

She felt her stomach contract as he stood and walked towards her, his hands in the pockets of his trousers. They shook hands and he didn't apologize for coming to her work, or seem embarrassed about appearing too keen.

'This is a surprise,' Nicky began to say.

'Don't be worried, I'm not after a job,' he said, flashing that devastating smile.

She gave him a rueful look. 'That's a relief. This isn't the place to be asking for jobs nowadays.'

'It's about my aunt. She's not got long left. I've been doing a bit of digging into her life, and I thought she might make a good subject for an obituary.'

Oh sweet, thought Nicky. She did believe Adam had a crush on her. Well, a mini one at least. She doubted very much that Adam really had anything of any use to her – people tended to overestimate how interesting their own family members were. 'Is that why you were trying to phone me earlier?'

'Yeah.'

They walked together to the revolving door and out into the summer heat. Nicky yearned for a sandwich and a drink on a bench in the napkin of grass round the corner. 'So when you couldn't get hold of me you decided to come and tell me straight away?'

Adam shrugged. 'Maybe I'm just a bit excited, that's all. Can I buy you lunch and tell you about her?'

Nicky put up a strong protest. 'Don't be ridiculous. You're not buying me anything. But you're very welcome to join me for a sandwich and a Coke. There's a good café—'

'Let me take you to lunch. Honestly, it's my pleasure.'

'I simply can't let you do that.' But she just couldn't manage to pack her smile away.

'I'm sure you think my aunt is just a line, but you're blunt enough to tell it to me straight. Either way, I'm buying you lunch.'

Nicky could feel the warmth on her back melting away the worries of the office and the blackness at home. She could sit under a tree with Adam by her side. 'OK, you win.'

'Fantastic.'

She set off for the park but Adam hesitated. 'Can we go somewhere else? Can I choose?'

'I've got one hour, no longer.'

'I don't want to stay in the open air; it's too visible.'

'Pardon?'

He looked uncomfortable. 'I'm sorry, but I've got a bit of a stalker problem and I don't want you to get involved.'

'A stalker?' She realized she must be looking very unconvinced as Adam began to walk round the back of the building and down an alley cast in deep shadow.

'I went out with a girl called Bea for a few months and it's been over for a while but she won't accept it. She sometimes follows me, makes silent phone calls . . .' He shrugged his shoulders with irritation. 'Sorry, it all sounds rather dramatic, but—'

'No, no, I understand.' Nicky was only half listening. She was thinking about the unread emails that were piling up in her inbox.

'She was particularly nasty to a girl recently—'

Nicky stopped walking and turned full on to Adam. 'What did she do?'

'I was seeing this girl, Rebecca. Bea followed her home and started screaming at her as she was trying to get in her front door. Really shook her up.' Nicky didn't reply. 'Needless to say, that was the last I saw of Rebecca.'

'I can imagine,' she said carefully, instinctively looking around but seeing no one. 'Well, if it's any help, I can take care of myself.' After Grace was murdered she had taken a self-defence course. Maria had said it was a way to channel her anger and make her feel less useless. The instructor had told her to stop pummelling the boxing punchbag so hard. She'd ignored him, and wordlessly venting her fury at Grace's death she'd ended up spraining her wrist.

While she didn't dismiss Bea completely, she did feel there

were perhaps some histrionics involved – the passions and dramas of those in their early twenties. But she didn't want her lunch ruined so willingly followed Adam. She knew what Maria would say if she recounted this tale: 'Bea won't bother you; she'll think you're his boss – or his mother.'

She waved at Bruton as he leaned against the back of the building, a cloud of real smoke drifting away across the concourse. They crossed an arterial road and Adam kept on.

'Where are we going?'

'A little place down here.'

'Which one? I know all the lunch places near my office.'

He turned up a street and round a corner. 'Here.'

He paused by some steps leading down to a cellar. 'Here?' She couldn't keep the disappointment out of her voice. It was a glorious summer day and they were to hide away in some cave. Nicky had been here eighteen months ago for another of the endless leaving dos – the place had smelled of cleaning fluid and the salads were limp.

He looked amused. 'Have a little faith.'

He ushered her down into a small and cosy restaurant with tables covered in white linen and a delicious smell seeping out of the kitchen. A friendly and efficient waitress led them to a table near a window that looked over a small basement garden and a high wall.

'It must have changed hands,' Nicky exclaimed.

'It's owned by the father of a friend of a friend. What do you want to drink?'

She asked for water; they ended up with champagne. The restaurant filled but she recognised no one. Their table was intimate, the food good. She felt she had been transported to another world, to a city where they were anonymous and deliciously alone. She told herself to stick to work. 'So, your aunt.'

Adam leaned forward, holding her gaze. 'You've heard of Tramps?'

'The nightclub?' Adam nodded. 'Of course, though I've never been there. I'm not posh enough or famous enough.' She asked for a glass of water and some red wine appeared with it. She gave up protesting and trying to stay sober.

'My aunt was a doorwoman there in the seventies and eighties. She ran all sorts of favours for people, was friends with famous people, dated top Hollywood actors, that kind of thing.'

'How long did she do it for?'

'I'm not sure exactly. She keeps saying there are loads of photos at the house of her with famous people at the club.'

'Did she say which people?'

'She was vague. She said people you wouldn't expect.'

The intoxicating smell of copy grew stronger. Nicky tried to remain casual. This was hard as she realized she was leaning over the table towards Adam and his knee was touching hers. 'It sounds like she had an interesting life. Can you get me these photos?'

'They're at the house. All Connie's stuff is there. I'd have to root through.'

'The house. That's an emphasis you use only if you've got a bloody great mansion.'

Adam laughed. 'Very perceptive. It does have a lot of rooms. It's near Bournemouth.'

'Did Connie grow up there?'

'Yes. She's my dad's sister.'

'Is your family very grand?'

Adam looked uncomfortable, or maybe he was trying to be modest. 'Not many of us left now. My mother's dead.'

'I'm so sorry.'

'With Aunt Connie on her way out it's just me and Dad now.'

Nicky gave a small shrug. 'I don't even know who my mum is.'

'What do you mean?'

'I'm adopted.' She waved away his look of concern. 'Don't worry about me. I have a great relationship with my adopted family. I don't have *issues*.'

'You've never had any wish to trace your real family?'

'None whatsoever.'

'That's unusual.'

Nicky smiled to cover the fact that she was lying. Sort of. It would be unusual not to have *some* issues. She loved her family but she had always felt different from them. She rolled the stem of her wine glass between two fingers. Part of her closeness to Grace had been because she was used to creating strong relationships in her life, rather than relying on blood ties to provide them.

Nicky was brought sharply back to the present by Adam placing his hand on hers from across the table. 'You look miles away.'

She put her hand back on her lap. 'Adam, I'm married.'

'You're not acting like you are.'

His words were like a slap, bringing her to her senses. 'I should go.'

'Don't you dare. I'm being silly. It's none of my business.'

'Really, maybe this isn't a good idea.'

'Please stay, Nicky. Please.'

She considered for a moment and relented. She fiddled with her fork, inspecting the tines. 'Sometimes it's difficult. Greg's wife was murdered. She was my best friend too.'

He said nothing but stared at her, the shock impossible to hide. 'Your best friend was murdered?'

'Do you remember the case of the body in the lake?' He nodded. 'That was her.' Adam's dark eyes were glassy; she couldn't interpret what he was thinking. 'Greg was married to Grace.'

Adam gave a small cough. 'I see.' He groped around for something to say. 'I'm so sorry—'

'Don't be.' Nicky waved her hand, wanting her fun lunch back. 'Things aren't always easy, between me and Greg. The past can be . . . intrusive.'

'Of course, of course, I understand,' he said.

Another glass of wine arrived. She struggled back to work thoughts. 'Have you ever looked through the photos?'

'No. She says there were politicians, actors . . . but the names don't mean a lot to me. She's got a condition that gives her a series of small strokes that affect her mentally and physically. Some days she completely lucid and at other times she rambles and it's impossible to get much sense out of her. She's not in a good way.'

'Could she do an interview, do you think?'

'I'm not sure. She lives with us here in London and has a carer, but I think she needs to go into a home soon.'

'Does she have children or a husband?'

'No.'

'Are there friends I could talk to?'

'My dad's the one. They were close, Connie and Dad. Now I think about it I'm intrigued to see these photos myself.' He leaned towards her, his gaze intense. 'You could come down to the house and see them in situ.'

There it was: the invitation and the challenge.

She sat back, high on wine and intrigue. She imagined Connie's photos, wrapped up in faded pink ribbon and stored in an old wooden trunk in a room with a rocking horse and something by Chesterfield. Her fingers were twitching to get her grip on this story. It could turn out to be perfect for impressing the new editor, toeing the new editorial line. And who knew, maybe those photos would turn up something really scandalous. I'm going to get to that house, she thought, glancing at her mobile. 'Shit! Is that the time?' She stood so fast her chair banged backwards onto the floor.

'Sit down, Nicky.'

It was the way he said it. He was so sure of himself, oozing youth, self-confidence and control. She righted the chair and sat down. She did what he said because when he talked like that she wanted to. The waitress came and put down the bill. Nicky grabbed it and Adam grabbed her wrist. They tussled, giggling for several moments over the table littered with the remains of their lunch. She felt a surge through her body before she gave in and let him take it. He was commanding, dangerous and sexy. She decided it was a fatal combination in someone so young. She understood how Bea could become obsessed by Adam. When he turned on the charm there wouldn't be many who could stand up to its force.

'Where the bloody hell have you been?' Maria asked when she slunk back to her desk.

'Finding an exclusive,' she replied.

'There are no exclusives on death.'

Nicky smiled. 'We'll see.'

She spent the next hour Googling Connie Thornton. She got a page from Debrett's and a couple of snippets from other websites. She took a crash course in Tramps, the place to see and be seen in the seventies and eighties. She noticed with interest that taking photos inside the club was strictly forbidden. She typed in Adam Thornton, and got an intriguing web page back.

'What's with the face?' asked Maria.

'I've just had lunch with the son of Judge Lawrence Thornton.'

Maria frowned. 'He sounds familiar.'

'The women's hero.'

Nicky watched as Maria searched her memory banks for the connection. 'Oh I remember. The first judge to find a woman not guilty of murder on the grounds of diminished responsibility because she suffered years of abuse . . .' Maria tailed off. 'You're looking far too pleased with yourself, you know. No good will come of this, Nicky.' Maria waved a finger at her and pointedly walked off towards the Foreign Desk with an oversized leaving card in her hand that they'd just signed.

5

Greg was packing his case for LA, a black Samsonite with a retractable handle and reflective stripes down the sides. So you could be seen. Everyone was so keen to be noticed – for their designer clothes, famous friends, shiny luggage. His fellow passengers were like a herd of narcissists disembarking on the other side of the world. Greg sighed. If you can't beat 'em, join 'em.

He threw his swimming trunks into the bag. Not that he ever went in the sea or a pool. He was too busy. How many pools were there in LA, he wondered. More than could ever be counted. You needed to be in the chlorine business in that town. That or palm tree maintenance. He hated palm trees. They were ugly and spiky and too tall, like a badly proportioned woman. He looked out of his bedroom window at the London plane bursting through the paving stones, its trunk so thick it obscured half of a car. Now *that* was a tree.

Nics was lying on the bed, supposedly watching him pack but she was fiddling with the tassel on her orange silk dress. Her bad mood was radiating out in waves, conflict bubbling just under the surface.

Impulsive, chaotic, beautiful Nicky. He felt a surge of love for her and then, as always, it was chased away by its old partner: guilt. He shouldn't have married her. He'd made a mistake. Sure, he adored her, but why hadn't they just kept things as they were, stayed living in sin, as his mum so disapprovingly called it. If only Nics hadn't asked. Why had she bloody gone and asked! Trapping him in that tawdry restaurant and grabbing his hand, rushing on about how it didn't need to be a leap year, as if he or she cared anything for shit like that. She'd cornered him in a burst of love and enthusiasm. She hadn't realized what she was doing, of course; how could she know? He'd been obsessive about the fact that she'd never know the full truth. But once the fateful words were out of her mouth he'd had to think fast. Nics wasn't stupid. She wouldn't buy some line about waiting. She had been thirty-two and everyone knew the score. The time was now. If there was something she didn't like, part of their relationship that didn't add up – she'd go. It would hurt like hell but she'd do it. That was Nics all over; she wasn't one for compromise. She deserved her happy ever after and she would go all out to get it. He'd sat there, fingernails digging into his knees, pretending to be surprised and flattered. If he'd said no, they would have been over, maybe not that night or the following week, but soon enough. Too soon. So he'd done a stupid thing. He'd said yes. He'd lied and feigned enthusiasm and agreed because he was a coward and he couldn't bear to lose her. He had thought at that moment that he could overcome what had happened and put it behind him. But what he'd done was worse, he realized now, much worse.

He'd left her in limbo, neither with him nor free. He couldn't ever tell her the truth, and the awful realization hit him that as the years pulled you further and further from what had happened the past never let you go. You didn't escape it; however distant it became it was still there, dank and hovering and brooding. He should never have lifted that perfume bottle to his nose – how stupid was that! The genie literally bursting from the bottle. He shuddered even though the day was hot. His union with Nicky was rotting away and there wasn't anything he could do about it. He couldn't open up to her, because articulating it made it real, and the only way he could cope was to hide it all away. So he was cut off from her in a travesty of a marriage.

The wedding preparations had brought back feelings of dread. Of course Grace was the spectre and the excuse for not wanting it big and white and public. Nics agreed immediately; she wasn't bothered about the traditional package or the sums that were spent. For her it was all about the emotion. She didn't need to float in a hot air balloon or hire a vintage car, bin a load of cash on a man who banged the dinner gong. So they'd had a small register office ceremony with just family and three friends each and he'd organized a surprise honeymoon, a secret trip. Because he was superstitious and paranoid – and rightly so, he told himself. They spent three weeks hiking in the Pyrenees, moving from lodges to small hotels and camping out in stupendous isolation – just the two of them. It was a glorious hiatus, the time of their lives. Because he knew it would begin to change once they came home. Once they came back to real life; once it became a daily fight to stay on top of the fear of the past.

Grace. She had been dragged to the lake, the police said. She had struggled before the end . . . He pushed the image away by folding a linen shirt and trying to get it in the Samsonite without creasing it. Fat chance.

'How are your nerves?' Nicky lay on the bed, her head propped up on her hand.

He gave her his best smile. Good old Nicky, bringing him out of himself. 'Jangling.' He reached out for the packet of Valium and popped two blue pills from the plastic blister. He threw them high in the air like they were peanuts and caught both in the back of his throat. An old pub drinking game he'd been a master at. He became absurdly pleased with himself and grinned at his wife as he swallowed them down with some whiskey. It was the little things. Concentrate on the little things and his big fat fear of flying would start to blur at the edges. The pills and the booze couldn't do anything about the other memories, but he knew that all too well. He'd learned the hard way.

'You've got an aisle seat?'

Greg shuddered theatrically and reached for the whiskey. 'So much for all those films you get to watch, I'm zonked from take-off to landing.' He put the Valium in his pocket. He felt the sweat bead on his forehead even as he thought of the name: Heathrow. It was another dose of his legendary good fortune, to be working somewhere that required a twelve-hour flight from home.

'Passport, ticket, money?' There was irony in her voice. He patted his jacket pocket. She looked away.

He shouldn't be going. She needed him. But he needed the work. Man was put on this earth to work, his dad used to say. Greg would have said it was more accurate that man was put on the plane back to LA to stop someone younger and hungrier taking his place, living his dream. Man – particularly this man – thrived on the competition. Bring it on! He picked up three pairs of balled socks and began juggling.

'Greg, we need to talk.'

He caught the socks and looked at her as she lay on the bed. So here it was, finally, the moment he had been dreading. The doorbell rang and he looked out of the window. 'That's the cab. What do you want to talk about?'

More tassel fiddling as he slipped the socks into a side pocket and started closing what seemed like miles of zip. He got no reply, just a sigh that seemed to say more than words could. She walked down the stairs after him. They stood in the corridor looking at each other. He couldn't have this conversation now, when the whiskey and the pills were pulling him away from himself.

She put her hand on his chest and fiddled with the buttons

on his shirt as if she pitied him. He felt a flash of his anger, a hard band across his chest. He couldn't stand pity.

'Make sure you put the alarm on whenever you're in – not just at night.'

He watched her nod, saw her eyes develop their telltale glaze. She just didn't get it. But then why should she? She had no idea of the depths of his paranoia and he was going to keep it that way. She might laugh when he made her put on the seatbelt in the back of a black cab; she might groan when he got the builders to put locks on all their top-floor windows so they opened only a few inches; she had even shouted at him on a holiday in France when he rejected a much nicer hotel room because it had a balcony. Too bloody bad. He was no longer cocooned in good luck. A normal life was something he could only dream of. The problem was that Nicky felt normal was within her grasp and she was getting desperate to live it. Their reactions to what had befallen Grace were different. Nicky was getting tired of fear being used as an excuse to avoid the things that were important to her.

He was a bloke, for Chrissake. He might not get the subtleties, but he got the gist. She wanted to talk about the big issues, the ties that bound them, their love for each other, where they were going, the state of their marriage. A luxury, Greg thought. I do not have the luxury of time to think. I do not allow myself time to think. I work, I stress, I work more, I succeed. Greg wondered how successful he would have to be to compensate for the things left unsaid. Pretty alpha, he concluded.

The doorbell rang again, making him jump, as if what he was thinking was shameful. He pulled her to him in an embrace and things unsaid swirled around them. 'I love you love you love you,' he said, gathering her hair into a ponytail and twisting it round his fingers.

'You need to show it, Greg.'

He grabbed her in a bear hug and picked her off the ground, swinging her round and growling into her neck. That way she couldn't see his face, couldn't see the despair and the hopelessness etched there. He felt Nicky limp in his arms. This time he wasn't pulling it off. He kissed the tip of her nose and Nicky said nothing as he walked out of the house, the Samsonite bumping down the steps behind him. He opened the taxi door and gave her a lingering look as he folded himself through it. She stood on the front step with one arm holding the other, as if she was protecting herself. She looked stunning in the evening sunshine. Women, he thought: the love and the tragedy of his life. The taxi pulled away and he watched her shut the door on their unfinished conversation.

When the taxi reached the corner Greg looked behind him to make sure she was no longer there. He slipped off his wedding ring and put it in his pocket. It was a habit he'd got into whenever he left the house.

6

Troy was trying to remember a Rolling Stones song about St John's Wood but the words wouldn't come to him. He lay in the king-sized bed and thought about Mick Jagger instead, imagining how many women he'd slept with; then he tried to think of his own tally. Troy was competitive, but the woman's yakking at the dog in the kitchen across the hallway was distracting him from his counting, and that annoyed him. Was she the oldest woman he'd had? Not by a long way. Was she the richest? She had a St John's Wood address but it was only a mansion flat. He leaned up on his elbows, his mind zoning in on the task ahead. She wasn't the richest, but he was going to make absolutely sure she was the most lucrative.

He pulled open the drawer of her bedside table. The Rolex glinted at him. He moved fast to her dressing table and opened the right-hand drawer (he'd noticed last night that she was right-handed, which meant she would store her valuables on that side), and scanned the contents. He saw some small rocks set in rings, a couple of gaudy Arab-looking necklaces, nothing too big league. She'd have a safe somewhere. He glanced round at the pictures on the wall, wondering which one it was hidden behind.

'D'ya take sugar?' she called. He heard the clattering of cups from the kitchen, the whoop of plastic on the fridge door as it opened.

'No thanks, Marcia.' It always paid to be polite. That

generation cared more for the niceties than his own, he reasoned. He repeated their names in the morning, to show that he'd remembered. The drinking of last night was an act, so his mind was clear. After all, he was at work; he wasn't going to fuck it up. She was from Detroit, had been in Dubai and had ended up in London with two fat divorces behind her. It hadn't been hard to follow her and her friends to the bar at the Hilton and alleviate her loneliness.

He started to dress, putting the pilot's uniform back on. Women of a certain age really did fall for that shit. It was a wonder to him every time. He'd carried her over the threshold last night and she'd given a little yelp of pleasure and desire. It's what they expected a pilot to do. His fake uniform drew women to him like moths to those smelly candles they were so keen to burn. He conjured up an era when flying was fashionable and elite; he helped them tap back into their younger selves, made them remember good times. She didn't notice that he'd memorized her alarm code – his old thieving habits were proving hard to break.

He wandered into her en suite and washed his hands carefully. He looked in the medicine cabinet, hunting for ammunition. He saw the usual array of products that attempted to stop the clock: an HRT prescription, extortionate anti-wrinkle creams, toothpaste for sensitive teeth, post-surgical bandages. Here was the toolkit of the sixty-something divorcee bent on keeping one hand on the mythical tree of youth. Troy wasn't going to condemn her for that. He admired her attempts to make the effort, because he understood. They were separated by a generation but their concerns were the same: they both had a desperate need to cling to physical perfection and the respect it brought. You couldn't be loved if you weren't respected. He slammed the bathroom cabinet shut. There had been a time when all that women wanted was a man who looked and behaved like him. A good-looking, good-time guy, flash with the cash and an animal in the sack. But now, at forty-two, he was constantly being asked about property: what he had, where it was, who really owned it. Women had changed; they wanted hard-cash money now, bricks-and-mortar wealth. He needed to get it as much as he needed to whiten those teeth. He grimaced in her backlit bathroom mirror and examined his gums. Receding. They were being beaten back by age and genes, crumbling under the pressure. Fuck that. He felt a rush of anger at his imperfections. Marcia was going to pay for a trip to the cosmetic dentist and add to his Caribbean retirement fund.

He heard her back in the bedroom, the yappy dog with her, and came out to meet her. She was dressed in something pink and too short, her hair a brassy yellow in the morning light. She had two cups on a silver tray and was keeping up the stream of banal chit-chat. It was probably one of the reasons Harvey ran into the arms of the blonde a generation removed from his wife. Troy vaguely remembered Marcia's replacement: lots of curly hair and she chewed gum.

'So what have you got planned for today, honey?' Marcia was teasing him.

'Marcia, tell me why you hated Harvey so much.'

The colour drained right off her face. Even the dog fell silent beside her. 'What do you mean?' Her voice was a whisper.

'Harvey. Your first husband. He fell from the twelfth floor. He must have done something to really piss you off.'

She had recovered slightly, her back stiff and formal. She tried to gather her babydoll at the neck to protect herself from his onslaught. 'How do you know Harvey?'

'Oh I don't. But I know you paid, and I know how much.' Troy pointed his finger at her. 'You clever little bitch. You waited and took your revenge long after he left you. The first flush of a new marriage is perfect cover—'

She was a fighter. She ran to the side of the bed and hit the panic button. 'Get out of here!'

Troy leaned back against the armoire and picked something out from beneath his nail. 'You paid £40,000 to Darek to have Harvey killed. Revenge, jealousy, pride, I don't care. You paid once, but now you're going to pay again.'

'Who the hell are you? You've no proof!'

'I've plenty.'

'Liar!'

'Room 392 at the Florina Plaza in Dubai. A hot night in March four years ago. Harvey took an unfortunate tumble from his balcony wearing only a bathrobe. Don't look so shocked, you know how I know all this. You hired and paid Darek, who paid *me* to do the job.' He picked up her mobile and threw it on the bed. 'Phone the security company.'

She was shaking, mute, ugly blotches of red on her cheeks, but she didn't move. Troy was calm, he still had time. 'Life with Harvey wasn't all bad – you have Arabella.' A strangled gasp came from Marcia. 'She's got a nice life partying in Chelsea. I wouldn't want to ruin that. This is simply a business decision, Marcia. I want what the middleman got.' Her face was now deathly pale again. 'I like you, Marcia, that's why I came to you before ruining Arabella's pretty face. You of all people understand the power of a pretty face. It made you your fortune. Now you're sharing a little of that fortune with me. This way, no harm done.'

Marcia was panting now, as if on a treadmill at the gym, but she didn't move. 'We can do it your way, if you want.' Troy moved to the bedroom door and made to leave.

His going shocked her into sound. 'Wait!' She grabbed the phone and made the call to the security company to cancel the alarm, then she dropped down on the bedcovers, her legs unable to support her. 'I haven't got that kind of money.'

Troy grinned. He had her right where he wanted her:

vulnerable in her babydoll get-up, in her bedroom. The fleeting passion of last night was like a soiled tissue she was keen to throw away. 'Open the safe.'

He saw her swallow nervously. 'I don't have a safe.'

'Oh Marcia. *That* wasn't very smart.' Troy slowly shook his head before moving swiftly to the picture hanging next to the built-in wardrobes. A bullfighter swirled a red cape in front of a charging animal. He tossed it to the floor to reveal the safe.

'How do I know you won't plague me?' She sounded old.

'Marcia, I'm a fair guy, I really am. It's just a shame that there are so many people who seem unable to play by the rules. I took the risk so I should receive the reward. But I have since discovered that the parasite in the middle gets the lion's share. Trickle-down economics is really just what it says on the tin. A trickle. So I want what Darek the middleman got. No more, no less. Now, let's start with the rocks Harvey gave you, shall we?'

Five minutes later he left with her cache of jewellery in a Louis Vuitton luggage bag. He started to walk towards Regent's Park, where a weak sun was beginning to shine. With each step he felt lighter, younger. It had worked like a dream. The crazy bitch had coughed it all up. He was nigh-on fifty grand richer because Marcia's phone number was on Darek's list. Darek, who was so anal he had kept a paper trail of the jealousies and hatreds of his clients and how much they had paid to try to alleviate those emotions that had set up home in their guts and weren't letting go. And now Darek was dead and he had the list. It could turn out to be the luckiest bit of paper he'd ever come across.

Knowledge is power – the truth can make you a king. Troy liked the feeling of wielding the sword of truth. It cut down everything before it.

7

Nicky ducked under the sign that berated passengers who came this far. She stared down the dark track and took a step back. He was mad. She wasn't going down there.

Adam retreated out of the gloom and came towards her, holding out his hand. 'Come on.'

'I'm not doing it. This is nonsense.'

'Do you want to see the graffiti or don't you?'

'Yes, but I want to live more!'

A train crawled past, slowing down for its approach into Charing Cross Station. He'd been so enthusiastic to show her a huge painting by a hot new graffiti artist that she had become infected by his energy and ended up meeting him near the river. The work, by 'The new Banksy', was painted on the bridge over the Thames, but now she'd realized how they were to get there she changed her mind. This was what twenty-year-olds did, not married women the wrong side of thirty-five.

'It's perfectly safe – how do you think the artist got over there to paint it?' He had a point. 'Come on!' He grabbed her hand and she liked the feel of her own in his. It was their first prolonged physical contact and she didn't want it to end. They walked over commuter litter blown down the tracks and past tools and barrels and boxes left by workmen. Another train passed, honking angrily.

They came out into the light of the bridge. 'Where are we going?'

'Just trust me and you won't go wrong.'

They edged out across the river, the sun glinting off the twisting mass of rails that disappeared into the distance and round a bend to Waterloo. She felt the fear of where they were again; this was one of the busiest stations in Europe, with trains coming and going all the time.

'How do you know about this place?'

'I followed a graffiti artist I recognized one evening and ended up here.' He gripped her hand tighter. 'Right, we're going to cross now.'

'Cross?' Nicky thought she hadn't heard right. Cross a mainline railway? She looked up and down the tracks, trains shifting between points, switching tracks, travelling at different speeds. It was like being in a demented computer game. It was madness. 'No. We can't cross.'

'Come on, Nicky!'

'I'm not bloody Lara Croft.'

'I think you've got potential. You might find you enjoy it.'

And the truth was that she understood what he meant. His disregard for safety, his desire for kicks and danger, his search for an adrenalin rush – she found she was responding to all this.

'Get back,' he said, shoving her hard up against the metal struts of the bridge as a train passed by them, so close she felt the wind it created brushing her cheek.

Grace's death had robbed Nicky of the remains of her youth. She had stepped over into a world where unspeakable horrors lurked in corners, where life wasn't carefree and consequence free. While she loved Greg, Adam brought the spontaneity and risk of her younger years bubbling to the surface. She didn't want a life half lived. She took a deep breath. 'I'm in.'

Adam held her face in his hands. 'You won't regret it,' he shouted as a train wobbled past them. 'Follow me exactly.'

He started out across the tracks.

'What about the third rail—'

'Don't touch *any* rail,' he interrupted.

The tracks were wider than they looked and the other side seemed far away. About a third of the way across fear began to expand inside her. She could hear the clanging of points as they changed, the hum of the shiny metal rails. She didn't dare look up, scared that what she saw would make her panic and run – and who knew then what danger she might be in? She gripped Adam's hand harder, his knuckles a bony lifeline. Finally they were across and she half staggered on the small loose stones piled by the side of the tracks. Her heart was pummelling the inside of her chest. She didn't let go of Adam's hand as he led her out over the river, because she couldn't bear to feel herself outside his comforting orbit; she didn't want reality to leave her exposed.

A little further on Adam turned into a triangular space with high cement walls made by the struts of the bridge below them and she could finally retreat a little from the trains. She looked around her at the spray cans that littered the ground as Adam commanded her to stand right back against one of the walls. Nicky gave a gasp. So this was why graffiti artists risked their lives for their art. The wall in front of her had a huge mural of Red Riding Hood painted on it, her red cloak fanning out behind her, her hair a blonde punk interpretation. In her hands she held a spray can of paint, aiming it like a gun, and above her head were the words 'Fear makes the wolf grow bigger'. Red Riding Hood's eyes contained a steely glint that it was impossible to ignore. The enclosed space, the inability to walk away from the work because of the train lines, meant its full power caught the viewer head on.

'Now *that's* what I call art,' Adam said.

They were suspended over the middle of the Thames, the

breathtaking view of the beating heart of the city flowing away beneath them, Red Riding Hood's blood-red cape caught in the wind off the river.

'It's amazing,' was all Nicky could say.

'Worth the danger?' Adam asked. Nicky nodded, adrenalin surging through her body. She hadn't felt so alive in years. 'Life is about taking risks, confronting your fears. Otherwise what's the point?'

Nicky laughed. 'Fear makes the wolf –'

They finished the rest together: '– grow bigger.'

He suddenly looked serious and grabbed her hand again. 'We need to go. The transport police will be here in a minute.' He led her back the way they had come and she felt at that moment that she would follow him anywhere. This day was a divine hiatus, a break from her real life. They walked back onto the platform past several gawping passengers. 'Shit! The police are here!' She followed his gaze and saw two policemen hurrying across the concourse. They sprinted down a walkway and out into Villiers Street. As she ran along she started giggling and then she started laughing and she found she couldn't stop. Such happiness surged through her that she had to double over near Embankment Tube. This was all so gloriously silly, so young at heart. Adults didn't run, they walked. Greg might stride, his sturdy legs eating up the ground, but he didn't run. There were probably moments when Adam skipped.

'Nicky Ayers, you've got some balls, I'll give you that! I never thought you'd go for it!'

'Then you really don't know me at all, Adam Thornton!' He was looking at her through his laughter with amazement – and desire.

They jogged across the river and down onto the South Bank, her heart only now beginning to return to something like normal.

They passed the National Film Theatre and Nicky went in to the bar to buy a bottle of water. As she inched forward in the queue she felt a swirling mixture of adrenalin, excitement and shock. Adam had taken her back to her younger self, her self before her marriage and before Grace's death.

Just as she was looking for her money for the water she was shoved roughly from behind, careering awkwardly into the woman in front of her in the queue. She turned round, astonished and annoyed, to find a small woman with spiky blonde hair, and wearing a cropped T-shirt that showed her taut brown tummy, balling her fists. 'Do you mind?'

'Leave Adam alone.'

Nicky realized in an instant who she was. 'Bea.'

'See, he's told you about me. We're still together, so hands off.' Her bottom lip jutted forward in a pout that Bea probably thought was attractive. And she had a kind of image that made an impression. There was a smattering of freckles across her nose, which was fine and upturned, and her skin was stretched tight across her cheeks. She looked like a vindictive elf.

Nicky could feel her anger mushroom. She wasn't going to be pushed around. She also didn't like the idea that she was being followed; it was creepy and unsettling. 'If you're still with him, go off and find him. He's just over there.' She pointed towards the river. 'And leave me in peace.' Bea narrowed her eyes, which were hard and unyielding; her small breasts sat high on her ribcage, exposed under the tight and see-through T-shirt; her skinny legs showed under the denim mini. She was an acrimonious bundle of hatred. Nicky sensed the wiry strength in her thin arms and had no doubt that Bea could fight nasty if she wanted to. Nicky glanced at the barman, who had suddenly found something of great interest to study in the ceiling tiles, while people behind her in the queue shifted and craned for a better look. She felt ridiculous, as if she'd been dragged back through the years into a teenage argument. 'You're not so sure now, are you?'

'I'm not giving up.' The queue shifted forward. 'I'll enjoy making your life hell.' She grabbed the water bottle from Nicky's hand and threw it on the floor, where it skidded and spun towards some stools. 'Bitch!'

'Just leave me alone!' Nicky was ready to vent her anger. She bent down to pick up the water and turned to see Bea marching out of the bar, her middle finger stuck skywards.

Every eye in the room was now upon her, waiting for what she would do next. She mumbled 'Sorry' and headed for the exit, head down. She found Adam a few moments later, buying them ice creams.

He gave her one glance and exclaimed, 'What the hell happened to you?'

'I just met Bea.'

'Bea Forrester? For Chrissake!' He looked around wildly. 'This is beyond a fucking joke!'

'It wasn't a pleasure.'

'I'm so sorry. Come on, let's go.' He handed her an ice cream, his face clouded.

'She's got it bad, hasn't she?'

'She's ridiculous. I feel powerless to do anything except wait it out.'

'Rejection is a very intense emotion.'

He was staring at her and Nicky felt a tension began to shimmer between them. She turned and headed towards the river, putting her hand on the wall that bordered the Thames and feeling the rough stone under her palm. They walked along, licking their ice creams, and slowed by some builders who were digging up paving stones and replacing a section of the wall. Nicky stopped by a line of red and white tape and busied herself eating so she didn't have to look at him.

'Nicky.'

Now she had to face up to the situation she had partly created. She looked at him, noticing a small scar near his lip, caught in relief by the sun. She had to make a choice here. He was handsome and keen – what more could a girl want? But Nicky was married, and whatever her problems she needed to deal with them with Greg. Nicky took a step back because she thought Adam was going to try to kiss her. It was a distraction she didn't need. She felt the red and white tape of the builders' barrier slide under her bum.

Adam opened his mouth, as if about to say something, when through the crowds of people on the Thames Path Nicky saw Bea loom up, cycling fast towards her. She gasped and instinctively took a sharp step backwards. As Bea screeched to a halt, Nicky stumbled and tripped on one of the paving stones, aware of the builders' tape breaking and pinging away under tension. She heard a workman shout out as she took another step backwards, trying to regain her balance, but her foot found nothing on which to land and her arms began to cartwheel in a useless attempt to stop herself falling. She was going backwards into the Thames with nothing to break her fall. She heard a woman scream – it might have been her – before the shockingly cold water closed over her head.

8

Nicky had heard many times that the Thames was a lot more dangerous than it looked. She knew that the tides pulling that huge body of water upstream and down swallowed at least one person a week, and those were the ones that were found. By the time she surfaced Nicky noticed with a jolt that she was already ten metres from where she fell in. She tried to swim to the bank, but her dress and shoes were weights dragging her down. She swam harder but got no nearer to the high, slimy wall. Even if she got there she couldn't climb out. She saw a line of boats and barges moored mid-river that had seemed almost within touching distance from the shore, but now that she was in the gunmetal water their distance was absurd, the expanse of broiling water between her and them impossible to traverse. Something pulled her sharply under again and she fought to get her head above water. She saw a bridge in the distance. If she was pulled under there she knew it was unlikely she'd ever come out because the vicious eddies and undercurrents would hold her down. She was swimming as hard as she could, rapidly losing strength and making absolutely no headway.

Nicky realized with a terrible sense of déjà vu how quick death could be, how decisive and unstoppable her journey towards it was, how puny her efforts to fight it were. People were shouting from the top of the wall, their arms and hands waving. They were too far away to help her. She heard a scream as someone dived into the river. Adam swept downriver to her and started shouting as he neared. 'Kick as hard as you can!'

Nicky was mute, with no strength to utter a word. She put all her energy into staying afloat and he reached out his arms in the water to pull her towards him. He cupped his hand under her chin and together they kicked for the wall. He was a strong swimmer and his legs powered away beneath her. She used the last of her energy to kick as best she could, while Thames water slapped over her face, making her cough and splutter. She turned her head and saw he was trying to use the current to aim for a large buttress of stone that jutted out at right angles into the river. If they could get there at least they would have a chance of avoiding being swept downriver under the bridge.

They smacked into the wall with surprising force, then Nicky grappled to find any handhold in the slimy brick, but she kept being dunked under by the current as it swirled against this obstacle. Water filled her mouth; the dank smell of rotting masonry filled her nostrils. Adam reached up and grabbed an old round boathook fixed into the ancient brick. He clung on to it with one hand and planted his feet wide against the wall. 'Hold my hand!' he commanded.

Nicky made a lunge for his hand as the water tried one last time to suck her around the edge of the buttress and back into the river. She climbed between his legs and he created a cage around her where she could gather her breath. She saw a line of faces peering over the wall and heard shouting that she couldn't make into anything meaningful. A few minutes later some workmen appeared and lowered a ladder over the side towards them. Nicky only had the strength to climb up one rung so Adam shoved her up by her bum from below. The builders pulled her up the wall with the energy of hopeless bystanders suddenly finding themselves useful.

By the time she was dragged over the wall and lay splayed on the warm concrete of the South Bank, panting like a fish landed on deck of a trawler, she realized she'd had the most extraordinary day. As a crowd of anxious and appalled onlookers gathered round, asking her if she was OK, patting Adam on the back for being the have-a-go hero he was, she burst into tears of relief and – at that moment of rescue – love.

9

Greg didn't believe in luck, he didn't like surprises and accidents made the hairs stand up on the back of his neck. He sat hunched over the computer in the hotel room while the LA morning sun bounced off the building opposite. Nicky's movements were pixellated by a bad Skype connection; she seemed manic and excitable, and, considering what she was telling him, he wasn't surprised.

'The Thames has got this funny taste, not what you'd expect at all.' She tried to laugh, but it didn't come out right. The spotlights in their kitchen accentuated dark circles under her eyes and made her look tired.

'I still don't understand how you fell in. Have you contacted a lawyer? You need to sue that building firm right now, their health and safety procedures—'

'Greg, listen to me, I'm fine. I've got one hell of a scratch on my knee—'

'Jesus! Have you been—'

'I went to the doctor for a tetanus injection. I had a shock, but I'm fine now.'

He watched her tuck some strands of hair behind her ear, bite a hangnail. All right, my arse.

'Hello? You still hear me?'

'I'm still here.' A stretchy silence opened up between them. 'Who was this guy who jumped in?'

She was shrugging her shoulders now, tracing a finger over a mole on her upper arm. 'He was called Adam, but I don't remember much else about him. I was in a bit of a state . . . there were a lot of people around. He said he was a strong swimmer and a bit impulsive so he just jumped in after me.'

She was a bad liar – good liars could always tell, and he was one of the best. It was all too implausible. Fit healthy women didn't just fall in the bloody Thames. He squeezed a stress ball in his palm, trying to keep a handle on his rising panic.

'Are you OK, honey? I know it's a bit of a mad story.'

'Who were you on the South Bank with?'

He noted the shrug of the shoulders, the telltale hesitation. 'I was on my own. I just wanted a quiet day on my own. Funny how things turn out.'

Greg squeezed the stress ball so hard his knuckles went white. Fear and superstitions swirled in his mind and he knew that hot on the heels of fear came the rage. The anger that it could happen again; why always to him? Saliva formed in his mouth and he swallowed it away. He was beginning to go mad. The past was playing its never-ending trick on him, laughing at his attempts to outrun it. The faster he ran, the harder he worked, the more he crammed into every day . . . and still it was there, mocking him.

'Nicky, I've got to go. I've got to get to set. You sure you're all right?' She nodded. She held her finger up to the small camera and he did the same. 'I love you. I love you more than I can say, more than you know.'

She looked sad and confused. 'I miss you.'

'Miss you too.'

Greg watched the Skype rectangle jump to black. He laid his head on his arms next to the keyboard, thinking through this strange conversation with his wife. The gulf between them was growing wider. Nowadays their conversations were short, perfunctory. How different from the early days when the distance of his jobs separated them. Back then she had fallen asleep with him listening on the Skype connection, had lain the laptop next to her on the pillow so he could watch her. They'd had phone sex and Skype sex and still it hadn't been enough. But somewhere on their journey together they had lost each other and, like so much, he knew it was his fault.

He sat in front of the black screen and thought through every nuance of that conversation. She hadn't said she loved him. He tried to remember if that was a first. He needed to insulate himself, try to get reassurance where he could. He wasn't a religious man, *that* would have been a joke, considering; but he even gave a little prayer. He picked up his phone and hesitated. He was trampling on the unspoken codes that underpinned his marriage. But then it wouldn't be the first time he'd gone beyond decent. Suspicion crawled across his hot skin. He called a number in London. The phone was answered after two rings.

'To what do I owe this pleasure?'

'Full of the joys of summer, are you, Liz?'

'You only ever call me if you need something.'

'You know me too well.' She was silent, refusing to pander to her brother. 'Oh come on, Liz, I'm away, and I'm not that bad.'

'Are you drunk?'

'I need a favour.'

'Oh! Here we go.'

'Hear me out. Pretty please, sis dearest.'

'You're such a wanker!'

But he could tell that she would relent. Liz was lonely and life had not lived up to the high standards she had expected. 'I'm worried about Nicky.'

'Oh?' Now she was interested, revealing an eagerness to know about problems and strife. 'How so?'

'I just want to make sure that she's OK. Can you keep an eye on her?'

There was a pause. Her voice was triumphant. 'You'll have to be a lot more specific.'

'I just need to know that she's OK.'

'Are you trying to tell me you want me to *follow* your wife?' She was dripping sarcasm.

'Liz, please, just for a while—'

'What do you think I do all day, Greg? I work! I've got Dan . . .'

'And you've got me too. You've always been there for me, Liz.'

'Greg, tone down the touchy-feely Hollywood – this is south London. I might gag.'

'Just do it for me.'

She swore under her breath. 'You owe me.'

He finished the call and stared uselessly out of the window. He wondered if the Californian sunshine could cleanse him of his disturbing thoughts.

10

Nothing attracts like a saviour, Nicky decided. Try as she might, Adam had become a hero, and heroes were hard to ignore or turn down. After the shock of a visit to A&E and a tetanus injection, then a change of clothes and borrowing money off Adam to go round to Maria's to get her spare door keys, she mooned around the house for the rest of the weekend, replaying her ditch in the Thames and her rescue over and over. She thought about making a complaint against Bea, but dismissed it almost immediately. She wasn't worth the bother or the paperwork, and despite what Bea might have wanted to happen, Nicky's fall into the water had been an accident. Plus, she had more practical issues to consider: she'd lost her bag and now faced a full day on the phone replacing her entire identity: bank cards, money, make-up, keys. In the midst of these jobs she got an email from Adam inviting her over on Wednesday – his dad was at home and if Connie was well enough Nicky could meet her.

After three uneventful days at work, and still waiting for the police report of her fall in the Thames to be sent to the accounts department so she could get a replacement mobile, she walked the short distance from Notting Hill Gate tube to the address at the southern end of Portobello Road. It was a warm sunny evening and she felt the long dormant feeling of excitement and anticipation at doing something new, meeting someone interesting, uncovering the layers. Lawrence's flat was down a cobbled mews cut off from Portobello Road by a large gate. She rang the bell on a brushed-steel door and a moment later someone clattered down the stairs. Adam was trying to keep his feet inside a pair of faded espadrilles and he shifted and hopped on the doorstep as he kissed her on the cheeks. He'd got browner in the few days since she'd seen him, and it suited him. 'Come on up.'

He took the stairs two at a time and she followed him into a large, open-plan living room-cum-kitchen. A row of sliding doors led on to a large patio beyond which a sumptuous view of a west London sunset could be seen. Several large, high-gloss photographs of tree canopies hung on the matt white walls. It was not what Nicky had been expecting; she had imagined an old-fashioned town house with stuffy chairs, leather books and patterned wallpaper, but Adam's father had defied the conventions of his age and class. An elegant black woman in her sixties, wearing yellow flip-flops and an abstract patterned skirt, was at the kitchen island boiling a kettle and someone sat at the dining table hiding under a red towel.

'Dad, this is Nicky. Nicky, this is Lawrence.'

Lawrence waved his arm at her as a greeting, his head still under the towel. A strong waft of Vicks VapoRub carried over to her. 'My darned sinuses are playing up.'

'He's such a bore about it,' the black woman said, spoon tinkling as she stirred a cup of something and brought it over, placing it on the table next to Adam's father. 'You'd think no one else had ever been ill,' she said with an air of resignation, quickly followed by amusement as she turned back to Nicky. 'I'm Bridget. Now for God's sake let's have a drink. I hear you're a journalist, so I presume you neck anything that's put in front of you?' Her eyes twinkled.

Nicky laughed and nodded.

'There's a bottle of red wine in the cupboard,' Lawrence

half shouted from under the towel. 'It's got a peacock on the front. Let's have that.'

'You shouldn't be drinking in your condition,' Bridget replied, walking over to a Scandinavian-style sideboard and opening the door. She ignored Lawrence, who was muttering to himself under the towel.

Nicky was enthralled. Their manners were so casual, their flat so beguiling, the sun somehow warmer and conversation just that little bit more fun. Visitors to her parents' house were rare enough to cause stress: fiddly snacks in little bowls, her mother stiff-backed in the Victorian chair by the nets, her dad offering the coasters with the best of British birds on them. Sometimes, when she was low or had had an argument with her parents, Nicky wondered what her real family had been like. She had never told anyone, but in her dreams she hoped they were a bit like this. Her dad was a loss adjuster, her mother a part-time librarian. Nicky knew she was falling for the allure of a life more interesting, a history more exotic than the one she had lived.

'Come and sit down,' Bridget said.

Adam was lying across one corner of the low grey sofa, his head supported by a hand, regarding her. She hesitated, unsure where she was supposed to put herself, when a high-pitched scream made her jump. She looked over at the doorway to find an old woman standing there, clutching the frame for support.

Lawrence swore loudly and threw back the towel. 'Connie! I've burned myself!'

Nicky was taken aback. The old woman was glaring at her. She glanced at Adam and saw that he was upright now, his shoulders tense, staring at his aunt. An awkward silence fell across the room.

'Pleased to meet you,' Nicky managed to say, wringing her hands together.

She looked at Lawrence and tried to smile. His face was puce from his vapour bath, droplets of water forming by his eyebrows, which were a striking black next to his grey hair. He sat stupefied. 'Oh, I feel dizzy now,' he said, touching his forehead.

'Just sit still for a moment and you'll be fine,' Bridget said with brisk efficiency and then she came over to Connie. 'This is Nicky,' she said, taking her arm. Connie pushed Bridget's offer of help away. She was a tall, slim woman, wearing red baggy trousers that looked expensive and a flowery shirt. She had a selection of large gold rings on her bony fingers and she still dyed her hair. Its chestnutty colour gleamed in the evening sun. The only evidence of her catastrophic health was in one eye, which had drooped at the outer edge – presumably the result of one of her strokes. It gave her face a strange lopsided appearance.

'She's not going to bite,' said Adam, coming to Bridget's aid, holding on to his aunt and trying to get her to sit down.

'What are you doing here?'

'Adam invited me round,' Nicky replied.

'Adam, your nephew,' Lawrence added loudly as he dried his face, his features hidden again beneath the red towel.

Connie frowned but let Adam lead her into the room.

As Nicky looked at Connie, she adjusted her age downwards. From her good eye and her skin Nicky decided she was probably only in her sixties. It seemed young to be so frail and dependent.

'You were fine earlier. You're having a good day today, Connie,' Bridget said, setting out glasses.

Nicky came towards Connie and held out her hand. 'It's good to meet you.'

Connie stared at her nephew. 'Good?'

'Sit down, Connie, for goodness sake,' Bridget said, irritated at the old woman's rudeness.

'Sorry about that. I'm Lawrence.' Lawrence put the towel down and came over to shake Nicky's hand. 'Excuse my sister.' His face was still red and blotchy from the steam, but he had a nice smile, which she found comforting in the awkward atmosphere.

Lawrence sat on the sofa, reached for a wine glass and poured a generous measure. Adam sat down next to Nicky and opposite Connie. Silence descended again and Nicky realized Connie was still staring at her. Adam had prepared her for how Connie might be, so it should have been no surprise the way she was acting, yet her stare was unnerving. She was confused, but her eyes, even though one wasn't straight, looked clear and focused.

'So, Adam jumped into the Thames after you,' Lawrence said.

Nicky smiled. 'Yes, he did, and I'm very grateful—'

'That's just like Adam, not appreciating the consequences of his actions,' Lawrence interrupted.

'*Such* a dangerous thing to do,' Bridget said, shaking her head.

'Anyone would think you lot *wanted* her to drown in the Thames!' Adam was scowling at his dad.

'Of *course* we don't mean that.' Bridget added for emphasis: 'I'm very glad you're OK, Nicky.' She handed her a glass of wine.

As Nicky tried to navigate the toxic cross-currents eddying through this room she decided that her own family really wasn't that bad at all. But she was here for a reason, so she just decided to get on with it. She turned to Connie. 'Adam has told me a lot about your life, Connie. It sounds fascinating.'

'Is she out to get us?' Connie looked at Lawrence in panic.

Bridget put her glass down. 'I'll get Tatjana. I think Connie's overtired.'

'No, don't. I want to hear what she's got to say,' Adam said, staring at his dad.

Nicky tried again. 'Adam told me that you used to work at Tramps, the nightclub.' There was a pause and she saw anguish pass across Connie's face. 'You must have met a lot of interesting people.'

Connie snorted, her eyes suddenly coming sharply into focus again. She was like a radio that wasn't perfectly tuned, her comprehension fading and returning in waves. 'Superficial and empty, it's all for nothing.'

'I see.' Nicky smiled with encouragement, realizing that this was going to be more difficult than Adam had made out. 'How many years did you work at—'

'Are you married?' Connie blurted out.

The room froze for a second and Lawrence muttered under his breath.

Nicky saw Connie staring at her wedding ring and she rubbed her hands in embarrassment to cover up the evidence. 'I . . . well . . . yes, I am. Have you ever been married, Connie?'

Connie narrowed her eyes. Adam came to her rescue. 'You were too busy, weren't you, Cons? Hanging out with all those glamorous people . . .'

'Who?' Connie frowned.

'You know, the guests at Tramps, the people who came down to the house—'

'They were all going to hell. I'm going to hell!' Her lip started quivering and tears sprang to her eyes. Nicky felt for the woman; she seemed terrified.

'I'll get Tatjana,' Bridget said, and she got up to leave the room.

Lawrence sighed. 'Not this again. There's no life after death, Connie. There's no heaven or hell—'

'Lawrence, please!' Bridget gave him a furious look from

the doorway and Lawrence threw his hands in the air with exasperation.

Nicky watched the old woman, who was still staring at her. Her face was expressive. Where a moment ago there had been fear, she now drew herself up and seemed defiant. 'I'm not going alone,' she said. 'Your husband's coming with me!' she added.

'Connie!' Bridget's voice was sharp. She called out for Tatjana and came back to help Connie to her feet.

Lawrence wasn't letting up. 'The punishments we deserve are given in this life only.'

Connie's mouth was working hard on things unsaid as a fleshy woman in a white uniform entered and started making soothing noises to her patient. Adam was sitting perfectly still, his eyes moving from his father to his raving aunt to Bridget.

Tatjana and Bridget began to lead Connie away while she moaned slightly. Lawrence picked up the towel and flicked it in frustration against a chair. He turned to Nicky. 'I'm a judge, as you know. Some of the things I hear in my court-room would freeze your blood. I've meted out punishment all my working life. You soon get to believe it's the here and now that matters.'

They sat in silence for a few more moments as Connie was guided down the corridor. Lawrence seemed to visibly relax once she had gone.

'I love my sister, but she drives me crazy. Isn't that always the way?'

'Is she always . . . like that?' Nicky asked.

'No,' Adam said, before his dad could answer. 'Often she can talk for quite long periods and be perfectly lucid.' He said this almost as a challenge to Lawrence.

'Though she's always been rude,' Lawrence added.

Adam jumped on his remark. 'That's not true—'

Nicky was keen to avoid getting caught in another father-and-son argument. She was guessing they happened with predictable regularity. 'Those are wonderful photos,' she said, pointing at the wall opposite her.

Lawrence banged his hand down on the coffee table and pointed at his son. 'You put her up to that, didn't you!' His face broke out in a grin.

'They're Dad's,' said Adam. 'He's very proud of them.'

'I love their scale.'

'Thank you. I develop them myself to get that size.'

'Dad's got a darkroom here.'

'He only photographs trees,' added Bridget, coming back into the room. 'What does that say about a man?' She rolled her eyes in faux horror.

'An oak tree spends three hundred years growing, three hundred years living and three hundred years dying. Show me a human being as magnificent.'

'He's been in court too long,' Bridget said. 'It does strange things to a man.'

Lawrence sat back on the sofa and regarded Nicky. 'I met your just-fired editor a few times, you know. Did you rate him?' Nicky took a deep intake of breath. Lawrence laughed. 'You don't have to answer that. I'm being mean. But I hear you're going downmarket – that true?'

'Remember that he looks like a pickled beetroot,' Adam said. 'You don't have to answer his silly questions.'

'You'll probably know before I will,' replied Nicky.

Lawrence sighed. 'My sister . . . Connie is vain,' Lawrence continued. 'She'd love the idea of an obituary, and I'm just sorry she's not able to help much.'

'I think lives like Connie's might be just what the new regime is looking for. People think obituaries are all about death, but we're really celebrating someone's life.'

Lawrence looked rueful. 'Whereas I deal with the nature

of a person's death. People think there are good and bad deaths, but they don't realize how many are true horrors – it's only in court that that stuff is revealed.'

Bridget shuddered. 'This is very morbid.'

'Morbid, but true,' said Lawrence. 'We all die screaming, one way or another. Do you know that, Nicky? We're pre-programmed to fight to our last breath. It's the human condition.'

There was nothing more to say after that. They all took a gulp of wine in silence, Nicky trying to block out the image of Grace in the black water. What the others were pondering she had no idea.

11

'I assure you, Mr Haynes, your teeth are not a reflection of your soul.' The young Asian dentist pulled the paper mask off her mouth and sat back.

'Imagine how black they would be if they were!' She laughed and he saw her own pearly whites. Her uncomplicated, unadorned face only accentuated the perfection of her smile. 'Dorian Gray has a lot to answer for.'

She nodded. 'Indeed. The idea that our true inner natures are reflected in our appearance is a Victorian idea that has proved very hard to shift.'

'Well, it keeps you in work. All of us, your clients, I mean, are really trying to make ourselves look –' he paused, searching for the appropriate word '– holier.' He gave her what he thought of as his wolfish grin, and she indulged him with another smile. He saw the wedding band on her finger with a touch of regret. He'd have liked to try it on with her. Success or failure, he loved the challenge and the chase.

'Now, let's take a look.' She pulled an overhead mirror towards him and he parted his lips. 'The veneers on these two side teeth give you a nice neat line that still looks natural.' Troy gazed at his five-grand grin. He ran his tongue over his new teeth, feeling the smooth outline. 'You'll notice how there's still a tiny gap between each tooth. That makes each tooth look real. This way you don't get that increasingly unnatural effect as you age.'

Not her too, thought Troy with a bolt of panic. Even the hot dentist was talking about him ageing.

'I've begun the bleaching, but you probably won't notice anything for a few days. It's a gradual process and we don't want to do too much too soon or you'll end up looking a little too "Hollywood" and it can make your teeth brittle.'

Troy nodded. He knew how easily teeth could break. And skulls; bones of all kinds, in fact. He'd grafted for his money over the years. Maybe that was what had aged him. It was time to stop working so hard. He rinsed and spat out a pink, strawberry-flavoured liquid. His jobs had not all been as easy or as fun as Marcia. But as he sat in the pretty dentist's chair in Harley Street he knew he'd still rather live this way; the alternative seemed grotesque and pointless – the drudgery and poverty of the nine to five, a jumped-up tyrant further up the greasy pole using his small bit of power to stamp on your manhood, and coming home to a nag who never turned the telly off. His brother and the grisly wife sprang to mind.

After school Troy had gone to work in the kitchens at the airport because he needed cash for women and drugs. There he clashed horns with the head of catering and, just like with the teachers and the headmaster at school, he didn't want to *be* that man when he was older. He parted company with the plastic chopping boards and nasty white hats pretty quickly, but not before noticing the private jet that would sometimes land or take off while he and his fellow grunts took their fag breaks out by the bins. He made it his job to come to the attention of the man stepping out of that private jet. Lyndon B was to Troy that completely alluring animal: a property developer. That Lyndon obviously had an eye for young men Troy soon turned to his advantage because Lyndon B needed a handsome helper on his plane, someone to be his 'biscuit chucker', his beck-and-call guy. What he did in his bedroom was up to him. Looking back, Troy realized Lyndon probably saw something in him, an amorality he could use, a violence lurking just beneath the surface that could explode with deadly results. Troy was a young man he could shape, and Troy was only too happy to go along. The airport was the perfect setting to be schooled not in flying but in crime. He smuggled for Lyndon, stayed loyal and kept his mouth shut as the nature of Lyndon's business dealings became clearer. Lyndon began to ask him for favours that extended after a few years to roughing up people and threatening others. He met Darek, who occasionally did jobs for Lyndon but ran his own stuff too. It was only a short and painless step to do work for Darek on the side.

The dentist lowered the chair and Troy stood up, helpfully handing her back the protective bib.

Troy's life had stayed this way for years, until three months ago, when Lyndon was diagnosed with a serious heart murmur. He holed up in a hospital in Monaco, leaving Troy adrift in London, and for the first time in his life Troy had too much time to think about the big things: death and love and money. If Lyndon died, Troy had nothing.

Uncomfortable thoughts about where he was going and what he had achieved were beginning to trouble him, when he got a call from Darek about a job. They met in a pub and, unusually, Darek was drunk and full of bitter recrimination about his girlfriend having walked out on him. Troy was an opportunist and he helped take Darek home; there, fuelled with another bottle of vodka, Darek became just a little too chatty. He let slip that the best job he'd ever done earned him half a million quid. Troy laughed and pretended to drink his vodka. He realized that at the end of that commission, dangling at the very end, had been him. The bottom feeder. He had only got thirty grand.

It was all about proximity to the money. The price of killing was flexible: a lowlife on a south London estate would kill a man for £200 and a wrap; murder for an oligarch and you got half a million. The act of pulling the trigger was no different and neither was the outcome. The only difference was the cash.

Troy washed his hands in the dentist's sink and used her hand cream. She held the door open for him and wished him a good day and he said he was looking forward to seeing her soon.

Troy had never been afraid of taking risks or of playing dirty, and he'd done both with Darek.

'Problem with this business, Troy, is you can't move up. One client gives you all the work and nearly all your cash,' Darek had said that night.

'What about the one-offs we do?'

'They don't make you any money. There's no repeat business.'

Troy walked down the steps of the town house in Harley Street. He paused, running his tongue along his teeth, and watched a limo with blacked-out windows draw up. He wondered who was coming for a nip and tuck in the discreet building opposite.

As Darek had slurred and farted on his sofa Troy had had his light-bulb moment: *I can force repeat business and they are rich enough to pay.*

It had taken Troy three days to get the information out of Darek, and then three hours of hunting for the safety deposit key when Darek could no longer talk. He'd washed his hands eight times after that.

The door of the limo opened and a woman in huge dark sunglasses, flanked by two minders, emerged. She stared straight ahead as she walked to the front door. The world looked at her, not the other way round.

Lyndon was still on a recuperative holiday in a special facility in the south of France, so Troy had had time to study

Darek's list and work out a plan of sorts. He walked down the street, the pavement on this side cast in deep shadow. He stopped. The phone in his left pocket was ringing. Darek's phone. He answered and a woman asked, 'Darek?'

'He's retired. I've taken over.'

The phone went dead. Troy swore, annoyed that a foray into this new line of business seemed to have ended before it had begun. But five minutes later she rang again. 'You still doing the same things?'

'Your problem, my pleasure.' It had sounded catchy to Troy earlier when he'd practised in his mirror and he was trying it out for the first time now. 'Where's the drop?'

'Paddington Green Cemetery, like before.'

Before. So Darek had lied. He did get repeat business. 'Be more specific.'

'The weeping angel grave. Aisle 1B.'

'It's all up front.'

'Of course,' she replied.

'It's the same price.'

She didn't disagree. 'I want it done fast.'

'OK.'

She paused. 'I'll have something there by three this afternoon.'

Troy smiled to himself. The drop was a bouquet with the money and the picture inside a plain envelope. '*Muchas gracias.* If you're bringing flowers, I like daisies, by the way.'

She snorted. 'The symbol of innocence. I prefer chrysanthemums.'

'What do they mean?'

'Death.'

Troy looked at the phone, but she had already hung up.

12

Troy didn't say hello, they didn't shake hands or do anything that might make people think they were together. This was all part of the game, part of the hiring: assessing people, taking precautions. They just picked each other out and fell into step.

'You picked a funny place to meet!' Struan had to shout over the horns and rattles that were going off all around them.

Troy leaned towards Struan and spoke in a low voice. 'Good cover.'

They tried to walk down the street but the crowds were hemming them in on all sides. 'What are this lot getting all worked up about, then?' Struan was aghast as hordes of people milled around, waving placards, holding up bed sheets covered with appliquéd lettering and moving at a snail's pace down the Strand towards Trafalgar Square.

'It's a student march,' replied Troy. 'Why do you think they're protesting? More money or fewer cuts. No one ever protests about anything else.' Troy held up his hands as if to join in. 'Enjoy. You probably won't ever go on another.'

Struan frowned, staring: a guy with piercings dotted across his top lip was walking arm in arm with a girl with a shaved head. 'Go back to bed!' he shouted. 'They all look like fucking freaks.'

Troy glanced down at Struan's forearm, where a tattoo of a snake with big fangs coiled round and round and ended under the strap of his gold watch. 'I guess it all depends on your point of view.'

Struan unstuck his shirt from his stomach. 'Fuck, it's hot! I'm a bit over it, to be honest. I saw someone collapse in the car park at B&Q yesterday. Louise had to go and help. I got tarmac all over my shoes. It was literally melting.' He shuddered. 'That stuff never comes off.'

Troy smiled. Struan hadn't changed. He was still too talkative, still with Louise. They had known each other a long time and while that didn't mean someone wasn't going to cast you aside if a better offer came in, it probably made things safer than with someone new. Because the fear that someone had switched sides, that someone was doing what they shouldn't, was always there. Struan was a former squaddie turned bouncer, working for a man from Essex who controlled the doors of every major upmarket venue in the West End. Controlling the doors didn't mean deciding which hen parties or footballers to let in, which paparazzi to tip off; it was all about which drug dealers were allowed to operate inside, and who was cut out. If anyone was found to be working independently and not sharing the proceeds with the owner it was Struan's job to sort them out, and whether it was immediately down a side alley or with a more organized hammering later, Struan was efficient and effective. Troy had met him when he'd driven Lyndon B to a club off Regent Street for a meeting with the man from Essex. As they waited for their bosses they'd had a few drinks, had a laugh, and found they had a mutual love of poker. They had started playing regularly together and things had gone from there.

'How's business?'

Struan swore. 'Bad. Numbers are down. They're all out in Shoreditch or at pop-ups in Hackney. Even the tourists are staying away. It's not like the old days. The party's over, mate.'

Good, thought Troy. Struan was still a pessimist, still had

money problems, was keen to earn extra however he could. Troy pulled an envelope out of the inside pocket of his linen jacket and handed it to Struan, who put it in a plastic Tesco bag he was carrying. 'Ten thousand.' Struan scratched his nose. They had met yesterday and Troy had outlined the job. Meeting today meant he had accepted.

Troy was busy going through Darek's list and was keen to extort the maximum amount of money in the shortest time. It felt like a piece of good luck that could run out if he didn't exploit it quickly. He needed to outsource this new job. He knew how time-consuming following a hit was and he quite liked the idea that he was too busy and important to do it himself. And so Struan had duly stepped in.

'Afterwards, call me from a phone box and tell me someone fainted at Homebase. Oh, and one more thing. Play rough.'

Struan shrugged and Troy felt a great urge to go and wash his hands.

'Hey,' said Struan, looking closely at Troy. 'You've had your teeth done.'

Troy was pleased. No point in paying for improvements if no one noticed. Stealth wealth was bullshit, as far as he could see. 'Yeah, I had a bit of work.'

'Eh, well, they look really good.' Struan was nodding, pleased that he'd worked it out. 'I'm gonna go for a few things myself . . .' He gave Troy a knowing look. 'Stops the girlfriend spending it, if you know what I mean.'

Troy agreed, but didn't show it. Struan looked like a meat-head but it was a mistake to underestimate him. It was a smart way to spend money. No one could take your nip and tuck off you. Troy wondered if it was the love handles or the double chin Struan would get sucked out. Maybe both. They were all moulding themselves into brighter, shinier versions of their real selves, doing their best to hide their warts: their dark, vicious secrets.

Troy listened to the horns and a few leftover vuvuzelas as he ambled down the road in the sunshine. His kills didn't affect him but he did remember them; the first one was hard to forget. He watched two girls in miniskirts link arms in front of him, their hair bouncing on their shoulders like in some shampoo advert. The first job would have been about their age. Must be more than ten years ago now. It didn't seem that long. He'd learned some valuable lessons from that one. Never hesitate, don't look them in the eye. She hadn't fought, but she'd begged. Normally begging left him cold; the mark's weakness made it easier to be done and be gone. But there was something about her . . . He'd spent too long watching her from behind the curtain, that was the problem. The old appreciation and impossibility of turning away from an attractive woman had temporarily distracted him from the job in hand. It had been a hot night then too and she'd moved lazily this way and that in the bed. Christ, he was only a man, and who could resist having a gander at that? Francesca – that had been her name. She'd suited it, with that tumble of blonde hair swishing against the pillow. It was the last thing he saw of her before the black night swallowed her up. He was nearly at the bedroom door before she hit the ground.

A man with a megaphone round his neck handed Troy a flyer, which he let slip through his hands to the litter-strewn street.

She'd sat up in the half light, gloriously naked. God, those breasts! It would have been romantic if he hadn't been there to kill her, the curtains billowing on the balcony in the warm wind off the ocean . . . Then she'd got up and stretched and he could see the roundness of her stomach, the child growing within.

A line of policemen at a junction brought Troy back to the present with a jolt. For the first time he wondered who had wanted her dead. That he didn't think about the past at all was no surprise, considering what was buried there. Be careful, he counselled; don't go soft in your old age. It wouldn't do at all to develop a conscience. Find that and you were dead in this business.

He had been working backwards through Darek's list, disturbing the past. Some of the information on the neat, handwritten sheet made instant sense to him because he'd done the jobs himself. An area code for a town he remembered, for example. There were few names (Darek had been careful), but Troy had been phoning these numbers and seeing what popped up. Now he wondered which was more valuable: a secret a few years old, or one buried long ago? How much more of a shock would it be to be confronted by what you did, what you desired and executed, in another lifetime? Was it time to resurrect a trail gone cold? Francesca. It was time to stir up the dust that had settled.

Troy's chat with Struan was over. They parted with only the briefest of goodbyes and Troy walked down to the Embankment. He stepped into an ancient red phone box and was almost beaten back by the smell of urine. He pulled out the list of phone numbers from a pocket and dialled the number next to Francesca's name. He was amazed that it rang; he'd been afraid it might have been disconnected many years ago. A voicemail clicked in after a few rings. 'This is Greg Peterson. Please leave a message.' Troy put down the receiver and turned back to the fresh air.

13

Nicky didn't pack an overnight bag as she was coming back the same day. She tried to calm herself: it was a glorious Sunday in high summer, she was on an intriguing hunt for information from the past and she was going to a country house. She put the roof down on Greg's convertible and drove to Lawrence's flat to pick up Adam. She had insisted on meeting in the street so she could avoid seeing the family again and being subjected to their scrutiny.

He let out a faux-impressed 'whoo whoo' when he saw the car, and jumped into the passenger seat without opening the door. 'Well, this is a lot flasher than I expected you to be.'

'It was Greg's choice.'

Adam stroked the leather seats and put his feet up on the dashboard. Nicky knocked them off with her hand.

'So Greg likes his Beamer box fresh.'

'Yes, he does.'

'So he's into status symbols.'

'Everyone's into status symbols.'

'I'm not.'

'But you're using that big carrot of a house to get me out of town for the day,' she retorted.

Adam laughed. 'Don't romanticize it. It's not what you're thinking.'

'You don't know what I'm thinking.' She smiled and started the engine.

'Can I drive?'

She laughed. 'No way.'

'Go on, let me drive it.'

'Over my dead body!'

'Go on. I can tell you want me to.'

'No, I don't!'

He had his hand along the back of the seat; he was unfazed and enjoying himself. 'Today is about doing something different, taking you out of your comfort zone. I can show you what this car can really do.'

'My comfort zone is huge, and I know what this car can do.'

He leaned towards her, whispering, 'Live a little.' She held his gaze. There it was again, his knack of bringing out in her an urge to be silly. She held her hands out, just like he had done in the plane when they first met. 'It's all yours, Adam, it's all yours.'

He grinned at her but didn't get out of the car, sliding across on top of her instead, so she had to wriggle underneath him into the passenger seat. They were already invading each other's spaces, breaking down the barriers. Nicky glanced back to see whether Lawrence or Bridget was watching. She felt shame slice through her at what she was doing.

'Put your seatbelt on, we're going for a ride.'

Nicky put her sunglasses on and felt the warm sun on her bare arm. They were happily silent for a while as they headed west, soon pulling up at a red light at a four-way crossing, pedestrians crowding the pavement and pouring across the road. Adam revved the engine aggressively.

'No dents,' she added playfully but Adam ignored her, seemingly in a world of his own. He muttered something under his breath and then without warning swung right, directly into the path of a people carrier, which screeched to a halt in the middle of the junction. A variety of people jumped on horns quicker than to the buzzers on *University*

Challenge and pedestrians froze in mid-stroll. Adam turned right on the red light and tore off down a side street, flattening Nicky to the back of her bucket seat. 'What the . . .'

The change in Adam took her completely by surprise. He swung expertly but very fast round a mini roundabout, sped through a series of side streets, and while waiting at another red light he flicked the switch that put the hood up.

'I was enjoying it down,' she snapped, annoyed and startled at his rash behaviour.

'I'm driving, it's my shout,' Adam replied. He leaned over and put some music on.

She didn't reply, watching instead as Adam drove like a man in a hurry 'Why did you do that?'

He didn't answer.

'Adam!'

'It was just a bit of fun.'

She stared at him, sure he was lying. She checked the wing mirror for the cars behind them but could see nothing out of the ordinary. She wondered if Bea had been following them and if he'd just lost her. Or maybe he was just a young man driving a fast car. She tried hard not to be so annoyed at his reckless posturing, so different from her safety-conscious husband. He began to show off again, accelerating to get through some traffic-calming columns and it took a further ten minutes for her to forgive him.

They drove for an hour and then he turned off the motorway and they began to twist and turn down a series of smaller and more minor roads.

'Are we getting close?'

He slowed and pointed to his left. 'That's the wall of the estate.' A large, grey-brick wall snaked along the road and Nicky felt the stirrings of excitement again. 'Wow. I thought you said it was near the airport. There's not a soul out here.'

He slowed almost to a stop then turned up a rough track

with no sign and they bounced along, a cloud of dust ballooning out behind them. He shook his head. 'Track's got worse.'

They drove for a while through some woods and eventually came to a high, wrought-iron gate. Adam got out a huge metal key and opened the lock.

'It's like something from *Harry Potter*.' Adam didn't reply as he swung the gate inwards with a screech. 'This is going to be amazing, I can tell,' Nicky said in a burst of enthusiasm.

'Hayersleigh House,' Adam said, and she realized it was the first time she'd heard the name. Of course, how silly – she'd never thought to ask. All grand houses have names. Her internet search may well have turned up more if she'd—

She didn't hear the noise at first because the car was running over gravel, but then they were surrounded by a roar so powerful it seemed as if it would flatten the car. Nicky instinctively ducked, the hairs on her neck jumping to attention.

'What the fuck . . .' As she turned the sun was obliterated by the underbelly of a plane and for a few seconds they were plunged into the feel of autumn. She could see the wheels above her head, the black oblongs into which they would soon retract, the shiny metal. The wind came after, hot and forceful and infused with petrol fumes, before it died down as the aircraft gained altitude. The BMW felt tiny and tinny and exposed in the face of such power. Nicky watched it go in stunned silence.

'Flight FR687 to Lanzarote. There'll be another in ten minutes.'

Nicky's hands were shaking. 'It gave me a fright.'

He turned and pointed. 'The end of the runway is beyond that wall. There's a bit of space and a load of barbed wire and fencing and warnings about trespassing, but it's over there.' He drove on down the drive. 'And the house is here.'

They came over a rise and the land fell away, and Nicky saw the sun shining off an ornamental lake in front of a large lawn that sloped up to a house made of the same grey brick as the estate wall. It was a house big enough to have wings and servants' quarters and stabling; things that the modern world had rendered obsolete. 'Welcome to Hayersleigh House, our English idyll under the flight path.'

'If you cover your ears,' Nicky added, and they both laughed.

The gravel drive ended in a comma of a flourish by the large central door but Adam parked at the back of the house near a side door and a ramshackle collection of outhouses and garages. They got out of the car as another plane came over. 'Where's that one going?' Nicky shouted.

'Sharm el Sheikh?' Adam shouted back.

He fiddled around in some pots of dried-up flowers by the back door, fished out a key and opened the door. Nicky stepped straight into a 1970s-style kitchen that wouldn't have looked out of place in a suburban three-bed semi. It smelled unused and looked unloved. She put her handbag on the small table in the middle of the room and followed Adam past a series of storerooms and then out to a grand entrance hall, bigger than a room in a normal house. Doors led off to the dining room, drawing room and the stairs.

'You've got a billiard room!'

Adam nodded. 'The felt's ripped. No one can play on it now.' He turned to the large double front door. 'Key's been lost for years,' he added.

'Did the ghost steal it?'

'No, the mad woman in the attic did.'

Nicky watched the dust billow in the sunbeams as she sat on a pew made of dark wood that smelled faintly of a lemon furniture polish. 'It's an amazing place, but why is it so run down?'

'My dad's life is in London now, Connie lived here until she couldn't do it any more, the planes have increased lots in the last few years . . . We're in a dispute with the airport about it.'

'What do you mean?'

'They've got the permission to expand, which means they want to buy the grounds. Dad's resisting. He's been locked in a legal argument with the airport owners for years now. He's driving Lyndon B mad.'

'Who's that?'

'A guy who owns some regional airports, here and in Spain. He's the next BAA, if he gets his way.' Adam opened a door opposite the dining room and walked into the darkness. 'It's not an exaggeration to say Dad and Lyndon hate each other.' Nicky followed him into the drawing room. It was gloomy, with shutters across the bay windows. She reached out for the light switch. 'Don't bother. There's no electricity. There's a generator if we really need it, but we're off the mains here.'

'Really?'

'Dad's convinced Lyndon's done something with our supply as it comes across what is now airport land. You know what I think? He just forgot to pay the bill, so Southern Electric cut us off.'

'The entrepreneur versus the aristo.'

'You're such a journalist, thinking in headlines.' He yanked at one of the shutters and it opened with a grinding clank. She crossed the room to help him as another plane made the windows rattle.

'Did you get used to the planes when you lived here?' she asked.

'I never lived here. I was sent away to boarding school and was with my dad and Bridget in London in the holidays.'

With each shutter they opened it was like breathing life into a mausoleum.

'It's such an amazing view,' Nicky couldn't help saying in wonder, as she scrunched her eyes against the sun now flooding the room. The opened shutters revealed a set of patio doors that led to a terrace and then to the grassy slope that ended in the lake, which the sun bounced off like beaten silver. Beyond that were flat fields with huge trees dotted here and there, and far away on the horizon a black line which must have been the wall, on the other side of which lay the airport. 'So no one lives here now?'

'No. Mrs Perkins is usually here, keeping an eye out, making sure no one makes off with the silver.'

'She must have a job vacuuming without electricity.'

Adam laughed a little sadly. 'She lives in the village, but she's on holiday at the moment. I keep telling Dad to sell, but he's a stubborn old man.'

'Who cuts the lawn?'

'What?'

'Lawns need lots of work and these gardens are huge.'

'The deer eat it. There's no one here, no one at all. It's just us.'

Their tour of the ground floor ended in the wine cellar, which was really a small room without a window sandwiched between the storerooms off the kitchen and the back stairs. Most of the shelves were empty, cobwebs dragging down from the low ceiling. Adam jumped down the three wooden steps into the gloom and began brushing dust off labels.

'Is some of this stuff valuable?' Nicky asked, bending her head to get in.

'I doubt it. Quantity not quality was the mantra.'

It was cool and dark in the wine cellar, the light failing to reach the furthest corners. Nicky held up a bottle, trying to see whether it was red or white.

'Got mine,' said Adam.

Nicky's eyes wandered over the many empty shelves, the wealth of this semi-cellar presumably quickly disappearing down the thirsty throats of Adam and his mates. The thought made her sad, somehow. It took years to build something, and but a few raucous nights to end it. She followed him up the creaky steps, wondering if this was an allegory for her marriage. He picked two glasses off a shelf and they began walking round the drawing room, pausing to look at the dark oil paintings of stern-looking men and women, or men with dogs, which were hanging on chains from the picture rail.

'I've never seen a picture rail actually used like that.'

'It's a way of never being able to get rid of the ancestors. Aunt Connie said that they used to give her nightmares when she was young.'

Nicky walked further along the wall, examining the paintings. 'They're all holding guns. What is it about the upper classes and their guns?'

Adam laughed. 'They're still here. There's a cabinet.'

'No way!' She followed Adam out to the hallway and by the billiard room there was a locker with a long glass front and two guns stacked against the supports inside. Nicky pulled at the door. 'It's shut.'

'There's a key somewhere.' Adam felt along the top of the case and a moment later found the key. He opened the door and pulled out a shotgun, aiming it at Nicky's chest. 'Stick 'em up!'

It was more unpleasant having a gun pointed at her than she had imagined; its power and connotations were impossible to ignore. 'Tell me that's not loaded.'

Adam shrugged. 'I've no idea.'

'Please put it back.' Adam didn't move. His grin grew wider. He lifted the gun towards her face, looking down the barrel at her. 'Stop it!' He didn't, and a long moment passed. 'Put that fucking thing away!'

A spell had been broken. Adam held up his hands in mock defeat. 'Relax, it's OK. I'm kidding.' The gun rested on his shoulder, pointing up to the ceiling.

She was suddenly angry. 'You never mess about with guns.' She tried to grab it from his hand, preparing for a battle, but he limply let her have it. It was colder and heavier than she had expected, the wood smooth in her palm. She bundled it back into the cabinet and locked the door, putting the key back where Adam had retrieved it from. When she turned back he was staring at her, looking hurt. 'I'm sorry. It's the total surrender it demands. The – I don't know – bowing before the great power of the fucking gun. These things kill, Adam!'

'It was just a joke,' he said quietly, and walked off into the drawing room.

Nicky felt bad, but she didn't feel in the wrong. He shouldn't point guns in people's faces. She picked up the key from the top of the cabinet and stuck it behind a photo on a bureau in the hall. She didn't want a repeat of what had just happened. It might be his house and she was a guest, but she was unnerved. Hiding the key was a way to keep things light between them. She looked at the picture in the frame and paused. It was Adam's mother, she was sure. Their eyes were the same shape, with the same intense stare, but hers were blue. She was looking up at the photographer, her hands clasping her elbows in a defensive gesture. She was wearing a frilly blouse that made her look a bit prim; her blonde hair was iron straight and long. She was beautiful and young and it brought home to Nicky the enormity of Adam's loss: a child without a mother. I don't have a single picture of my mother, thought Nicky suddenly. Not even one.

She looked round at the grand old house, steeped in gener-ations of family history, ancestors on the walls, photos in frames, stories, anecdotes, a lineage recorded in Debrett's. It really brought home to Nicky, for the first time, that she was without history; she had been stripped of her own story. If you don't know who you are, can you know where you're going? She was affected by this and retreated to the toilet, shaken.

That these unresolved feelings about her unknown family should appear so strongly here, of all places, was a shock to Nicky, and she would have spent longer thinking it through but she was soon distracted by her admiration of the trompe l'oeil wallpaper in the toilet, some of which was peeling at the sides with the damp. Guns, dogs and horses – the motifs of the upper classes. A representation of her upbringing would have been a drinks trolley, a chicken brick and those British bird coasters. She weed on the curly blue lettering in the toilet bowl that advertised the workshop that had fashioned the ceramic. 'Pissing on the workers, are we, Nics?' That's what Maria would say when she told her. But Maria, despite her fashionable flirtations with revolutionary politics in her youth, would be rapt. This set-up was every girl's dream, however much they pretended otherwise. She'd seen Maria steal *Country Life* from the Art Desk, just as she had done. She was hanging out with a handsome, passionate young man with a crumbling estate and a tragic past. In many ways Adam and Greg were similar – no wonder she was attracted to him. She was dealing with high emotion and chaos and it was a heady combination.

She came back into the billiard room and looked at the huge painting hanging on the back wall.

'My mum painted this.'

'Oh bless.'

'It's awful, really awful.'

'Yes, I see what you mean.'

It was a view of the estate seen from the side, where a huge willow tree dominated a section of lawn. It was a timid and literal representation of the view. It was sludgy and sad, but not in an arresting way. Nicky tried to find something positive to say. She admired anyone who had a go and thought sniping at someone's ambition, however poorly executed, was mean, but she couldn't help thinking of the striking, modern prints in Lawrence's London flat – so much better than these.

'Let's get Connie's stuff,' Adam said and they wandered up the broad turning staircase to the bedrooms on the first floor, passing more paintings by Adam's mother of the lake and other views of the estate, some seen through a first-floor window.

They were on the top landing now, sun cascading through the floor-to-ceiling windows, where a much better, larger oil painting, of a cavalier knight, hung on the landing wall. He was staring sternly out of the canvas, his hand on the hilt of a huge sword. 'Oh we have to do something funny,' Adam said. 'Close your eyes. Go on, close them.' Nicky gave a nervous half giggle. 'Go on, it's an old family game. Everyone plays it when they come here, it's a Thornton ritual. Just stand here on the landing and close your eyes.'

'I'm in.' Nicky liked silly games. She put her hands over her eyes, listening. She heard nothing. 'Can I open them yet?' There was no answer. 'Adam?' She waited a few more moments and then took her hands away and looked around. The sun was still shining, the dust dancing lightly on the rising summer air. She looked down both corridors that led away from the landing but Adam wasn't there. She leaned over the banister but he didn't seem to be downstairs. A plane began its low drone over the house, the noise reaching its crescendo a short while later. The silence crept back. She sensed Adam was near but she couldn't work out where. She heard a faint noise by the picture of the cavalier and took a step towards it. Where was he? She stared at the picture and gasped. Its eyes were moving! She burst out laughing as

Adam rolled his eyes theatrically in the cavalier's head. 'That is brilliant!'

Adam opened a hidden door in the painting, made to follow the outline of the knight's armour, and Nicky joined him in the secret room. It was larger than expected and the only light came from the two holes in the eyes. She looked out at the corridor and the top of the stairs. 'When I came to stay we had such a laugh scaring people,' Adam said. 'Look, here are the eyes you put back.' He held up a piece of wood with the eyeballs painted on it and pointed at the little shelf that it sat on.

'Who painted this, then?'

Adam sniggered. 'Certainly not my mother!'

14

Greg woke in his bed with a start, clawing his way to consciousness. He lay panting in the wet sheets, his heart hammering. He had been falling, twisted and contorted . . . He wondered if he had been screaming, and if anyone in the hotel had heard. He reached out for the ringing phone and dragged himself to sit upright on the side of the bed.

It was Liz, her voice crisp and accusing. 'I've got some news.'

'Yeah?'

'She picked up a young man this morning in the car.'

'Who is he?'

'How should I know! She met him on Portobello Road.' Greg frowned. He opened the Evian bottle on the bedside table. 'Then they drove off.'

'Where did they go?'

Liz paused. 'I don't know.'

'You mean you lost them?'

'Yes, Greg! This isn't an action film! I'm not exactly trained to do this! He was driving. He suddenly took off.'

'He was driving my car?' The silence hung heavy in the air. 'He was driving my fucking car?'

'They swapped when she met him.'

Greg began to squeeze the small plastic bottle in his hand. A cold pebble of hatred and jealousy formed in his throat as he thought of Nicky. He was stuck here, working seventeen-hour days, seven days a week, while back home his wife was letting her toy boy smear his hands over the gearstick of his beloved motor. She knew how much he cared for his car, and he didn't apologize or feel embarrassed about that – it was what men of his class and age did: care, covet and show off. Why else did men buy Kevlar bicycles and flat-screen, sixty-inch, high-resolution TVs with surround sound? He squeezed so hard on the tiny Evian bottle water splashed onto his fist.

'They were driving west when he suddenly ran a red light, turned right across two lanes of oncoming traffic and sped off. He nearly hit a pedestrian. It came out of the blue. She looked as surprised as I was.'

Too much saliva was draining into Greg's mouth. Surprises in his life had never been good; unexpected news was, to Greg, simply tragedy by another name. After what had happened to Grace it was no wonder. The anger was being chased by fear, the claustrophobia of not knowing, of having to imagine. 'What did he look like?'

'He's got dark hair, kind of tall, really young.'

'How young?'

'Mid-twenties, I'd guess.' Greg thought back to his Skype call with Nicky after she nearly drowned in the Thames and was rescued by some young buck. It was the same jumped-up little fucker, he was sure of it. 'She didn't take a bag with her. She wasn't planning on going for long.'

'Hang on.' Greg put his mobile down as the hotel phone rang.

'Mr Peterson, your car is waiting for you, sir,' Sheri's or Diane's or Trudi's sing-song voice trilled from reception.

'Thanks.' He turned back to the call from London.

'Maybe it's nothing, Greg. He was probably just showing off.'

Greg's feeling of impotence was redoubled by being thousands of miles away. He picked his trousers off a chair and put them on. His plan had made a twisted sense at the time: keep far away from Nicky and the bad karma that surrounded him couldn't contaminate her. He had thought their love could survive the distance. After all, he had survived things that would have broken other men; as a consequence he believed he was not like other men. He veered wildly between amazement that he was still here and fear at what tomorrow might bring. But now he felt that in trying to protect her he had simply lost her. All that effort and pain was for nothing! A surge of hatred for this young man flowed through him. Jealousy had a power and a logic all its own. He knew he shouldn't be asking Liz to keep tabs on Nicky, but he had been separated for ever from normal by Grace's murder and by what had gone before. He wiped his sweating brow. Was it so wrong that he was trying to buy a little insurance? Why me, Greg thought. For the millionth time the unanswerable question came back to him . . . He had lost Grace, and now, because of how the past was shaping him, he was in danger of losing Nicky too . . . The anger he tried so hard to control swamped him.

'Greg?' His half growl, half grunt and the sound of breaking glass was clearly audible down the phone.

'I'm still here.' Greg stared at the shards of the vase that had stood on the mantelpiece above the instant fake-log gas fire before he'd hurled the doll-sized Evian bottle at it. Against all the odds, he was still here, he was still clinging on; on the surface he was a success, a man with a wife and a future that was his to control, if only he could forget his past . . .

'I'm not sure I can do much more, I have to work tomorrow.'

'OK, thanks, Liz.'

'Greg? I'm sorry.'

Greg looked out of the window at the weak sun struggling to shine through the pollution layer. La la land. Helio was downstairs waiting to drive him to the shoot, where he'd have breakfast at the catering van. The public would watch from behind the lines set up to keep them at bay. He'd shoot images today that would remain cast for ever in cinema history. A smooth, slick, fantasy representation that bore no relation to the effort required to make it. He needed to remember that. He rang off and phoned reception. 'Can you tell the cleaner to watch out? I accidentally broke a vase this morning. I don't want her to get hurt.'

15

Upstairs they walked past a series of bedrooms, some of them habitable, others filled with broken chairs and old trunks. A large damp patch stained part of the corridor. 'I guess all Connie's stuff would have been kept in here,' Adam said, opening the door to a bedroom that overlooked the lake. The room had a single brass iron bedstead with a blue satiny cover, a faded Indian rug on the floorboards and a wardrobe.

Adam began rummaging through a series of trunks, unearthing clothing and cloche hats and papers and dust.

'Was she an organized kind of woman?' Nicky asked, having a sneezing fit.

'No. She thought of herself as too bohemian to bother about order or anything. The room at Dad's is a comedy of junk and stuff she won't throw away. It drives Bridget mad because it spoils her modern, clean-line aesthetic. There are to be no wonky standard lamps in Bridget's eye line!' He shook his head. 'It's pathetic what little is left at the end, in the end.'

'I completely disagree. My whole job is about showing how much there is to celebrate and to remember.'

Adam opened a large box of photographs and started rifling through them.

'Maybe. We'll take this box outside on the terrace, but first let's see what else there is.'

Nicky pulled a suitcase out from under the bed. Inside

were about ten faded red notebooks. She picked one out at random, opened it and began scanning the first page. It was a description of repairs to the estate wall by the airport and of the trouble the builders had getting some machinery across the parkland. The passage was dated June 1988. She opened a page in the middle of the book and skim-read about a dinner party at the house. A date had been added here too. 'It looks like she kept a diary.'

Adam leaned over her shoulder to look. 'That's not Connie's writing.' Nicky turned to the front of the notebook but it was blank. She flipped through to the last page, finding it empty. Nicky picked up another notebook and looked at the first page and the last, but again they were unmarked.

'My God, my mum . . .'

Nicky turned to Adam, who was holding one of the notebooks. On the inside back cover she saw the marks of a fountain pen. In scratchy lettering was Catherine Thornton's name.

'These are hers? You never knew they were here?'

'No. I had no idea.' He knelt by the suitcase and put the notebook back in.

'Are you going to read them?'

Adam sat back on his heels. 'Not now, maybe not at all.' He looked at Nicky and gave a nervous half laugh. 'It feels weird.'

'A bit like an intrusion into something private from long ago.'

'I guess.' He gave a little shudder and closed the suitcase lid, then pushed it back under the bed. 'Come on, let's go outside.'

They lugged the box out into the afternoon shade and pored over the photos from the Tramps doorway, and others from parties here at the house. They ploughed through another bottle of wine as they laughed at letters of thanks from cabinet ministers, written on headed paper, handwritten notes that meant nothing to them from people they didn't know. At one point Adam pulled out a photo and turned to Nicky. 'Look at this.'

The photo summed up the late seventies: it was full colour, Connie was wearing a blood-red jumpsuit and large hoop earrings and her lips were glossy. She was pictured in a doorway, presumably of the club, a cigarette dangling from her lips. Half out of shot was a top Hollywood actor of the day, sunglasses, sideburns and all. The picture was taken at an angle and was full of movement and life.

'This is great. It's a good basis for a piece if I can talk to a few more people who knew her.'

Adam looked sad for a moment. 'I can't believe that's her. Not a trace of her old self remains . . .'

Nicky felt it best not to comment, but she didn't agree. Connie no longer had youthful, even features – the stroke made it hard to see any physical resemblance at all – but the eyes were the same. The hard, unyielding stare had remained until the very end: it was the stare she had given Nicky at the flat. 'She's had a good life, that's all you can hope for.' He looked away and said nothing.

They ate a picnic of bread and cheese and pickles as the shadows of the trees lengthened across the grass. She had enjoyed the day, but her thoughts started turning with increasing regularity to going home. Adam was stretched out on a sofa they'd dragged out from the drawing room behind them. She didn't want to go, but the longer they remained the more problems it would create. 'We need to be leaving soon.'

Adam looked up. 'I've changed my mind. I'm staying here.'

She was surprised. 'You're not coming back to London?'

'Not today, no. There're some things I need to do here so I'm going to hang around for a few days.'

'Oh.'

Nicky couldn't keep the disappointment from her voice, but she dismissed it quickly. Of course he could stay. 'I really need to go.'

'And leave all this?' He threw his long arm out lazily to take in the wide sweep of the estate. 'You simply can't go.'

She smiled at his insistence. 'How long are you going to be here?'

He leaned up on his elbows and looked at her, shrugging. 'As long as you are.'

His T-shirt had ridden up and she could see the flat hard planes of his stomach. She forced herself to look away as a bolt of desire shot through her.

'Stay another hour. Then you can go.'

'I suppose the traffic will be better if I leave later.' She paused, feeling the sexual tension.

As the dusk began to creep around them they retreated indoors to the drawing room. Adam found a box of matches and lit a variety of stubby candles. The smoke drifted towards the ceiling as shadows danced across the walls and over the unsmiling faces of the ancestors.

'Have you had a good time?'

'It's been amazing.'

'I take it Greg doesn't know you're here.'

Nicky shifted, embarrassed. 'No, he doesn't.'

'I guess we all have secrets from those we love.'

His mocking tone seemed to slap her to her senses. She stood up. She was much older than him, a married woman. It was time to take control. Whatever problems Greg and she were having, this wasn't the way to deal with them. She needed to banish the grey, the unspoken . . .

'Adam—'

'Don't. I don't need or want your pity.'

'It's hardly pity.'

'I fancy you rotten, is that such a sin?'

'No. But it's why I need to go. I'm married. I'm not in a position to get embroiled—'

'Come on, admit it: you fancy me.'

She smiled. 'I don't think it's helpful if I answer. It really is for the best.'

'For you.'

'For us both.' Adam said nothing. 'I really need to go.' She stared at him lying on the sofa, those dark eyes boring into her. He'd be good in the sack, that much was obvious. She forced herself back to the issue in question. 'If I misled you, I'm sorry.' He was silent, staring at her with something that for a flash of a moment looked like hate. For the first time Nicky felt a flicker of alarm. 'Maybe I shouldn't have come.'

That roused him. 'No, no, not at all. I'm delighted you came. It's just I . . . there's so much more I want to know about you.' He looked at her again. 'Of course you need to go. It's what you said you'd do.' He flung his feet to the floor and stood. 'I'll make you a coffee. We can't have you falling asleep at the wheel.'

She didn't answer; she was too busy trying to interpret that last comment. Odd, and aggressive. She dragged her hand across her face. She'd had too much to drink, or too much sun. She watched him stride out to the kitchen. No, he was a gent, a special person. She luxuriated in the what ifs of having lived a different life, of being a decade younger, of being unfettered by marriage, Greg, her career, of having the ability to throw it all up in the air and watch where it fell. She had been that person once; it was a privilege to glimpse her again, hazy with wine and heat, but deep down she had no desire to *be* that woman again. The flirtation was over. It was time to go home.

Adam came in with a delicate coffee mug, stirring in sugar. 'Sorry, there's no milk, but this'll make it taste better.' She wrapped her hand around the mug. He sat down on the floor opposite her, his legs crossed. They chinked drinks, his with wine, hers with coffee.

'I think this should be the last time we see each other, Adam. And I say that with a lot of regret.'

His expression was impossible to read. 'Have you done many things in life you regret?'

She paused. 'Oh loads, probably. But they pale next to not saving Grace. That's the thing I most regret.'

'The person who killed Grace, how do you know they're not coming for you?'

She was so shocked she couldn't reply for a moment. 'What do you mean?'

'Exactly that – her death had no motive and no reason, so how do you know you're not next?'

Nicky jumped to her feet. 'Adam! That's a disgusting thing to say!'

'I thought it was a logical question . . .' He tailed off when he saw the look on her face. 'I'm sorry. I didn't mean anything by it . . .'

Nicky slammed the mug down but was overcome by a wave of dizziness. She half fell backwards onto a chair.

'Are you all right?' His voice came from far away but she could see him bending over her, close. The image of him swam in her blurred vision, blending with the shadows and the candlelight. 'Nicky?'

16

Troy was getting angry. He could feel the heat begin in his belly and expand outwards. RJ was looking scared, turning almost green as he huddled on the rank armchair in the small room that stank of enclosed spaces and cigarette butts. The rumble of a skateboard's wheels bled through the window, followed by swearing and a clatter as someone young took a tumble on the walkway.

It had been harder than he imagined trying to track RJ down on the estate. No one knew who he was and Troy understood why: he was too poor for anyone to notice him. Eventually he'd ended up at this hovel. With the first slap he'd confessed readily enough to hiring a hit man to kill his business partner. He talked openly about his past life as if it belonged to an entirely different person. His eyes had turned almost dreamy as he recalled it.

'I got divorced, had a breakdown . . .' He tailed off, having trouble forming his thoughts. 'Been here for three years now.' It was as if he wanted the company. 'Never see the kids, the taxis are long gone.'

The anger spread hard and fast across Troy's chest as he punched RJ in the jaw. He heard the bone snap. His plan was being derailed by the man's weakness, by his inability to keep going in a crisis. People paid if they had something to lose, but this bastard was just waiting to be put out of his misery. There was obviously no money here. Not a sou.

Darek had kept records of his work as an insurance policy,

he told Troy proudly that night they were downing vodka at his flat. Names, dates and numbers, as much information as he could, sealed up in the box at the bank. Some of the jobs Troy had done himself; RJ's he had not. Darek had also kept records of the amounts that were paid, so Troy knew exactly what was due – and exactly what he'd been denied by Darek. It made him even angrier. Troy never met the client; he never knew their names, faces or what they did. All part of the know nothing, tell nothing mantra. But he had been the one taking the risk and getting a fraction of the reward. That had all been going to change . . . But the idea that RJ still had anything like the twenty grand he'd paid was laughable.

He thought about killing RJ, but what was the point? He gave him a punch in his left eye which knocked him clean out. RJ never heard his cry of anguish from the bathroom when Troy discovered that there was no soap in the flat.

Troy reeled along a south London arterial road searching for a pub or café. He couldn't get back in his car and touch his steering wheel with his dirty hands. About a quarter of a mile further on he found a parade of beaten-up shops and a greasy spoon and hurried to the bathroom past a series of plastic tables stuck to the wall and chairs bolted to the floor. He washed his hands four times with the liquid soap, scrubbed his nails on one hand with the backs of his nails on the other. He calmed right down instantly and came back out into the café. A square lady with large sweat circles under her armpits was manning a boiling urn. He slid into a plastic seat.

The square woman came over. 'What can I get you, handsome?' she asked, licking her finger and flicking the pages on a dog-eared pad.

'Tea.'

'Right you are.' She shuffled off.

Troy knew it wouldn't all go to plan. He knew that not every contact on Darek's list would be lucrative, or found. He thought of Lyndon, probably being massaged by a Moroccan juvenile under an orange tree. Well, he wanted his own tropical verandah and personal services. And by God, these conniving, lying, greedy, murdering motherfuckers were going to give them to him.

'Penny for your thoughts?' The square woman slid the cup over towards him. He smiled thinly.

Troy had only one: Greg Peterson.

17

Nicky struggled to keep her eyelids open. The room had turned ninety degrees. She sat up, disoriented, and a pain in her head exploded. She was on the floor of the drawing room, still in her clothes, an animal fur draped over her. The rough hairs of a big cat whose descendants were nearly extinct poked her palm. Her neck was stiff and her hip numb. The candles had burned down to black stains on the plates and the grey dawn was breathing a new day into the room. A plane rumbled overhead, drilling into her headache. Adam was not here. Had she spent the whole night on the floor? She had no idea. She stood in a hurry, annoyed and alarmed that she was still here. She saw a glass of water and drank it greedily, then tried to stagger to the door, but the sofa appeared before her and she sank down into pleasing softness. Better than the floor, was the last thought she could process.

It was Adam rubbing her arm that woke her fully in the end. The day was acid bright, the dawn long gone. 'You need to wake up. You've been out for hours and hours.' He pulled her upright. 'I made you a black tea.' She took the cup without answering and drank it down. 'Do you feel all right? You suddenly fell asleep last night and I couldn't wake you. But it's nine now. You've been asleep for more than twelve hours. Do you need to see a doctor?'

'I'm fine.'

She ran her hands distractedly through her hair,

embarrassed. Sitting side by side like this on a sofa had all the awkwardness of the first moments of the morning after the night before, without any of the pleasure to look back on. She desperately tried to remember what on earth had gone on, but it was all a blank. 'What happened last night? Why did I suddenly fall asleep?'

Adam shrugged, but he didn't meet her eye. 'I think you had too much to drink.'

The silence was heavy between them with things unspoken.

'Remember that when you nodded off I spent the night by myself.' He was defiant now. 'Not so much fun in that.'

Nicky said nothing. She was still trying to compose herself and banish the cotton-wool feeling from her head.

'Do you want a bath?' He was smiling now as he changed the subject.

'I thought there was no electricity.'

'There are no lights. There's a gas boiler that heats the water.'

She felt grubby and stiff and a soak would wake her up. He led her to an upstairs bathroom where there was an old roll-top bath. It had fat taps with the metal flaking off and a precarious plastic bridge linking the sides, bending in the middle with the weight of old shampoo bottles and dried-up bits of soap. The water was boiling and as she made shampoo peaks in her hair she tried to make sense of how she could fall asleep so soundly for so long. She had a blank, funny feeling in her head. She felt aware of how fragile she was, how she needed to be handled carefully. Misgivings she couldn't articulate swirled around. Had he drugged her? He was part of the Rohypnol generation, after all. She forced the thought sharply from her mind. 'Get a grip, Nicky,' she scolded. She rubbed herself dry with a towel so threadbare it made her skin turn pink.

When she came to the kitchen he was carefully lining up

slices of bread under the gas grill, humming a tune she didn't recognize. She did the washing-up as he cooked. She picked up a cup and was about to tip the contents down the sink when she realized it still had the remains of her coffee from last night. Adam had his back to her, buttering toast. She sniffed the contents, and then sniffed again. An aroma of coffee hit her. She watched the black liquid swirl away down the plughole. After a moment she sat down.

'Since you're still here, I can show you the grounds. We can swim in the lake.'

'I don't swim in lakes.'

'There's nothing to be frightened of. The bottom is sandy—'

'I don't swim in lakes,' she said, far too sharply.

He didn't reply. For the first time their conversation wasn't flowing; she felt guarded and suspicious. He turned, opened a cupboard and pulled out a tin of treacle, then sat at the table. 'There's no jam; it goes mouldy when no one's here. But this is just like honey.' He opened the tin and plunged in a knife, drawing out an elongating strand of black treacle, runny in the heat. He scraped it across the toast. Nicky had to overcome an urge to gag. She shoved her chair back so violently it crashed to the floor, making Adam jump.

'What's the matter?'

Nicky felt the sweat break out across her chest. An image of Grace, lying on the lawn in the moonlight, her blood as black as treacle as it ran over her lifeless chest, came to her with such force that she stumbled as she raced for the toilet and hurled violently. A moment later she heard Adam behind her.

'Are you ill?'

She was shaking all over, that horrific night coming back with brutal force. She sat on the toilet seat and tried to get a grip on her fraying imagination. She must be sick. How could she have fallen asleep for so long and now be a shuddering wreck, haunted by images she had spent years of her life trying to erase? She wanted to connect to the outside world, to hear familiar voices, to phone work and apologize for not being there.

'Can I borrow your phone?'

He paused. 'Who are you calling?'

His tone of enquiry was all wrong. 'Does it matter?' She was often quick to rise and couldn't keep the irritation from her voice.

'It's just that there's no way of charging the battery, so I try to keep calls to a minimum while I'm here, otherwise it'll run out.' He reached into his trouser pocket and pulled out his mobile. 'But here, of course you can use it.'

Nicky looked at the small black lifeline and felt ashamed. This was a man who had saved her life just over a week ago, who had jumped into a swirling river and risked his own neck for her, who had put her up in his house and spent an evening alone as she snored away, drunk on too much red wine. She made a quick call to Maria but she wasn't there. She left a message explaining that she was ill but would be back tomorrow.

'If you're sick, I can look after you.' She watched him blocking the doorway of the toilet. He was so large she couldn't see the hallway beyond him.

18

'I really don't want you to go.' Adam was playfully trying to pull her handbag off her shoulder as she approached the car. The shadows were lengthening across the grass again as the hot day wore on.

'But you know I have to.' Her shoulders were warm where they'd caught the sun when she and Adam had lounged on his terrace. Her misgivings about her night asleep had faded, but sexual tension was building and Nicky knew she had to be going. She didn't want an affair; she didn't want to lie any more to Greg. It was time to go.

She opened the car door and looked back at Adam. He wore a pale blue T-shirt that accentuated his deepening tan, the fabric taut across his chest. I'll probably never kiss anyone as beautiful again, she realized. Suddenly, with a last burst of enthusiasm that a reluctant party guest discovers when they know they can finally leave, Nicky reached out and kissed him goodbye.

It was a mistake. He was a much better kisser than she had been expecting. As he wrapped his arms around her and pulled her to him she thought she was being playful; she thought his youth and looks meant he didn't feel and couldn't be hurt. But he was giving his all, and she was acting like a child.

She pulled away sharply and got in the car. She started the engine and the roof began to recline. She felt herself blush to the roots of her hair. She could feel Adam's eyes boring into her. Nicky suddenly very desperately wanted to leave. She was playing with fire, and she would get burned.

She put the car in reverse, turned and started down the drive without looking back. In a few moments she would be away from the house, the shame of how she was manipulating Adam would start to lessen, her guilt at how she was testing her marriage would recede. She tried to accelerate but something was wrong; the car felt unbalanced, veering to the side. She stopped and got out and saw that the front tyre was completely flat.

'Something wrong?' She heard his feet crunching towards her.

Nicky said nothing. She bent down and examined the tyre, tracing her fingers over the grooves in the rubber. 'Is it flat?' She heard his voice above her, his shadow falling in the afternoon sun across her shoulders. Her finger felt the long gash in the rubber without her having to see it. That was no nail or shard of glass. She stood up and opened the boot with cold efficiency. She was angry but thought it best not to show it; she felt it was important to pretend. Beneath her calm exterior something darker and more sinister was growing: alarm.

Nicky yanked at the protective cover over the spare wheel. She knew about cars. She wasn't some sap who needed to call the AA if she got a flat. Her dad had tinkered with a series of broken-down cars in their driveway all through her childhood. She'd hung out with him for hours, watching and helping him. Adam didn't know that. She felt a sour thrill of petty victory. Adam came from a generation where cars were built by robots in Osaka and a rite of passage for a young man didn't include getting greasy under a bonnet. She knew something he didn't. She would get the spare on and get the hell out. She needed to be out of here – *now*. Tomorrow morning at the office was looming in her mind. Deadlines and office politics and news round-ups and washing and ironing were where her thoughts were turning now.

She started yanking at the spare until Adam came to her rescue. 'Let me help you. Don't fight it.'

He pulled it out and together they rolled it towards the front of the car. Nicky went for the jack. She opened the bag and pulled out the piece of heavy metal. Adam was crouched down looking at the front wheel.

'You've got a problem.'

'No shit, Sherlock,' she snapped.

'I think this is what's called a space-saver tyre. Look, it's smaller than the one on the car. It saves room in the boot, but means you can only drive very slowly once it's on and you probably shouldn't drive back to London with it. It's designed to get you to a garage where they can deal with it.'

'Well, let's get it on and then I can deal with it.'

Adam shrugged, as if he was indulging her. He set up the jack for her and she began to try to undo the bolts on the wheel. They wouldn't budge.

'Let me try.' She watched with mounting frustration as his forearms strained against the bolts. 'They're mechanically tightened, you know.' He put all his effort into trying to get one to budge. He didn't need to add that getting the wheel off was going to prove impossible.

She swore loudly as a plane began its roar over the house. 'Give me your phone, Adam.' He didn't move. 'Please can I use your phone?' She held out her hand.

'You don't need to go.'

'I don't need to go. I *want* to go.' Nicky folded her arms.

It was her way of keeping control, of not flying off the handle, which she was about to do.

'There's something I don't understand. You seem so keen to get home, but what for?'

'What for? For my job, my husband, my family, my friends, my plants. For me, Adam.'

'Greg's thousands of miles away. He won't even know that you're not there. Just stay a few more days. I need you here, I really do. We'll have fun—'

'Give. Me. Your. Phone.'

'I'll get it if you promise to stay for longer.'

'Don't try to blackmail me.'

They locked eyes and Nicky didn't look away. He gave in. 'It's all cool and the gang.' He walked back into the kitchen, then returned and handed over his mobile, with only a third of the battery life left.

'You'd do better phoning the garage tomorrow. It's just past six so they're closed now.'

'I'm going to phone the AA.'

'Wait, wait. Before you waste any more of that battery, think for a moment. They can only put this spare on for you, which won't get you back to London anyway. Wait till the morning, phone the garage and they can do the whole thing for you. Then you won't have the hassle of getting a new tyre in London. And the tyre won't appear on Greg's bill. You can avoid some awkward questions.'

She thought for a long moment. What he was saying made perfect sense, of course. This was one of life's irritations that were sent to test one. She was acting like a spoiled child. If she phoned for a taxi to a station and took the train home she still had the problem of Greg's car being stuck here. It would mean a return journey at a later date. She knew it was better to get it sorted tomorrow, and leave then. She took the business card that Adam held out to her, looked at him defiantly and dialled the number. He frowned. After two rings a recorded voice announced that Mason's Garage was closed and gave their opening hours. She felt reassured; the outside world was there, after all.

'I guess you're right,' she said. But it didn't feel right.

19

Nicky went off for a walk. She needed to calm down; she needed to keep things pleasant. One more evening, that's all it would be. Maybe this was for the best. She'd leave feeling desperate to go. The fields were turning brown in the heat, crisping slowly, transforming into France. The pleasant weather was giving way to a heatwave and the plants had had too much of a good thing. She wondered if this was an allegory for her . . . flirtation. She could hardly call it an affair.

She suddenly wished she had never gone to Spain, never sat next to Adam on that flight . . . She was annoyed at herself because there was no one else she could blame. This was all her own doing; she had brought this situation entirely upon herself. She came upon a series of outbuildings to the side of the house and saw broken equipment and an old bicycle leaning against the wall of the barn. The air was heavy with abandonment and decay. She walked under the large willow that his mother had painted in the picture that hung in the billiard room, and paced around under its leaf curtain. She could simply walk away – leave the stupid car, walk across the grounds and out to the road. But Nicky felt she was someone who saw things through, who stayed the course. She reluctantly went back to the house.

He was standing in the drawing room staring out at the lawn.

'Let's have a drink,' she suggested.

His eyes screwed into slits and he shrugged. 'You asked for it, Nicky.' They headed to the wine cellar.

She picked up a bottle and dusted off the label. She was not a connoisseur and had no idea what she had chosen. She was examining the label as she walked up the three steps to the entrance, when she heard a cracking, and with a lurch she plummeted forwards and down. She saw Adam jump with the noise and turn, but then her attention was taken up by the broken bottle under her hand, smashed against the stone floor as she'd tipped forwards under the broken stair tread. She gasped as blood ran down her palm, mixing with the red wine. Then she screamed as the pain in her leg reached her brain.

Adam pulled her out by her armpits. She groaned and swore as he pulled her leg from the broken board. She leaned against a cupboard, frantic for breath, looking back at the rotten stair. Her palm was gashed, but she tried to remain calm as it didn't look deep. Adam swore and ran off. She heard him clattering around in the kitchen. He came back with a tea towel which he wrapped round her hand. She tried to put her foot on the floor, and pain shot up her leg.

'Fuck fuck fuck!'

'Calm down.' He bent down and looked closely at her leg, at the bright red scrapes running up her shin.

'They're smarting like hell.'

'They look awful. Can you put weight on it?'

She tried and gave a yelp. 'No.'

'I'll carry you.' He lifted her up and put her on the sofa in the drawing room. 'Keep it high.'

He picked up cushions and put them under her foot. He left her and she untied the tea towel, squeezing blood from the wound in her hand. The flow was slower now so it didn't need stitches. She shivered violently in the heat and realized she'd had a proper shock to her heart. As she looked at her ankle she fancied she saw it expanding and she experienced a feeling of utter hopelessness. Tears sprang to her eyes. She couldn't blame anyone for what had happened. She'd walked down the stairs fine; he'd walked up them fine. It was not Adam's fault. *You asked for it, Nicky* . . . She shook her head. No, he hadn't meant it like that, had he? She heard the kitchen door banging and wiped her tears away. She didn't want him to see her like this. She wanted him to see her strong.

He set down a bowl of warm water and some cotton wool in a plastic packet and sat down at the end of the sofa. He handed her a packet of paracetamol. 'Take three.'

She took four.

He began to bathe the scrapes on her leg in a strictly professional manner. 'First aid was part of the circus-skills training.' She winced. 'Sorry, sorry.'

He handed her a bottle of wine. 'It's for your leg – hold it against it. I don't have any ice.' The bottle was cool at best but it was better than nothing. 'Can you wiggle your toes?'

She nodded, watching him as he untied her sandal. 'Well, it's not broken. It's a sprain. You need to rest it.'

'I need a drink.'

He laughed nervously. 'Yes, of course.' He came back with a bottle of red wine and two glasses. She reached the bottom double quick, sour self-hatred swirling round her brain.

He bandaged her hand and fixed it with a safety pin.

Nicky looked at the wounds on her shin and the scabbed-over remains of her fall into the Thames. She now had a gash in her palm and a ruined ankle to accompany them.

'You're lucky you didn't break your leg. You wouldn't be able to drive, then.'

But I should have already been away, Nicky thought silently. She tried to keep things light, though inside she was fuming at . . . she knew not what. 'Well, I can see the view from here at least.'

Adam sat staring out of the windows. 'Do you mind if I go and do something, Nicky?'

She shrugged. 'What?'

'I'm looking for something.'

'What?'

He patted her leg and headed off. She crossed her arms and sat in a funk. Typical. Now she didn't even have any company. She pressed the bandage harder on her palm and then began counting the pictures on the walls. Twenty-two on the back wall alone. She tried to think how many she and Greg had in their entire house. She thought about Adam at boarding school; he'd only just left, really. His phone never rang. He didn't want to look up Facebook or email anybody. He seemed strangely alone for someone of his class, looks and health. Unconnected. She looked round the living room, seeing it with a fresh pair of eyes. She thought hard, back to the times they'd spent together. He'd never mentioned friends, of any kind. There was mad Bea, Davide in Spain, and his family, and that was it. He didn't have a job. And now she was semi-trapped in a house far from human contact. Yet he knew where she worked, had quizzed her carefully about Greg, her family, had poked around inside her tragic history with Grace. There was no balance. She'd haemorrhaged information to him. Something wasn't right. The problem was that Nicky didn't know what, because she realized she didn't know anything about *him*. She was pretty much trapped in the house of someone who was as much of a stranger to her as the person she sat next to on the tube. She'd made the most basic error: she had been taken in by a pretty face, a tidy body and a big house. You're a journalist, Nicky; find out. For your own safety, said a deeper voice.

She picked up Adam's phone to call Maria.

A revving noise distracted her. She was about to get off the sofa and hobble to the door when she looked through the French windows and saw a tractor chugging across the lawn, Adam driving. He drove to the furthest corner of the garden, by the lake, and as he passed the windows she saw something attached to the back, something metal that glinted viciously in the late evening sun. When he got to the corner where the rough grass began to rise up the slope, he took a while to reverse and turn and manoeuvre into position He jumped from the cab with the motor thrumming and unhitched a part of the metal contraption he was pulling behind him. It was a plough. She watched in amazement as Adam climbed back into the cab and drove along the lowest part of the slope skirting the lake, the plough turning the ancient lawn into a vicious brown streak in his wake. At one point he stopped and climbed back down, adjusting bits of metal and blades, before continuing to the end near the old jetty and turning in an awkward circle. He didn't look at her; he didn't look at the house once. He was a man possessed, destroying the thing he professed to love.

Nicky heard him reversing and revving up the slope as she hopped and hobbled out into the hallway. By the bolted front door she found what she was looking for: an umbrella stand crammed with walking sticks. She took two and could make quite good progress across carpets and floors. She came out through the French windows.

'What are you doing?' she hollered above the noise of the engine.

Adam didn't respond so she shouted louder, waving her sticks. He ploughed another furrow, the dry earth throwing up clouds of grey dust that sat like mist in front of the lake. She started screaming at Adam, testing how loud she needed to get before she was heard, but he seemed in a world of his own as he cut up the garden.

He drove to the far end and stopped. The silence returned with a vengeance once the engine noise died.

'What are you doing?' He looked up at her, got out of the cab and walked back up the garden towards her. His face was set, stony.

'I'm looking for something.'

'What are you looking for?'

'I don't know.' He paused and stared at her. 'Yet.'

She felt Adam's phone in the pocket of her dress, resting against her thigh. Its weight gave her the means to beat back her fear. There was something deeply wrong about this wanton act of destruction.

'It's not very rational, Adam, what you're doing.'

He continued to stare at her, and as an unfamiliar door swung open in her mind she glimpsed something horrible lurking behind it. 'Maybe. Maybe not.'

'What does that mean?'

'It depends on what I find.'

'Or whether you find anything.'

He looked out at the ruin of the garden and bit his lip. 'I wanted us to do it together but time's running out.'

'Excuse me? Help you do what, Adam? I don't understand.'

'It's under the lawn. My mum said it was under here.'

'Your mum? How can your mum have told you anything?'

'When you were asleep I read her diaries.'

'And your mum said that there was something buried under the lawn.' Adam nodded. 'So what is it?'

'I've no idea.' He laughed a little. 'The answer – to life, the universe and everything . . . to your life.'

'What? My life? Adam, what are you talking about?' But he walked away across the lawn and started examining the furrows he'd ploughed.

Nicky struggled across the lawn after him. 'Adam, you are digging up a beautiful lawn that has taken hundreds of years to cultivate, that you toddled across as a baby, that generations of your family have nurtured and enjoyed, because of something you read in those diaries upstairs?'

'Yes.'

'So it's something valuable?'

He shrugged. 'I don't know.'

The little beat of alarm, the insistent tap, tap in her mind grew louder. 'What else did you say just then . . . why is time running out? Adam!' He looked back at her, almost surprised to see her there. 'What's your dad going to say when he comes back and finds this?' She pointed a stick at the dirt.

'He doesn't come here. No one comes.' And with that he walked along the furrow he'd just ploughed, methodically searching, occasionally kicking at small stones and picking up clumps of dried earth to crumble in his hands. Nicky stood with her foot throbbing, watching him, waiting to see how far he would go. There was no hesitation in him, no moral battle over what he was doing. She hadn't anticipated this; she could not have predicted he would act like this.

No one comes, he had said. But Mrs Perkins comes, doesn't she? The garage will come. They will, they will. She wasn't sure she believed herself. The sun dropped behind a large tree on the other side of the lake. Night was closing in.

20

They ate an omelette and the remains of the bread for dinner and drank a bottle of wine. They didn't talk much and the mood had changed; gone was the flirty banter, the suggestion of sexual possibilities. Even though he was physically closer to her than ever, swabbing her skin, changing the bandage on her hand, even carrying her through to the kitchen, he seemed more distant, more serious and preoccupied. Nicky felt she was drawing into herself, concentrating on her physical shortcomings and how to overcome them.

She told him she wanted to go to bed early and he helped her as she struggled to the bathroom on the first floor. He was waiting in the corridor for her as she came out, and she felt like he was her carer in an old people's home. He led her to a spare room next to Connie's bedroom and placed her sticks carefully against the wall. 'Hang on a minute.' He disappeared and came back a moment later with a white nightie. 'This was my mum's, but you can wear it.'

Nicky felt the last dregs of physical attraction drain away as she took Adam's dead mother's nightclothes from his hand. The differences between them – their age, their class, their experiences, their passions – yawned like a chasm. Nicky felt the red shame of embarrassment spread across her cheeks, quickly followed by the thought of how she would regale Maria with this story of a passionate two days loaded with flirtatious possibilities gone horribly, farcically wrong.

'I'll sleep next door,' he said, his hand on the doorknob ready to close it. 'If you need anything, just call out.'

'I need a light.'

He paused. 'Yes, of course.' He came back with three candles and some matches and then rather formally said goodnight.

She heard him closing up the house for the night.

She woke hours later in the unfamiliar bed, with a start. It was very dark and her ankle was sore, her hand throbbing. She sat up and heard the bed creak beneath her. She was thirsty from too much wine and drank greedily from the cup of water on the table by the bed. She reached out and groped about for Adam's phone. It glowed green in the darkness with the battery bar still showing signs of life, the reception bars rising like a stair. One thirty a.m. She'd forgotten how dark the countryside was – she couldn't see anything beyond the low green circle of light. She wanted to phone Greg. She held the phone to her ear and imagined dialling his number. She wanted to hear his voice, to be taken out of herself by his upbeat outlook, to groan at one of his bad jokes. She shut her eyes. She knew she wasn't going to call him, for she was in a strange bed in another man's house and his Beamer, his pride and joy, was lying punctured in the drive. No, this was certainly not the time. Her foot hurt so she took another paracetamol. She'd have to take a taxi to work for the rest of the week. It would cost her a fortune. Her mind turned to practical issues looming in her immediate life. Once she'd got out of here.

She lay back and listened to the silence. It was complete. The window was open because of the heat. She wished for a moon that might shed some extra light, but that thought stayed only for a moment. There had been a time when she loved moonlight. Stop it, she told herself sternly, forcing herself not to go down that dark road to Grace; she wasn't strong enough tonight to cope with it. Instead she concentrated on the fact that for the first time there were no goddamn planes. It emphasized the solitude, allowed her to feel what a magical place this must once have been when it had a family creating happy memories in it, before it was abandoned to rot away. A night creature, probably an owl, screamed outside. She felt jealous of its freedom; she wanted to be walking across a beautiful lawn, feeling dew between her toes. She wriggled her swollen foot. Not tonight, Josephine. She rolled over and began to think of Adam asleep in the bed on the other side of this wall, his dreams peopled by nubile girls the right side of twenty-five. She felt the unfamiliar ruffles on the nightie she was wearing. She had put it on to protect herself from she knew not what; she always slept naked at home, but she was far from home now. God, she had been so stupid, selfish and vain, testing her marriage to Greg in such a foolhardy and pointless way. Grace would not have approved. Grace would have expected better. A tear formed and slid across the bridge of her nose and down into the pillow. She had tried to live up to Grace, to live a better life in memory of her. But as she lay in the dark, she worried that she'd failed.

Nicky opened her eyes and tried to adjust to the blackness. She blinked twice before fear washed across her in a wave. Someone was in the room. She could just make out a shadow by the door. Before she could cry out the figure took several quick steps across the room and Adam loomed out of the gloom. He put his finger on her lips and bent down close to her ear.

'Don't leave this room.' He was across the bedroom in a moment and out of the door.

She sat up in bed, her heart hammering in her chest. She was disoriented and bewildered. She groped for the phone

on the bedside table, desperate to know the time, to get a
handle on her fear. She couldn't find it. Her fingers probed
ever more frantically, but didn't touch it. It was so bloody
dark in this house she couldn't even make out a phone on a
table. She was swinging her feet out of bed when she heard
a shout. Was that Adam? She froze, transfixed. Sounds of an
argument ebbed and flowed for a few seconds before a
smashing noise ricocheted up from below, the sound hide-
ously loud in the rural silence. Somebody else was in the
house. As she stood her senses were assaulted by a series of
noises, each more violent than the last: grunts and guttural
shrieks, something heavy rebounding off furniture, she
guessed. In her confusion and in the dark she couldn't
remember where the walking sticks were so she hobbled to
the door. She heard a groan and something that might have
been swearing. Scrabbling noises were interrupted by a thump
as an object fell to the ground and rolled, a faint light swinging
up the wall and lighting the stairwell. Someone had dropped
a torch.

She started down the corridor, trying to use the wall as
a support for her sore foot. The noise below was intensifying
with deeply unpleasant sounds and she was bewildered,
unsure what to do, whether to stay in the bedroom or fling
herself into the melee below. She knew that noises could be
misinterpreted, that her visions of what was occurring at
the bottom of the stairwell might be very different from
reality.

'Adam!' She screamed involuntarily and immediately
wished she hadn't. The scuffling lasted a few more moments
before the faint light from the torch died. It was pitch black
in the corridor now. She held her breath, straining to get
beyond the white noise in her head. She jumped as she heard
creaks, then she realized she could hear another sound. It
was her own whimpering. She was frozen, not knowing

whether to retreat or go forward, her mind unable to provide a rational explanation for what might have occurred downstairs in the middle of the night. She waited, trying to hear what was happening, and all the while her fear was mounting in her chest. Someone else was in the house, someone uninvited. What if Adam was injured downstairs? What if he needed her help? The myriad of unpleasant possibilities froze her to the spot. She was unable to process them all at once. However hard she strained, the darkness didn't lift. The agony of her indecision was swiftly brought to an end when the torch went on again, throwing ghostly jumping shadows round angles and up walls.

Someone was climbing the stairs.

Slowly, with a heavy tread.

Nicky tried to run. She retreated down the corridor, limping painfully, making for the back stairs. Anything was better than passively awaiting whoever was coming up the main staircase. She bumped into a chair in a corner – she couldn't have advertised her presence more clearly if she'd tried. The back stairs had a door at the top and she scrabbled for the handle, yanking it open and pulling it shut behind her before plunging into the pitch black. Clutching the banister for support she half fell down the whole flight, then spent a frantic few seconds trying to open the door at the bottom, but the latch wouldn't lift. Finally she tumbled out and for the first time could see the faint outline of objects in the hallway beyond. The door was opening at the top of the stairs so she forced herself to keep moving, the pain in her foot a dull ache that fear and adrenalin rendered her unable to even feel.

She actually tripped over the body. Tumbling to the floor in an uneasy mess, she could feel the warm fleshy undulations beneath her bare knees. She had fallen on his stomach, but he lay unmoving beneath her. As she tried to right herself light beams bouncing off the ceiling announced that the person pursuing her had arrived.

'Nicky!' Adam's voice came in little more than a whisper from the stairs. He approached, holding on to the walls as he went, gasping for breath and clutching his stomach. His torch threw wild shadows on the scene around them but she still struggled to take it in.

She sat on the floor, her legs almost touching a middle-aged man who was lying face up on the carpet. He wore a black windcheater, black jeans and dark shoes; beneath his feet one of the hallway rugs rumpled in waves, the sign of his final desperate attempts to dig his heels into life. His eyes stared ahead, unseeing.

Adam was struggling to speak, strange gurgling noises coming from him. He was almost doubled over and must have been punched in the stomach. She could see a ballooning black eye forming.

'What happened?'

He nodded his head towards displaced furniture and over-turned chairs. It seemed the effort of doing that was too much and he sank to the floor against a door frame on the other side of the dead body. 'I jumped on him from the stairs, but he was stronger than I expected.'

'Do you know him?'

'What? Why would I know him?'

'You were talking.'

Adam shook his head. 'He saw me on the stairs as I came down but he didn't run.'

Nicky leaned forward and felt for a pulse on both sides of the man's neck. 'He's dead, Adam. The sound of the fight was horrible, just horrible!'

'He attacked me. It was me or him.'

'When you came in to my room, what had you heard?'

'I was lying awake in bed and I heard noises I didn't like.'

'Are you hurt, are you injured?'

'I'm fine, I'm fine. You?'

Nicky felt her heart still jackknifing around in her chest, adrenalin making her breath come fast and shallow. 'It scared the shit out of me. The noises . . . God, that was horrible.'

Adam didn't, or couldn't, reply. He seemed in no hurry to move, he was probably in shock, but she was becoming desperate to end this nightmare.

'How did he get in?'

Adam looked around and closed his eyes. 'I don't know.'

Nicky tried to stand, and pain exploded anew in her foot. But she had things to do now, a huge list of things to organize if order was to be reimposed on this chaos. She ignored her foot and took the torch from Adam's limp hand. The beam of light fell on a crowbar lying under the bureau, and its black metal glinted. It was then she gave a cry of disgust. As the light shifted back to the dead man she saw he was wearing latex gloves.

She looked carefully at his face. The mouth hung slackly; there were livid scratches in his skin; a trickle of blood stained his teeth under a blond moustache; a darker and larger stain was spreading backwards across the carpet under his head. Her hands shook as she closed his eyelids.

'How did you . . .' She tailed off, unable to say the word.

'I hit him with that.' He pointed at the crowbar. 'And that.' He pointed at the broken bits of ceramic from a bowl that had been thrown in the fight.

Nicky forced herself to get going. She began to haul herself up the stairs back to her bedroom to get the mobile.

'Where are you going?' Adam's voice sounded desperate.

'To phone the police.'

He struggled to standing. 'No. Don't do that.'

She turned to face him from the stairs and her hand

clutching the banister was rigid. 'Adam, we must phone the police.'

Grey tinges of dawn had begun to seep into the hallway, turning the centre of the room pale. She could see Adam standing over the dead body in a possessive way. 'We can bury him. He'll never be found.'

Nicky had a sensation of the world tipping and never righting itself. She heard her voice coming from far away. 'Adam, we must go to the police. What's happened is not your fault. They will understand. I will back you up. But we must call them *now*. Adam, we are in this together.' She kept using his name. She'd heard that this was supposed to help those that were becoming unhinged.

'No.'

She gripped the banister even more tightly, to keep herself from losing control. 'Adam, you've had a shock, so have I. This man broke into your house and attacked you. This is what the police do; they help people in this situation.'

'You think so?' He snorted with derision. 'Lucky you. You're going to help me bury him. You're as much a part of it as I am.'

'You've lost your mind! This isn't a sane reaction! I'm going to get the mobile and we *must* call the police!' She turned and started up the stairs again, cursing over and over that she wasn't fully fit. The phone was just a few metres away and an end to this horrible night was—

'It's not up there. I've got it, and we're not phoning the police.'

She turned and looked down on him looking up at her. She was plunging down a dark tube into a world she had no experience of – and didn't want to. She stood in a dead woman's nightie in front of someone who was strong enough to have killed another man, someone who had just won a fight for his life. She looked again at the rucked carpet under those worn shoes. How hard had he struggled to stay alive, she wondered. How much extra strength had he summoned? How vicious is a fight to the death? As nasty as it gets. And here was a man who wanted to cover it up; to deny it ever happened.

Be careful, Nicky's inner voice counselled. Be very careful indeed.

She was strangely calm. Some of the pretence had fallen away. They were standing on opposite sides of an ever-expanding chasm. Soon it would be impossible to jump over, soon it would be impossible to speak, because to do so would articulate how far apart they were from each other – how mad he was. If she couldn't get him to change his mind she knew, as surely as night follows day, that he wasn't going to let her go. And where that led . . . well, she couldn't even let her imagination take her there.

'You have killed a man. In self-defence – I will back you up on that. But even this man, whoever he is, had a family and a life and people who will mourn. And you're scaring me, Adam.' She was testing, seeing how far she could push it. 'You cannot cover this up. It is madness to even try.' She took a step down the stairs. 'One phone call away is all the kindness, counselling, sympathy and resolution that you could wish for.' She took another step, getting bolder. 'You are one hundred per cent in the right on this. You've done nothing wrong.' She took another step. 'Make the call.'

'No.' He looked up the stairs straight at her. 'Maybe he wasn't here to burgle the place.'

Nicky stopped her walk down the stairs as a thought came to her, a thought so horrible it robbed her of her ability to move. Grace. It was not rational to think of Grace at this moment, but that's where her mind took her. Someone had come for Grace that night and Nicky had not known until it was too late; she had not understood what was happening.

'You don't get it, Nicky. I'm doing this for you. I'm saving you.'

'Saving me from what, Adam?'

He paused, looking pained. 'I'm not sure.'

There was to be no revelation here, Nicky realized. This was simply the ravings of a madman. 'Adam, see sense. Maria knows where I am. She knows I'm with you.'

Adam bent down under the bureau and pulled out the crowbar. For a hideous moment Nicky thought he was about to swing it at her and she lost her footing as she tried to duck, giving a helpless little cry as she stumbled on the stairs. He put the crowbar on the bureau. 'You thought I was going to hit you.'

She looked up at him, bewildered. 'I don't know, Adam. Were you?'

He made a scoffing noise and began to trace the ballooning skin around his eye. 'I did this for you, Nicky. You need to trust me, not fear me.'

'But how can I do that, Adam, when I'm injured and cannot leave your house, and you won't phone the police?'

'You'll live.' Adam let out a huge sigh and stared down at the man he had just killed. 'I just hope you're worth it.'

'What did you just say?' But he had closed his eyes and was swaying in the doorway. 'Adam? *Adam*?'

He opened his eyes and stared at her and Nicky felt a swoop of terror down her back. 'I'm going to make some tea. Come with me.' Nicky sank slowly down onto the stairs, the strength in her legs failing. 'Now.'

She got up again, fast. The tone in his voice left no room for dissent. She limped after him into the kitchen.

She sipped her tea dully as the first shafts of dawn broke across the house. As the summer light began to flood their world the night-time horror became almost impossible to recreate in her mind; it took on the hue of melodrama. She could see the corner of the dead man's shoulder from where she sat at the kitchen table. The kernel of an idea began to form. 'He might have ID on him.'

Adam looked up from tracing random lines across the Formica with his finger. She felt a little bolder and got up and limped over to the body, sensing Adam following behind, watching.

'I've checked him for a phone,' Adam said.

Her heart sank, but she knelt down and opened the man's jacket, avoiding looking at the caved-in side of his head. She dug around in his pockets for a wallet, but found only a packet of chewing gum. His trouser pockets were empty, he wore nothing round his neck and he indeed carried no phone. There was an inside pocket on the windcheater and as she dug around in it her hand caught on a plastic oblong object. It was a car key, so he was parked nearby. It was a tiny lifeline but she clung to it as Adam tracked her every move. 'He's got nothing on him at all. Don't you think that's strange?' She looked up at Adam, feigning surprise as she folded the key into her fingers and started babbling. 'Should I take off his shoes?' She pulled her hand from his inside pocket, the key caught in her palm. 'Maybe his watch will tell us something?' His watch was a Seiko and running underneath it were the fangs of a large snake tattoo. She made a great play of taking the watch off to see what was engraved on the back. There was nothing. She looked again at the latex gloves, aware that Adam was staring at her as she did this. 'He came with that torch?'

Adam nodded.

She felt protective of the body, even while knowing he had broken in. She wondered whether she'd rather have taken her chances with him. Nothing made sense. This guy was a burglar, but he had no bag. How was he going to get his takings away? He would have seen the car, the open shutters . . . Why burgle the house on one of the few occasions that anyone was in it? And Adam had talked to him. What can you possibly say to a burglar you meet in your hallway in the middle of the night? She kept these thoughts to herself.

A little while later they began to walk round the ground floor, trying to work out how the man had got in. He didn't leave her side, and the tension between them began to ratchet up. In the downstairs toilet they found a jimmied window.

'Do you know why he was here?'

'He's a burglar.'

Nicky stayed silent. Adam had calmed down now; he could present an image, stick to a story. But just after he'd killed that guy his tone had been very different. Nicky wasn't sure that the man was a burglar, but, if he wasn't, what was he doing here, she wondered. She tried again. 'Why is it so important that no one knows he was here?' He didn't answer, looking engrossed instead in thoughts best left alone. 'Is this something to do with what you're looking for?'

'I can't tell you yet.'

It was a small lifeline but one she grabbed at. 'I don't understand. Help me to understand, Adam.'

'I need you to help me find it.'

'What?'

'I don't know yet. But when we find it we'll put him under the lawn.'

Nicky felt bile rise in her throat and she fought to keep it down. He needed her to complete whatever plan he had concocted, that much was clear. But once that was over . . . She looked out at the bone-dry grass, at the wetter, colder earth that had been turned over yesterday and was still a black scar against the green. Today it would bleach and fade to grey, mingle with the earth around it. She was aware of the warmth of her own body, her heart beating its eternal rhythm. But she knew at that moment that unless she was lucky she was going to end up under that lawn, her body rotting away until it too was indistinguishable from its surroundings. The pain in her injured foot radiated up her leg. They would spend today digging that earth, tilling soil and discarding rocks, his eyes constantly on her, the odds on her ability to escape stacked against her.

She would be digging her own grave.

21

The walking stick made a whistling noise at it smacked into the back of Adam's head. Nicky hit him so hard it bounced out of her hand and he pitched forwards into the ploughed earth with a yowl. By the time he hit the ground she was already running as if a hot wind from hell was on her back and about to smother her. As a schoolgirl she had been a county-standard sprinter: over one hundred, two hundred metres, there had been few who could have beaten her; those long legs gave her the physical advantage to get her down the track to the finish line first. She hadn't sprinted in at least twenty years but she took off in an explosion of speed, her breath coming out as ragged gasps, and she pumped her arms higher, straining over the uneven ground. Her foot was numb now with the pain but she'd taken this course and she had to see it through. For nearly three hours she had been digging up the lawn in the late morning heat, waiting for the perfect moment to make her escape. Now she was running for her life.

She arched her back, waiting for the hand to grab her or her legs to be rugby-tackled from beneath her. Five steps, ten, twenty, sixty. She risked glancing behind her. He was sprinting back to the house. She hadn't expected that and fear of the unknown leaped up her spine. She tried to slow to a fast jog, to conserve the energy she'd need. She wanted as much space between him and her as she could get. The dead man's car key jiggled in the pocket of her dress.

She ran on round the lake, heaving her bad foot, falling
and stumbling as a plane came low and fast overhead. Her
lungs screamed with the effort suddenly required of them as
she came up the rise to the drive; her thighs burned beneath
her. The grey wall of the estate came into view two hundred
metres away. She could see Adam still moving up the lawn
to the house. He was in boots that would slow him, and he
was going uphill. She was panting now, every stride getting
harder. When she hit the gravel drive she'd already run a
quarter of a mile and her heart was doing something horrible
in her chest. A vicious pain started in her side. The drive
curved away and soon Adam was out of sight. She got nearer
the wall, saw more clearly how high and smooth it was. There
was no easy way to climb over. She tried to focus on the
only thing that mattered: getting to the gate. Her feet slapped
against the gravel; she was going downhill now and she saw
the curve in the drive leading to the entrance. Four hundred
metres . . . three hundred and fifty . . . She would hide in
the woods. She knew that on a good day and with a head
start she could give even a man a run for his money. But
with her injured foot she was severely hampered; and he was
in his prime, with vigorous muscles and youth and the fear
of the consequences of her escape on his side. A game of
cat and mouse in the trees was the only way she'd get away.
She looked behind her. She was alone. She allowed herself
the first tiny flutter of something dangerous: hope.

She heard the engine with two hundred metres to go. If
she could have screamed in anger and frustration she would
have. He was driving the tractor, cranking up the gears as
he bore down on her.

She bent her head and pushed on to the gate. Every cell
in her body hurt now. He was gaining, but slowly. He was a
hundred metres away. The gate looked monstrous as she
slammed her hands into it and yanked, howled and yanked

again. It was locked. He must have come out in the night and locked the gate. She swore as she started to climb, slotting her sandals into the rococo metal curves, hauling herself skywards, the gate rocking and swinging as she climbed. The tractor was fifty metres away. Adam was leaning out of the cab, holding something in his hand and shouting. Through her exhaustion she sensed exhilaration. One leg was over, avoiding the row of spikes at the top. She was nearly there. She gave a yelp of surprise when she felt something close around her biceps and tighten. She felt a sharp yank across her shoulders that almost toppled her right off the top of the gate. It was a rope. He had lassoed her. She flailed madly, the ground a dizzyingly long way away, then her hands clawed to hold on.

'Get down, Nicky,' Adam shouted, pulling on the rope. He was walking towards her, the rope spooling by his feet. She tried to hook a finger under the binding round her arms but he was yanking so hard that she slithered down the gate, scrabbling for a handhold or a foothold. He walked closer and with one hard pull prised her from the exit. She fell leadenly back to earth, the breath knocked out of her, her arms pinioned to her sides.

'Why did you do that?' He was angry, the first time she'd seen him like that. 'You could have been killed!'

That wasn't the end of it. Oh dear God, no. He made her run back to the house.

She watched him tie the lasso to the plough, in a daze; her brain was unable to function, too starved of oxygen by her heart and lungs. He climbed back into the cab, turned the tractor round and started back to the house. The rope began to slither through the grass. She watched it passively for a moment or two, unable to process what it meant, and then her eyes followed the end and she staggered to her feet, although she could hardly move. It was then she realized that fear had as many levels as love or pain. With her arms tied to her sides she couldn't balance well, but if she fell, she died, because he didn't bother to look behind him.

She tasted blood as she jogged along, probably from her fall from the gate. She felt the rough gravel beneath her soles. Her physical sufferings fell away as she concentrated only on the task of staying on her feet. If there was a worse way to die than being dragged along a gravel road, she couldn't think of one, couldn't think of anything beyond keeping pace with the tractor and saving her life.

The drive rose slightly as it approached the house but he didn't slow.

He drove the tractor to one of the outbuildings beyond Greg's car. The first premature leaves of autumn had floated on the summer breeze and come to rest on the bonnet. He stopped the engine and she slumped to the ground. Her vision swam with exhaustion and through the pounding in her head she could hear him jump down from the tractor cab and start swearing and pummelling the huge grooved tyres with his boots.

'This isn't a game, Nicky! You think I'm playing a game! What the fuck do you think you're doing! You're staying here! Don't go out there!'

She tried to regain her breath, looking dully round the yard. She was too tired to be scared. She didn't reply, mainly because she couldn't and she had nothing to say.

He untied her and she let him carry her into the house as she couldn't walk. Livid, smarting marks covered both biceps; her foot, now that she'd stopped her absurd abuse of it, was throbbing. He stepped over the dead man on the floor and laid her out on the drawing-room sofa, then left. She could hear him moving around in the kitchen. As the physical thumping of her heart receded fear began to take its place; she had space now to feel the fear. The shades of grey in their relationship had exploded into harsh black and white, into complete clarity. She could no longer cling to a hope that her series of mishaps were accidental, that the puncture wasn't deliberately inflicted, that the wooden step in the wine cellar wasn't prepared, just in case she might, as she duly did, hurt herself on it. Hope was a delusion. She was not in the country house of a beautiful, thoughtful, carefree youth who offered her a tantalizing and affirming glimpse into life's possibilities. She was locked in a brute struggle for survival with a man she barely knew; a man who had no limits.

Adam came back into the room and when Nicky saw what he had in his hands her body found the strength to scream. It was an animal sound from the pit of her stomach.

He was holding a pair of handcuffs.

The room was large and he took a long time to cross it. She got off the sofa but there was no fight left in her; she was consumed by terror. Snot and tears mixed as he pushed her up against a radiator on the back wall while she keened and moaned in protest. She kicked out at him with her good leg but she couldn't stop him locking her arm to the radiator pipe.

'I've got to dig and, after what you've done, I have to tie you up.' He grabbed her feet and pulled off her sandals, throwing them into the corner of the room. 'There'll be no more running.' He was acting as if nothing had happened, as if this was all normal. As if a dead man in the hallway was no more unusual than a parcel left by the postman, that tying up a woman was as ordinary as pouring her a drink.

She sank down the wall to the floor, sobbing and crying. 'Let me go, Adam. I beg you, don't do this to me. Please!'

He stood unmoving above her. 'Don't beg, Nic. It's not in your character to beg. You're not being honest if you beg.

It's what I love about you. You're strong, you can cope. It's unconventional, I admit—'

'You're mad!'

'You don't understand, but I'm doing you a favour.'

Incapable of words she screamed in pure anger at him; it was a brute rage at her helplessness that left her spent a few moments later.

He sat back on the faded Persian carpet a few metres from her and stared at her, and she thought that just for a second she saw indecision there. An expression of something she couldn't catch passed across his features. He rubbed his head where she'd whacked him with the walking stick. 'That really hurt.'

'Good!'

'You're a fighter. You've got such self-possession.' He shook his head as if in wonder. 'You're amazing.'

'Fuck you!'

He got up and left the room, returning with a glass of water and a packet of pills, which he put in front of her. 'I've only got paracetamol, but it'll help your foot. It must be very painful.'

She spat at him. It was the only thing she had left.

He paused and she felt he was about to say something. But he opted for silence and slowly wiped his face, regarding her the entire time. He walked off and a few minutes later she heard the tractor start up and saw it pass the windows on its course across the lawn, every turn bringing him closer to the house.

Nicky willed herself to calm down. She wiped away her tears, blew her nose on her dress and tried to summon the energy to think rationally. She pushed the pills out of their blisters and downed several, emptying the water glass. She breathed deeply. I am connected to people, she said to herself. She breathed deeply again. I am someone who will be missed.

I have family, friends and a job. They will notice and they are the kind of people who, if they kick up a fuss, will be believed. She felt herself growing bolder. Greg would notice first, but he was several time zones and thousands of miles away. By the time his worried messages began to filter back to London, days would have passed – an eternity. She saw the tractor backing up as it turned at the edge of the lawn. She didn't know if she had several days.

She looked beyond the torn earth at the lake and the fields beyond. The countryside was full of people, particularly in this weather. Someone would come. Perhaps he would make a mistake.

She shifted and the handcuffs clanked against metal. She needed better odds than 'perhaps'. She thought back to when she was hanging off the estate gate, and her stomach churned again at the giddy feeling she'd sensed as the gate had swung on its rotten hinges. She'd nearly made it. He hadn't foreseen that; she had surprised him. She didn't know him, but he didn't know her either. She was going to turn that to her advantage.

He might be laying out the rules, but, as Greg would say, rules are meant to be broken. An image of her husband flooded her heart and she felt his absence like a physical blow to the stomach. He had overcome the hardest challenge life throws: Greg had lived through the murder of his wife. Now she had to believe she could live through this. Defiance flamed inside her as she rubbed a chafing arm. She could see the dead man's feet from behind the sofa and through the drawing-room door. He was evidence of what happened in a head-to-head fight with Adam. She studied the ruffles in the carpet again.

A blackness swamped her. Maybe she had been lucky. And luck eventually runs out. Greg's deep and mature voice came to her then: 'Think, babes, what would Bruce Willis do?' He'd wear a cut-off T-shirt and blast the bad guy with an Uzi,

Nicky thought. She turned to the hallway and imagined the gun cabinet. She dismissed it a moment later. Greg wasn't always right. She'd never even held a gun until two days ago, didn't know if they were loaded or where the bullets were kept. Even assuming she could get unchained she needed a different tactic to get out of here. She'd have to talk her way out.

Or something else. He might have put her in his mum's nightie but he'd fancied her at one time and that itch had never been scratched. He was young, he was male, he was stressed and she was desperate.

The sound of the tractor faded. Her heart started thumping again and she saw him walking slowly along a new furrow, his face cast in shadow, searching. What was he searching *for*? Someone who wanted something this badly was someone who could be used, was someone with a weak spot. She would have to turn that to her advantage. She took a deep breath.

'Adam!' she called out, but her voice was a dry croak. She swallowed and tried again. 'Adam!' Louder this time, more insistent and sure. He looked up from the ground. 'Adam! I'm hungry.'

22

'If you try to escape I'll get much angrier than I did before.' Adam was crouching on his haunches near her, watching for her reaction, rubbing his palms together thoughtfully. The dried mud on his fingers made a scratchy, scraping sound and fell in a fine dust on the rug. There was no trace of his earlier anger; he looked like a man enjoying working in his garden. She nodded and he unlocked the cuffs round her wrist and helped her to stand. She gave a yowl when she tried to put her foot down. It was much more swollen after her sprint on it.

She limped along as they made for the kitchen, wincing with every step. As they got to the door of the drawing room he tired of her gasping, awkward passage and picked her up in his arms, then carried her the rest of the way to the kitchen. Nicky consciously stared at the skirting boards and held her breath. Their physical closeness seemed absurd after the traumas of the day. He set her down by a kitchen chair and she sank onto it.

'What do you want?'

'Bread and cheese is OK.'

'Put your hands on the table where I can see them.'

She did as he told her and watched him as he washed the mud off his hands in the sink and moved round the room, gathering plates and provisions. The sun cast long lines of light into the room and Nicky was struck again by the absurdity of her position. One moment things seemed almost normal between them, the next they tipped over into a dark horror. She ran her hands through her hair, tucking it back behind her ears. Her lips were chapped from the sun and too many days of drinking too much. She might be a prisoner but Adam was sociable; he'd want companionship if it was available, conversation to keep him entertained. She would give it to him.

He handed her a glass of water and she realized how thirsty she was. She downed it in one and asked for another. He smiled at her as he refilled the glass and put the food down. She ate a lot, and as the food hit her stomach it made her feel a bit stronger and almost began to drag her back to the ranges of normal. He got up, crossed to the counter and picked up an apple. 'Here.'

She looked up and he tossed the apple to her, giving a low cheer when she caught it. He came back and sat down with a bar of chocolate and snapped a piece off for her. She noticed the dark matted stain of old blood in his hair from when she whacked him with the walking stick earlier. Despite everything he had done to her, a feeling of shame came over her.

'Does your head hurt?' He stared at her as he touched the cut with a finger. 'Do you want me to clean it? There's blood in your hair.' She saw the battle in him over whether or not to trust her. 'I'll just wash it.' He stood up and got a bowl and some warm water and the cotton wool. He pulled his chair closer to hers and bent his head sideways so he could look at her as she cleaned away the blood. As she stared at his gleaming, dark hair she forced herself to concentrate on the positives. She was no longer tied up. If she could stay unchained she had a chance.

'It's a lot to dig up the lawn on the strength of something in a diary from over twenty years ago.' He shrugged, non-committal. 'Can I read your mum's diaries?'

'No.'

He pulled away from her dabbing, looking morose and grey, as if a mood was coming upon him. He seemed to be sinking further away from her and she tried to bring him back.

'You only look for something if it's lost. What's lost, Adam?'

'It's not what's lost; it's what's found.' In the fading sunshine of late afternoon his dark features looked sallow. 'What's so special about you, Nicky, eh? Why's it all about you?' He was sullen, his eyes mean and staring.

She stayed silent at first, wondering if this was the safest thing to do. She took a deep breath and let it out slowly. Keep control, don't lose control, she urged herself. 'There's nothing special about me—'

He stood suddenly and she reeled back against her chair. 'I fought that guy for you! I ended up killing that guy for you! I've got a heap of shit this big on my head because of you!'

Oh God, thought Nicky. Oh God . . . 'You know him, don't you, Adam?'

'No, I don't, but someone does!'

'You were talking to him.'

'Yes, I was! You think it's a coincidence he's here? Bullshit! What was he looking for? He was trying to take it.'

'Take *what*?'

His anger was overwhelming him now, coursing through his strong arms and making the veins on his neck stand out. 'Are you for real? I mean, are you for fucking real?' He started pacing the kitchen in a trance. 'Connie's not that mad – maybe she's the sanest of all of us. Maybe fucking Greg deserves to go to hell for all I know!' He picked up the chair he had been sitting on and threw it in a rage across the room, where its back legs became detached and landed broken in the corner.

Nicky sat very still on her seat. Change the subject, change the subject, her mind jabbered . . . It would be a victory if she got out of this room in one piece. 'Shall we light the candles? It's getting dark and I'm scared of the dark.'

This simple request pulled him back towards her. He leaned against the kitchen units and dropped his head. 'We need some more.' He rooted through a cupboard and found some in a bag and a moment later carried her into the drawing room, lit them and then stuck them to the plates. He didn't give her the matches. They sat on separate couches and watched the long sunset and listened to the roar of the planes in silence.

Eventually he stood up. 'It's time to go to bed.' She sat up in alarm. 'I'm going to have to tie you up again.'

'Adam, please . . .'

'You can't leave, Nicky. I don't want to do it, but –' he touched his head where she'd hit him '– I don't trust you.'

'If you don't want to do it, then don't. I know the way you're behaving isn't you. We can end this now if—'

'Stop it.'

She did.

She made her long and weary way up the stairs for her night-time incarceration, Adam behind her carrying the candles. Their shadows jumped and wavered across his mum's paintings as they went, the dead body an indistinct, dark shape below them on the hall floor. She slowed to a stop outside the bedroom, the thought of the long, black night to come a crushing weight on her soul. She didn't know if she had the strength to endure it. 'Please don't do this, Adam.'

'I've been left with no choice.'

He led her into the bedroom and pulled the handcuffs out of his pocket. She began to whimper, pleading with him not to do it. She backed up against the wall as he came towards her. 'Tell me one thing, what did you mean about Greg? Earlier you talked about Greg going to hell.'

But he didn't answer; he simply handcuffed her to the bedpost and closed the door.

Her night was scored with the dull clank of the metal handcuffs against the bedpost, a never-ending reminder of the desperate position she was in. She slept little, the house a silent and brooding prison. As dawn broke and the outline of the room became solid, she remembered watching a TV programme once about a lone hiker in the Canadian wilderness who was pursued by a grizzly. The hiker couldn't outrun it, couldn't climb a tree or cross a river to get away from it. He had to find a way of scaring that bear, or he was going to end up never being found. Exhausted, petrified, thirsty, cold and backed into a ravine with no exit, he tried one last-ditch ploy: he extended his tent poles, strung his canvas across the poles and fixed them like wings, then turned and ran screaming straight for the grizzly. He made himself bigger, scarier and bolder than he really was. The bear turned and fled.

Nicky thought back to the graffiti Adam had shown her by the Thames. 'Fear makes the wolf grow bigger.' She spent the rest of the disappearing night forcing herself to beat back her terror.

23

He knocked on the door at eight a.m., like a timid owner of a B&B bringing her breakfast in bed. He was in the same dirt-stained T-shirt and trousers he had worn the day before and he looked exhausted. Clearly she wasn't the only one who hadn't slept well.

'Here, I made you some tea.'

She stared at it suspiciously, wondering if he'd put something in it, but then he unlocked her handcuffs and sat next to her on the bed and she was so glad that her hand was free that she took the tea and drank it.

'What fun things are we doing today?' She couldn't keep the sarcasm out of her voice. The idea of being chained up again, or digging for hours in a futile search for who knew what, overwhelmed her spirit.

'I'm sorry, Nicky, really.' He couldn't meet her eye and gazed awkwardly through the door instead.

Nicky stood up and put her foot down. He grabbed her to keep her steady, but she pushed him away and held the bedframe instead. She limped to the door, wincing with pain, but the truth was that her foot felt almost normal. She was going to keep this advantage to herself.

They came round the curve in the stairs and the sight of the dead body in the hall shocked Nicky more than she could say. She stared down at the blood, now black and matted in his hair, and saw the corner of his mouth was stained green. The flies would soon be feasting. She turned to Adam and drew herself up tall. She felt nothing but contempt for him.

He seemed to wither under her gaze before looking down at the body. 'I'll tell you why you're here,' he said.

'What?' He had spoken so quietly she wasn't sure she had heard him right.

'Help me dig this morning, and I'll tell you why I'm keeping you here.'

'Tell me now.'

He shook his head. 'Not yet. But I will tell you.'

'Does this have something to do with Grace?'

He looked stricken, almost ill. She could smell his old sweat on his clothes. She saw his indecision as he looked at the man he had killed. 'I'll tell you later.'

'You're going to bloody tell me now!'

But he was walking away from her down the stairs and Nicky simply had to follow.

They spent a boring, hot and exhausting morning digging up the lawn, Adam driving the tractor and Nicky hobbling along barefoot behind, not knowing what she was looking for in the furrows. It was a succession of stones and broken tree roots and endless black mud. The highlight was a bundle of ancient nails, rusty and disintegrating as she touched them. Her mind was mulling over Adam's promise on the stairs. She feared he was setting her up for nothing. Her rational voice knew there was no revelation to come, knew that there was no excuse for his actions – they were unjustifiable.

Eventually, once they had ploughed to the end of a furrow by the lake at nearly lunchtime, Nicky stopped and shook her head, stretching her aching back. 'I need a drink and a rest,' she said.

Adam got down from the tractor cab and nodded. 'I'll carry you in.' He picked her up in his strong arms and walked with her across the remaining lawn and into the kitchen, placing her down gently by the sink. He poured two large glasses of water.

'I want some wine.'

'Good idea,' he replied. He paused. 'Thank you for helping me.' His rage of the previous day, his see-sawing between sullenness and anger had gone. He was more like the Adam of old.

He picked her up again, although it really wasn't necessary, and carried her to the door of the wine cellar. It was as if he didn't want to let her go. He put her down slowly. 'Nicky . . . I—' He had his hands on her shoulders and he pushed her tenderly up against the door. She was about to reject his advance when she felt something hard sticking into her back. It was the key to the cellar door. Nicky made a split-second decision. Make it believable, she told herself. He leaned in towards her and she pulled him to her and kissed him.

Several things happened at once. Nicky found she couldn't stop herself. After all the physical discomforts and the fear and the crushing loneliness, she responded to Adam more than she'd expected. She wanted the feel of another human being close to her, she wanted to feel alive. He jammed her up against the cellar door, his erection prodding her in the stomach, her small lifeline poking her in the back. She ran her hands through his hair. He was a very good kisser and his hands started to wander down her body, cupping her under her bum and pulling her closer to him.

He might notice the key.

She gasped with desire and with fear that her one tiny hope might be crushed, and pushed him to arm's length, her hands splayed across his chest, feeling the hard planes of his torso.

He was staring at her. 'Nicky, I—'

'I need a drink.' She peeled herself off the door and made to go into the cellar but it was as if all the blood in her limbs had pooled between her legs and she didn't have the strength to stand. She staggered against the wall.

He flung open the door and jumped down over the broken stair. One step, two . . . he was in the room.

The rest happened in slow motion. She tried to pull herself together, to tell her body to stop revelling in unexpected pleasure and to act. She grabbed the door as he began to turn. And she shut it before he understood what she was doing. She heard him shout as she leaned against the door, grabbing the large old-fashioned key and turning it in the lock half a second before his body weight slammed into the wood.

'Nicky! Don't do this, Nicky!'

She had crossed over. The spell was broken. Her body changed from pleasure to flight. She raced through the kitchen, knowing it wouldn't be long before he broke down that door. Her mind was working with complete clarity. This wouldn't be a blind race for the gate. She hobbled to the barn, even though there was the possibility she would be trapped between it and the kitchen door if he got out. She yanked at the old bike propped up against the wall, hoping wildly that the chain was still on. She swung her leg over and started pedalling across the gravel, skidding slightly as she went. She gained speed as she edged away from the house. The gravel path ran down to the lake but she saw a walking path heading left through some chestnut trees. The path was flat and she made good progress, bumping along, getting nearer to the high grey wall. She saw a folly of stone a short distance away, the moss encrusted on its sides grown shrivelled and yellow in the heat. A plane began to roar above her. The sound of it made the hairs on her neck stand up and she pedalled with all the strength she had. At the folly she turned right towards the wall.

She took a second to look around and guessed she was maybe half a mile from the house. She was hidden in the trees and bushes and he wouldn't know which way she had come. She leaned the bike against the high, smooth wall and grabbed at a small stone protruding from the stonework. She balanced on the bike seat and put her left hand on the top of the wall. Trying to find another handhold, she drew on all her limited climbing experience. Bare feet were actually an advantage here. Another little victory over Adam surged through her. She tucked her dress into her pants and put her big toe on a rough stone. She inched upwards; one more move and she had two hands on the top of the wall. She felt wildly for another handhold, a crevasse or hole worn away by wind and frost, but didn't find one.

Nicky knew that climbing wasn't about brute strength but more of a mental puzzle. It was about balancing in a precarious position and, instead of ploughing forward if the way was blocked, doubling back and finding a fresh path. She put her foot back down on the saddle, wincing, and studied the wall. She started this time with her right hand, reaching up for a handhold and hugging the side of a small cement ledge with the side of her left foot. She inched upwards, swinging her hand onto the top of the wall. This time she got it right, and, turning her head, saw a stone for her right foot. She scraped the skin off her knees on the rough stone as she pushed higher. She swung her hand out and finally had two hands on the top. A few moments later she rolled her body across the top of the wall. She looked around at the direction she had come. There was no noise, no movement in the buzzing afternoon heat. She looked over at the ground on the other side and dropped down as far as she could, then swore and let go. She landed heavily in a pile of bracken, winded but unharmed.

Thirty seconds later she was hobbling away from Hayersleigh through the woods.

24

Nicky was running along as best she could when she saw a track ahead through the trees and dropped to the forest floor. She was disorientated, unsure whether this was the drive to Hayersleigh or another that ran through the woods. If the track bent at any point, she might well have come back upon it. She cursed silently. He might be near. The thick vegetation was a good cover at this time of year, the bracken an almost impenetrable thicket she could move through. She came to the track and paused, straining for any sound of him. The noise of the forest was all that came back to her. She kept the track in sight as she crawled along. After a hundred metres she saw a red car parked in a passing place. She pulled the key out of the pocket of her dress. Did they match? The car was facing the way she had come so she reckoned she'd have to three-point-turn it to get away. If she broke cover he might be on her. She forced herself to bide her time, listening, straining for any foreign sound.

Nothing.

She put her hand out and pressed the 'door open' button. The lights on the car flashed. She couldn't hold out any longer; her means of escape was right in front of her. She went for it.

She sprinted on that darn sore foot for the driver's door, on the far side of the car. She was round the bonnet, grasping madly at the door, then she was in, key jabbing at the ignition slot. She found the button to lock the door as she got the key in the slot and turned it, her foot slamming on the accelerator. A horrid grinding noise filled the car. The fucking thing wouldn't start. She turned the key again and felt the engine spark to life just as a dark shadow broke free of the bracken across the track and Adam ran at her window with a big stick. She rammed the car into first and had just got the handbrake down when the crunch of cracking safety glass exploded by her face. She screamed as he drew back for another hit. His next blow was stronger, breaking through the glass now as she roared away up the track. She saw him running towards her in the rear-view mirror as the closed gate of the house came into view round a curve. She swore as she began a three-point turn. She shoved the nose into bracken, slammed the car into reverse. He was sprinting hard, a baseball bat in his hand, not a piece of wood as she had first thought. If he breaks the windscreen I won't be able to drive it, she thought. The back of the car hit a tree with a smack. She ground the gears into first as he got to within ten metres. She juddered forward, the fear ramping up the closer he got. She couldn't get the front of the car all the way round. She swore as she realized she should have stayed straight and reversed out. He was at the window now as she reversed the car again.

'Nicky!' He had his hand in the broken window, trying to pull the key out of the ignition.

She tried to fight him off with one hand, the mantra of 'Don't stall this car, don't stall this car' racing through her head.

'Your life's in danger!'

He jumped on the bonnet as she slammed the car back into first gear. They stared at each other through the dirty glass for a second before she floored the accelerator and the car jumped forward. Adam was thrown to the ground. The tyres squealed as she flew off down the track. She risked a glance in the mirror and saw his dark figure splayed out in the dust from her car wheels. She changed into second and picked up speed, a dizzying elation beginning to flood her. She'd done it. She'd got away. The car bounced madly over the potholes as she screamed a roar of defiance and thanks for her escape. She began to skid on the dry gravel and turned the wheel madly to try to stop it, telling herself sternly to slow down. Victory was so close now.

At that moment, as she came out of the skid, bits of bracken trapped and flapping in the broken window, she wanted to kill him. She wanted to pummel him to death with her bare hands, reduce his head to the kind of mess she used to watch on *The Sopranos*. Her sense of outrage over what he did to her, what she was reduced to, flamed inside her as she roared. That sick bastard was going to pay, he was going to jail for what he did. Murderous thoughts were competing with elation, with the sheer, unbridled joy at the feeling of being free, of having survived. As she drove further away from Adam and his house her feeling of specialness, the sense of how lucky she was, overrode everything else.

An in-car air freshener in the shape of a fir tree swayed with the bouncing car, the scent long ago dried up. She was driving a dead man's car. A cup of old coffee sloshed in the cup holder. Who was he?

She popped open the glove box and pulled at papers, getting the first glimpse of the tarmac road ahead. She should have put her foot on the brake, changed down into first, but she couldn't take her eyes off the bit of paper that she'd pulled out. The familiarity of it socked her in the guts.

The photo that had spilled from the dead man's glove box was of her.

The photo was medium-sized and clear. Nicky couldn't tell whether it was taken by a digital camera or a phone. It was taken somewhere from a distance, but it was unmistakably her. She glanced back at the road, then back to the photo. She stood smiling at someone off camera. She stared at the picture. Where was the building behind her? It was a modern, steel-and-glass tower, indistinguishable from every other office block, and as she stared at the photo, trying to understand what it might mean, she shot out of the tiny side road.

Troy was trying to tune into a local radio station. Make that any bloody station. It was as if he'd hit the Bermuda Triangle here in the English countryside; his digital radio was picking up sweet FA. Troy liked music, it was the playlist of his life, it changed his moods, gave him his feelings. It also reduced his anxiety. Struan hadn't called and that made him nervous. He should have done the bloody job himself, he was thinking. He had to take action. The drive to the house was near here and he was going to park, have a walk on this fine day and find out what the fuck was happening. He slowed as he approached a bend in the road, and finally he happened upon a station playing James Brown. Instantly his anxiety faded as the thumping beats filled his car, masking the noise of Nicky's engine as it raced along in too slow a gear. He still had one hand on the volume control when a red blur of a car appeared out of nowhere and slammed into the side of his beloved black Toyota Rav4.

25

Troy was livid, so steaming angry he wanted to punch the seats in his car till he nearly broke the leather. He was going to fucking strangle this mad bitch who'd just totalled his car, but he was reeling from the impact and the unfamiliar feeling of grappling with an air bag. So he sat stunned as he watched her jump from that piece-of-shit rust bucket with the smashed-out window and scream at him for his phone like the banshee she was. He wouldn't have let her touch it with her filthy hands, not for all the lager in Bournemouth, but the impact had sent his I-phone 4 flipping skywards from the passenger seat to land on the dashboard near the passenger window, allowing her to see it mid-rant and snatch it up in her claws and call the law.

He undid his seatbelt and tried to open his door, but he'd been shunted tight up against the hedge and had to climb across the car to the passenger side to get out. He staggered as he stood, shock from the impact coursing round his body and his rage multiplying as he reached open air. She was gonna pay for this, every fucking penny was coming from this tart.

He checked himself for injuries, ran his tongue over his new teeth and balled up his fists. He was going to fucking deck her, this bitch with the wild hair and filthy clothes. This gypsy country whore, fingernails ingrained with black, was holding his phone! But then he tuned into what she was saying to the police and then he stood transfixed. She'd been kidnapped, held against her will for three days at Hayersleigh House. An Adam Thornton was coming down the road to get her. He'd killed an intruder. And then she said her name, repeated it three times, louder and louder into the small I-phone microphone. He hadn't recognized her from the photo he'd handed to Struan, so changed and distressed did she seem.

Troy took a step towards her as another car screeched to a halt on the country lane. She rang off and started shouting at him: 'I need to make a call!' Great sobs racked her body. She was holding out his phone, pleading for him to unlock it. He did so immediately, handing it back to her with all the concern of an upstanding member of the public. With shaking fingers she dialled a number as he watched a couple tumble from the other car, their faces telegraphing concern, a shout of enquiry that he batted off with a wave. He stood awkwardly in front of her as if he might have to catch her if she fell. 'Honey, it's me, it's me. Please pick up, please!' Troy could tell her man wasn't there. He wondered idly if he was with another woman. She hung up and started to cry. He pulled her dirty face towards the lapel of his pristine linen suit and patted her on the back, offering words of comfort and encouragement as she sobbed and shook with fear and relief.

His mind was crunching through scenarios. So Struan had been struck out. He was going to have to finish this off himself. As if he didn't have enough to do. He looked back at his buckled side panel, the cracked window and the deflating air bags, and then actually kissed the top of Nicky's head.

Now he had two reasons to kill her.

26

Nicky couldn't work out what time it was in LA and she didn't care if she woke him up. She wanted to speak to Greg so badly, to hear his voice. The perspex bubble of the phone booth was scored with scratch marks. She doubted many pleasant conversations had been heard by this receiver in the corridor outside A&E. She had been checked for concussion and had her ankle dressed, her scabs and scrapes dabbed and disinfected. The policewoman had given her some coins as she had no money or ID and no phone; the bindings to an understandable life had been severed. She had never felt more exposed, less prepared.

She heard his phone ringing and the tears sprang to her eyes as he answered. 'Greg? Greg it's me.' He groaned and she couldn't tell if it was from panic or pain. 'Greg it's me.'

'What? What time is it? Christ! Nicky, you're alive?'

She was taken aback. 'Why wouldn't I be?'

'I . . . Jesus . . . I don't know—'

'I'm running out of money. Call me back on this number.' He mumbled, hunting for a pen as she read out the digits. 'Call me back.'

She replaced the receiver and stared at it as if it might suddenly attack her. *You're alive?* For the first time a suspicion about her husband began a slow crawl up her back. It was roasting in the hospital, the smell of fetid bodies and old food flourishing in the heat. She waited a long couple of minutes before the phone rang and she picked it up.

'Nicky? Hi. How are you? Having a good time?'

Her call had dragged him from sleep; had he unwittingly revealed something while struggling to consciousness? Now his voice was perky and fake, a million miles from the warts-and-all reality of where she stood. She'd caught him unawares with the unknown number, but he'd spent a while phoning her back. He'd been composing himself.

'I'm OK.' She coughed. 'Yes, I'm good, I suppose.'

'Well.' There was a pause on the line. 'That's just dandy.'

Dandy? Her misgivings deepened. He was being sarcastic, she was sure.

'I really miss you. I miss you terribly.'

Silence. 'I miss you too, Nicky.'

Nicky's eyes filled with tears. Twice in the past two weeks she had come perilously close to dying. She thought about that moment when she keeled over backwards and there was nothing there to break her fall except the river. It didn't make any sense. Why had Adam jumped in to save her that time if he wanted to hide her away a week later? The second time terror drilled through her guts as she fought to stay alive and get away. She had a vivid image of Adam hanging off the car as she floored the accelerator to escape. What had been his parting shot? *Your life's in danger*. It didn't get clearer than that. He was mad, bad and dangerous, but what if part of what he was saying was true? The brutal reality was that she couldn't be sure that it wasn't, she couldn't be certain that Greg's reaction to hearing her voice hadn't been tinged with surprise – and disappointment.

'Greg?' She felt overwhelming foreboding and horribly alone. Even while on the phone to her husband, all that filled her mind was Adam. She knew this was irrational, maybe a reaction to the trauma she'd experienced earlier in the day, but it was powerful nonetheless. 'I'm going now. I'll phone you soon.' She hung up before he did.

As she put the phone down she saw the policewoman who had taken her original statement – was it Sandra? – watching her from the plastic seats lining the corridor. Nicky's hand moved to her dress pocket and she fingered the battered photo of herself. She gripped the dirty plastic to stop herself keeling over. How did she know that Grace's killer wasn't coming for her? The answer was that she didn't. She didn't even understand what questions she should be asking.

The policewoman sitting a little way away gave her a smile of sympathy, an invitation to revelations.

All Nicky could think, as she stood injured and alone, was that no one was above suspicion.

27

DI Jenny Broadbent turned the AFC Bournemouth mug round so that the chip in the rim was away from her lips. It was the last clean cup in the staff kitchen – their rota system for washing-up had proved as successful as the local football team. She stared at the fruit tea bag floating in the hot water. The contents looked like things cleaned off a stable floor. Raspberry and Echinacea, Sondra had said: a good way to cut down on the caffeine. Jenny needed a caffeine shot in the veins right now as she skim-read the report in front of her. This was a situation that was confused at best. They were dealing with a night-time break-in and a fight that ended in death. These were talking points enough at this small station, or, as Sondra had said excitedly, 'A posh bloke in a huge house. They're the worst, aren't they?'

Jenny didn't agree. She could think of plenty worse, but then Sondra was younger and fresher and had yet to rack up the years of experience Jenny had behind her. She sniffed the mug carefully; like most healthy things, it smelled of nothing at all, as if it didn't exist. Other accusations were flying around: kidnapping, hit and run, hints of sexual violence. The force had swung into action, squad cars screaming off down country lanes. The victim, a Nicky Ayers, was involved in a car crash and had been taken to hospital; the alleged perpetrator was here at the station with none other than his father, Judge Lawrence Thornton, to represent him. The women's hero with a sexual molester for a son? The station was humming with rumour and it was Jenny's job to set the record straight.

She picked up her mug and approached the interview rooms, knocked and entered. This side of the building had high, south-facing windows and she walked into a wall of heat. A fan spun uselessly in the corner. The two men across the table automatically rose as one and then sat back down. Jenny pushed the record button on the huge black tape recorder that took up half the desk they were sitting at. Jenny introduced herself and stated the date and the time as she sized up the men in front of her.

She found it easy to put herself in other women's shoes, to see things and scenarios as they might. Adam Thornton was a person in whom two potent attributes collided: good looks and youth. The first she had never enjoyed and the other she had said goodbye to a while ago. He was deeply tanned with a livid bruise over one eye and an arm in a sling. His T-shirt was torn and dirty and his arms were covered in scratches. That was some fight, she thought.

'You've been seen by a doctor, have you?'

Adam nodded. She looked at his forearms, muscled and sinewy. Jenny liked generalizing; it made the world ordered, understandable. She thought it was a great asset in this job. A punch from this guy would do great damage, as the dead man had found to his cost.

She looked down at her notes. He had gone to a top boarding school, the family owned the country house where the incidents took place, and he was living temporarily at his father's house. The father's address in the capital was in a smart area she'd heard of. Adam was a walking embodiment of privilege, with a big inheritance coming his way and a nice bit of countryside property to impress the ladies with.

Jenny figured that if this guy turned his attentions on you he would be hard to resist.

'We're trying to establish what exactly happened on Tuesday morning.' Jenny paused and looked down again at the notes. 'So you wake in the middle of the night, you hear a noise, you come down the main stairs and you see Struan Clarke.'

'I saw he had something big in his hand – I couldn't see what exactly because it was dark. So I picked up the vase from the landing and I threw it at him.'

'Which way was he facing when you threw the vase?'

'He was facing me. He had started to come for me.'

'And then you jumped on him?'

'He was coming right at me.'

Jenny let out a silent groan. This kind of case was the worst. It was not as clear-cut as she would have liked. Adam had used fatal force but she'd like to see this stand up in court. A householder on trial for killing an intruder in his home? It never played well. The media howled with outrage, politicians jabbed fingers, the police and the CPS were made to look like fools. And here was the defendant: young, attractive, and posh to boot, with no prior convictions. The contrast between him and Struan, a tattooed bouncer with a criminal history, was all too evident. Jenny leaned forward to try to unstick her skirt from the back of her thighs. 'Tell me in your own words exactly what happened next.'

'We fought. He was trying to kill me, no doubt about that. He was swinging that crowbar around, but I got it out of his hand in the end. I punched him a few times and we were on the ground, rolling this way and that.' Adam illustrated by swaying in his seat, his shoulders feinting and ducking. 'He tried to strangle me at one point but I got him off me and my foot hit the crowbar – it was really dark down there – and I picked it up and hit him with it.'

'During this fight where was Nicky?'

'She must have been upstairs. I told her to stay there. She had a bad leg too.'

'Why?'

'She fell on the wine-cellar steps that day and couldn't walk properly.'

'Why did you tell her to stay upstairs?'

'I was worried for her safety.'

'Why? Why were you worried? You had no idea there was even someone in the house at that point.'

'How is this relevant to the chain of events?' Lawrence asked.

Jenny paused and let it go. 'Would you describe your fight as vicious?'

'It was a fight for life.'

'Would you describe yourself as a man with a temper, Adam?'

'When someone's trying to kill me, yes.'

'Struan Clarke was a bouncer. He was used to throwing young men like you around for a living, tossing you off the steps of nightclubs. He was used to fighting, but you managed not just to injure him but to kill him.'

'Again, I ask what is the inference of this question? You are implying my son is at fault, when the intruder broke into a private house and attacked my son – my client – with a weapon.' Lawrence Thornton was leaning forward, calm but determined.

'I meant only that—'

But she didn't finish her answer because Adam interrupted. 'Like I said before, it was me or him.'

There was silence.

'Did you know him, Adam?'

'What?'

'Have you ever seen him or met him before?'

She sensed his discomfort; it was impossible to hide. 'No, never.'

'Nicky Ayers says she heard you two talking before you started fighting. That's a strange thing to do with someone who's broken into your house in the middle of the night.'

Adam looked surprised. 'I never said a word to him. I may have shouted when I saw him. I don't remember; it was a very tense and frightening situation.'

'Struan Clarke lives in London. Why would he be burgling your house? How would he even know about your house?'

Adam shook his head. 'I have no idea.'

'Are there valuable things in your house to steal, Adam?'

'Yes. I suppose so.'

'What happened after you'd killed Struan? You had your phone at the house. I've heard that reception's fine there; it's not a mobile black spot. Surely you called the police immediately?' Adam began rocking back and forth in the chair and didn't respond. 'Adam? Why didn't you call the police?'

'I'm not saying any more.' Adam glanced at his dad and looked away.

'Nicky says you wanted to bury Struan under the front lawn. That you were digging up the lawn to put him under it.'

Adam leaned forward across the table. Jenny instinctively leaned back. There was something about him that made her uneasy. She sensed an animal rage running beneath the surface. An image of Nicky and what she'd put in her statement flashed unpleasantly across Jenny's memory. She spent a second or two imagining how terrifying it would be to be this man's captive for days on end.

'When Nicky wanted to call the police, why did you stop her?' Jenny couldn't help glancing at Lawrence. He was wearing a pale linen suit that was rather crumpled and gave him the air of a man who had just returned from a punt along a river and had dropped his hamper by the back door, opened that door and found his rectory trashed. He was making an effort to stay unaffected by what he heard, but it wasn't working. If she hadn't worked as a police officer for nearly twenty years and had her heart hardened to all manner of things, she would have felt sorry for this father. He was looking after his son's interests here, but he looked grey and crushed. The overriding emotion that was present on his face was shame.

'No comment.'

'Adam, try to answer the question,' Lawrence said.

Jenny saw Adam flash his father a look she couldn't interpret. 'Did you kidnap Nicky Ayers, hold her against her will?'

He said nothing.

'Did you handcuff her to a radiator? Did you puncture the tyre on her car so she couldn't leave your house? '

'I—'

There was a knock on the door and Sondra came in. 'Excuse me, I need a word.'

Jenny leaned towards the tape recorder even though she knew it picked up sound perfectly well. She did it to hide her irritation. 'DI Jenny Broadbent leaving the room.' She stood and excused herself and turned to Sondra when they were out in the corridor. 'This had better be good.'

'She's changed her mind. She's retracted.'

'What?'

'Nicky Ayers wants to give a new statement. She's now saying she wasn't held captive.'

Jenny swore. She went back into the room and ended the interview. Lawrence followed her out immediately, smelling a hitch. 'What's going on?'

'You and your client will have to wait, sir.' She walked off stiffly down the corridor, Sondra half jogging to keep up with her.

'She's adamant,' Sondra said.

Jenny swore softly to herself again. 'I haven't even met this woman and already she's pissing me off.'

'She's waiting for you,' Sondra said.

The first thing Jenny noticed about Nicky when she entered the room was her dress. It was ripped and stained with mud and dust but it was a summery, designer piece in almost comic contrast to the cheap and heavy black courts she had been given as emergency footwear. One of her ankles was bandaged. 'Miss Ayers? I'm Detective Inspector Jenny Broadbent. Please don't get up.'

Jenny sat in the chair next to Nicky and saw a pair of startling blue eyes regarding her. 'I understand that you want to give a new statement?'

Nicky said nothing.

'I'd like to go over some of the details again, if that's OK. It's quite a complicated story.' Jenny carried on, her voice soft but firm. 'You and Adam Thornton went to Hayersleigh House on Sunday. You don't know him very well, and you suspect that he drugged you on Sunday night to prevent you leaving and then slashed the tyre on your car to prevent you leaving on Monday. On Tuesday morning an intruder broke in sometime around four a.m., there was a struggle and Adam Thornton killed him. You didn't actually see this fight, but listened to it from the top of the stairs. When you found the body you insisted that he phone the police and he refused, saying he was going to bury him in the garden. When you disagreed with this he then kept you prisoner for the rest of that day and night, handcuffing you first to a radiator and then, overnight, to a bedframe. You stole the dead man's car key, managed to lock Adam in a wine cellar and escape to beyond the estate wall, found Struan's Clarke's car and attempted to drive away in it, while Mr Thornton came at you with a baseball bat. You drove away and in your panic crashed into a car on the road.'

Jenny watched Nicky watching her.

'I can confirm that as of two hours ago Mr Adam Thornton has been in custody – he is no threat to you now.' Nicky didn't move. 'I do need to warn you that wasting police time is a serious offence. But if things happened as you described, then this man has broken many laws and can – and will – be sent to prison for a long time. I don't want you to feel scared, or intimidated. He can't hurt you any more.'

It was hot in the room, Jenny thought, so goddamn hot it was hard to concentrate.

'I think in the heat of the moment I misinterpreted what really happened.'

'You seemed to think it was pretty clear-cut only a few hours ago.'

'I believe this Struan Clarke broke in to burgle the place but Adam woke up and they fought. I think the shock of having killed him – I'm sure it was in self-defence – gave him a funny turn.'

Jenny looked down at the original statement. 'It says here you thought you heard them talking before they started fighting.'

'I . . . I'm not sure.'

Jenny shifted forward to the edge of the chair. It was a police issue armchair with a saggy, plasticky middle that made her thighs splay uncomfortably on the hard edge. 'Well, were they talking, or weren't they?'

'I'm afraid I really can't say for sure. We should have called the police the moment it happened but we . . . we didn't.'

'Why didn't you?'

She shrugged. 'I think he was very stressed at what had happened and acted irrationally. He had been injured in the fight and I think he was horrified that the man had died.

Of course he knows he should have called the police immediately but maybe that would have made it real, if you know
what I mean. My car had a flat tyre . . . We were trapped,
essentially . . .' She tailed off, frowning and looking at the
floor.

'Nicky, did he handcuff you? Imprison you so you couldn't
report the incident?'

She paused. 'I think the longer the indecision went on, the
worse it got for him. He had the phone and wouldn't listen
to my pleas of calling for help.'

'You didn't answer my question. Did he imprison you?'

Nicky shook her head. Jenny watched a fat tear roll down
her cheek. 'Today I had had enough and we had a fight and
I ran away.'

'A fight so violent that he broke the side window of the
car with a baseball bat and tried to break the windscreen?'

Nicky nodded, not meeting her eye.

Something uneasy moved within Jenny. This woman was
lying and she thought she knew why. She started to get angry.
Why was shame still a woman's default response to abuse?
The number of rapists she'd seen escape justice, the men
who pummelled the life out of the mothers of their children
. . . These animals rarely went to jail and it made her ashamed
of her job. She thought of her daughter, Isla. If any man
dared do that to her she'd kill him with her bare hands. When
she worked at the Domestic Abuse Unit it had been hard to
stay uninvolved. She'd come home from work and watch Isla
bounce Barbie in her wedding dress down the aisle in the
corridor and make the doll kiss Herbie the toy caterpillar at
the altar, while Disney cartoons showing princesses dancing
with handsome suitors played on a reel in the lounge. And
she'd have fresh images from her shift of what those women
had endured at the hands of their husbands and boyfriends:
violence and pain and exploitation masquerading as love.

Jenny's skirt was sticking stubbornly to her legs again. Then there was the age difference. Nicky was thirty-six and the kidnapper wasn't yet twenty-three. In the conservative light of a courtroom she could be made to look ridiculous. Of course this woman with her expensive clothes and sports car – a BMW, she read in the report – didn't want this story to get out. She would be keen to keep up appearances, probably keen to salvage her marriage.

'What are those marks on your arms?'

She saw Nicky stiffen. Her short sleeves had ridden up and the welt marks could be seen running around her biceps.

'Nicky?'

'Who was Struan Clarke?' Nicky was on the offensive.

'A fifty-three-year-old bouncer and former soldier who served in the Falklands. He has no connections from what we can gather with this part of the world. Most burglars operate very locally.' She paused. 'He was a long way from home, Nicky. But don't worry, we'll be looking into why.'

'Did he have a family?'

Jenny was getting irritated. The power of the police had swung behind this woman to help her in her predicament: no money or effort had been spared to protect her, arrest the perpetrator and lay charges. Her team was the mark of a civilized society taking care of its citizens. But only a few hours later her retraction made Nicky the enemy – and none of them would forget it.

'He had a girlfriend who is at this moment being told very unpleasant news.'

'Does Adam have a police record?' And here she was, acting like a journalist and thinking she was in a position to ask questions.

Jenny stared at Nicky. Something about this woman didn't add up. 'You do realize that if you change your statement

Adam Thornton will most likely walk out of here soon and I probably can't keep your – or his – name out of the papers. Are you prepared for that?'

Jenny watched Nicky jut her chin forward in an act that looked like defiance.

'I'm as ready as I'll ever be.'

28

Jenny excused herself from Nicky's room and came back out into the corridor, where Sondra was fanning herself with a copy of *Police Review*.

'What do we do now?' Sondra asked.

'We charge her with wasting police time, if I get my way.'

'Do you believe her?'

Jenny sighed, more irritated than she could articulate. 'There's a big fat lie going on somewhere here. For a start, why didn't she leave until the following day, why did she take off in the dead guy's car, and who the hell is this bloke who ended up dead anyway? He's got a record for GBH from ten years ago and he served two months inside, but that's all. Adam killed him, so they say, but she's all beaten up—'

'Do you think *she* killed Clarke?'

Jenny smiled. That's why she liked working with Sondra. The girl had ideas that were out-of-kilter with everyone else's, but whether they would serve her well as she tried to forge her career in the years ahead wasn't so clear. Jenny herself had learned the hard way that original thinking didn't get you far in the force. In fact, it was a positive disadvantage. 'She killed him and got Adam to lie for her, to protect her nice life?'

'Maybe.'

'But then why did she claim he kept her prisoner?'

'Because he did. He was playing funny games with her. Did you see those marks on her arms?' Sondra shuddered and made a disgusted sound. 'He's into subjugating women, gets a power kick from it, and she's calmed down now she's away from him and realizes what a serious charge she could face, so is backtracking, hoping he'll understand she hasn't squealed on him and will stick to his side of the deal.'

Jenny sighed. 'All I know for sure is that it's too hot to think straight.' She lifted her hair away from the nape of her sticky neck. 'Maybe it's Stockholm Syndrome.'

Sondra turned to look at her full on. 'Nicky's been kept prisoner and is now siding with her captor?' Jenny nodded. 'So in her mind the fact that he didn't kill her has become the belief that he saved her?' Jenny nodded again. Sondra let forth a low whistle, a strange sound, and Jenny knew that it was men who whistled, as a rule. But then, Sondra tended to break the mould. 'I thought that took a long time to develop?'

'Not necessarily. It's the intensity of the experience rather than the length of the imprisonment which creates the conditions for it. It can be as short as twenty-four hours. I studied it as part of my work in the Domestic Abuse Unit.'

'Does it have anything to do with how charismatic the kidnapper is?'

'Yeah, it all helps. It's the situation combined with the person. After all, you're more likely to believe a handsome guy than an ugly one, right?'

Sondra made a funny face. 'I don't believe any man, troglodyte or Justin Bieber.'

They were interrupted by Lawrence Thornton approaching. 'May I ask what's going on?'

'Miss Ayers is preparing a new statement. She was apparently not held against her will and she's unsure whether Adam ever wanted to bury Struan under the lawn. Her account now tallies with his.' Jenny couldn't keep the sarcasm from bubbling to the surface.

Lawrence gave a look like he'd seen it all before. He held out his arm in a silent gesture of apology for the work he knew they'd put in and for all the tedious paperwork someone was going to have to complete now to lay it all to rest. He frowned slightly. 'I really don't believe there is much you can keep my son in on. He is no threat to the public, he has no prior convictions and he will cooperate fully with your investigation, as he has done all along. And after all he and the woman have suffered considerable trauma from the break-in and the defence of the property.'

Jenny chewed a hanging bit of skin on the inside of her cheek. It stopped her blurting out things best left unsaid. Today Lawrence stood on the other side of the law and order divide. He wasn't to blame; they just happened to be on opposing sides in a battle neither of them had sought and that Jenny had in all probability just lost.

No, thought Jenny, despite the trauma she'd obviously experienced, the person who had packed her secrets away was Nicky Ayers and it didn't look like Jenny could prise them open.

'I'll be waiting in the interview room,' Lawrence added as he walked away.

The two policewomen stared ruefully at each other once he had gone. 'I need a coffee. Two sugars,' said Jenny.

29

Jenny stood in the hallway of Hayersleigh House, trying to give instructions to the scene of crime officers, but she had to pause as a plane passed overhead.

'Those planes would send you mad, surely?' Sondra said after it had faded away.

Jenny didn't reply. She looked at the dried bloodstain on the wood-panelled floor and the Persian carpet. The body had already been removed. In this heat no one wanted to hang about. She looked at the stairs and saw the tall, narrow table on which the vase had stood before Adam had hurled it. There was probably a name for that bit of furniture, but Jenny had never lived in a house big enough or grand enough to need one.

'Imagine growing up here,' Jenny said. 'Amazing, but weird.'

Sondra looked up the stairway at the pictures that lined the walls. 'I know I don't know nothing about art, but those are really rank, aren't they? This whole place just feels . . .' She grappled for the correct word.

'Unloved?'

'Yeah, that's it. Sad and unloved.'

'Houses reflect the mood of their occupants, don't they? Is that what Adam is, sad and unloved?'

'My dad never loved me,' said Sondra. 'He bunked off when I was two. But I'm not sad.' She grinned playfully.

'Adam never had a mother. Did you know that men who lose their mothers when they are children are twice as likely to end up with mental health problems, become drug addicts or be violent?'

Sondra flared her nostrils in disgust. 'Poor biddy-biddy baby. My mum works double shifts at the Co-op, takes in ironing . . . He's bloody privileged. There's always a choice.'

Jenny walked into the drawing room and looked out at the mess of garden, where the plough stood abandoned, the turned clods of earth a grey scar in the landscape.

'What was he *doing*?' she asked no one in particular.

'He's got a screw loose, if you ask me,' Sondra replied. 'A silver screw, to be exact.' Jenny felt Sondra's hand on her arm. 'Look.' Jenny followed Sondra's pointing finger. A pair of handcuffs lay on a side table.

'But does that make him a killer, or a kidnapper?' asked Jenny.

Sondra scrunched up her eyes against the sun and enjoyed a few moments in the heat. 'Well, he killed a man, but I doubt he'll ever see the inside of a cell.'

Jenny looked around at the large room. 'Fighting for your life to defend all this.' She paused. 'This case is likely to be dropped before it ever comes to court and since Nicky's withdrawn her statement there's no kidnapping charge either.' She shook her head in frustration. 'What I mean is this: is this going to come back in a few years and haunt us? Are we – and the Ayers woman, for that matter – letting a dangerous psycho off the hook?'

'You know she's an obituary writer?'

'I tell you, if this goes bad, you'll be reading my career obituary in *Police Review*.'

'Want me to check if there are any other bodies poking out of the ground over there?'

Jenny tutted. 'We need to continue to investigate Struan.' She gazed over the lake to where the wall separated the estate from the airport. 'Maybe Struan's connection was through someone at the airport. Did Struan ever work at Heathrow? It's one of the biggest employers in west London, I bet. Maybe that's how he heard about this place, rotting away with little to protect it.'

'It's odd though, why burgle the place when there are people in it? Most of the time it's empty. If you turned up and saw the shutters open and a car, wouldn't you just come back another time?'

Jenny frowned. She walked back out to the hallway and shouted for an officer. 'Did Struan have a bag with him? Something to carry what he wanted from the house with him? It was a long walk back to his car.'

The man shook his head. 'Found nothing like that.'

Jenny and Sondra looked at each other and turned back to continue their tour of the house. They passed the wine-cellar and spent a moment regarding the splintered door; it had been broken in half. Jenny walked upstairs. She wanted to put herself in Nicky's shoes, to stand at the top of the stairs and just feel the situation for a while. When she passed a first-floor window a few moments later she saw Sondra walking along the furrows, taking a look, just in case.

30

'Are you OK?' Lawrence felt Bridget's warm hand on his knee and he covered it with his own. She was driving, her black eyes hidden behind gigantic sunglasses. The bushes lining the country lane were a blur, impossible to focus on. He reasoned he lacked perspective: on Adam, on Hayersleigh, on the hateful and bullying Mr Barnsley, who was straining at the leash to gobble up his land in his airport expansion. Even his name gave Lawrence the shivers. Lyndon B. It was the name for some kind of pop star crossed with a footballer. He was Connie's kind of man – a man without history, making it up as he went along, reinvention being the great and ongoing act of his life. He was like the playboys and actors Connie had known when she still had a job. Connie had actually met him. She had wanted to sell, take the money built up in the bricks and vistas of the house, and spend it on transient things. But then the tragedy hadn't been hers, had it? Her relationship with the house would never be what his was.

Bridget grabbed his hand and bounced it up and down on his knee and he felt the terrible pressure, which left him fighting for breath whenever he got close to the house, beginning to ease as they motored away.

'Thanks for coming.'

She smiled. 'I would always come, you know that. Lawrence, this is not your fault, remember that.' She squeezed his hand, then added, more insistent now: 'I know you don't agree, but it's the bloody truth.'

He didn't reply. His own son, fighting and killing a burglar in that blasted house . . . It didn't shock him. He'd lost the capacity for shock many years ago. When the worst thing that you can ever imagine happens, the rest is only noise. He felt only a great disappointment. That children were a joy was the great con of the age. His own flesh and blood – the only thing Catherine and he had created together that had lasted – was flawed . . . as deeply flawed as she had been.

A twist of fate had robbed Adam of a mother's love, and in this confessional age his son had ended up mourning an idealized relationship he had constructed entirely in his imagination; Lawrence had had to endure the loss of the actual thing. Cathy could be nothing but a saint to Adam, and saints weren't real. Cathy had been vain and bored and flighty as well as charming and bright, but he had loved her all the same. He had adored her faults: the risible paintings, the snobbery, the wittering. And he would have adored them now.

At times it was as though her death had happened five minutes ago, but at other times it felt so long ago it seemed impossible she had ever existed. The time expanded and contracted like a piece of origami. She had lost her life; he had lost the person he had been. I am an exile, he thought, a refugee from my own life. He saw Adam as a baby in Andy Pandy dungarees crawling down the shallow steps that led from the terrace to the lawns beyond, falling one day as he tried to drag the duck on wheels with him, and cutting his lip. He had felt his son's pain acutely then. The scar that had remained had been visible through Adam's tan at the station today. Lawrence had looked and felt nothing. Their child should have sustained him, but he hadn't. People in grief talked about losing their anchors, their lodestars. He hadn't known it then, but realized it all too acutely now, that he had lost his future. He had suffered a break in the continuity of who he was that could never be repaired.

Bridget said it made him a better judge. He feared it made him the worst kind: he was emotional, when the law worked only because it was entirely without emotion. He saw so many sides to grief every day in his calling – the blank faces of the victims' relatives, their hands, whether bony or fat, rigid with a tissue crumpled inside them. He heard their shouts of rage when the legal system tied his hands and he couldn't deliver them the justice they deserved. But success was often no better: if he sent someone down for many years their faces would crumple with exhaustion. What now, they silently said. And he could provide them with no answer.

The car sped up as Bridget turned onto an A road heading for the motorway. Lawrence rolled up the window to stop the wind. 'Maybe it's a good thing that he called you,' Bridget ventured. 'Maybe this is his way of reaching out to you, of beginning something new.'

Lawrence and his son had lived together since Adam left university and began to dabble in this and that. They had been together through Connie's illness and her deterioration. He tried to think positively. Adam couldn't be bothered to get a job or do training (that circus course surely didn't count), but he spent hours with Connie, making her last months more comfortable, talking to her, keeping her company. He had shown great patience – love, even – to her. He hadn't expected that, because he and his son were strangers who didn't understand one another. They were civil, even perfectly pleasant to each other, and they put on a show for visitors and relatives, but the hard truth was that his son was unknown to him. Bridget was right. The phone call had come as a shock; what he heard when he got to the station was even worse.

Who *really* was Nicky Ayers? When he'd met the two of

them the previous week their attraction to each other was obvious, his son and the older woman. She brazenly walked around with her wedding ring on. When they had left Bridget had done that thing with her eyebrow that he liked – raised it to her forehead like the curl of a question mark. They had both thought they had known where that was going, but they had both been wrong. Something dramatic and unpleasant had happened out at the house, but he didn't know what it was.

He looked out at the trucks roaring past in the opposite direction. Bridget's words struck a chord. Why had Adam phoned him? Was it a cry for help, or to rub his nose in the shame and discomfort? Lawrence didn't know, and that, he realized, was his answer. I've raised a stranger, he thought. Another tear for his lost son dropped into the lake of disappointment.

31

Nicky's life began to return to something approaching normal when Sondra appeared about seven in the evening with her handbag, car key and shoes, which had been retrieved from the house. She greeted them like old friends. Sondra stood by the door swinging a car key in her hand. 'There's nothing more we need from you today. You're probably keen to get home.' Nicky nodded. 'I can give you a lift to the station, if you want. Your leg still looks sore.'

Sondra watched Nicky out of the corner of her eye as they drove down the high street. She was preoccupied, or maybe just shattered.

'Have you been out to the house?' she asked. Sondra nodded. 'Did you find anything unusual?'

Sondra turned to her as they stopped at a red light. 'Nothing I haven't seen before.'

'Does Adam have a criminal record?'

'I'm not allowed to disclose that.' Sondra waited while Nicky picked dried mud from under her nails. She was searching for clues, doing her own investigation.

'What *was* he looking for under the lawn?'

'I have no idea,' Nicky said.

'You really don't know him at all, do you?' Nicky didn't reply and there the conversation ended. Sondra drove away, watching Nicky limp into the ticket office from her rear view mirror.

✶   ✶   ✶

Two hours later Nicky was back home. She locked the door behind her, turned on the alarm, drew the curtains and then dragged herself up the stairs, shedding her filthy clothes and shoes as she went. She spent half an hour under a scalding shower, scrubbing viciously at her skin. Lurid images of what she had been through over the past few days were impossible to block out. She sat on her bed in a bathrobe and tried to think rationally about what had happened, but her hands were shaking and she was crying. She was having some kind of low-level panic attack, her thoughts a crazy jumble that jumped with no direction or reason between the present and the past.

She tried to concentrate on the strictly practical and dared to take a look at herself naked in the bedroom mirror. She looked pulverized. Bruises and scratches covered her torso, arms and legs from her barefoot run through the forest; she had a nasty graze down her shin from falling on the cellar step; the gash in her hand still throbbed; her biceps were ringed with yellow and purple bruises and weeping rope burns, and she was sunburned. She got out the first-aid kit and dabbed antiseptic on her wounds, redressing them as best she could, then rubbed moisturizer into her leathery skin and drank lots of water. She cooked a hot meal and forced herself to eat it.

The phone rang but she hardly noticed. At past midnight she finally crawled into bed, but not before she'd taken her largest kitchen knife and put it under the bed. She was asleep before her head sank fully into the pillow and she didn't wake till a car skidding in the street dragged her from sleep at ten the next morning.

She sat in her kitchen listening to the kettle reach boiling point. The fridge hummed, a laptop light blinked. She revelled for a moment in the pleasure of pulling energy from the National Grid. A shaft of hatred for Adam bolted through her but she pushed it away. She'd made a choice yesterday and she was going to have to stick to it. Because of what she'd said Adam wasn't facing serious charges of kidnap and assault; he was probably being portrayed this morning as an upstanding, have-a-go hero valiantly defending his property from a vicious intruder, someone so shocked at what he had been forced to do that he didn't report the death for two days. He would be out of custody soon, and who knew where.

She picked up the photo from Struan's car and turned it over slowly in her battered hands. Why was her picture in a burglar's glove box? Was Adam right, and protecting her, rather than trying to do her harm? The rings round her biceps throbbed at the thought. He had said he was going to tell her something, but she had not believed him. She had seized her chance for escape instead and that had been the right choice. She felt a headache coming on and reached for the Nurofen. The kettle clicked off with a sharpness that made her jump. But Adam had said other things. That maybe Grace's killer was after her: the assassin that had never been unmasked. Was it really a case of first Grace and now her? And if so, why?

She moved the photo, its shiny surface reflecting the light, obscuring her face and then the building beyond. Why had she not shown this picture to the police? Why hadn't she told them what Adam had said about Grace?

Greg distrusted the police. In fact, that wasn't strong enough to describe his feelings. He hated them. They were corrupt, stupid, lazy, racist and incompetent, and he had thought that before Grace had died. Their treatment of him after her murder, the circle of suspicion tightening ever closer round him, as they could find no other suspects, had deepened that enmity still further. Nicky had thought Greg's manias endearing when she first knew him, but, inevitably, close proximity to them meant that some of his feelings had rubbed off on her. And what evidence could she actually show them of someone trying to do her harm? A picture in a glove box? She made a cup of tea as her headache began its rhythmic bashing against the inside of her skull. No, as things stood, she had nothing, even though what had happened to her was far from nothing.

She picked up her filthy dress in a fit of useless energy and threw it and her shoes in the outside bin. She'd never wear them again without being reminded of things she would rather forget. She slammed the bin lid down. She had better be right – her gamble had better pay off – because if she was wrong she'd let a dangerous psycho roam free.

Nicky checked her watch. She should be at work, but there was somewhere she needed to go first.

32

When Liz opened the door the smell of burning toast wafted out behind her in a cloud. 'This is unexpected,' she said, folding her arms across her ample chest and leaning on the doorframe.

'Can I come in?'

'Of course.' She paused. 'Are you all right? You look like all hell.'

Liz had such a way with words, thought Nicky. The searing heat was showing no sign of breaking and she was uncomfortable in a long-sleeved top with a high neck and jeans. She wanted to hide her injuries from the world, but the scratches on her hands she could do nothing about. 'I fell and hurt my leg, but it's getting better,' Nicky said, making light of her wounds.

'Come through. Dan's being "creative" in the kitchen.' Liz waved her hand in a sarcastic flourish down the narrow corridor. 'The way he's going we'll need the fire brigade.'

Nicky followed her sister-in-law down to the back of the house and said hello to Dan, who grunted and wandered off with his plate of toast, a pile of burned toast shavings, like coal dust, scattered on the surfaces.

When he left there was nothing to distract the two women and Nicky stared awkwardly at the floor. 'Come, come, sit down,' Liz said, pulling out a chair. 'So. You been busy?' Liz was looking at her accusingly.

Nicky gave a small laugh. 'No, but I've got some time off,' she lied.

'And on a roasting hot day you came all the way to south London to see me.'

Nicky smiled and acknowledged the dig. 'There's something I wanted to talk to you about.'

Liz leaned back against the kitchen cupboards and kicked distractedly at a door with a stubborn hinge that wouldn't close. 'Well, start at the beginning. That's usually best.'

'What was Greg like when he was younger?'

'Greg?' Liz looked surprised and uncomfortable. 'That's a funny question. Why do you want to know?' There was a hint of steel there, a suspicion.

Lies always work best when they're based on truth, Nicky decided. 'Well, to be totally honest, Greg and I are having difficulties in our marriage and I thought that maybe if I knew more about his past I could . . . use it to help us.'

Nicky saw Liz looking keenly at her. 'I'm sorry to hear that. Really I am. Believe me, I know how difficult it is to keep a marriage on track. You're lucky you don't have children – that makes it ten times worse.' Nicky shifted awkwardly in her chair. 'Sorry, sorry! I didn't mean that!' Yes, you did, thought Nicky; that's exactly what you meant. There was an awkward silence. 'What problems are you having, if you don't mind me asking?'

Embarrassed, Nicky traced her finger through the burned crumbs on the table. 'Oh I don't know, Liz, he just seems so different now we're married. He's so distant . . . cut off from me, somehow.'

Liz let out a theatrical sigh. 'I think he's scared. After what he's been through, it's no surprise.'

'Maybe he needs to have more counselling, but he won't go. It's an argument I've lost.'

'He can be very stubborn.'

'So . . . prior to Grace?'

'Grace . . .' Liz paused and took out a ham studded with

cloves from the fridge. She picked up a boning knife and began to cut slices from it. 'Well, there were lots of women – you know Greg!'

Nicky nodded. Grace had said as much.

'Grace was young and fun and attractive, but she had more to her than that too. She wasn't just a pretty PR dolly or someone who dabbled in the art market, yet with all her doting dad's money behind her she could well have been.' Liz was talking as if Nicky had never known Grace, but she stayed silent and listened. Nicky could well see how that kind of girl made Liz spit. 'She had a bit of grit to her.' She paused and picked a clove from the back of the ham.

'She was very driven,' Nicky added.

'I guess she was. He was very happy with her, I really believe that. He's a different man now. She changed him, she brought out his ambition, gave him the funds and the drive to succeed. She carried him along, so to speak, and after she'd gone, he never stopped.'

'What about before Grace?'

'Oh. God, I can't remember their names. There was never a break in the women. There was a homeopath and then a dancer. I think he left her for the mad one.'

Nicky sighed. 'He's a man who makes sure he has hold of the next vine before he lets go of the first, so to speak.'

Liz smiled, picking up a slice of ham from the plate. 'Like Tarzan, swinging through the jungle, vine to vine,' she said playfully, shaking the slice of ham to and fro in front of her face.

'At least I'm not a jumper,' Nicky added. She was thinking about her own love history, how she had always prided herself on not lining up a boyfriend to replace one she had tired of. She was strong enough to live life alone if needs be.

'So he told you about that?' Liz was staring at her intently, the piece of ham dangling in front of her mouth.

Nicky waved her hand to play for time. Told her what exactly? 'Yeah, he told me all about that.'

Liz let out a sigh of relief. 'Thank God. I told him he had to tell you. Relationships can't survive secrets like that. It would have sent him mad.' Nicky's mouth was dry. She'd only wanted to score some small petty victory over Liz and suddenly she was staring at a chasm of secrets. 'When did he tell you?'

Nicky hesitated and made a split-second decision. 'Quite recently.'

'I'd take that as a very good sign. He always swore to me that no one else was ever going to find out. If he's opening up to you, it's a sign of great progress. Even Mum and Dad don't know and he never told Grace.'

'Why didn't he tell them?'

'I think he felt a failure, in Dad's eyes in particular. He thought that maybe they'd think it was somehow his fault. He would have been such a great dad.'

Nicky felt as if she had been punched in the stomach. She fought to stay nonchalant. 'Yes, a lot of what ifs. How old would the child be now?'

'Oh, about ten, I guess.'

Nicky shook her head, reeling. 'Was she very different from Grace?'

'Francesca?' Nicky nodded, though she had no idea who Francesca was. 'Well, she was another blonde, of course. God, my brother's such a cliché, love him as I do. They've all been blondes. You've all been blondes! I didn't meet her very often.' Liz popped the ham into her mouth. She gave Nicky a sly grin. 'I don't think any of them liked me. I was Greg's big, loud, older sister. I don't do the kowtowing to the young blondes very well.'

'You've certainly never kowtowed to me, and for that I'm eternally grateful.'

Liz finally revealed a smile Nicky took to be genuine. It softened her face and made her look almost maternal. 'To be honest, I thought he got together with Grace too soon. She looked like Francesca and I wondered if that was the overriding reason they were together. But I do think they were in love, desperately in love.'

Nicky was leaning forward, hanging on Liz's every word. She realized that even though she was married to Greg, she knew very little about his romantic history. A baby. Greg nearly became a father. She didn't know who Greg had dated or when. The past was filled with Grace, the agony of her; she was impossible to move beyond, and there had been precious little room for anyone else. Now Liz, unwittingly, was revealing another life before Grace, with a drama and heartache all its own. It was like she was reading chapters of Greg's life, the pages finally opening and divulging how he became the man she married; the man who could keep secrets so totally from her.

'To suffer like that, it's bound to affect him. He's become so safety-conscious, so superstitious! He tells me that he never stays anywhere but the ground floor now! I mean, honestly!'

Nicky played along. 'He makes me turn off every fuse in the fuse box when I change a light bulb.'

'There! Told you!' They both laughed.

'You love your brother very much, don't you?'

Liz gave up pulling delicate strips off the ham; she cut a thick chunk and began chewing vigorously. 'More than ham itself.'

They both giggled, a sound Nicky had never heard from Liz before. There was a softer side under the harried and efficient social worker and single mother. Maybe Liz could be an ally in the work that needed to be done to understand Greg. 'Where's Francesca now?'

Liz slapped her piece of ham back on the worktop and

folded her arms. She stared at Nicky, her eyes narrowed. Nicky swallowed. Something had just gone wrong. Silence filled the kitchen. When Liz spoke again her voice was flinty. 'You little bitch. He didn't tell you any of it, did he?' Nicky opened her mouth but could think of nothing to say. She found she was shrinking back against the chair as Liz took a step across the kitchen. 'You're out of your depth, little girl. You'll drown if you go any further.'

Nicky got out of her chair fast and grabbed her bag. Their chat was obviously at an end. As Nicky fled down the corridor Liz called out again. 'Ignorance is bliss, Nicky. Keep it that way.'

Liz felt the walls of the house shudder as the front door banged shut into its warped-wood frame. She walked down the corridor and checked up the stairs. Dan's bedroom door was closed. There had been no witness, but she was still angry at herself for getting caught out in such a basic way, and after she'd kept her counsel so efficiently over the years. But then that was her all over, Liz felt: covering up others' mistakes, repairing those who were broken, doing the difficult, unseen work that was never recognized. There would be no televised, black-tie gala for her work, she knew. Her back was never going to be slapped, her ears would never ring with fatuous applause. She walked stiffly back into the kitchen, picked up another piece of ham and stared at it, the fat running through the meat like veins in marble. They were like mistakes winding through a life; you could try to cut them out but traces of them always remained. She dropped it back on the plate, her appetite gone, and picked up the phone. She jabbed at the speed dial and left a terse message. 'You need to look out. She's on to you.'

33

Troy had given a false name and pulled out some fake ID when the policeman got round to interviewing him after the ambulance had taken Nicky to hospital. Various scenarios had churned through his mind. He'd watched the officer taking down all his details. Seen in black and white he didn't want his name associated with this in any way, however tangentially. A squad car had driven off down the lane to the big house, the two uniforms, having got the garbled story off Nicky, looking as apprehensive as if they were hunting down Jaws.

He would have asked questions, tried to get extra information, but he could tell this lot knew even less than he did. Struan seen off by a poshie! If he wasn't brown bread he'd have been embarrassed. Struan had made the fundamental error Troy himself had never made: he'd underestimated his opponent. He guessed Struan hadn't anticipated the aggressive butchery of a man on the ropes in his own property. But Struan's casual approach now presented Troy with a problem. Things had suddenly become a lot harder, the stakes a lot higher. There was a trail to find if you dug far enough; there was always a trail. Troy had started to mentally tick off separations that would have to be made, safeguards he would have to employ to distance himself as much as possible from Struan.

He had had no idea how the woman would react to a delay in the job, or, God forbid, to the publicity that might be generated. She was an unknown and he was exposed, which was not a feeling he liked. For the first time in a long time, Troy had felt fear. His attempts to cash in and gather that retirement fund were looking more delusional by the minute. Bloody Struan. He had begun to feel as stressed and irritated as any other manager trying to corral inefficient and under-performing employees. Troy couldn't share others' pain or feel their anguish, but he could put himself in other people's shoes on a practical level. He suspected that once this got out the woman would want to cut all ties with him as soon as possible. And Troy knew exactly how he himself would tackle that task.

And then there was the day job. Lyndon B was still his employer. Even though he was recovering from a heart scare and was in the south of France, and so Troy didn't have to go anywhere by plane with him, things had a funny way of travelling back to Lyndon, and he was someone Troy never wanted to get on the wrong side of. Lyndon had known Darek, the supplier of the list of hits that had led him to the woman, but Troy had no idea how they all linked up, if at all, or how Lyndon might react if he discovered what free-lance work Troy had been attempting to take on the side. Trying to think through the ramifications of this had given Troy a headache of monstrous proportions.

This was not a moment to be weak; it was a moment to be ballsy. He had watched the metal arms of the tow truck begin to tighten round the belly of his motor, the man in Day-Glo adjusting the straps. Troy currently had one advantage: no one knew what had happened – yet. He had to turn that to his favour. As his car had been hoisted off the road and out of the hedge with a tearing, metallic judder, he had made his decision.

34

Nicky fled back home from Liz's house to find Greg's car being unloaded from a recovery truck. A cheery man in overalls made her sign some papers before revving the engine and driving away with a wave.

She sat in the living room staring at Greg's car in the street. Liz's words wouldn't leave her head; her abrupt transformation was . . . horrifying. She was a guard dog snapping at anyone who got close to her brother's secrets. But Liz had made a mistake, and now Nicky was on a trail of discovery. I am his wife, she thought with outrage; you can't keep me out. It was time to start digging.

She started in the study, a room she never used as she preferred to work on a laptop on the kitchen table. Greg had imposed a kind of shambolic order and she knew the photos were stored in a filing cabinet. Her drawer was the bottom one, Greg's the top. It opened with a dependable screech and she started sorting through the mess of dog-eared envelopes filled with negatives and photos, half the packets ripped through age or neglect, stray photos or negative strips popping up at odd angles. She began to dig back through the strata of Greg's life, the ages before digital. As she sifted, years of her husband's life seemed to be absent, and then she'd open a package and an afternoon or an evening of the thousands that had gone unrecorded and unremarked would jump right out of the past and make itself felt. She found a fat envelope filled with photos of a single afternoon on a foreign beach: fresh-faced twenty-somethings gurned and sprawled; there were blurry shots of people moving too fast or everyone looking the wrong way; a woman in a bikini bending over to adjust a towel. She recognized no one except a shockingly young Greg: skinnier, sometimes smoking, often in sunglasses.

A few packs further down she found a series of moody, black and white shots of Greg in a fisherman's hat and cropped trousers. He could have been no more than twenty-five. The rococo balcony in the background and the geraniums made it unmistakably Paris. Below that she found some photos of a woman's pubic hair triangle, and there were two shots of Greg laid out naked on a bed in a brown room, a livid sunburn on the tops of his thighs. The next photo was a blurry close-up of balls and a dick. She turned it this way and that, resisting the urge to laugh. She didn't know if it was Greg's or not, surprised she couldn't remember what her husband's own member looked like. Underneath were a few professional head shots from his agency, and then right at the bottom, in a reversal of the fresher-to-the-older order of memories were the photos of his wedding to Grace, the ones that hadn't made the cut into the album downstairs. A lump formed at the back of her throat. She closed the drawer quickly to choke off the flashbacks.

It struck her that she didn't recognize many people in this drawer and the most common subject apart from Greg himself seemed to be Liz. Greg didn't carry friends through life. In all the time she'd known him she had never met a friend from school or an old university pal. Most of his work contacts were now in the States and she'd never met them. Greg wasn't a keeper: he shed friends and created new ones without any sense of loss or pain.

Did this tiny sample from the complexity and length of a person's life hold any picture of Francesca? Nothing was written on the back of any of the photos; Greg didn't collate or organize, he wasn't the type to alphabetize or label.

There were almost no photos of herself, apart from their official wedding ones. She knew why: those were on the computer, sealed up in a hard drive rather than in a drawer like this. She'd drawn a blank.

She started a hunt through Greg's desk, inspecting filming paperwork, his tax minefield. Finding a white A4 envelope she opened it and the funeral service for Grace fell out. She froze, that hideous day jumping to clarity in her mind. She was always holding someone's hand at that service, and other hands continually patted her on the back or gripped her shoulder, as if everyone at that funeral needed the touch of another to survive it. The only time she had stood alone, physically unsupported by someone else, was when she had followed Greg's funeral address with her own. She still to this day did not know how she had done it.

Or how Greg had done it. He had seemed calm, in control, adjusting his shirt sleeves under his black jacket.

The envelope was full and she pulled out the contents: correspondence from lawyers, the copy of a writ served on a national newspaper for insinuations that could prejudice a future trial, condolence letters.

The dam holding the tears back was beginning to crumble. What was she doing, rifling through Greg's stuff, digging through his history, feeling grubbier and nastier the deeper she went? Finally the dam burst and she sat in the study amid all the old and yellowed paper and she wept. She wept for Grace, for the people who had loved her, and in a good dose of maudlin self-pity she wept for herself and what had happened to her over the past few days at Adam's hands. She began to pile the paperwork back onto the desk and that was when she found it: a funeral card inside another envelope that had been thrown in amongst everything else.

Another life lived, another life ended. Francesca Connor, Mountain View Cemetery, Oakland, Ca, 3 September 1999. And there was Greg, giving another eulogy. Nicky had to sit down on a chair because the strength in her legs drained away. Grace *and* Francesca. The room seemed to still, even the dust particles rising on the summer air seemed to pause on their lazy way.

The man who lost two blondes.

How had Francesca died? She looked at her dates on the pale yellow card. She had been twenty-five years old. Grace had been married to Greg so he got all the official correspondence, but Francesca had been Greg's girlfriend so, according to the law, she was still the property of her parents and Nicky found nothing more than the funeral card. What was it Liz had said? Something about jumping. She did an internet search on Francesca's name but came up with nothing. She phoned the library at the newspaper and insisted they look in their files, claiming it was research for a story, but that also turned up a blank. She was an American citizen; finding the truth wouldn't be easy.

She made a cup of tea and tried to put her thoughts into some sort of coherent order. She listened to the home phone's answering service and found a message that shocked her more than she thought possible. Greg was coming home, he said; he'd be back in London on Saturday. Something uneasy moved deep inside her. He must have spoken to Liz. She had the sensation of being in a pincer movement, closed in by Greg on one side and Liz on the other. What was so important that he'd abandon a film shoot and come home?

She pulled out of her pocket the photo of herself that came from Struan's car, and stared at it again. It didn't reveal anything at the moment, but she began to wonder if it would.

35

The lift door hadn't even shut behind Nicky when Maria saw her and was up from the desk and over in a flash. 'Where the hell have you been?'

'What, not even a hello?'

'The managing editor was here, asking where you were.' Maria spoke theatrically *sotto voce*, looking round the desks like she was an East German spy at Checkpoint Charlie.

'I sprained my ankle.'

Maria sighed and tapped the side of her head. 'You left me a message that you were ill. At least keep to the right cover story.'

Nicky stood and drank in the image of Maria, stressing before 9.30 a.m. She reached out and gave her a spontaneous hug. 'You have no idea how happy I am to see you and to be back.'

'It's too early for sarcasm,' Maria snapped. 'Now put your back into that limp, Nics. Wince a bit more. Oh, and your phone's finally arrived. It's on your desk. That bloke with the pimples in Accounts brought it up. Isn't that nice?'

Three hours later Nicky was editing the early career of a lord who founded an ethnographic museum in Cairo. It really was good to be back. She craved work to stop her mind going crazy thinking over the madness of the past week. Last night had been sleepless as she tossed and turned, trying to process the revelations about Greg's previous girlfriend, and Adam's actions and her reaction to them.

*   *   *

Maria clunked the phone receiver back into the cradle and groaned. 'It's a freelancer chasing a late payment. It's all bloody Accounts' fault. I don't write the cheques, but they phone me when their money hasn't arrived.'

'And you get shouted at.'

'Oh, quite the contrary. She's always so polite, so apologetic that she's bothering me, which makes me feel even worse. We both know that underneath she's seething with resentment that her pay has stayed the same for the last ten years. She should be giving an earful to Bill Gates, or online news sites, or Twitter or something, though I'd like her to find a phone number for them any time soon.'

'Any more rumours while I was away?'

Maria waved her hand dismissively. 'Oh the usual threat of further "reduced head count". We're not even complete bodies any more.'

'We're the past, aren't we?' Nicky said, looking with regret round the office.

Maria waved her finger in a note of caution. 'Careful. The past can be more trouble than you might think.' She leaned forward, a glint of defiance in her eyes. 'And it fights dirtier. This old dinosaur would love to be too much trouble to sack.'

Nicky was thinking about past secrets, was thinking that she needed to talk to Maria and unburden herself, when she saw Bruton, the news editor, leaning on the back of an office chair and pushing it like a Zimmer with wheels across a large area of carpet where a phalanx of sub-editors used to sit before their work was outsourced to Shipton-on-Stour. Bruton was back from a fag break. She got up and joined him.

'Feeling better, Nicky?' he asked half-heartedly, his voice like a stone grinding flour.

'Yes, I sprained my ankle, but it's much better now, thank you.' He nodded. 'I need a favour.'

'Mm?'

She followed him and the office-chair Zimmer back to his desk, which was dominated by a large ornamental glass ashtray brimming with paperclips and bits of gnawed pen and chewing-gum wrappers. It looked almost insulted at being used as a receptacle for desk junk. 'I really need your help.'

Bruton looked up at her, she was much taller than him, or maybe he was just so stooped that it seemed that way. 'That's a first.'

'Indeed.' She smiled. Bruton didn't suffer fools so it was better simply to ask. 'You used to work the crime beat, I hear,' she said, pulling up an office chair and sitting across the desk from him.

'Crime beat! You make it sound like I was here back in the 1930s!'

'You weren't?' He began coughing in reply. 'I need to find out where someone lives.'

'Is this for work?'

'No.'

Bruton shook his head. 'You know I can't do that, Nicky. There are processes, security procedures—'

'Get a contact of yours to do it.'

He paused to sit down in his chair, twisting slowly this way and that. 'Why do you need it?'

'So I can kill them, of course.' She paused for a beat. 'But I didn't say that.'

Bruton smiled and tapped the edge of the ashtray with his finger, as if knocking ash off a phantom fag. 'I really can't do it, Nicky.'

'Of course. But you'll do it anyway.'

Bruton opened a new chewing-gum pack and put one of the rectangles into his mouth. 'What makes you think that?'

'Because you and I are very similar.' Bruton guffawed loudly. 'I'm an addict.' Bruton looked surprised. 'I'm addicted to passion, intrigue, pointless high and lows, fleeting romances, none of which are good for me.' She paused. 'And I know you know all about addiction, Bruton.'

It was cheesy and lame but she hoped he'd go for it, and deep down she wondered if there was a grain of truth about what she was saying. Why else would she have gone on such a mad and reckless test of her marriage if she wasn't some of those things? She had been, at least, very severely punished for it.

Bruton grunted and coughed. He held up his right hand so she could see the yellow stain between his fingers no soap or pumice stone could remove. 'I've smoked forty a day since I was probably sixteen years old. I once worked out that I must have smoked at least half a million cigarettes in my lifetime. I've spent about three years of my life smoking.' He paused and shook his head slowly. 'And by God, I've enjoyed every single minute.'

Nicky picked up the glass ashtray and tipped the cluttery contents into the waste bin next to the desk. She buffed the glass with the edge of her shirt and put it back, pride of place on his desk.

Bruton shifted slowly in his chair. 'You know, that ashtray was given to me by a famous footballer back in the days when I covered sport. We must have put fifteen cigarettes in it during that one interview alone.'

Nicky stood up, reached across the desk and patted Bruton on the shoulder. 'If we can't beat it, at least we can enjoy it,' and she handed him the bit of paper with the name on it.

Two hours later he passed her desk on the way to the lift, an unlit fag dangling from his lips, and wiped down a Post-it with an address in Hackney on it. 'This is ten years of purgatory for me,' Bruton said.

'I'll buy you some duty-free when I next go through,' she said. For the first time all day, her biceps didn't ache.

* * *

The flat was in a red-brick mansion block with iron railings leading up a small flight of stairs to a communal door. The door was once fitted with small coloured squares of glass but the panes near the lock were a variety of cheap clear-glass replacements after numerous break-ins. There were eight doorbells on a panel on the left, with various surnames taped next to some of the bells. Nicky rang but there was no answer so she waited across the street in an entrance to some public gardens. She heard the slap-slap of flip-flops on a variety of young women, then a couple of young men in Hawaiian shorts strode by, followed by a hobbling wino. Windows screeched open, doors banged. There was activity aplenty in this street, a contrast to the quiet opulence where she lived with Greg. She had never even seen her neighbours on one side. She once saw a Daimler slide out of their car parking space, and that was the sum total of her interaction with her neighbours. She was trying to decide if this was a problem when a moped drew up and a girl in hot pants and ballet flats flicked down the stand and got off. Nicky peeled her back off the wall, her senses tingling.

The girl took off her helmet and ruffled her hair back down. Caught unawares Bea looked like an extra from *Roman Holiday*. She picked her hot pants out of the crack of her bum, then did a little youthful jump up the steps and unlocked the door. A moment later Nicky crossed the street and rang a variety of doorbells until she found someone to let her in.

Bea's flat was on the first floor. Thrash metal blared out from behind it. She had to knock loudly three times before Bea heard her and opened the door. Nicky jammed her foot in the entrance before Bea had a chance to slam it back in her face. Bea's mouth was a mean line, her eyes narrowing dangerously.

'Get your foot out of my door.' She had to shout over the music.

'Let me in.'

'Piss off.'

'You're lucky you're not in jail,' Nicky shouted. 'I could have had you arrested for that stunt you pulled at the river. You're going to talk to me, however long it takes.' Bea tried to stare her out, but after a long moment she gave a sarcastic little laugh and opened the door. Nicky followed her into a living room and watched as Bea sank into a low sofa covered by a throw, under a dirty window. She tucked her legs underneath her like a fawn and started fiddling with an earring.

'Turn the music off.'

'What?'

'Turn the music off.' Nicky said it louder this time.

Bea waved dismissively at the iPod on a shelf unit made of reclaimed wood planks and brick struts and after Nicky turned it off they were plunged into a silence so profound it was as if Nicky had been thrown into a swimming pool. 'Did you take photos of me, of Adam and me?'

'Why the fuck would I do that?' She spoke quickly and spat out the words. 'Why would I want your ugly face near me?'

'Did you get someone else to take a picture?'

Bea stretched her legs and flipped her shoes off onto the wooden floor. They landed next to a half-drained cup of coffee. 'Worried your husband might find out?'

'Just answer the question.'

Bea paused, but not for long. 'I didn't take your bloody picture.'

Nicky sat down on an armchair covered in a matching throw to the one on the sofa. It seemed more conversational to sit and she wanted to get Bea on side. She was facing a fireplace where the grate and the mantelpiece were gone, and the square hole was filled with magazines and books. A blue neon sign that said 'hurt me' hung above the hole, a black wire trailing away behind the bookshelf. 'How long did you go out with him?'

'More than nine months.' She sounded indignant. 'We were very, very close. We shared a lot.' She said it as a challenge.

'How often did you go to the house?'

'You mean Hayersleigh?' Bea picked up a cushion from the sofa and twiddled with one of the tufts at the edge. 'Have *you* been there?'

Something in her voice made Nicky pay greater attention. 'Yes.'

Bea looked like she'd been given news that was unpleasant. 'Well, well.' Her voice had turned quiet as the envy, plain to see, churned through her heart. 'He won't stay with you, you know. You're way too old.'

Nicky didn't rise to the insult. 'So you went out with him for nine months, but he never took you to the house.'

'He doesn't love you! I've known the family all my life. Adam and I go way back; we practically grew up together.'

'I thought you said you'd never been to the house?'

'My parents are friendly with his dad. We used to hang out in London in the holidays when we weren't at school. And then when we met up again recently . . . well . . .' Her voice paused so she could rub it in. 'We got together pretty quickly.'

'So you're a real pal, trying to frighten his girlfriends like you do.'

Bea pulled herself up to vertical on the sofa. 'You're not his girlfriend!'

'No, I'm not. So tell me, did you and Adam plan that I should end up falling in the Thames?'

A cruel little smile spread across her face. 'That was funny.'

'Did you plan it?'

'What do you think? Of course not! I was nowhere near you, anyway. I never touched you.' She paused. 'I hear your balance starts to go funny when you get old.'

Nicky counselled herself to not get sidetracked into a

pointless slanging match, however tempting. 'Did Adam talk about his family much? Did he talk about the house at all? I really want you to tell me about him.'

'Yeah, well, Adam hasn't had it easy, has he? You know *that*, don't you?' She could layer on the sarcasm as thickly as a Vegas showgirl her make-up, Nicky thought sourly.

'Bea, you know him better than I do.'

'Yes, I do!'

'So please, tell me about him. Tell me some of your stories.'

Bea sat back on the sofa. Most people relished being asked for their expertise, however banal the subject. She ran her hand down her tiny shins and grabbed her ankle. Bracelets clanked on her skinny wrist. It seemed she really wanted to talk about Adam. Nicky listened to a story that Bea was excitedly relating about a music festival they'd been to together when their car got stuck in the mud and had to be pulled out by a tractor, but she was thinking about another scenario. Were the photos of Connie an excuse to get her to the house? Why had she been taken there? What was so different about *her*?

Bea's music festival story ran out of steam so Nicky asked, 'Did he go to the country house often?'

'No. No one goes there much. Adam and his dad constantly argue about that place; Adam wants to sell but his dad won't hear of it. There's some long-running dispute with the airport owners. If they ever sold the airport would buy the land as they've been given permission to expand. Adam's always saying the guy who owns the airport is a crook who should be in his dad's court. His dad refuses to sell to him. It's a mess.'

'How did Adam's mum die?'

'He never talks about it. An accident when he was tiny. That was all I heard.'

'What about his friends, his family?'

'Aunt Connie was a substitute mum before she got ill . . . and there's Rob from circus training, Davide—'

'Was he at school with Davide?'

Bea nodded. 'Yeah, they go way back.'

'So is he Adam's closest friend, would you say?'

'Kind of. They hang out a lot.'

'Even though he lives in Spain?'

Bea frowned. 'What do you mean?'

'Doesn't Davide live in Spain?'

'*Hello!* Not that I've heard.'

The bump in the legs from the man behind. The hand on my bag as we shoved it in the locker. 'Here, let me help.'

Had he planned to meet her on that plane? Had Adam not met her by happy accident? Had he set her up? And running through her mind was the desperate question: why? Why? Why?

'Er, like, hello? I haven't got all evening!' Bea was leaning forward and staring at her. Nicky sensed she thought she'd got the upper hand.

'Did Adam ever tell you he was looking for something at the house that explained his background or his family?'

Bea ran her fingers through her spiky hair. 'There's nothing to explain, that's the tragedy. His mum died when he was eighteen months old. It totally fucked his father up because they were really in love and now he's had to live his life without her, and Adam never had a mother. That's enough to be getting on with, isn't it?'

'Did he ever tie you up?'

Bea's eyes widened. 'I'm not telling you that, you twisted cow!'

'During sex? At other times? Did he ever handcuff you?'

She snorted, but she was listening, her eyes taking Nicky in, assessing. She was jealous, only she had no idea how far from the truth her overactive imagination was taking her.

'You're married. I'm going to tell your husband what you've been doing, you dirty slut.'

'Cut the self-righteous crap, Bea.'

'You know something? You're talking about him as if he no longer exists. It's already over between you, isn't it?' A vindictive smile spread across her small features. 'Did your fuckerama of a weekend not go as planned?'

'How did you know we went away for the weekend?' Nicky rose slightly from her seat, sensing Bea had unwittingly revealed something. 'How did you know?'

Bea closed her eyes and hesitated for a moment too long. 'Adam told me.'

'No he didn't.' Nicky felt she was beginning to understand. 'You've been following me – or him.'

Bea didn't disagree, and she was the sort to disagree violently if she felt the need. 'Have you got a car?' Something about their journey to Hayersleigh had stuck in her mind: the way Adam squealed away from that junction in Chelsea.

'No.'

'Do you know Struan Clarke?'

'Who?'

'Struan Clarke. Middle-aged guy with a tattoo of a snake on his arm.'

Bea wrinkled her nose as if the idea of anyone that old was distasteful to her. 'No. Never heard of him.'

'Ever heard of Greg Peterson?'

'No. Leave Adam alone, he's mine. We're soulmates, we have a connection, we depend on each other.'

'Sure you do, Bea. Don't worry, you can have him. Once the police are finished with him.'

'*Police*?'

'That's right. The police have been questioning him about bludgeoning Struan Clarke to death with a crowbar. You obviously mean so much to him that he called you first, isn't that right, Bea?'

She had no answer to that and sat mute on the sofa. Nicky rose and let herself out of the flat. As she came down the steps of the building, her mind a swirl of unpleasant revelations, she heard the angry scrape of a sash window opening above her. Bea's spiky hair poked out. 'He's ashamed of you. That's why he took you to the house. To hide you away.'

Nicky hurried down the street as Bea's voice became shriller and louder, a witch's cackle behind her. 'He was planning to hide you away because you're so ugly!' And the terrible thing was that Nicky couldn't disagree with her. Amongst the diatribes and the hate and the jealousy was the kernel of truth: Adam had had a plan. He had set out to meet her and had manufactured their sitting together on the plane; then he had saved her when she ended up in the river, and maybe he had saved her from Struan Clarke . . . and it was rough justice indeed to hide her away, but what was he hiding her from?

A thought so horrible came to Nicky that she stopped dead in the street and it seemed as if the people walking past her speeded up. Had he also saved her from her own husband?

The man who had lost two blondes.

Outrage tore through her heart. She was going to find out why. She was going to find out. Her steps echoed on the hot pavement below her, beating out a new determination.

36

Maria had buzzed Nicky into the building and was now standing at the door of her flat, a bright flowered apron covering her summer dress. Her dark features were a question waiting to be answered. 'Something that couldn't wait till next week?' She swung the door wider and beckoned Nicky inside. 'I'm so glad you called – now we can eat together.' Whenever Maria was in she cooked, and she did it very well. With parents who were originally from Calabria, she retained a reverence for and expertise with ingredients that rendered Nicky's attempts in the kitchen amateurish at best.

'What is that divine smell?'

Maria laughed. 'You know I only ever get visitors at mealtimes? Sardines stuffed with raisins. Sounds disgusting; tastes divine.'

'Do you need a hand?'

Maria gave Nicky a look of pity. Don't insult the master, the look said. 'You have to soak the raisins to get the cloying sweetness out of them. English raisins don't really work in this.'

Nicky smiled. English supermarket ingredients were always inferior, tasteless, mushy. Nicky took Maria's word for it.

Nicky suddenly felt exhausted and slumped into a chair next to Maria's small kitchen window. Geraniums in the window boxes fluttered lazily in the warm evening breeze. Maria's flat was tiny but perfectly formed – a bit like Maria herself.

'Come on, spit it out,' Maria said kindly, pulling a bottle of white wine from the small fridge. Maria was in her mid-forties; she was a friend, a colleague, and was known for dishing out not only good food but also very good advice.

So as Maria swished raisins around a Pyrex dish filled with warm water Nicky told her everything about the last few days: falling in the river, what happened with Adam at the house, her changing the story she told the police, her talk with Bea, and the most recent revelation that Adam had not met her by accident. By the time she had finished Maria was sitting opposite her at the tiny café-style table, the raisins long forgotten, her mouth an O of shock.

'Where's the photo?'

Nicky pulled it from her handbag and put it on the table. Maria stared at it for only a moment. 'Are you a fucking psycho?'

'Excuse me?'

'You let this man go? You changed your story to the police and now he's free to either hurt you again or attack someone else!'

'I know it sounds weird but I think there's more to the story that I have to try to uncover—'

'Nicky! Listen to yourself!' Maria shook her head as she realized how she sounded. 'God, Nicky, I'm so, so sorry. You've been through a terribly traumatic few days. I'm horrified at what you have endured. It's not right, or at all just. You were basically kidnapped by some power-crazed –' she struggled for the word – 'maniac, who by the sounds of it psychologically tortured you. We need to find you someone who can help you get over it. A counsellor, maybe.'

'I . . .' Nicky was at a loss for words. 'But he saved me from that intruder—'

'You said he was talking to him!'

'I . . . yes, but—'

Maria leaned nearer to her. 'Nicky, listen.' She put her hand on top of hers. 'This man must go to jail. He will have done this before, and will almost certainly do it again. It is a pattern of behaviour. Being good-looking simply gives him the opportunity. He is the worst kind of predator.'

'But Adam saved me. Didn't he?' She saw Maria make a great effort at self-control. Nicky hadn't expected to meet such opposition, but she rallied. 'Why was my photo in that man's car?'

Maria shrugged. 'Because Adam gave it to him? Sounds to me that they knew each other and were planning . . .' Maria changed the subject fast. 'And what about this mad girlfriend? She basically pitched you into the Thames. They're working together, which is even worse!'

'Well, what about the other stuff? Turns out there's more than meets the eye about Greg! There's another dead bloody girlfriend – and this one was pregnant!'

'Oh Nicky,' Maria's voice was barely a whisper. 'We are talking about what happened over the last few days, not about something from – what? – ten, fifteen years ago!'

'Liz told me to stay out of it. She completely changed when I found out about Francesca. Something is going on, I can feel it.'

Maria leaned further across the table and shook her by the arms, making Nicky wince. 'You are a journalist. You work in facts. You respect the truth. R-e-a-l-i-t-y. This is not something you feel!'

'Greg has been acting really weird. It's like he . . . like he knew what had happened to me!'

'OK. OK, OK.' Maria looked ashen. She was still holding Nicky by the tops of her arms. She stopped and traced the outline of the bandage under Nicky's thin, long-sleeved top. 'Take this off. Now.'

Nicky tried to protest but her heart wasn't in it. Maria

pulled her top over her head and stared at the bandage still on one bicep and the livid bruises and scrapes visible on the other. There was a long silence and then Nicky saw that Maria's eyes were full of tears. 'He did that to you?' The silence told her all she needed to know. 'Nicky, is there anything else you want to say?' Nicky shook her head. She couldn't meet Maria's eye. There was a long pause. 'Where is Adam now?'

'I don't know.'

Maria looked like she'd had the life kicked out of her. As if she'd discovered that something she had always believed was based on a lie. 'You think this is connected to Grace, don't you?'

Nicky nodded.

'I want to make sure I've got this right. You think Greg did something to that girl, Francesca, that he was involved in Grace's death, and that he is somehow connected to Adam or Adam knows what Greg's done, and that even though Adam kidnapped you and you had to fight for your life to get away he was trying to help you in some way.'

'I don't know.'

'You do understand that if you believe this, you are saying you are married to one of Britain's serial killers? Do you really think Greg is a multiple murderer? That he murders the women he loves, and his sister covers it up?'

'He's coming back. He'll be here tomorrow. He left a film shoot to come back after my conversation with Liz!' Nicky looked out through the window as a bumblebee that should have gone to bed hours ago banged itself continually against the glass, smashing its head and body against an invisible obstruction, killing a little bit of itself with every knock. She felt a roar of voices in her head, rising in volume to a scream. She felt Maria's hand on her wrist.

'I phoned Greg to tell him I was worried about you. I

didn't know where you were! That's why he's coming home!'

'Christ!'

Maria still held Nicky's hand. 'Nicky, listen to me. The world is full of bad men, brutal men, psycho men. They are young, old and in between. You had the misfortune to meet one. You escaped with your life; you were very lucky. But life isn't a game of joining the dots. There is no pattern. There is no relation between this and Grace or Greg. There is often no tying up the ends in life. Grace's death is a question you will probably never know the answer to. With each year that passes, the likelihood of a resolution fades still further. Time is the great killer of the truth. Her death will resonate with you always, particularly if justice is not served.' Nicky felt a tear roll down her cheek. 'Remember, when you think about this later, that the reason you like me is because I tell it to you straight.' Nicky felt Maria grip her hand almost too tightly. 'Does maybe a part of you *want* to tie your experience to what happened to Grace?'

Nicky stood abruptly, as if what Maria said had scalded her, and she snatched her hand away. 'How dare you say that to me!'

'Nicky, you have had a terrible experience.' Maria stood up on the other side of the table. 'I think you need help. I get a bad, bad feeling about this. Changing a statement is serious stuff. I just hope you haven't caused yourself a lot of trouble for the future. I really do.'

Nicky roughly pulled her top back on. 'Your fish are burning.' As she marched in indignation from the flat she heard a grill pan being slammed on a hard surface and Maria cursing the Madonna.

37

'You'll just have to leave it here and they can drive round some other way.' Jenny pushed the *A–Z* off her legs and tried to stuff it into the side pocket of the passenger door, but it was too large, so she threw it into the seat well in frustration, wiping the sweat off her neck. Sondra coasted the car to a stop behind a police car stuck behind three more cars stuck behind a police van. Both sides of the narrow one-way road were bumper to bumper with parked cars.

Sondra craned to see if there were any parking spaces further up the street.

A car behind them honked angrily.

'I hate this city!' Jenny hissed under her breath. When they'd got the call from the Met this morning about a murder at Struan's address, she'd lost no time in getting to the scene, but it hadn't been easy or pleasant. They'd got lost three times getting here, after sitting nose to tail in Saturday jams on the M3, the heat radiating up from the tarmac in waves. They'd stop-started across giant roundabouts as Sondra struggled to interpret a jumble of road signs at knocked-about angles. They'd been frustrated by one-way systems, by no-right-hand-turn signs – the *A–Z* was no bloody good for that, was it? – and now they were finally here her bad mood could expand to meet the ugliness of the place. She felt hemmed in already, a haze of dirt and pollution hanging over the row upon row of terraced houses, giant wheelie bins blocking the pavement and skinny front yards in a never-ending battle to recycle the tons of rubbish produced by all these people crammed in too tightly together. It was the fag end of summer and the whole place felt like it needed a bath.

Jenny got out of the car and approached the Astra behind her. 'This road is closed,' she snapped at the Sikh in the driving seat. He groaned loudly as he stared back at the long reverse he would have to do.

She turned back to Sondra. 'It's number 197,' Sondra said.

'We'll just have to leave the car here,' Jenny said and they trudged down the road towards the blue and white police tape fluttering in the Saharan wind. 'I probably couldn't afford to buy a flat in this street,' Jenny added sourly. Sondra tripped on a broken paving stone as they approached Struan's front door. Detective Inspector Martin Webster came out to meet them and they all shook hands.

'Flat's upstairs,' he said. Martin was large and cheerful and must have got overexcited by the weather recently as his nose was red and peeling with sunburn, Jenny noticed with a touch of disapproval.

'You've got a traffic problem out there,' Jenny said, nodding her head back at the street.

Martin shrugged. 'It's the weekend. People kill for parking spaces round here,' he replied with a smile, and called for someone upstairs to go and sort it out.

'No one broke the front door,' Jenny said, eyeing the cheap door that covered the bottom of the stairs.

'No sign of a break-in but there was a fight,' Martin said as they climbed the stairs and came into the living room. Two men were still dusting for fingerprints, a woman held a camera and was taking pictures, but the majority of the team dealing with murder cases had already left with the forensic evidence they needed.

The bay window was covered in net curtains that were clean and bright and a modern sofa in grey sat along the back wall. There was a modern shelving unit at right angles to the window; it was lined with DVDs and photos in frames and a cuddly toy that said 'Easy tiger' on it. A glass coffee table was at a skewed angle. The blood splatters had reached as far as the large and expensive flat-screen in the corner.

'Someone was eating a bowl of crisps,' Martin pointed out and Jenny tracked the scatter pattern of crisps across the wooden floor, a bowl and a cup accompanying them, and saw several women's weekly magazines scrunched on the sofa and floor, some scattered with blood. 'And that scrape on the wall –' both women turned to see a grey diagonal line in the magnolia paint – 'we think this mark was made by the end of the gun that they were fighting to get control of. From the angle of the blood splatters on the TV we think Louise Bell was pushed backwards over the coffee table and then shot. Best estimates so far are that death occurred sometime Thursday afternoon, between one and three.'

'One of my team interviewed her after Struan's death,' Jenny said. 'She'd been going out with Struan for at least five years.'

Martin nodded. 'Her mother called her every day. They were like sisters. After the death of Struan Clarke she didn't want to even leave Louise alone, she said, as Louise was too upset. When her mother hadn't heard from her she simply came round and let herself in with a key that she's got. She got a nasty shock.'

'Louise claimed she couldn't understand what Struan was doing out in Dorset in a country house in the middle of the night,' Jenny said. 'It was a total shock to her.'

'Louise's mother says the same,' Martin added. 'Far as she knew, Struan was just a bouncer.'

'A shotgun makes a very loud noise. No one heard anything?' Sondra asked.

Martin shook his head. 'The neighbour below is in Greece, those either side were either out or away. Those across the garden at the back don't speak any English and we're waiting for a Tagalog interpreter to arrive from Kensington.'

'Tagalog?' said Sondra uncertainly.

'It's a dialect of the Philippines,' he said. 'There's no remote entry system so she would have had to come down the stairs, open the door and bring the killer up.'

'So it's likely it was someone she knew.' Martin nodded. 'And this shotgun—'

'We're still waiting for the full report, but it's a Beretta 687, a pretty standard make, the kind of thing you'd find on many farms . . .' he paused, 'or estates, and I don't mean the types on the other side of the main road.'

'There are two shotguns registered at Hayersleigh,' Jenny added. 'Both are still there, but the place is chaotic to say the least . . .' Jenny tailed off. Most crime, particularly violent crime, was obvious, brutal and sordid. Passion made people into animals – the human race was not sophisticated. All the education, fine clothes and opera in the world couldn't prevent the violence lurking inside most people from exploding with lethal force if the circumstances were right. Jenny didn't know what had occurred here in west London, but she wouldn't be surprised if it tied up in the end with what had happened at Hayersleigh.

'And then there's this.' Martin grinned as he pulled some photos of the body out of a file. 'A necklace.' He started sorting through them. 'It's been bagged and tagged. Mother doesn't recognize it. Here.'

Jenny heard Sondra make a clucking noise of satisfaction. 'Would you look at that?' Sondra said, holding the photo aloft for Jenny to see.

The necklace was a thin chain and nestling in the centre of it was a name, each letter joined to the next by a little piece of silver. The silver letters spelled out 'Nicky'.

'I doubt it belongs to a Debra,' Martin said cheerfully. 'That's a stupid thing to leave behind at a murder,' he added.

Jenny didn't answer. Over the years that she'd worked murder cases she'd learned that the most obvious suspect usually was the perpetrator, the most obvious evidence was irrefutable. Leaving your own necklace in the dead woman's grasping hand wasn't so surprising after all; it was banal and stupid and real. She stared at the photo. Nicky Ayers wasn't stupid, but she was clearly out of her depth. The necklace was something for teenagers, or someone like Kate Moss. She could see Nicky in this necklace. On herself such a thing would scream out 'mutton dressed as lamb', but Nicky could pull it off without looking ridiculous. Jenny could see Nicky in a nightclub, come to that; she would have clothes suitable for a club full of teenagers. Was that where she'd come across Struan and Louise?

'Whose flat is this?' asked Sondra.

'Louise rented it. She's lived here for three years and it is in her name. She was a midwife.' Martin rubbed his sunburned nose. 'Louise Bell isn't your case, but now you've come all this way why not wait and hear what Nicky Ayers has to say? It could be illuminating.'

38

G reg was still woozy with the pills he'd taken to survive the flight and also hungover from his whiskies as he tried to fit his key into his front door. He didn't need to bother as Nicky opened it and started shouting at him before he'd even put the handle down on his suitcase.

'Who's Francesca? Who is she, Greg!' He backed up against the wall, trying to process his shock and surprise at that name being bandied about by his wife. 'Come on, tell me, Greg!' She looked livid, with staring eyes and wild gestures.

This homecoming was so different from the fantasies he indulged in during the long lonely hours it took to get back home. He would imagine them hugging each other on the doorstep, right where she was shouting at him now, then they would take a bottle of wine and go upstairs, and he would pull off his uncomfortable travelling clothes and they would go to bed even though it was only the early afternoon and he would just lie there, nuzzling her, coming back to earth. But not today.

She kept up the attack. 'Francesca. She was your girlfriend, wasn't she?'

Greg nodded, sobering up fast under her questioning. 'Yes, she was.'

'She was pregnant, wasn't she?'

Greg sensed his heart beginning its slow thump, thump

of alarm. There had better be a good reason why this had all come out. The weather must have been hot, Greg thought, because she was sunburned, which was unlike Nicky, and she looked different, though he couldn't put a finger on why. She seemed a bit wilder, a bit . . . stronger.

'You've got nothing to say? This bit of information isn't worth commenting on?' Nicky came closer to him, pointing her finger. 'Why did you never tell me and why did you never tell Grace?'

Greg was big and solid and could have shoved that physicality in people's faces, but he walked away from a fight and very rarely used his strength for baser purposes. He walked past her, towards the kitchen, to gain some space to think. 'Did I ever lie to you? Did I ever?'

'A total omission is just as bad!' She was a pace behind him as he retreated to the back of the house.

'Bullshit! I never lied.'

'But you hid it! You were never going to tell me!'

'No, I wasn't.'

'Your girlfriend died!'

'Yes, she did.'

'How could you never tell me, never talk to me—'

'This is bullshit! Talking? That's clap-trap dreamed up by people trying to steal your money, though they call it counselling! I had to forget, otherwise I'd go mad. Always onwards, always forwards, Nicky, that's how I cope. I don't dwell, I don't think about the might have beens. Nothing corrodes me like thinking that if only I had done something different, something cleverer, I might have saved her. So forgive me if I don't put flowers on a grave or build a shrine to dead love in my fucking garden. I'm doing it my way!'

Greg could feel his face reddening, his rage coursing through his veins as he turned to face her. 'Cut the crap,

Nicky. I'll ask you the same question. Have you ever lied to me? Come on? Have you ever? Anything you want to confess?'

She ignored him and went back on the attack. 'Why was Liz so angry when she unwittingly told me? Why should it be a secret?'

'It's not a secret!'

'She acted like—'

'Liz is Liz. For Chrissake, she's a pain in the arse at the best of times, and now I've got to be judged on my sister? How do I know why she said those things? She's probably a bit like me and wants to protect you from it.'

'Protect me from *what*?'

'Pain and grief, that's what! Don't tell me you understand, Nicky. Don't tell me you know how I feel—'

'I've *never* said that to you!'

'I wouldn't be with you if you had! People expect grief to play out as they see it in a film. If you don't act a certain way they feel cheated – if you don't cry they think you don't feel; if you cry too much they tell you to pull yourself together. You don't know what I've been through, you can never know! And remember, I had those detectives sitting opposite me at that fucking table, assessing my every reaction to Grace's death, scrutinizing me for faults, trying to find chinks, and your charming workmates were doorstepping me, phoning my friends, insinuating rubbish—'

'You don't have a monopoly on suffering! Grace was my best friend! I had known her all my life!'

That pulled Greg up short and he began to moan and drag his hands across his scratchy, jet-lagged eyes. 'I know . . . I know. I'm sorry.'

'How did Francesca die?'

Greg took a deep breath and ran his hands through his hair. He was standing by the sliding glass doors that led to their large garden. It was the kind of London garden that millions must covet: wide and long, with mature trees at the back that shielded them from the neighbours, who were never there anyway. A secret, hidden place that children should play in, a garden that his unborn child should have enjoyed. 'She fell off a sixth-storey balcony. We were on holiday in Morocco.' His voice was flat, expressionless. 'I had gone to the chemist's because her mosquito bites were itching. She was scratching them too much and I was worried about them getting infected. She was found naked in the grass by the edge of the pool. Twenty-third of August 1999.'

Nicky paused. 'I'm so sorry. Did you have any idea she was suicidal?'

'She wasn't.' He spat the words out.

'What?'

'She didn't kill herself.' He made a funny movement with his shoulders, halfway between a shrug and a gesture full of defiance. 'She had been treated for depression in the past and could be very up and down, but I don't think she would ever have done that . . . I mean, it must have been some kind of accident.'

'I don't understand.'

'Neither do I. She had no reason to . . . Maybe she was disorientated . . . The bloody hotel . . . They were just so keen to cover it all over because it was bad for business.'

'No rooms above the ground floor . . . It makes sense now. But how—'

'I don't know. I don't understand, OK? I can't explain it to you, any more than I could explain it to her parents!' He was shouting now, his voice harsh in the afternoon heat. 'There was a queue at the chemist's, an Australian was dithering about buying waterproof plasters or something . . .' He tailed off, his eyes glazing over. 'When I got back she wasn't there.' He turned to Nicky. 'It was at least ten minutes before I heard shouts outside the window and leaned over that bloody balcony.' He paused. 'You'll never get the details you want because I can't even begin to explain it to you. I don't have the words!'

'I know how it can be difficult to explain things, to reveal things that are not straightforward . . .' She looked crushed.

'Nicky?' She was silent for a beat too long. 'Nicky?'

'I'm so, so sorry.' She looked about to cry.

'I don't want pity. I can't stand pity. So I didn't tell you or anyone. I was away in California a lot then – that's where she lived – and we'd only occasionally stay in London, but we were on holiday in Morocco. The police never asked about it because it never came up in their searches, and I never told them.'

'She was going to have your child.'

'But she didn't, Nicky! She never did have that child! I might want to pretend otherwise, but that child never existed! She was five months pregnant when she died and I used to feel that baby's elbow under the skin, feel those tiny feet pushing against her stomach . . . But there is no name for that child, that child has no sex, it has no birth certificate and it has no grave!' Greg was angry now, so angry that blotches were appearing on his face. Nicky had never seen him like this before. 'I've just got back from a twelve-hour flight during which I sat sweating in fear the whole time. I'm jet-lagged. And I don't need this inquisition about things in the past I'm trying to forget from my *wife*!' He picked up his jacket and jabbed his arms roughly into the armholes. He nearly ripped the fabric in his haste. 'Don't you think I spend enough time in hotels? You think I want to come home and spend my first day back in a fucking Novotel? Cos that's what you're making me do, Nicky!'

'Please stay here so we can talk about this.' Nicky was pleading with him now. 'You're cutting me out and I'm trying to help.'

'Oh really!' He wheeled round to her. 'You're telling me you're not like all the rest? When you found out about Francesca you thought about Grace, didn't you? And you thought: *two* dead women? No one can be that unlucky! That's what this is really all about. You suspect me, just like everyone else!'

He marched to the front door, feeling for his wallet, but it wasn't there so he whirled back to the kitchen and swiped it from the island while she stood in the hallway. He put his hand on the front door and turned towards her. Now his voice was low and menacing. 'You thought I'd killed both of them, didn't you? But you didn't answer my question, did you? Have you ever lied to me?' He leaned forward. 'Where were you phoning from when you woke me up the other day, eh? And then you rang off without saying anything at all.'

'I . . .'

'Have you ever lied to me about something that happened recently?'

'Yes. Yes, I have.' She said it loudly, without any shame or embarrassment.

'God help you,' he said in a whisper as he slammed the door behind him.

Troy used a reverse directory to find the address that connected to the phone number that had taken him to Greg Peterson's voicemail. His heart beat a little quicker when he saw the postcode: Maida Vale was a pricey part of town. Troy didn't like to give in to intuition, he didn't trust it, but every so often he had to admit a feeling would come over him and excitement and hope would soar in him. This just *felt* different

from that loser RJ, who hadn't been able to stump up a sou
in payment for his past sins. A secret taken to the grave was
about to reach out of the cold earth and grab at Greg Peterson
in his very own *Carrie* finale. Troy couldn't wait. But first
he had to get prepared – for success and for failure. However
excited he might be, the potential for fuck-ups was ever
present. Struan's snake tattoo flashed in his mind, but only
for a moment.

39

Greg's elbow slipped off the edge of the bar at the Crown in Cricklewood and he had to make a bit too much of a bum-shuffling adjustment to stay on the stool. How the mighty fall, he thought. The fiasco of a reunion with Nicky was not what he had planned. His temper had got the better of him, but then it wouldn't be the first time. Anger and managing it had been a problem all his life. He just hid it better now that he was older and slower, presumably with lower testosterone. What was testosterone? Where did it live? In the balls? In the glands? He should have paid more attention in biology, but he knew why he hadn't: he would have been trying to chat up some girl or other, back in the days when he was cocky and sure of himself and so, so young. There was an irony there, if he cared to search for it. And he didn't care, not tonight; he didn't care at all. Desire was brought on by what hung between his thighs: his need for love; his failure to keep it.

He slugged back a shot of Jim Beam given to him by the barman, who looked about fifteen and had a silver name tag on his uniform. The lettering was too small for Greg to read and he was too drunk; things were beginning to slide in and out of focus.

'What's yer name?' He managed to get that out in what sounded like English to him.

'Vladek,' the fifteen-year-old replied and turned away in pity from the old soak drowning his sorrows.

The bar was so empty it wasn't like there was a dishwasher to stack or lemon to chop. Greg realized with a shot of drunken clarity that the guy wanted nothing to do with him. 'You and my wife,' he said. Vladek didn't turn. Music he didn't recognize played from the walls. What a homecoming – just what he'd spent twelve hours on the red eye for: a bunk-up in fucking Cricklewood. He could have gone central, marched into the Hilton or the Dorchester, binned cash and had them fawning, but he wanted to indulge his moroseness, caress it, and that would have been harder in a place where he might have bumped into someone he knew. He leaned his head forward and wiped the sheen of sweat from the back of his neck. Christ, it was hotter here than in California. At least there the breeze off the Pacific cooled him at night, or the air conditioning shouted its efficiency. This heatwave had given London a stench reminiscent of Tangier; the council needed to sort out their bin policy.

He swilled his ice cubes and burped. He should be thinking about Nicky, about how they had drifted apart, about how love can flourish so strongly and then wither – but he was worrying about Camden's environmental waste issues. It was a sign, as if he needed it, that he'd hit middle age. He'd slammed right into it like a rubbish truck into the bollards on the Kilburn High Road. But he knew what Tangier smelled like because he'd been there with Francesca.

He saw some peanuts in a silver bowl further along the bar and pulled them towards him. What the heck. He tried to throw one skywards and catch it in his mouth but he never even saw it come back to earth. Peanuts probably grew in Tangiers. Film catering trucks didn't offer peanuts: too many allergy lawsuits waiting to happen, too calorific for the talent. Were there six types of wee on LA peanuts and, if so, was it a better class of wee than Cricklewood's? He shouted at Vladek for another shot. He wasn't in California any more.

He'd bailed from a film shoot! Liz's terse message and Maria's worried one had sent him walking right out! After that stunt he'd probably never work again. *You'll never eat lunch in this town, buddy* . . . After what had happened to him, was it any wonder he was paranoid and superstitious and difficult and – he hardly dared say the word but it reverberated round his drunken skull anyway – cursed. Cursed, contemptible Greg, trying to keep the demons at bay with underhand tactics like having his wife followed by his own sister and hiding his hurt and anguish behind a wall of silence. He crunched down on an ice cube. Maybe Liz took a little too much pleasure in playing the guard dog.

So, here he was, alone, in Cricklewood. The old anger flared brightly within him. Good fucking riddance to all of them, Nicky included. He drank another slug of whiskey and found his hand was shaking. He was teetering on the abyss, but he had stood on that abyss many times, too many times; it was as if he could feel the hands of those dead women trying to pull him over!

We live our lies, Greg thought. They are our defence mechanism. Tell a lie for twenty years and it turns into the truth. He had created his own truth, however twisted. He had only done what any man would have done. What *had* to be done. He refused to feel guilty for that.

Why did he have a thing for blondes? Maybe if they had been redheads his life would have turned out differently. He would be married with a couple of kids and living in Essex, and his neighbours' wives would be the hotties. But real or bottled, there was something about a blonde. All his girlfriends had been that honey colour. It was the colour of desire, a symbol of his drive and ambition and he wasn't going to apologize for that.

The whiskey burned his throat. He did have things to apologize for, but he blocked those thoughts from his mind.

The whiskey would tear down the barrier later that evening, and the fear and guilt and recrimination and pain would flow unhindered and unwitnessed through him, but with considerable mental effort he got the barrier to stay upright for now.

'Vladek, leave the bottle.'

Vladek gave a nod. 'I'll charge it to your bill and you can take it to your room, if you wish, sir.'

There it was, the polite 'Get lost', issued by a fifteen-year-old. Oh my, he was a lush to be hidden away in shame. His elbow slipped off the bar again and he stood up and managed to weave his way through some rather complicated seating arrangements to the stairs. They were curved and he felt ridiculously pleased that he got to the top without a stumble.

Occasionally there were nights when the memories took over, when the guilt visited him, worse than the worst acid trips he'd had as a student. He gave into the feelings that crashed over him, let them soak through him. He was not a religious man but these were the nights that the terrors stalked him: the what ifs, the what might have beens, the how close he came to walking a different path. In the past he'd used Liz as a crutch to get him through, but their relationship had been tested and had worn away over the years until only a bitter shorthand of it remained. He sometimes had dark thoughts about his sister, wondered if her increasing bitterness and distance towards him was because she thought he didn't suffer enough. Her support had helped make him more successful, had stretched the gap between their respective lives to a greater degree than she'd ever expected, and maybe this had made her bitter. She had Dan to worry about and an ex-husband to hate. For Liz hate had been a cleansing passion. He was under no illusions that his dear sister would have killed her ex-husband if she'd only known how. If only she'd had the guts. No, there was no Liz tonight. He was middle-aged now; he was on his own.

He didn't have children, the ties that hold a person to a place or a routine; he had dead bodies, memories he tried to blank out, regrets that never lessened, hopes that had been crushed, over and over again. And now Nicky had gone and done it all on her own . . . she had found his way of being wanting.

He swayed along the corridor to his room and fumbled with the card key to open the door. The room was as stuffy as the bar. 'Welcome to London,' he said to the walls and sank back onto the bedspread, Jim Beam slopping over his hands. 'Come on, then! Come and get me! All of you!'

40

After Greg had stomped off Nicky had assumed he was coming back. The first hour had dragged by and when he hadn't appeared she was angry – she'd jumped on his travel bag and kicked it across the corridor, she'd paced up and down, swearing at her husband in his absence; ninety minutes later she'd phoned and pleaded on his voicemail with him to come home. Two hours later she'd collapsed on the sofa and let the love she felt for Greg course through her veins. It was painful. She loved him so much, but he seemed ever more separated from her. The revelation of an entire story before Grace had sent dark shards of suspicion deep within her.

When the doorbell had rung and she had run to the front door, she had told herself that she wouldn't accuse, she would fold herself into his arms and they would work it out. Her fear and panic at the hospital had been a psychosis brought on by her experiences at Adam's hands. How could Greg possibly have seemed suspicious on the phone? She'd disturbed him in the middle of the night. She would sit Greg down and she would tell him everything. And he would forgive her. They could start anew.

She had been so sure it was Greg that she had opened the door without looking through the spyhole.

It hadn't been her husband. And the rock that had formed in her throat as she had opened the door had grown in the hours since and was still growing. It was now so big she didn't know how she could continue to breathe.

Inspector Broadbent was sitting across from her now but the interview was being led by a big man called Martin Webster.

'You have no idea who Louise Bell is?' Martin was repeating all his questions for emphasis.

'I've never heard of her, and this picture doesn't help. I've never met her.'

Martin had a box file in front of him. He pulled out a plastic bag with something inside it, turned it round and laid it in front of Nicky. 'Is this your necklace?'

Nicky instinctively put her hand to her throat. Her necklace. It really did look like hers. She picked up the bag. The weight felt right, the thickness was as she remembered, but when had she last seen it? She couldn't remember. 'Yes . . . I guess so. Or one very similar. Where did you get it?'

'The clasp is broken.'

'It wasn't broken when I last had it.'

'This necklace was found clutched in the hands of Louise Bell when she was shot dead in her flat.'

'That's not possible. I . . .' She saw the lawyer turn towards her, waiting. They were all waiting for her. She was the centre of attention. She had been wearing that necklace when she first went to Hayersleigh. She remembered with a vividness that was painful spending time getting ready in the bathroom before they left for the country that day. She had thought through her outfit, played out scenarios in her mind. So many different outcomes, except the actual one. She had put the necklace on because it made her feel young; she had put it on because Greg had given it to her, and she thought maybe it might stop her straying too far from the righteous path. She took a little bit of Greg with her on her day's escape to the country—

'Nicky?'

And the contrast between her arrival there and her exit – barefoot, injured, scared half to death, scaling walls and crawling on hand and knees in the dust like an animal – could not have been greater. Had she been wearing the necklace then? She had no idea. But it seemed pretty clear now what had happened. 'I wore that necklace when I first went to Hayersleigh House.' She couldn't bear to even say his name. 'I think it was taken off or I lost it there.'

'Where were you on Thursday, twenty-fifth of August?'

'Two days ago? I went to see my sister-in-law in Brockley.'

'What time were you there?'

'I went in the morning. I left there about midday.'

'And after that?'

'I was at home.'

'All day?'

'Yes.'

'Anyone with you then? Anyone call on you?'

'No.'

'We'll need your mobile phone to corroborate what you say.'

'I didn't have a mobile then.'

'You don't own a mobile?' Martin was looking sceptical.

'I had lost it before that and I didn't get a replacement till I went back to work the next day.'

'Do you own a gun, Nicky?'

'A gun? Of course not.'

'A shotgun?'

'No.'

'Are there guns at Hayersleigh House?'

Nicky paused. 'Yes.'

'How many?'

'Two. They were locked in a gun cabinet.'

'Did you ever see Adam using a gun?' She paused, thinking

of the moment he had looked down the gun sight at her. 'Did you ever see Adam firing a gun?'

'No.'

'Louise Bell is Struan Clarke's girlfriend.' Jenny saw the shock on Nicky's face. Impossible to hide, but possible to fake? If she was faking, she was bloody good at it.

Nicky shook her head. 'I don't understand.'

Martin snorted. 'When you were interviewed by DI Broadbent only a few days ago you went to great lengths to change your statement, wasting hours of police time. Juries don't like women who change their minds. What's the real story here?'

'I don't know this woman!'

Martin got angry. 'I don't think you realize how serious a situation you're in. This is being treated as double murder! Struan's death could be taken as the result of an intruder break-in, but Louise? She was gunned down in her living room holding *your* necklace!'

Nicky felt fear then: a great immovable alarm. She was completely out of her depth, a piece of flotsam that events tossed from one disaster to the next before she could draw breath.

'Your husband is Greg Peterson?'

'Yes.'

'Whose former wife was Grace Peterson. Murdered.'

'Yes.'

Martin paused. 'How long after her death did you and Greg get together?'

Nicky leaned back in her chair, sensing something particularly unpleasant was coming. 'I don't understand.' But she did, completely. Now she was on the receiving end of the insinuations, the puffed cheeks of scepticism, the glances and pauses.

'Oh, it's quite simple. How long was it before you got together?'

'Six months.'

She saw Jenny making a note. 'Grace's brother says it was four and a half.'

'That's not true.'

'How soon after she died did you get married?'

'Two years.'

'What's it feel like to spend your dead friend's money?' Nicky gasped but Martin didn't let up. 'Greg got the lot, didn't he? And it was quite a lot.'

'What's your point?'

'Patterns of behaviour are my point. Transgressions from what most people think of as decent. For example, your best friend is barely cold in the ground, but you go off with her husband. Did you always want him? Were you always jealous of her?'

'No—'

'Now you're carrying on with Adam Thornton – husband knows, doesn't know, who cares? You obviously don't. Most people would think that a transgression from the norm. See the picture I'm painting for a jury? A woman not to be trusted. A cheat and a liar, doing things others find offensive.'

'I am not and never have had a relationship with Adam Thornton. I went to his house to look at photos for a newspaper obituary. Not a bit of what you say is true.'

Jenny watched Nicky carefully. It wasn't her investigation now, but she was sitting in anyway, because she was intrigued and part of her wanted to know how the supposed big shots at the Met handled a murder investigation. So far she wasn't too impressed. She didn't believe you got the best results by throwing your weight around, something Martin seemed keen to do.

'As a member of the public do I have a right to see police notes on an investigation?'

And here she was, thought Jenny, straight back atcha.
'Get real!'

'Does my husband, Greg Peterson, have a criminal record?'

Martin slammed his hand down on his files. 'I'm the one asking the questions here!'

'Where's my motive? I've got no reason to kill her! I've got no reason to kill him! I don't understand how my necklace ended up at the scene!'

'It doesn't look good, Nicky, it sure doesn't look good.'

'We've been going a long time,' the lawyer said. 'Let's have a dinner break.'

Jenny rose sharply and exited the room. She found Sondra waiting for water to drip into a small plastic cup from the gurgling water cooler in the corridor. 'What's happening?' Sondra asked.

'She's giving as good as she gets. She's a toughie, this one,' Jenny said.

'I just phoned the station. Adam was taken in for questioning from the house. He was still digging up that damned lawn. He's got no alibi for the time of Louise's murder. He's being questioned now.'

'Did he go willingly?'

'Apparently so. Stunned, was the word I heard.'

Jenny leaned in closer to Sondra. 'Why are you whispering?'

Sondra looked around guiltily. 'I didn't realize I was.'

Jenny smiled. 'Don't be intimidated by this lot.'

Sondra nodded and finished her water. 'Do you think she did it?' She was still whispering.

'I think she's capable, but there's still no reason as to why. Struan could have been lured to the house, but Louise?' She shook her head and pointed at the water cooler. 'Can I have some of that?' Sondra extracted a half beaker of water from the partially blocked machine and gave it to Jenny. She drank it as she watched Martin walk down the corridor humming an R&B tune. He handed Jenny several bits of paper and began rocking from side to side and circling his arms slightly as if dancing to a tune only he could hear.

'I've got the details from Louise's flat.'

'OK, what have we got?' Jenny asked.

'Nothing, so far. We know the necklace was wiped clean, and we found no fingerprints we could identify apart from Struan's, Louise's and the mother's. The bullet hasn't given us anything either. We'll have to wait for fibre samples. Either they've been watching a lot of *CSI*—'

'Or they weren't there.' Jenny scanned the papers and handed them back to Martin.

'Two steps forward, one step back.' Martin smiled as he moved his feet forward and back. 'We've got a warrant to search her house so we'll see if we find anything interesting there.'

'Let us know what turns up,' Jenny replied. 'It's been a long day.' She turned to Sondra. 'I think we need to be getting back.'

'The later you leave it the better,' Martin added kindly. 'The bank holiday traffic will be murder.'

They watched him dance up the corridor, his papers flapping as he went.

41

It was six a.m. when Greg woke up, his heart beating double quick with a sickening anxiety. Jet lag and a vicious hangover had pulled him from oblivion. The room wouldn't straighten. He was so thirsty his tongue seemed cemented to the top of his mouth. The worst thing was that he had nothing to do. No work to keep him occupied, no audience to keep him in line. The abyss beckoned again.

An hour and a half later, when he pulled up in a taxi outside his house, he saw so many people he thought Nicky had already called the removal men and was on her way to a new life without him.

He was halfway through the front door before anyone thought to confront him.

'Can I help you?' a man on a mobile asked him.

'This was my house, last time I looked,' Greg snapped. He knew instantly it was the police. The manner, the practised ease with which they moved through the rooms – he'd seen it all before.

The policeman ended his call. 'Husband's here!' he shouted down to the kitchen, then he turned back to Greg. 'Step in here, please, sir,' the man said, inviting him into his own living room.

Greg's headache was pounding but no amount of ibuprofen and aspirin and something else the pharmacist had given him would make it go away. He was quick to anger today. 'This is my bloody house!'

'Just a minute, sir, if you would.'

'Where's Nicky? Where's my wife?'

'We're undertaking a search of your house. We have a warrant.'

'For fuck's sake don't you let ever let it go? What have I done now?'

The policeman looked surprised. 'Nothing, as far as I know.' He handed him a piece of paper on which floated words he couldn't read, as another man came into the room.

'Mind if I ask you a few questions?' Greg waved his hand as it was easier than talking and watched a notebook being produced and flipped to a blank page. 'Recognize this necklace?'

'That's Nicky's. I gave it to her as a present.'

'Where was your wife on Thursday, twenty-fifth of August?'

Greg shrugged. 'At work, I'd guess. I was in LA.' He heard the sound of footsteps in his bedroom above him. 'What are you looking for?'

'Do you own a shotgun, Mr Peterson?'

'No.'

'Does your wife?'

'Of course not. Where is she?'

'She's been taken in for questioning over the murder of Louise Bell.'

'Who's that?' The policeman didn't answer. 'What the fuck is going on? I have to see her right away.'

'I'm afraid that won't be possible. She's still being questioned.'

Greg reeled through into the kitchen to see a policewoman pointing a long needle into the earth round the pot plants. 'Who's representing my wife? Why wasn't I called?'

'Sir, it would be best to go down to the station to get an answer to those questions. Do you know Struan Clarke?'

'Who?'

Greg had had his personal possessions searched before. They'd crawled all over his flat the last time, insinuating, pulling apart his relationship with Grace, hunting for the murder weapon, asking their friends if their love was real. And like everything else in Greg's life, the bad bits just got repeated, over and over again, like some terrible loop film on the aeroplanes he travelled on.

He felt nausea rising in his gut and raced for the downstairs toilet, barging past a man hunting through the medicine cabinet.

'Don't mind me,' the man snapped as Greg retched and heaved. He'd kept so much from Nicky, but maybe his fear at revealing things meant he hadn't noticed how much she was keeping from him. Jet lag pulled at him from every side. Maybe he'd met his match; maybe this was a great cosmic joke at his expense. He staggered back into the front room. When the police team left three hours later Greg was still fast asleep on the living-room sofa.

Nicky held out her hand for a taxi in a daze. The police had finally let her go as there was no evidence with which to keep her in any longer. She'd walked straight out of the front of the police station. She saw a taxi pull over and begin to coast to a stop, but she waved it away. She leaned back against a shop front and almost laughed. Where did she have to go? She realized she didn't know whether to walk left or right, to home or away; she didn't know whether home was a hazard or a haven. She put her head in her hands to stifle a scream. She hadn't slept all night, she felt stiff and grubby and scared, and the rock in her throat wouldn't be dislodged. She gulped down some fresh air and tried to control herself. She got into the next taxi.

42

Troy pulled up in his car and stared at the house. Sunlight bounced off the white stucco. The houses opposite and either side had drawn curtains. Bank holiday weekend and just as he had hoped, no one was home. He locked the car and walked up the front steps.

Troy liked the harsh sound the doorbell made. It was a sound that was difficult to ignore. A bit like himself, he liked to imagine. He was about to ring again when the door opened a few inches and strained against the chain. He glimpsed a man with bleary eyes and a five o'clock shadow. Someone who was afraid of who came calling, Troy decided. His heart beat quicker. He held up his fake police ID.

'What do you want now?' the man asked.

'Are you Mr Peterson?'

'You know I am.'

Troy smiled. 'I'm sorry, have some of my colleagues been here recently?'

'For Chrissake,' the man said and closed the door to open it. He leaned on the door frame rubbing his cheeks as if trying to warm himself up.

'I'm sorry, Mr Peterson, can I come in? What I'm going to explain might take a while.'

Greg put his hands in his pockets and stood defiantly in his doorway. 'No. Let's do it here.'

Troy glanced up and down the street. There was no one anywhere. Hell, if he wanted to do it here, Troy didn't mind. He had a gun with a silencer on it in the back of his trousers, if things got out of hand. He watched Greg cross his arms and take up a wide stance on his doorstep, his chin jutting defensively. He looked suspicious and awkward and Troy took this as a good sign. 'I'm not a policeman as such,' he began, watching Greg for a reaction. 'I'm more a technical analyst working on behalf of the Met. You may have heard in recent years that the police can solve old crimes by finding new DNA traces on evidence that can be up to twenty years old, in some cases even older than that.' Troy could see that Greg wasn't really paying attention, that nothing he was saying was having an impact yet. 'My job is to look at old technical data around major crimes, data such as telephone or fax numbers, and see if they can throw up emerging patterns.' Troy's heart began beating more quickly. The guy's eyes! They were like saucers.

'Old crimes?' asked Greg.

Troy saw Greg's right eyelid begin to twitch. His eyes slid to the ID badge on Troy's chest.

Nicky swayed forward in the taxi as it slowed for the road hump. The air coming in the window she'd pulled down felt almost solid. A storm was coming, the pressure was falling, her headache increasing. She was two streets away from home and felt a panic attack building. She had to get out, get out and try to breathe in the sticky city air. She paid the cabbie and stood on the pavement, shaking. She started walking, trying to clear her head and think. Maria sometimes said that journalists and policemen were the same kind of people. It was about making connections, seeing people for what they were. It was about asking the right questions. The problem was that Nicky had too many

questions; they floated round her head and refused to lie in
any order. And at the base of it all was Grace, an image of
her. What happened to her? Was Maria right, and there
was no connection between this and Grace's death? Were
there no dots to join?

Nicky weaved down the street, her head a swirl of
unpleasant thoughts. DI Webster's words rang over and over
in her head as she mentally called out to Grace: *It wasn't like
that; we hadn't seen it coming. Greg and I fell in love only after
you'd gone.*

Nicky was ten houses from home at a point where the
road curved slightly, a broad sweep down a hill. Something
she saw made her instinctively duck behind one of the thick
trees on the pavement. A hot wind gusted up the street and
deposited dust in her eyes, making the edges of her vision
blur. Greg was talking to a man on the doorstep. Nicky was
still some way away, but it was the shape of his shoulders,
the height of him and the colour of his hair that made her
sure. It was unmistakably the same man she had crashed into
outside Hayersleigh. So what was he doing talking to Greg
so amiably in front of her house?

'It might be easier if I come in to explain, sir,' Troy said.

Greg said nothing. He stood his ground, but Troy could
feel the tension in him. He seemed ready to pounce. Troy
could feel the gun pressing into the small of his back. 'One
of the cases that we're looking into might have a connection
to a Francesca Connor. Does that name mean anything to
you, sir?'

Troy could have sworn Greg Peterson went white. The
colour drained right out of him. 'Computers now allow us
to create patterns that it would be impossible to see when
police officers are only looking through paperwork. In 1999 a
drug dealer called Gary Obett was murdered in the West End.

He was part of a large drugs ring and his murderer has never been caught. The police at the time made a log of all mobile phone numbers and calls made in the area around where he was killed, hoping that the killer might have actually made a call shortly after committing the crime or had a mobile with him. They came up with nothing, but we've now cross-referenced every number used in the vicinity of Obett's murder with other crimes to see what gets thrown up.' Troy paused. 'And we've found that one of the numbers in the vicinity of Obett's death was once called from the landline registered to this house, sir, where Francesca Connor stayed.'

Nicky watched as the man talked to Greg. Greg was rapt. And then the most extraordinary thing happened: Greg seemed to pitch forward and give the man a hug. They were hugging on the doorstep, two giants leaning against one another, their bums stuck backwards in the awkward lean-and-emote stance.

Her mind took her back to the dreadful moments in the road outside Hayersleigh, to the moment when she escaped her captor, and ended up crashing into that man now standing on her doorstep, then how she had finally got a mobile into her hands, her connection to—

Nicky had a sensation of falling forward, as if the world and herself were suddenly moving at different speeds. She remembered grabbing the phone from the dashboard, dialling the police, feeling an unstoppable surge of elation that for the first time things were going her way, that there was an end in sight. She remembered that man unlocking the phone and handing it back to her; he was asking her questions and she couldn't hear what they were; there was the sound of another car approaching as she dialled Greg's number. She swallowed as she recalled that she was shaking so much from the adrenalin in her body she could hardly touch the right digits on his phone . . .

Nicky thought very hard about that exact moment. It came to her clearly now. She had not been mistaken.

Greg's number was already in his phone.

Their home phone number diverted automatically through to Greg's mobile so he never missed any calls that came through while he was away filming. To call Greg she simply typed in their home phone number. That day outside Hayersleigh, and a second before she put the phone to her ear, a name had appeared on the screen, not simply the numbers she had just dialled. What was the name? She couldn't recall it. She took a step out from behind the tree. She couldn't conjure the name, but she knew it hadn't been 'Greg', because she was sure she'd have noticed that. She started walking.

Why was their number in the man's phone? Why was he here in Maida Vale? She'd made the call to Greg, he hadn't been there and that man had gently, really quite gently, taken the phone from her and gathered her to him in the kindly gesture of passers-by called upon to help a woman in distress.

The warm wind whipped along the street, tumbling crisp leaves with it. What had the man said? Platitudes, he'd murmured consoling platitudes at her, held her as she cried. She thought of what the policewoman had said: 'You're lucky he was driving so slowly, otherwise you could have been seriously hurt.' She stopped in the street, staring at her door-step. Why was he driving slowly? Because he had been waiting. Waiting to turn? Driving past?

Greg knew where she had been. Greg knew what she had been through. And then for the first time a really horrible thought hit her. He didn't come back because of what Liz had told him; he came back because he was told what had happened at Hayersleigh. There was a connection between Greg and Adam – she just didn't know what it was yet.

Nicky began to run.

'Are you OK, sir?' For a split second Troy believed Greg might faint. This mark was so soft he had reached out for a cuddle. Making up a bullshit story about a drug dealer and bringing up Francesca's name had pitched this grown man right into his arms like a baby.

'I'm sorry, I'm sorry. It's a shock . . .' He was casting around wildly, unable to settle his eyes on anything. 'It's been such a long time since I heard that name, and now in the last two days I've had to relive . . .' He tailed off, running his hands through his hair. The man looked stricken, physically ill. 'My God, Francesca . . .'

'Indeed. Francesca.' Troy bared his new teeth. He was closing in.

Troy saw Greg stare at him. Now he seemed to be trying to recover what little was left of his manhood. 'A phone call from this house?' There was a pause. 'But I moved in here three years ago. Francesca died just over twelve years ago.'

'Well, to be exact, it was a phone call from this number. Did you transfer your number when you moved here?' Greg looked blank. Troy tried again. 'Did you live near here and transfer the number from your old home?'

Greg seemed to be able to answer only the obvious questions. 'I lived in Maida Vale. So, yes, I took the number.'

Troy nodded. 'What was your relationship to Francesca?' He got out a notebook and started making notes. When he looked up Greg was staring at him with a look that made Troy take a step back.

Greg spoke slowly, as if his mind was only now waking

up to what had been said. 'But Francesca's death was an accident. She died in Morocco.'

Troy remembered the evening well. She had been pregnant too. Troy shook his head slowly. They were getting to the bit he enjoyed: the confrontation, the action. He took a step towards the door and then saw that Greg's pupils had dilated with shock at something over Troy's right shoulder.

Nicky's rage increased with every stride. The terror she'd felt at Hayersleigh, her fear at the unfolding events that she had no control over – all these thoughts collided as she raced for her own front door. She'd show them. She bounded, three at a time on her long legs, up the steps of her house and shouted something incoherent as she shoved the man in the back.

Troy felt himself pitch sharply onto Greg, who fell backwards into the corridor.

'You little shit, you've been following me!' she shouted. 'And you –' she pointed at Greg, who was trying to get up off the floor – 'I know what you're doing. How could you?'

Nicky saw the look of complete surprise in Troy's face but she didn't stop her tirade against both of them.

Troy tried to stand but Greg was clambering over him in a desperate bid to get to his wife. Sometimes clichés said it all. He literally couldn't believe what he was seeing. The woman he had been hired to kill, here! With the bloke he was trying to extort money from for a previous kill! He wanted to lie back on the warm doorstep and laugh and laugh.

Greg was shouting at Nicky, trying to grab her. 'What's going on? Who's Louise Bell?'

'Your number's in his phone, Greg! You two don't even bother to go in the house to talk about me. See how you like it!' Nicky pulled out her phone and that's when Troy really did try to get to his feet, fast.

She was taking a photo of him – and that was something that he couldn't stand. God, how he wanted to do her, right now! He could have shot her right here and made it look like the chump husband, Greg, did it. But today was his birthday, Christmas and pay day all rolled into one. Because now that Troy realized Greg was married to Nicky he did believe he had discovered a man who more than once had hired killers for his wives or girlfriends, and that meant that Greg was going to have to pay very handsomely for that information to stay secret. Greg was Troy's retirement fund.

Greg turned to Troy, confusion still dulling his reactions. 'Why is my number in your phone?' He turned to Nicky. 'How do you know my number's in there?'

Nicky retaliated. 'What's your name?' she asked Troy. 'What's his name, Greg?' A name meant someone was traceable.

'I don't know him!'

'More lies! I can't stand any more lies!' And with that she turned and ran down the steps and into the street.

Greg took a couple of steps after Nicky and then seemed to change his mind. He turned back to Troy, his face hard. 'Who are you?'

Troy leaned back on the railing, nodding. 'Oh you know who the fuck I am.'

'I don't understand.'

'That's what they all say.'

'Who's *they*? Where did you meet my wife? What's this *phone call* anyway?'

'She crashed into me on Wednesday outside Hayersleigh House, down in Dorset. She was in a great hurry to—'

Greg took a step towards Troy, layers of misunderstanding beginning to peel away, like old paint on a door bleached by the sun. '*Where* did—'

Troy had seen that look in a face before: confusion giving way to understanding and then passing through anger or indignation and on to fear. But he'd had enough already and he didn't want Nicky to get away. Troy gave Greg a quick and decisive punch in the face that sent him straight to the floor and bundled him into the corridor. He calmly shut the door and walked away.

43

Nicky's call was blunt and to the point. 'Liz, I need to see you now.'

'I'm sorry, Nicky, I'm busy today. I'm on call.'

'Cut the bullshit, Liz. Saving the babies can wait.' She heard Liz's sharp intake of breath. 'We need to talk about your brother. Meet me in Hyde Park by the pirate ship.'

'Typical that you'd want to meet way out of my way, at that playground full of tourists and Eurotrash—'

'Just be there. I've got something that'll test your hero worship for your brother. And otherwise I'm going to the police.'

There was a pause. She could tell Liz was wondering whether it was worth starting a fight over the hero-worship bit, but she let it slide. 'I'll be an hour.' She hung up without saying goodbye.

Nicky chose a table away from the ice-cream queue and sat down to wait, pigeons pecking at the crumbs on the seats around her. She phoned Maria and cursed as she got the message service. In contrast to her indecision outside the police station, she felt full of conviction now. After ten minutes she saw Liz walking purposefully from the south, up the wide avenue flanked by beech trees, her face with its frown giving no hint that this was a hot, sunny bank holiday weekend and that it was almost impossible not to be enjoying yourself. They didn't hug or kiss as she sat down, mutual suspicion still swirling after their last meeting.

'Urgh, air rats.' Liz waved her hand aggressively at the pigeons and they fluttered half-heartedly just out of arm's reach. 'What's so important that I've been dragged half across London on my day off?'

'I thought you were on call.' Liz's lips thinned. 'I want to talk about Grace and Francesca.'

Liz let out a bored sigh. 'If we must.'

'Did you ever think their deaths were connected?'

'I can't be doing with these histrionics, Nicky, really.'

Nicky shook her head. 'You can't have it both ways. If you act smart all the time you can't play dumb when it suits.'

Liz frowned and slowly took off her sunglasses, folding them carefully and placing them on the table. 'Why are you asking?'

'When you stood there at Grace's graveside, did you also think about Francesca? Did it cross your mind at any point that Greg could have—'

'See sense, Nicky! Greg was thousands of miles away when Grace was murdered.'

'The police back then never found out about Francesca, did they? They never made the connection and he – and you – never told them. Why not, Liz?' Liz didn't reply. 'I believe my life is in danger, and for me that's one coincidence too many. I don't understand why Greg would be killing his wives and girlfriends, but I can find no other logical explanation.'

'You're not the first person that springs to mind when I think of "logical",' Liz muttered. She held out her hand to stop Nicky protesting at her jibe. 'It really is all a bit far-fetched, don't you think? We didn't tell the police because it would simply have brought Greg more unwanted scrutiny when he was half drowning under the grief and pressure anyway. Francesca was a depressive and it's terribly sad what happened to her. Grace . . .' She tailed off. 'Grace I can't explain. No one can.'

'Ever heard of Louise Bell or Struan Clarke?'

'No.'

'They're dead, and the police think I'm involved.'

'Who are they?'

'I have absolutely no idea. I'm this close –' Nicky held her thumb and forefinger together in front of Liz's face – 'to being charged with murder. So for the love of your brother, come clean and tell me what you know about his past.'

Liz looked like she'd tasted something bad. 'Greg's the victim, let's remember. I'd like to see other men cope so bravely and so stoically with the misfortunes he's endured. Don't become a tired cliché like others, Nicky, and start to think he's somehow responsible.'

'Has he changed over the years?'

'We've all changed. It's what we do,' Liz said sharply. Nicky looked round at some shrieking toddlers, each grasping for possession of a cheap plastic toy. They were grappling unfettered for what they desired; as they aged, as they watched and imitated, they would learn the subtleties of getting what they wanted without a bare-knuckle fight. 'Let's get back to basics here. What evidence have you got?'

'He hires people to do it for him.'

'Oh please!'

'Do you recognize this man?' Nicky opened her phone and showed Liz the photo of crash man.

'No.'

'He's been following me. This morning I found him talking to Greg on our doorstep!'

Liz put the phone carefully down on the table, her movements slow. 'What does Greg say?'

'He denies it, a flat denial. He simply claimed he had no idea who he was even talking to!'

'I'm not sure I have any idea what you're talking *about*.'

Nicky decided to try another tactic. 'If you heard tomorrow that I'd died, are you telling me that you wouldn't be just a little bit suspicious?' Nicky watched as Liz put her sunglasses back on. Liz's eyes were now covered with mirrored glass in which Nicky could see only a dishevelled version of herself, but she could sense Liz's indecision. Liz was a woman who prided herself on always having a view, who knew exactly where she stood on every moral issue. She didn't back down and she was never wrong. So Nicky understood that it took a great mental leap for Liz to pick up her phone and look again at Troy's photo. 'I think Greg's hired him to follow me and . . . well, I don't know what else.'

'What's happened to make you so convinced your life is in danger?' She homed in. 'Have you been playing away, Nicky?' Liz gave her shark's smile: cold and wide. 'Unless I know the full story how can I help you?'

Nicky hesitated. How much should she confide in Liz? Her allegiances were with her brother. 'Who's Adam Thornton?'

Had she just seen Liz stiffen? The mirrored glasses threw her own reflection back at her. 'I've no idea.' Liz shrugged and paused for what seemed to Nicky like a second too long. 'Look, I'm a fair person. What you say about this man in your phone sounds strange. Let me look into it, let me talk to Greg.' She looked around. 'Is there a toilet here? I'm desperate.'

'In there.' Nicky pointed inside the children's play area.

'Wait here, I'll be back in a sec.' Liz got up, opened the gate and walked stiffly past careening children to the toilet block.

Nicky got up as soon as she'd disappeared from view and followed her. Liz was standing with her back to the basins, phone clamped to her ear.

A second later Nicky grabbed it from her hand. 'That desperate for the toilet, are we?' She looked and saw Greg's was the last number dialled.

'Give me back my phone.'

Nicky handed it to her and marched out into the sunlight, Liz following.

'Who is he, Liz? Who is Adam Thornton?'

'I don't know.'

'Bullshit.' They were both walking fast now towards the gates of the park.

'I met him recently, Liz. He sought me out. I've been to Hayersleigh.'

Liz jerked her face towards hers.

'Who is he, Liz?'

Liz suddenly grabbed her arm. 'Stay away from him, Nicky!'

'Why? What is going on?'

'I . . . I don't know. I can't say.'

'Tell me!'

'I don't know what's going on, but I can tell you this – stay away from that man, Nicky!'

'On the contrary, I'm going back there. There's something at the house, isn't there? What is it?' Nicky ripped her arm away from Liz's grasp.

'Nicky, stop!'

Liz cursed sourly under her breath as she watched Nicky turn from the gates of the park and jog west towards Notting Hill Gate. She could see Nicky ahead of her, running through the clumps of people on the wide pavement, thunder rumbling ominously. Liz had never felt older as she tried to catch up. The crowds had started to thicken; it was Carnival Sunday. She shouted repeatedly after Nicky, trying to get her to stop, but after a few hundred metres she pulled up at the closed tube station, panting and sweating. Nicky had the advantage of fewer years and a manic, misplaced zeal about her. The contest wasn't equal. She wasn't going to get to Nicky like this.

She pulled out her phone and looked up at the building clouds, at the rain that was sure to come. So Adam Thornton had been in contact with Nicky. Pretty close contact, from what she'd observed. Loyalty to Greg flamed intensely inside her. Her brother's silly wife and her search for self-fulfilment could ruin Greg. But something deeper, a more worrying concern, was niggling her. She typed in some numbers and made a call.

44

That Liz obviously knew Adam meant Nicky had another piece of the jigsaw but the picture it was a part of was as jumbled as ever. She pulled up at the top of Portobello Road and called Greg. She swore when she got no connection. Hundreds of people crowded round her, streaming down the street to the Notting Hill Carnival. The roar of the huge street party just a few blocks away carried towards her on the sultry afternoon air. She needed more jigsaw pieces; she *had* to complete this picture and she knew where she needed to go.

She rang the bell at the entrance gate of the mews and was buzzed in. She crossed the courtyard and rang the bell on the flat. The door clicked open and she headed up the stairs to Lawrence's flat. Adam had told her his parents always had a party during the carnival and sure enough a waitress opened the door and offered up a tray of cocktails topped off with umbrellas and chunks of fruit. Nicky snatched at one before the girl had finished describing what each contained and gulped it down. 'Would you like another?' she asked with a smile, but Nicky was scanning groups of people weaving between the grey sofas and in and out of the sliding glass doors. A small steel band was playing on the patio next to a barbecue, where chicken was frying. A waiter walked past with a tray piled high with barbecued and caramelized sweetcorn. The Thorntons were getting into carnival spirit and she admired them for having a go. Most of the inhabitants of this wealthy part of west London hurried away for the bank-holiday weekend with the panic of the medieval nobility fleeing the plague pits and only returned once the noise, the crowds and the mountains of rubbish had been cleaned away. Nicky took a step further into the party. Through the patio doors towering clouds of the imminent storm could be seen building.

Being in this flat flooded her with memories of the last time she had been there, in circumstances so different – before the madness at Hayersleigh, before the revelations that had led her back here. A Nigerian woman in a yellow headdress walked towards her with a piece of jerked chicken wrapped in a napkin. 'Don't stand there being a wallflower, come in! Eat now before the rain douses the barbecue.' Nicky felt the damp slick of sweat in her armpits. 'I'm Minty.'

'Nicky. Have you seen—'

'Jonas!' Minty hugged a tall man with a big nose and Nicky found herself surrounded by a smiling group of strangers. Minty began to introduce her, waving her piece of chicken like a baton.

'No complaints about the noise yet?' Jonas asked.

Minty threw her head back and laughed. 'Ask Bridget!' She turned to Nicky, pointing the chicken drumstick at her. 'Were you here last year?' Nicky shook her head. 'An angry neighbour came round and said if they didn't turn the music down he was going to call the police and we'd end up in the papers! You can imagine what Lawrence thought of that!'

'"Judge takes the rap", didn't he say?' finished Jonas.

'Guilty of noise in the first degree?' a man with thick-rimmed glasses quipped.

'Wait . . . QC is the MC?' offered a young woman.

'Not bad! "Judge me by my bass bins"?' Minty and Jonas and the others roared. They were having fun, on holiday and at a party, but Nicky couldn't even force a smile. She hunted for Lawrence with her eyes.

'The man of the hour!' Minty shouted and she turned to see Lawrence approaching. He looked older but he was battling it, smiling at everyone and shaking hands. He gave her a puzzled, searching expression. He was surprised to see her here, that much was clear. He began to wordlessly lead Nicky away, but Minty called after them, 'Nicky, where are you taking him? Bring back our host!'

Lawrence cocked his head, gesturing for her to come with him. She excused herself and followed him down a corridor and through to a study, where he shut the door behind them. It seemed very quiet with the door closed.

'Please, sit down.' He offered her a felt-covered chair, while he stood leaning against a bookcase. 'I'm very surprised to see you here.' He was formal and strained.

'Adam told me this was an annual event. I'm sorry to barge in.' He didn't reply. 'Where is Adam?'

He looked incredulous. 'He's still in the police station. I assume you've only recently been discharged yourself.'

Nicky nodded. 'You're not representing him?'

'This is murder, Nicky! This is as serious as it gets! I've got him the best lawyer I know. Of course I have. I'm waiting for a call any moment now to say that he's been released.' He paused and looked at her, his hands in his pockets. 'You know, I can't help feeling that if my son had never met you none of this horrendous stuff would have happened.'

It was an outburst of frustration and suspicion. Nicky stood and faced Lawrence full on. 'I believe that your son is innocent and that he was trying to protect me from . . . from certain people.' Lawrence looked unconvinced. 'I came here today to ask you a favour, a massive favour really.' Lawrence raised an eyebrow and waited. 'Five years ago my best friend, Grace, was murdered. Grace Peterson. She was known as the body in the lake. Maybe you remember that?'

'Adam told me. He never stops talking about you.'

'I want to see the police files on that case. Can you get them for me?'

Lawrence frowned. 'I'm a judge, Nicky! I can't do that!'

'I think my husband might have had something to do with her death. My husband is Greg Peterson and he was Grace's husband when she died.'

Lawrence took a big intake of breath. 'If you have concerns about your husband you should go to the police. Right now, in fact.'

'The problem is that I don't have enough evidence – yet.'

Lawrence threw his hands up in a gesture of despair. 'The police, Nicky—'

He was interrupted by the door opening. 'Lawrence, there you are. I was—' Bridget came up short when she saw Nicky. 'My God, what on earth are you doing here?' She closed the door behind her and stood side by side with her husband. Her expression was cold.

Nicky ploughed on. 'I changed my statement after what happened at the house because I believe your son is innocent. I don't understand what's happening, or what the connection is between the man Adam killed at your house, Louise Bell, your son and me. But what's in that file might help.'

'You've given me no reason to see a connection. And at this moment my only concern is my own son and helping him clear his name—'

'He's coming back here,' Bridget interrupted. 'He just phoned. They've released him.'

Nicky stood up. It was time to go. 'What was Adam looking for under the lawns at Hayersleigh?'

'You're going to go back there to look, aren't you?' Bridget crossed her arms as if she was trying to protect her new family from this danger in the room. 'Do I really have to remind you that it's private property—'

'Adam is looking for something that isn't there.' Lawrence sighed. 'He's young and fanciful, prone to romantic, grand gestures that mean little. It's what being young is. When you have your own children, Nicky, you'll understand.'

'Your late wife's diaries. What's in them?'

'I have no idea! They're twenty years old! Really—'

'Adam read something in them that made him start digging up the lawn – that made him try to keep me there at the house.'

Lawrence drew himself up. 'What happened between you two at the house I don't wish to know about.'

'I do,' said Bridget, unsmiling. 'I want to know exactly what went on there. When it causes this family such distress it's my business to know.'

Something occurred to Nicky. 'Where's Connie?'

Lawrence looked away. 'She became very distressed when I told her Adam had been questioned by the police about murder. We thought it would be better if she was moved to a private clinic.'

'Is there any way that Adam could know my husband, Greg?'

Bridget made a sound that was irritation mixed with impatience. 'I have to get back. Goodbye, Nicky.' She opened the door and the music boomed in before returning to a low thump, thump through the walls.

'He keeps asking about you.' Nicky opened her mouth to say something and then closed it again. Lawrence exuded quiet authority: the older, wiser judge. 'A married woman years older than him, from a different background, much more savvy and experienced than him. A better father than me would counsel him to stay away.'

'Lawrence, please! Your son saved my life when I fell in the Thames. I want to pay him back. Is there any way you can help me?'

He stared at her for a long moment, weighing up whether she was a friend or foe. 'I'm not promising anything.' But he asked for all the details of Grace's murder and he took her number.

'I hope you enjoy your party,' she said as he opened the door to the study.

'A friend of mine says that a father can only be as happy as his unhappiest child. This is Bridget's day today. Quite frankly, I'd rather be alone.'

They parted once they were back in the living room and Nicky pushed her way through a crowd to the front door. She turned to look back at the throng around her and then, between the backs of two people by the kitchen, she saw Bea staring at her. She watched, horrified, as Bea traced a finger slowly across her throat.

Nicky stuck two fingers up at her in return and slammed the door behind her as she left.

45

Liz had grown up with Greg. She'd seen him soil his pants as a toddler, lie on the floor screaming in a tantrum, pout through the awkward teen phase. She knew him very well, but she had never seen him panic like he was panicking now. 'Calm down for Chrissake, Greg!' She was in the street with him as he paced up and down the pavement, unable to coax him inside. Liz liked to think she was unfettered by convention; she was someone who had on occasion revelled in making a scene, making sure she was noticed. The biggest sin for Liz was to be a shrinking violet, something she had made sure she was never called. It was a badge of pride to be called a mad cow, an angry woman, but she glanced up at the neighbours' windows, wondering if they were being watched. She was not used to her brother making a scene. And Greg had really lost it.

'Nicky was at Hayersleigh! She's been there! Why would she have gone there?'

'She was taken there by Adam Thornton, I'm sure of it. I think that guy she drove off with was him. He's the right age.'

'For fuck's sake!'

'Calm down!'

'I've got to find her right now—'

'There are a million people in Notting Hill now. No phones will be working. The mood she's in, she won't answer you anyway. Don't go on a wild chase round the carnival. It's pointless.'

'Liz, I don't understand!' He was rubbing his sore chin back and forth as he paced. 'Some weirdo pretending to be a policeman came to the door and started asking questions about Francesca. Nicky arrived and claimed this bloke had been following her and then he decked me! He was claiming somebody phoned a *hit man* from my flat years ago . . .'

'From your old flat?' Liz narrowed her eyes, assessing her brother. 'A hit man?'

Liz saw Greg glance up and down the street before he came close and whispered in her ear. 'Most people never knew I was even with Francesca! Most of our time was spent abroad, what with my work and Francesca living in California. How could he know about her?' He started pacing again, dragging at his hair.

'Phone the police.' Liz crossed her arms and waited. 'Phone them and explain.'

Greg hissed in her ear. 'You know I can't! They'll drag Grace's death up again, try to link the two things – and then Hayersleigh! My marriage to Nicky won't survive that.' Liz stared at her brother. 'Stop looking at me like that! Nicky took a photo of this bloke with her phone. He didn't like that at all. We've got to find Nicky and get that photo.'

'OK. I will go and look for Nicky; you stay here and keep phoning. She'll come back soon, probably. Lock the door and wait. Take a Valium or something.'

She turned to head off. 'Liz,' he called out to her. 'I don't know what I'd do without you.'

She scowled. 'I've got a pretty good idea.'

Troy was getting edgy. He'd lost her, and every hour Nicky was alive with his picture in her phone meant danger to him. He would wait for dark and take her at the house. He was wondering which end of the street to cover when the phone rang. A minute later he was turning the car round and heading for Notting Hill. He'd just been told where she was. His client was keen. He thought about the photo she'd taken of him and the intensity of his thoughts and feelings cranked up. There would be no more mistakes. Nicky Ayers-cum-Peterson was out of time.

46

As Nicky pressed the buzzer to open the gates and come out of the mews into the swaying crowd streaming down the road to the carnival, she saw crash man coming towards her. In that split second Nicky wondered about the marvel that is the human brain, its capacity to scan thousands of faces and find each one uniquely individual. To be able to instantly recognize a face you've seen before. At that moment, as Troy bore down on her and his eyes locked on hers there was no mistaking their intent. He was coming to kill her.

This time Nicky didn't hesitate. She raced for the junction, realizing that after the next road down the crowd would be too big for her to really be able to run any more. At the first crossroads she risked a glimpse behind her. He was fifty metres away, but she could tell by the way he moved his arms that he was fit, with a long stride. He was a match for her and outrunning him in empty streets would be hard to do. The side streets were quieter but he was too close to risk going that way. One option was crossed off. She ploughed into the thickening crowd.

A great thunderclap erupted above them and people shrieked. The weather wouldn't hold; an English summer was finally upon them. Fat raindrops started bouncing off the awnings over the shops. Nicky started pushing aggressively against shoulders and backs, the pulsing sounds of samba wafting over the air.

She was slim and agile and made good progress but she

left a trail of complaints and tuts behind her. Her pursuer was tall and easy to see from twenty heads behind her. His eyes were always on her. People were beginning to put up umbrellas and hold them high above their heads as they swayed in time to the music. Far from running for cover, it was as if the long hot summer made people desperate for a change to the familiar, for the ability to groan and complain.

Nicky glanced over her shoulder but he was still there, elbowing his way through. She pushed on, panic taking hold. She had no plan, no way of ending this absurd situation. She saw a grey, sweaty man with a whistle in his mouth and a look of a three-day party hanging on him. She shoved past and flicked his fedora off the back of his head into her hands, then ducked low behind a large striped umbrella.

Troy didn't take his eyes off the target ahead. He was calm, almost enjoying himself. He wished it wasn't raining, but rain probably gave him an advantage. People would look around less as they tried to keep themselves dry. He could see the panic in her movements as she flailed through the crush ahead. He just needed to take his time; there was no hurry. He felt the knife in his jacket pocket. In a seething mass like this it would be easy. That hat she'd just picked up wasn't fooling anyone.

Nicky emptied her mind of everything bar getting away from crash man. Crowds of people were not her friend today. In a mass of thousands, no one can hear you scream. There were police on every corner and lining the parade route – there were probably thousands of police here today – but they were fixed on public order and keeping the peace, not trying to half listen as she stuttered out her convoluted story. She pushed on.

The crowd was crushing tighter and tighter, as they were

funnelled by crash barriers through a narrow section to allow space for a local radio station's sound system. She was thirty metres from a junction. Two large black umbrellas were being waved in front of her. She saw a tall woman with blonde hair under one of them and she shoved towards her. A rasta wrapped in a Jamaican flag was on the other side of her. She got under his umbrella and grabbed the flag. The Rasta whipped round, surprised. 'Sista, what you—'

She shoved a ten-pound note from her pocket into his hand. He glanced at the money and shrugged, turning away. She popped the fedora on the blonde's head and then held the flag up behind her and took two long strides for the corner.

Troy saw two umbrellas tilt towards each other in time to the music and saw a flash of blonde hair beneath a black hat. The umbrellas parted and he stared at the black hat through the rain. It took him a few seconds to register that the woman wearing it wasn't Nicky. He started tracking the crowd, fast. He reached the corner, where the swarm of people was wider and looser. He let out a low curse under his breath. He'd lost her.

Nicky kept the flag extended above her and walked quickly away from the corner as the crowd began to thin. She risked a glance behind her as she walked. She couldn't see him. She broke into a run.

Troy stood on the corner and scanned the masses. Crowds have their own rhythm, he decided. Here the flow was relaxed even in the rain; there was a slowing down, a discarding of the determined pace of the city. She was scared so her rhythm wouldn't fit. He would see her. He glanced down Blenheim

Crescent and saw a black and green flag pulling away at speed. He'd got her.

Nicky reached the corner of Blenheim Crescent and Kensington Park Road to find a group of teenagers arguing in a doorway with a huge bouncer wearing sunglasses. From the upper floors of the four-storey building party goers hung out of windows, a thumping bass clashing with the sound system set up in the street. A crowd on the roof terrace was dancing and shouting at a party on the roof of the building opposite. She elbowed through the people surrounding the bouncer and tried to get inside.

A massive hand landed on her shoulder. 'Tickets only.' She looked back down the street and swore. Crash man was bearing down on her again. He can't get in, she thought. He's too old, the wrong sex and the wrong colour. He was thirty metres away and gaining.

She threw the flag over the bouncer's face and ducked under his raised arm. She heard a shout as she dived for the gloom within. She hit the stairs and headed for the roof.

Troy saw her go in and pulled up at the door. The bouncer was acting like Mike Tyson, growling as the crowd around him surged forwards and back in an unruly wave. Troy stepped up to him and held out his fake police ID badge. 'What the fuck you trying to do to me, man . . .'

'I'm only interested in that woman. There'll be no trouble for anyone else – if you let me in.'

Nicky reached the roof, stepping over metres of cable gaffer-taped to the floor. She ran to the end of the roof terrace where a wall of sea-grass matting acted as a fence between this building and the next one along. She hoiked herself over by pulling at an aerial fixed to the chimney. She ran across the roof to the next door along but it didn't open. She vaulted a small fence and crossed a roof garden where tomatoes grew in a row of pots and a small shed had been erected to store this urban gardener's tools. Could she hide here? No. She yanked at the door to the stairs: locked.

Panic began to build again. She was practically at the end of the terrace – there was only one more doorway left to try. She threw aside a kid's tricycle and pulled at the door, which thankfully opened, and she barrelled down the steps.

Nicky only just had time to register that she was actually running through someone's house when she hit the first floor and saw through an open door into a room where ten people were sitting eating lunch at a long table. They sat staring at her, some with forks to their mouths, while she stood frozen on their landing.

Then she heard the bang of the door upstairs and the temporary spell was broken.

'Emile!' a woman shouted as Nicky flew down to the ground floor. Her hands reached the heavy brass lock and yanked it back. She heard shouts and swearing in French and felt bad at leading crash man into this house, but she was a desperate woman. She slammed the door behind her and ploughed on into the mass on the street.

Her desperation increased. He wasn't easy to shake off, and the thought tearing away at her was that she would never be rid of him. She would be for ever on the back foot, for ever living in fear of what was coming around that corner.

She barged east again, back to Portobello Road. It had stopped raining now and a weak sun pierced the clouds for a moment before fading away. She moved north for a couple of blocks and passed under the raised Westway motorway that snaked away to Oxford, its giant concrete girders blocking the sun.

★   ★   ★

Troy headed under the Westway flyover, the sound of music bouncing off the concrete undercarriage with renewed force. He was sick of running and he was getting tired of the crowds and the noise and the mayhem. He threw a twenty-pound note at a stall holder and grabbed a tasselled scarf that would have looked at home on a youth throwing rocks in Gaza. He tied it round his head. It was time to end this.

Nicky followed the curve of the overhead motorway. The crowds were so thick here she could hardly move through them. She could see the tops of the carnival floats as they moved in procession down Ladbroke Grove, the brightly coloured tips of the dancers' costumes bobbing like buoys at sea. She drew up next to a building covered in scaffolding and looked around, but couldn't see crash man. She glanced up and saw the legs of a reveller hanging over the planking of the scaffolding. She jabbed at his dusty Doc Marten boots and he looked down at her. She held out her hands, pleading for him to lift her up, and he leaned down and grabbed her hands. She reached out with her leg for a foothold on the hectoring sign warning of a security firm's instant response if the scaffolding was climbed and as she swung round to put her other knee on the boards to get up, she felt her phone slide from her pocket into the crowd below.

Troy saw Nicky being pulled up on the scaffolding and – it couldn't be – her phone actually fell out of her pocket to the ground. He barged through the crowd and grabbed it.

Nicky lay flat on the planking one storey up and couldn't move or cry out for someone below to hand her phone back, because at that moment she saw crash man right below her, looking around. Had he seen her? She cursed, long, hard and silently, for her lost phone. She saw crash man walk away from the scaffolding towards the motorway as she climbed an orange steel ladder to the second floor. The sheeting covering the scaffolding was wet and sprayed water on her as it flapped in the gusty wind. Could it be that he hadn't seen her? She tried to force open the windows on the second floor. Nothing budged. She couldn't throw anything through them, either; they were double-glazed against the roar of traffic from the Westway.

Troy stood by the girders holding up the motorway and studied the scaffolding. He could see a dark shape on the second storey. Game over. He'd shoot her. A crowd and noise like this was perfect – if unconventional – cover. Troy began a thorough and methodical check of the buildings around him for CCTV cameras and faces at windows. The thousands of people were focused on the parade, not on what the bloke in the scarf was doing. The angle was perfect. He put his gun with its silencer inside a discarded plastic bag. He was free to take the shot.

Nicky jumped as someone banged on the window behind her. An old lady in a dressing gown was making shooing gestures to her from the other side of the glass. Nicky knocked on the window, pleading with her to open the window, her arms in a praying position. The woman came to within two inches of Nicky's face and banged on the glass. 'Help me!' Nicky sobbed. The bullet smacked through the window three inches above Nicky's head and ricocheted off the ceiling of the woman's bedroom. They both stared mutely at the hole, at the cracks in the glazing running crazily across the pane. It was the woman's screams that shocked Nicky into action. She crouched low and tried to scurry to the other end of the scaffolding as another bullet pinged noisily off metal. Nicky raced up the ladder to the third storey and lay flat on the planking. She was out of room. There was nowhere to go and crash man was below, trying to pick her off.

She watched the cars speed past on the Westway: normal people cocooned in the bubble of normal lives. How far removed she felt from them, how insuperable the chasm. She wanted to scream with the frustration of her predicament. How badly she wanted to cling onto life. She couldn't see him below now; she didn't know where he was. She crouched and began to pull at the planking. Now that there was a hole in the old lady's window maybe she could smash her way through it. She hoped the woman's heart was strong enough to take the shock. She pulled up a board. It was longer than she was expecting and more unwieldy to move. It was too long to swing and she dropped it, its end sticking out at right angles to the scaffolding. Then, worried in case it fell on people below her, she jammed the end of the board under the fixed piece of planking that she stood on. She looked up. Suddenly the concrete wall of the Westway didn't look so far away from the end of the board.

Grace came to her then. What she had suffered; the questions that were never answered; the fact that the architect of all this would get away with it. Justice would not be served. She backed up against the wall. And in that split second Nicky ran. She sprinted away from the building with all the explosive speed her muscles were capable of, out along the plank into nothingness.

Troy was taken aback. He jerked his head a fraction too much and shot too high, firing over Nicky's left shoulder into air.

Nicky long-jumped off the end of the board and cartwheeled her arms to gain the maximum distance towards the grey cement of the motorway wall. She was so scared of not reaching it at all that she misjudged and her speed took her clean over the top of the motorway barrier onto the hard shoulder, where she landed with a sickening thud and rolled into the slow lane.

Gemma Woodhead had one hand on the steering wheel and was picking at her nose ring with the other as she drove along the Westway. It was sore and she wondered if it was becoming infected. She should have made sure that Jezza had disinfected the needle properly. But then that was quite like Jezza, a bit slapdash, a touch too casual. It's what she'd liked about him at the beginning. That seemed like a long time ago now. She was meeting him at Camden Market, T-shirts for sale in their plastic wrappers in the back of the car as requested. Make that demanded. The turquoise ones were better than the multicoloured ones. She'd tell him that when they went for ale later, not that he'd listen; he never listened to her, or took her advice, for that matter. She'd tell him a lot of things over the eight pints they'd sink. She was still mad about the timing, that their T-shirts were finally printed and packaged at the end of August. The hottest summer for years and they hadn't been ready to capitalize on it.

Gemma felt her nostril throb as a weak sun was cut off by a cloud. She needed to be more forthright, say what she really believed and not be steamrollered by Jezza. She would start today. She was going to put her own needs first for a change; it was her money that had printed the T-shirts, after all. Gemma was thinking that Jezza sitting up and taking notice was as likely as seeing pigs fly, when over the wall of the motorway came a bright awkward shape that tumbled across the hard shoulder and into the slow lane. Gemma's first thought was that it must be a piece of costume that had caught on the wind and separated itself from the carnival somewhere on the streets below her. She didn't brake because she thought it might float away again, like a plastic bag in wind, but then she realized the shape was very, very solid and – oh my God, it was a woman. Gemma Woodhead slammed on the brakes of lazy Jezza's Polo and the car began a vicious skid on the slippery road.

Nicky's first thought on feeling the hard road beneath her was how much it hurt to survive. She was winded and could only lie motionless, staring at the white sky. The screech of brakes came to her slowly and as she turned her head she saw wheels bearing down on her.

Gemma tried to swerve into the middle lane but she clipped the front of an Ocado delivery truck and began to spin down the road. The truck came to a screeching halt on the tarmac as Gemma pulled up in a spray of brakes and noise a few inches from the central reservation.

Nicky tried to stand as a woman with red hair and a long gypsy skirt got out of a yellow hatchback and began running towards her. Euphoria flooded her as she realized she'd survived a death leap and got away from crash man.

'My God, oh my God, oh my God,' was all the woman could say. 'Oh my God, you're bleeding.'

The Ocado delivery man was walking over, on the phone. 'I'm calling an ambulance,' he shouted.

Cars were beginning to stack up behind them, a queue lengthening away down the motorway as people gathered.

The woman had nearly reached Nicky and was gawping at her. Nicky started walking towards the woman's car.

'Oh my God, are you OK?'

Nicky stared at the yellow car. Then she turned to face the redhead. 'I need your car.'

'My car?' the woman repeated, the words meaningless.

Gemma felt the woman grab her elbows. She looked panicked and wild, her hair was wet and her arm was a scraped-up mess, but her deep blue eyes seemed filled with determination.

'I'm really, really sorry, but I need your car.' Gemma felt the woman's warm hands on her skin 'Please forgive me, but I'm going to take it.' The woman seemed so intent that Gemma nodded, shock still reeling through her veins. She watched speechless as the wet woman ran to her car, got in and took off in a wobbly squeal of brakes down the Westway. As she watched Jezza's wheels and all of Jezza's T-shirts fade into the distance, all Gemma could think was that the woman had been so polite, so forceful yet so polite. Oh my God, so unlike Jezza.

Gemma stood in the middle of a stationary Westway, realizing she still had a lot of work to do on her new dedication to assertiveness.

47

Troy experienced with a shock an emotion he had never felt for a woman before: admiration. As he melted into the crowd and pushed his way away from Ladbroke Grove, keeping his head down to avoid the security cameras, he felt stunned. What a jump! That didn't mean she was okay; there was a good chance she was badly injured or even dead, but the problem was he had no idea what was happening up there on the Westway and no way of finding out – for now. Nicky Peterson was one ballsy girl: he wouldn't have done it.

His mind flashed back to consoling her in the country lane outside that big pile, his hands expertly massaging her shoulders, feeling the muscles in her neck, reaching under her long blonde hair and across her wide shoulders, fingertips passing over the bump in her clavicle to unclip the necklace and fold it in his large hands: an insurance policy. He had spent a long time later holding that necklace, weighing it in his palm. It was attention-seeking, bold, a bit trashy. It reminded him of her. She was strong, someone who could fight back: a worthy opponent.

He almost laughed as he began to jog east, clearing the worst of the crowds. Boy, did she pick the wrong men! A husband who had taken out a contract on her, and a toy-boy lover who had tied her up – and he could imagine the rest. But she was still standing, taking the blows. That appealed to Troy. He would have liked to have been with a woman like that.

He heard the impatient whop-whoop of a police car and three uniforms ran past him. His temporary good mood evaporated as he realized he had made a mistake: he should have shot her at her house when he had the chance. He had given her just the tiniest opening and she had taken it. He had underestimated her. Women. They were meaner and harder than men. Desperate women were the most dangerous of all. He picked Nicky's phone out of his pocket. She had made a grave error dropping that, but he needed to tie this all up – find and kill the bitch. And he knew where he had to go for that. He began to head back to Maida Vale.

When Troy was less than five minutes' walk from Greg's house Nicky's phone began to ring so he pressed the answer button.

'Nicky? Nicky, can you hear me? Thank God. Where are you?'

It was the husband. 'Surprise, surprise.'

'Where's Nicky?' Greg's voice was a whisper.

'She dropped her phone and I kindly picked it up.'

'Is she with you?'

'Not now.'

'Where the fuck is my wife?' Greg shouted down the phone.

Troy smiled. 'You're going to take me to her.'

'Who are you, what do you want?'

'What do I want? Money.'

'I'm not paying you a fucking penny—'

'Francesca and your wife . . . you're going to hand over plenty for both of them.'

Greg made a noise that Troy couldn't catch. 'I don't understand—'

'Oh shut up! You fucking hired me!'

'I hired you?'

'She your new bit on the side, the woman who called me? You can give me a bell in a few years when you need her doing too, eh!' There was a long pause and Troy thought the connection had gone. 'You still there?'

'I want to be with you.'

His tone had changed. The high-pitched, desperate denials had gone; his voice was now low and flat. This was better, the pretence was over and they could simply get down to business.

'That's not how I work.'

'I want to be there when you—'

'No.'

There was another long pause. 'I hired you, I paid you, and you owe me. You punched me in the bloody face.'

Troy thought for a moment. It was unconventional, but he reasoned it meant more money or safety. If the husband was having second thoughts, he'd have to kill both of them in the end anyway. He'd already lost Struan on this job; if he kept him close he could make it look like Greg had killed Nicky and then himself. He could tie up all the loose ends. 'What car do you drive?'

'What?'

'You heard me, what car?'

'A BMW. Why?'

'Open your door.'

'What?'

'Open the front door.'

A few moments later the door of the white stucco house swung open and Troy saw Greg, phone still to his ear, standing on his doorstep, craning up and down the street. He leaned back against the warm metal of the BMW convertible parked in the road outside.

'Nice wheels. I hope you've got the key in your pocket – we're going for a drive.' Troy saw Greg open his mouth as if to say something into the phone, but no sound emerged. 'Fuck with me and I'll blow your head off.'

'No fucking,' he heard Greg reply.

Troy grinned his five-grand smile.

48

Nicky stopped the car on the rise looking down at Hayersleigh House. There were no cars in view, the shutters were drawn and the windows she could see were closed. Ripples ran across the surface of the lake, which looked cold and deadly, and the brown scar of newly turned earth on the lawn was now a black slash in the rain. She thought about the last time she was here, running for her life, scared out of her wits. She wasn't that Nicky now; that woman had died with every new revelation about Greg's past, with the danger she'd only just escaped at the carnival. She drove on to the house and parked the Polo near the back door. She got out and stood for a moment, listening. She walked to the barn, the only noise her feet crunching on the gravel. The tractor had been put away, its job done, and the bicycle that she'd used for her final escape was propped up in its original place. The barn door creaked in the wind.

The rain began to fall again, the scorching summer already a distant memory. She skirted the back of the house, peering in windows, steeling herself for what she was about to do. The police must have come and gone in their search for the shotgun used to kill Louise. The kitchen door was locked but the key was in the flower pot as before. A moment later she was standing in the kitchen, inside the lion's jaw.

The house looked different under cloud: its colours muted, the atmosphere stiller – and deadlier. She knew that she was alone, yet the house gave her the creeps nonetheless. She went and stood in the hall, right on the spot where Struan had died. Doorways into gloomy rooms with their windows shuttered surrounded her. She looked at the brooding outline of the gun cabinet and saw an image of her terrified self chained to the radiator. Not again, never again. She picked the key out from behind the photo on the bureau and opened the door, took one of the guns out and cocked it. There were no bullets. She opened the drawer underneath and found a box containing cartridges. Their golden metal ends glinted up at her before she loaded the gun and shut it with a snap. It sounded horribly loud in the country silence. She closed and locked the cabinet and put the key in her pocket.

She turned to the large cupboards outside the kitchen and dug around in several drawers until she found a torch, then she began a slow ascent up the stairs, listening all the time. The wind was getting up and the house was groaning and creaking like a yacht tossed on the high seas. She paused on the top landing and headed on silent feet down the corridor to Connie's bedroom. The room was shuttered and she needed the torch for extra light. She left the door open and pulled out the suitcase containing Catherine's diaries. She sat down in the corner under the window facing the open door, propped the gun next to her against the wall, and began to read.

The entries covered a fifteen-month period from June 1988 to September 1989. Nicky had seen Catherine's dabbling in the artistic life in the paintings downstairs, but what she now realized was that Catherine was a much better writer. The notes here began when Adam was a tiny baby, presumably her one great creative act spurring her on to record her life as well. She wrote quite movingly about her love for her son and the small triumphs, irritations and tiredness of early motherhood. She didn't write every day and there were whole weeks that passed without an entry, but an idea of the life of a typical upper-middle class woman with a large house to look after came through. There were dogs and a horse, a part-time housekeeper and a gardener who argued with Lawrence. Connie was often staying and helping with child-care while she took flying lessons.

After half an hour Nicky started to get frustrated. These red books were not offering any revelation of anything. She put them down for a moment. What were diaries for? Nicky didn't keep one, had never had any urge to. She didn't know anyone who did keep one. Was it generational? A class thing? What Nicky did know was that if she did write one it wouldn't be like this: lacking hatred and malice and family squabbles. This was a portrait cleansed of life's battles and frustrations. It wasn't real. These were books for public consumption – or books Catherine knew were being read.

Nicky picked up the last notebook and raced past a large dinner they'd held at the house; after that there was a week of no entries and then the tone changed.

I know you're reading this, Connie, though you'll never admit it. You never liked me, and you've tormented me ever since I came here. I know what you want – but you can't have it. You like playing games? Well, here's one. I've put something of his under the lawn. Now you're desperate to discover what it is. You know you want it. It'll tell you so much: the depths of what I know and what you don't, what I've got that you'll never have. And if you ever find it you'll never dare tell, because this family likes to bury things so deep that they're never dug up. Go on, you think you're so clever . . . try to find it.

The yellowing pages were blank from here. The entry was 9 September 1989: her last. She must have died soon after this, Nicky realized. *Under the lawn*. Adam had taken this note literally, and from this small piece of text he had literally dug up his own lawn. So Connie and Catherine hated each other, that much was clear. A plane roared over the house. What was Adam expecting to find? Had he already discovered it? Whether he had or hadn't found what he wanted, she was as much in the dark as before.

She stood and put the diaries away in the suitcase and pushed it back under the bed. Then she went along the landing, the gun in her hand, past Catherine's row of sludgy pictures. *Under the lawn, under the lawn . . .* What now? A banging noise from the billiard room froze her to the spot. There it was again. She crept down the stairs, eyes locked on the door, which stood lightly ajar. She crossed the entrance hall and steeled herself to push at the door with the barrel of the gun in one hand, torch in the other. She heard three bangs in quick succession as the door opened and she turned on the torch. The beam of light bounced off armchairs and the huge table and she saw that one of the shutters hadn't been closed properly and was moving back and forth in the wind.

She clicked off the torch as daylight flooded the room with the shutter swinging open, and dropped the heavy gun to her side. She should leave – drive away in the Polo and take her experiences and her terror at the carnival to the police; she could get no further information from this cursed house. She looked at the huge picture of the willow that Cathy had painted, a shaft of grey light falling across it, and she thought back to that blistering day when she had first become alarmed at Adam's behaviour and had gone and sheltered under that canopy for real. If only she had walked away then and there, had stridden across that lawn in the burning heat—

The lawn. Nicky took a step forward. The willow dominated the painting, but the foreground was a pale green strip of lawn. Hadn't Adam said this was the last picture she'd painted? She went across the room and touched the painting in its heavy and ornate frame. The room darkened as the shutter swung closed. Lawrence had said today that Adam was looking for 'something that isn't there'. Had Adam taken his mother's words too literally? She felt round the edges in the gloom, knowing that what she was doing was ridiculous, but doing it anyway. She tried to lift the painting away from the wall but it was stuck fast; it must have been attached halfway up each side with screws to carry its great weight. She couldn't get even a little finger behind it. Maybe she could poke something behind the frame. With an increasing sense of urgency she turned on the torch and rooted around in an old bookcase filled with vases and hardbacks for a ruler-shaped object but found nothing suitable. She went into the hallway, wondering where to look next, when her eyes came to rest on the photo of Catherine. She flipped the picture out of its frame and with the cardboard back that had held Catherine in place for twenty years she started poking up behind the painting. Towards one end she stopped as the cardboard hit an obstruction. She pushed harder, could hear Sellotape ripping . . . and the corner of a piece of brown paper poked out below the frame. She pulled.

The afternoon was grey and silent and Greg was cold, still in a T-shirt that no longer fitted the mood. Autumn had swept over the land in six hours, pulling the temperature down ten degrees. The unnamed man sat behind him on the back seat, a silent and deadly passenger. Greg hadn't seen a gun but he didn't have to; it was there, somewhere, the fatal force that could end his life. Greg thought of himself as an actor – he'd played a part for so much of his life – but today was his hardest role of all. As soon as he'd opened the door and seen the guy leaning so nonchalantly on his BMW he knew he was out of his depth. Show the guy a moment's doubt about what he was doing, any hint of indecision, and this guy would kill him and Nicky. So he'd walked down his steps like a condemned man and got in the car. When he'd been passed Nicky's phone to unlock it and get rid of the photo, he'd done it without complaint.

Greg had tried conversation, had offered inane icebreakers in an attempt to ease his tension, had tried to engage him in conversation, hoping he would reveal things that could be useful later, but he didn't respond. Now he drove on auto-pilot, following the man's instructions, wondering how many people Troy had killed – and in what way.

He headed south, eventually leaving the motorway for a succession of A roads and then a series of smaller roads until finally he turned onto the winding country lane that led to their destination. Greg felt sicker and sicker the closer he got.

He pulled slowly into the drive that led to Hayersleigh House, drinking in every change. The sign was gone but he knew where he was going. He had driven here in his dreams, or nightmares, that summer that changed the course of his life – and that of others – for ever. The road was pitted and overgrown, the bracken that carpeted the forest yellow and drooping. It had been hot that summer too. The images in his memory were jumpy and the colours bleached, like in a nineteen seventies cine film.

They reached the open gate as the rain began to fall again. Greg heard a plane overhead but couldn't see it through the low cloud. Had they been that loud back then? His twenty-year-old self wouldn't have noticed, or cared, yet now he shrank like an old man, loud noises ringing in his worn eardrums.

They reached the rise and he saw the lake and the house before them. It was the same, and yet so different. He was no longer impressed; his own wealth and success and life's experiences had dulled the grandeur of the place, made it seem tired and ordinary. How dazzled had been his first impressions, how intense had been his feelings as a young man. The romance and the excitement of it, the heady rush of the new – all harder and harder to recapture as the years rolled on.

My happiness ended here, he thought. I have never been happy since that summer. And there had been so many summers since; his attempts at running away from what had happened here, of escaping, had been pathetic. Now that he was back she was as vivid to him as if it had all happened yesterday.

Nicky ripped open the dusty envelope in her hands as a volley of rain splattered the shutters. She pulled out a photo. When she looked at it she didn't understand at first, but she was a huge step nearer. There *was* a connection between all of this – between all of them. Catherine Thornton had known Greg. She had known him very well. Nicky stared down at an image of Greg lying naked on a bed here at Hayersleigh, the strut from the four-poster bed in Adam's room visible at the edge of the picture. He was looking up at the camera, his blond hair tousled against the sheets, his cheeks fuller and his twenty-year-old body slimmer. He seemed caught in the act of saying something, his front teeth just visible over his lips. The scene was intimate and he was relaxed; this was not the first time they had done this. Catherine had indeed hidden her laughing lover beneath the lawn. *The depths of what I know and what you don't, what I've got that you'll never have . . .* She was tormenting Connie, gloating about her experience of love and passion. *You'll never dare tell . . .* Nicky heard the rushing in her head that came as she thought through the ramifications of this discovery, but was interrupted by another lower noise, increasing in intensity. She listened for a few more moments to make sure she wasn't mistaken: it was a car.

Greg drove over the uneven gravel towards the house. There was the double front door, still painted that shade of bottle green. She'd stood in her white dress, banging one half of that double door with her heel, as he had grappled with a stuck bottom lock. Her feet had been bare and brown with dots of pink nail polish on her toes. He'd grabbed her ankle. Her giggle crowded his head. He felt sick and took his foot off the accelerator.

'Don't stop,' Troy said.

But Greg was in a trance. He got out of the car. How often had Liz told him he was not to blame? That Catherine's death was not something that should trouble his conscience. And yet it had, whatever she had said. He couldn't move beyond it, and that had set the pattern for all of his disastrous relationships that were to come.

A light rain fell on his face as he stood and listened. This place had a silence all its own; the planes only accentuated it when it returned. A bird gave a mournful cry as it swooped across the fields. This peace had been so profound and appealing after his parents' cul-de-sac with its revving cars and screeching garage doors. He couldn't describe that silence. Liz once sneered and called it the sound of money, but that wasn't it. It was the sound of his youth and he'd never have it back.

The vain delusions he'd had that summer, of what he was capable of, of how life and love would be . . .

'Get back in the car.' Troy was standing with the door open. Greg did as he was told and drove on to the house and parked by the front door.

Nicky moved fast, but carefully. She put the photo in her pocket and put the picture of Catherine back into the frame on the bureau. She picked up the gun from the doorway and headed for the stairs. She was halfway across the landing when she heard someone trying the unused front door. It was someone who didn't know the house. She moved to the landing window that didn't have shutters and glanced out to see Greg and crash man. Together, here, walking side by side. The terror she had felt jumping out from the scaffolding onto the Westway came back to her with a force that socked her in the guts. And following on was the darker, more persistent memory of the dead weight of Grace as Nicky flailed around in that inky lake, screaming with all the energy she possessed for someone to help her. She gripped the barrel of the gun. She had failed that day, she had failed Grace. She wouldn't let it happen again. A surge of pure rage filled her. That Greg could do that to Grace, play the tragic widower when he knew what he had instigated . . . Her husband was the man who killed every woman he touched, the man who had spent a lifetime getting away with it, the man with a sister who kept his secrets. She heard the back door opening.

Nicky ran across the landing, opened the door to the hidden room and moved into the gloom. She turned towards the laughing cavalier and carefully removed the small block of wood with the painted eyes. She stood looking out onto the landing. I'm finally in control, she reasoned.

Which was why, when the hand closed over her mouth from behind her in the shadows, she couldn't understand how she had got it all so wrong.

49

DI Jenny Broadbent looked at the two white boxes on Asda's homeware shelf. 'This one's got the cage thingy that you pull out,' she said to Isla. Isla didn't reply; she was texting, leaning with her foot up on the lower shelf, where a wok was in danger of falling to the floor. 'Whereas this one's got something called an auto-defrost function.' There was no reply. 'Isla!'

Isla pressed send and turned, blinking, to her mother. 'They're just toasters, Mum. Get whatever.'

'*Which*ever.' Her mobile rang. 'Find me some barbecue tongs,' she said, waving her hand in a get-to-it motion at Isla. Isla thumped off down the aisle, boredom radiating off her. There was too much choice, Jenny thought, always too many options. It weighed one down, stopped one thinking straight. 'Hello?' It was Sondra. 'What's up?'

'London got a call from Nicky Ayers's sister-in-law. It's been passed on to us. She's concerned about Nicky's safety and seems to think her life might be in danger.'

'Did she say who from?'

'Her brother. She was very insistent. She also said she thinks Nicky's back at Hayersleigh House and the husband's followed her.'

'Why has she gone back there?'

'It turns out Adam Thornton's mother had an affair with Nicky Ayers's husband about twenty years ago.'

Jenny sighed. 'Where's Adam Thornton?'

'We don't know.'

'OK. Get a squad car.'

'Do you want me to pick you up?'

'Yes, please.' Jenny started walking down the aisle towards her daughter.

'It's raining today, if it's any consolation. Wet weekends, they're the worst,' Sondra added.

'I don't know, I like the rain,' said Jenny, looking at her daughter. 'When it's raining you know the weather at least can only get better later.' She hung up and watched Isla fiddling with a pair of tongs. Affairs caused more damage than anyone understood. Human desires that couldn't or wouldn't be kept in check. Isla's dad certainly hadn't kept it in his pants. She wasn't proud of how she'd punished him, of how she'd made it difficult for him to see Isla until he didn't bother to try any more. She had been eaten up with trying to throw the pain he'd inflicted on her back at him, with trying to make him feel the pain of his rejection. She regretted her behaviour in silence now that Isla was older, but she couldn't turn back the clock. Every time Isla badmouthed her dad Jenny felt the blush of shame. We hurt the ones we love, she thought.

'Look, Mum, these only open if you point them downwards.' Isla flipped the tongs this way and that, their metal sides clacking in the warehouse space. Her daughter could still find excitement in the little things. Jenny felt a gush of love for her.

The fallout from her failed relationship with Isla's father would last a lifetime; and hers wasn't the only one. It sounded as if murderous motives were at play at the big house too. Husbands intent on harming their wives – it was a time-honoured act. 'Love kills,' she muttered to herself. The state employed her to mop up the mess from overwhelming passion, from adoration that more often than not got warped and twisted over the years. Today was no different. 'Isla, I have to go.'

'Really? Can I go to Ella's?'

Jenny nodded at her thirteen-year-old. 'I'll drop you off on the way home.'

'Brill. So, which ones?' She pointed at the rack of barbecue implements.

Jenny reached out and blindly picked up a pair of tongs. Too much choice. She would argue long and hard about whether it made anyone happier.

Greg tried the back door and it opened. He crossed the kitchen uneasily, sticking close to Troy. He couldn't let him out of his sight. The ground floor was empty. He paused for a moment by the photo of Catherine in the hall and turned away. He saw Troy watching him.

They began to climb the stairs, Troy bringing up the rear, but a search of the rooms turned up nothing. No one was upstairs. They went back along the corridor and Greg stared at the paintings on the landing. His eyes came to rest on the laughing cavalier. He stopped, overwhelmed by a sensory memory of what they had done together in that secret room while her husband was working in London during the week . . . Troy's hand jumped to his waistband. He'd picked up a hesitation in Greg's movements which made him wary but he calculated that the threat came from the bedroom door on his right. He wasn't expecting the picture in the landing to burst open and spun a fraction too late.

Greg saw Troy blown back against the wall by the shotgun blast. He cried out but couldn't hear his own voice; he was deafened by the noise. He stumbled, almost in sympathy with Troy, and fell to his knees amid the burning smell of the spent cartridge. A livid splatter of blood rose up the wall in an arc behind Troy, who was slumped back against the skirting.

Lawrence stood holding the gun.

Greg shouted over and over, 'Where's Nicky? Where's Nicky?' but no sound penetrated. As the smoke began to clear he could see the beginnings of a smile on Lawrence's face.

50

Lawrence had often thought about this moment, when the villain who had ruined his life would be begging on his knees before him. He had remembered a big man, cocky and eager and naive. Jealousy was distorting, he realized. He was pleased to see that the cowering figure on the carpet below him bore no resemblance to that threat from the past. His actions had had an effect and from that he gained some comfort.

'Where's Nicky?' Greg's voice was getting through now, the shotgun blast radiating away. Lawrence pointed the gun at Greg's chest. 'You won't fire. That'd be too easy. Have you killed her?'

Lawrence lowered the gun. 'Not yet.'

'Where is she?'

'I'll take you to her. On my terms.'

Greg groaned. 'Fuck you!'

'We're going to play a little game, Greg.'

'Did you kill Francesca? Tell me!'

'You remember the Thornton family game, don't you? I know she'd have played it with you.'

'You killed Grace, didn't you?'

Lawrence watched Greg as he crouched awkwardly on the landing, fear making him pant and tremble, the realization of what had been done to him and the women he'd loved giving his face a mask of despair. And Lawrence felt

omnipotent. A great peace came over him. It had been worth
it. He had had his retribution; he had done this for her.

'The laughing cavalier game, it was always so much fun,
wasn't it, Greg? Stand on the landing and close your eyes,
find the secret hiding place.' Lawrence backed into the secret
room, keeping his eyes on Greg and pulled out a bottle and
a lint cloth. 'Now close your eyes, or she dies and this time
you'll never find her.'

'This is all because I fell in love with your wife?'

'You killed Cathy.'

'Yes, I did, and I've paid for that my whole life!' Greg sat
there staring up at the gun. The barrels looked huge to him,
like a gaping monster about to swallow him. But he also,
finally, felt a liberation. Nicky had done this, had forced the
issue, got Lawrence to come out of hiding, had finally made
the picture clear. She had been the one close to solving the
riddle of his life. He had been so wrapped up in bitter regret
and denial that he had been incapable of understanding the
depths to which the jilted husband had sunk. He felt a surge
of love for his wife and he knew then that to gain just a little
more time for Nicky he would close his eyes and put that
cloth over his face all by himself.

51

Jenny and Sondra drove up to the front door of Hayersleigh House and parked next to a BMW. Both women got out and looked about.

'Is that Nicky's car?' Sondra asked.

'Or the husband's,' Jenny replied. A plane began to drill its engine noise into her skull as they moved round to the back door. She saw Sondra raise her head and mime an oath at the racket overhead.

Jenny knocked loudly on the door with her knuckles for a time, but no one appeared so she tried the door. It opened and they stepped inside. 'Is anybody here?' Jenny called out. 'I'm a police officer.'

There was no reply. They walked together into the hallway and then Jenny stopped and sniffed. It was a faint, familiar trace. She sniffed again. Gunpowder.

She took the stairs two at a time, calling out Nicky's name as she climbed, Sondra behind her.

She saw the blood first, arcing up the wall and smeared across the skirting board, and then she saw the body on the floor. A white male lay in a spreading pool of dark red, his hands clutching his stomach. Jenny crouched down low by his head so she was as close as possible to him. 'I'm a police officer. An ambulance is on its way. Who shot you?' His face was waxy, his lips drained of colour, but he was still clinging onto life.

Jenny could see the man's mouth working, that a great and

final effort was being made. 'Stay with me, stay with me!' She could hear Sondra on the phone, calling in all the backup they needed. 'Who did this?'

The man's mouth opened and he said something, a whisper Jenny couldn't catch. She leaned closer, willing him to repeat it.

A roaring sound filled Troy's head, underscored by the frenetic beats of a samba band. It was the sound of a crowd of thousands, pressed together in a west London street. The last image Troy saw before he died was of a figure flying through the air above him, her blonde hair splaying out behind her. It was Nicky hurling herself off scaffolding above the roar of the carnival, her longs legs stretched, her arms cartwheeling in the air.

Jenny saw the man's neck relax for the final time. She stared down at him. Had he just said Nicky's name? Maybe, but she couldn't be sure. In this job it was important to be sure. She felt the familiar rush of frustration that they were too late; so often they were too late. She stood up and looked at the shotgun that had been dropped a short distance away. A blast in the stomach was a nasty way to die. She caught Sondra's eye as she finished her call. Where was Nicky now? The sick feeling of being too late yet again swamped her.

They did a quick search of the top floor but found no one else in the house.

They came downstairs and Jenny looked through the ground-floor rooms and then followed Sondra outside. The girl was standing by the kitchen window, staring into space. 'You OK?' Jenny asked. Sondra didn't reply. Jenny realized that this would be Sondra's first dead body. As an initiation, it wasn't pleasant. He would have been in a lot of pain for probably nearly an hour. Jenny patted Sondra on the shoulder. 'It gets easier, you know.'

Sondra looked at her in surprise. 'Oh, I'm fine. But I was thinking . . .' She tailed off and took a few steps forward. 'We know from Adam's statement that the front door doesn't open, so anyone who knew the house, including Nicky, would park round here by the back door, right?' Sondra bent down low to the gravel. 'So I think Nicky wasn't driving that car out front.'

'Go on.'

'These marks.' Sondra pointed to four long streaks in the gravel that gave out after a few metres. 'Strange, aren't they? Something heavy's been dragged out of the back door. They suddenly stop, like when you put something in—'

'A car.'

Sondra nodded. 'Bodies are heavy . . .' She shrugged. 'It's just a thought.'

Jenny swore and pulled out her phone.

52

L iz was grappling with an unfamiliar sensation: indecision. She was a woman who worked in black and whites, who was comfortable with moral absolutes. She liked people or she didn't, dismissed them or embraced them, believed them or didn't, but now a weird feeling chewed at her guts. Was Nicky right? Was Greg not the man she had always thought he was? The idea that she could have been wrong was a shock to Liz; she revelled in her self-righteousness, the pleasure of her own point of view, knowing it was the right one.

She had come back to Greg's house after a couple of hours of fruitless searching for Nicky but he was no longer there. Neither he nor Nicky would answer their phones and so she'd made a decision that had been difficult but necessary. She had phoned the police and told them what Nicky had told her, and then she had followed the path set by Nicky and driven down to Hayersleigh. Now she was barred from entering by a policeman standing by the large gate. Something huge was obviously happening for there to be a guard on the gate. 'You can't come through, madam,' he said.

Liz looked witheringly at the man in his uniform that was too big for him. He was barely out of his teens. Liz's life had been a long and righteous battle to do the right thing: student protests through her university years, anti-racism marches, ban the bomb sit-ins, never-ending arguments with her dad about patriarchy and sexism. She'd been fighting men like this all her life. Now they looked like children. She got out of the car. 'Get me the head of the operation here or I'll make sure you're tapping on the Job Centre window next week.'

Liz watched a middle-aged policewoman hurry towards her. 'I'm Liz Peterson, Greg Peterson's sister. I think Nicky's life is in danger.'

'That's a very bold statement, Ms Peterson. You need to give me all the details you can.' They paused as a police van came past at speed, racing down to the house.

'What's happening? Is Greg or Nicky at the house?'

Jenny shook her head. 'We are very keen to talk to both of them. Do you have any idea where they might be?'

'Someone's died in there, haven't they? Who is it?'

'We're not sure yet, Ms Peterson, but the situation is very serious. I want you to tell me everything you can about why—'

A plane began its droning roar above their heads and instinctively they both looked skywards, their conversation shrivelling with the interruption. Liz watched the hard grey underbelly of the plane above her and felt memory and family history press upon her. 'I know where Nicky might be.' She saw the policewoman waiting for her answer. 'She's at the airport. Take me with you in the car and I'll tell you why on the way.'

53

The pins and needles in Nicky's legs woke her up in the end, but it was the churning weightlessness, the sudden drops in altitude that she had experienced on a rollercoaster that jerked her head this way and that. She was lying on the back seat of a small aeroplane, Lawrence at the controls, a black rucksack strapped to his back. In the seat next to him Greg was slumped, head on chest, unmoving. They were flying through dense cloud, a wall of white and grey, buffeted by the storm. She struggled to get upright and realized her hands were bound tightly behind her. The plane plunged sickeningly again and she gasped involuntarily at the crazy movement and at finding she was tied up. Lawrence glanced back at her, his hand on the plane's flight yoke.

'Untie me!'

'I can't do that, Nicky.' She started to struggle with her bindings, trying to clear the fog from her head and mind. Her mouth was dry, her head pounding.

'Where are we . . . what . . .?' She was thinking back to the last moment she could remember, trying to process where she'd been. Inside the laughing cavalier . . . she'd been looking out at crash man and suddenly . . .

She stared at Greg. Nicky felt sick, as if she might hurl as the plane was tossed around by the weather. She tried to pull at the knots behind her back with her fingers. 'Is he dead?'

'Not yet.' He didn't turn round.

'What are you doing?' She pulled blindly at a piece of nylon cord, trying to find an end.

'I want to make you understand the man you married.' Lawrence stared ahead at the cloud. He seemed calm and unconcerned. Fear began to chatter in her brain.

'Where are we going?'

'France. Le Touquet.'

'Why?'

'Sometimes it's important to go back to the beginning.'

'The beginning of what?'

Lawrence turned to her. With the headset and the mike in front of his mouth he looked every inch the respectable pilot. He seemed younger and more alive than when she'd seen him earlier in the day. Was it only today? It felt like years ago. 'So he's never told you about Le Touquet? I suppose it's not a surprise. A liar hides things as a force of habit.'

'Hides what?'

Lawrence smiled slightly. 'I want you to see, Nicky, what the actions of selfish people can do.'

'I don't understand.'

'Greg killed my wife, Nicky. And when he did that he killed me in a way, too.'

Nicky looked across at her husband, at his broad, still back. Could this be true? Was Catherine the first in a long line of women to suffer a violent end at the hands of the man she fell in love with? With her thumb and forefinger she managed to pull a piece a rope from the knot. She needed to keep him talking, if only to beat back her fear.

Lawrence looked over at Greg. 'It was the selfish act of a stupid young man, for which he never paid his proper dues. For killing Cathy he spent not a day behind bars—'

The plane suddenly lurched viciously to the side as it hit turbulence and dropped away. Nicky's stomach slammed into her chest and she was pitched sideways, while Greg lolled forward onto the instrument panel. Nicky saw that he too was strapped in with his hands tied behind his back. Lawrence fought to keep control of the plane as her fear became a roaring party in her head. We're going to die up here, she thought. We're going to die.

'When he killed Cathy he imprisoned me – it was a double injustice.'

'What did he do? '

Lawrence laughed. 'You really don't know? I've presided over hundreds of criminal cases in my career. My life's work has been about delivering justice, yet I myself have received none. I'm not alone. Many times those that should have ended up in jail have walked right out through the front door; other times the wrong person entirely has sat in my dock. The law is blunt and ineffective and sometimes plain wrong . . . After Cathy died I was left with no alternative but to implement my own justice. For myself, for Cathy and for Adam.'

'Your own justice? That's just revenge!' Part of the rope she was fiddling with behind her back was snagged on her engagement ring. 'You took the law into your own hands.'

Now Lawrence was getting animated and he swung round to stare at her. 'You think that point of view's crazy? The world is crazy. I see it every day in my court. I really, really loved my wife. I would have died for Cathy. But he took her from me and I've had to live my life without her. Tit for tat, an eye for an eye – call it what you will.'

'You're going to kill me as revenge for Cathy?'

'Like I did with the others.'

She got it now, but could hardly believe what she was hearing. 'You killed the women Greg loved because of what he did to Cathy?'

'Yes.'

Nicky could feel the rage bubbling up with the force of a geyser, unstoppable. 'You killed Grace for that? You killed

Francesca, a pregnant woman, because of something her boyfriend did years before? I've never heard anything so sick in all my life!' That Grace, entirely innocent, had had her life cut so brutally short, that she herself had flailed around in that black water in her futile attempts to save her because of events entirely unrelated to either of them, made her want to puke. 'You murdered Grace! She was a woman with everything to live for—'

'So was Cathy!'

Nicky screamed with all the power she could muster. She screamed incoherently with frustration at his point of view. She screamed for the pointless loss suffered by Grace and by Francesca, and for that unnamed, unknown child of Greg's.

'That man who came to Hayersleigh with Greg, he was coming to kill me, wasn't he? That's how you did it, wasn't it? Hiring others to kill for you. You didn't even have the guts to do it yourself!'

'Greg had an affair with my wife in the early years of our marriage, at the time Adam was born, at the time we were creating a family, building the foundations for all our years together that were to come. He broke up my family at my moment of greatest joy.' Lawrence looked at the slumped-over Greg with contempt. 'I've watched your husband over the years. I've studied him, even. I know so much about him. Always a girl on his arm, so many passing fancies, so many flirtations, but I waited, waited until I knew that one in particular was special, waited until he had committed, had exposed himself to the potential for lasting pain. He never married Francesca but she was going to have his child; they were as good as linked for ever. Grace he did marry. I made him pay for playing with Cathy by making him lose the women who meant the most to him.'

You didn't have to kill a person to destroy their life, Nicky thought. 'It's over, Lawrence, this is so over! You can't get away with it!'

'Oh I can, Nicky, and I will. Greg's clothes have shotgun residue on them from when he killed the hit man. His fingerprints are on the steering wheel of the yellow car in the hangar at the airport. I'll say he made me take off, then once we got up here there was a fight and I got the parachute but you two crashed into the sea, because there's not enough fuel. I think it's time you really felt what Cathy endured at the end.'

A great groan came from Greg then as he woke and took in where he was. He turned to Lawrence and tried to head butt him from his seat.

'Greg!' Nicky screamed but he didn't notice.

He had let himself look for a moment out of the window and let out a low howl of panic. He started to hyperventilate, his fear of flying overtaking every other emotion.

Lawrence looked incredulously at Greg, sweating and moaning in the seat, his face turned away from the window. 'Are you scared of flying?'

Greg bent and twisted in his seat, trying to get free. He stared back at Nicky and shouted, 'He's trying to kill you!'

'What did you do, Greg? What did you do to Cathy?' Nicky was desperate to hear an explanation from her husband about what had happened all those years ago, what had made Lawrence pursue his twisted course.

Greg lunged at Lawrence again. 'You sick fuck! You tried to destroy me but I'm still here. After everything you've done I'm still standing, Nicky is still here—'

Nicky felt one knot fall away behind her. Her wrists were no longer clamped together so she could unwork her bindings faster. 'Your revenge has gone wrong, hasn't it?' She felt a surge of triumph. 'Adam rumbled you, didn't he? Your own son saved my life at Hayersleigh . . . he was trying to put right all the shit you created, wasn't he? He killed a man to protect me! Your own flesh and blood ruined your plan!'

Her voice died in her throat as the plane suddenly dropped again through turbulence. Nicky felt herself lift off the seat and was then slammed back down on it, their flimsy metal cage shuddering as the engine screamed with the effort of flying. Nicky felt a sudden release in her shoulders – she'd got the rope untied. 'He knew, and he rejected your scheme!'

Lawrence groaned and reached round and grabbed Nicky by her clothes as Greg began screaming again. 'Throw me out! Kill me, not her – she's done nothing wrong.'

Nicky used surprise as her weapon and smacked Lawrence hard in the face with her newly released hand. He reeled back into the yoke, the headset bouncing off his hair and dangling from the control panel. The plane pitched downwards.

'Get off me!'

Lawrence tried to hold Nicky back with one hand as he adjusted the yoke and fought to bring the plane back to horizontal. He was panting hard, panic and anger coursing through his body. 'This will never be over, Greg! You *will* pay!'

'You did all this for the most precious thing you and Cathy had left – Adam – but he hates you!' shouted Nicky. Lawrence mumbled something Nicky couldn't hear, took his hands off the yoke and undid the straps across his chest. 'What are you doing?' He pulled his arms free of the parachute and slammed it into Greg's feet. Greg's mouth dropped open.

'No!'

'I'm not sorry. I did it for her. It was a way of keeping her alive. Grief and anger eat up your life and destroy you from inside, but revenge is cleansing. The unfortunate thing for you, Greg, is that there'll be no one for you to take revenge on.'

Lawrence leaned over and pulled at the catch that opened the door. Nicky screamed and lunged forward to stop Lawrence throwing himself out. She wedged her feet under her seat and tried to pull Lawrence by the waist as he pushed at the door, the wind resistance making it hard to open. Nicky clung on. There was no way on earth she was letting the only person who could fly this plane throw himself out of it. 'Don't do this! You alone can end this, Lawrence. I beg you—'

'But you didn't do this alone, did you?' screamed Greg. 'Someone rang the hit man who killed Francesca, from my flat. Who was it?'

'Me. It was an insurance policy. Pinning the hit on you wasn't bad for me.'

Greg lunged forward again, the veins in his neck bulging with rage as he fought to free his hands from their bindings. 'But someone helped you. The hit man said a woman called him. Who was the woman? Who was it who made the calls to him? Tell me!' Greg was hollering at his nemesis as the door flew outwards. Nicky held on for dear life to Lawrence, who had his hand on the side of the plane, one leg out of the door.

Lawrence smiled at Greg, his hair whipping this way and that in the ferocious wind. Nicky's feet were beginning to slide away from under her seat. Slowly, slowly, she was coming away from her anchor. 'One parachute and a broken fuel line,' Lawrence shouted. 'A fitting end, don't you think?' He looked at Nicky. 'We all die screaming, Nicky, remember?' And with that he yanked Nicky's hands away, leaned back and dropped out through the door.

54

Nicky cried out so loudly she thought she would go hoarse. The noise and the wind were terrible, the plane careening and bumping. Nicky knew with absolute clarity that she was going to die, but she went through the motions of struggling against her fate all the same; the survival instinct is strong, and she would fight on until the very, very end. She climbed over the seat backs into Lawrence's place while the plane rocked crazily, her fear that she might be pitched out after Lawrence almost paralysing her. She grabbed Greg's arm and tried to reach out to the door to shut it. She couldn't get there.

'Untie me, untie me!' Greg was shouting. 'Leave the door – you won't get it shut – we can fly without it. Hurry!'

Part of the knot was undone, and she sat back and clawed at the ropes holding Greg's hands. But with the wind flinging stray items round the cockpit, blowing her hair into her eyes, her mouth, she knew that with no one to fly it they were going to die trying to land this plane. The knots finally came away and she reached out to snatch at the flight yoke.

'Leave it! Don't touch it!' Greg yelled with new conviction. 'Swap seats with me.' Nicky hesitated. She could see the dark water below them as the plane cut through a gap in the cloud. They swapped places in an untidy sprawl over the seats, the sea coming ever closer. Blind panic swamped her. 'Yank it, yank!'

'No. It'll start a spin.' There was no sky visible in the

windscreen as the plane pitched for several seconds closer and closer to the sea. Nicky slammed herself back against her seat in a puny attempt to delay the end by a millisecond, then the nose inched upwards and she saw the coast of France, a smudge on the horizon.

She stared at her husband as he inched the plane back to horizontal. His face was set, his jaw straining under his skin, a bead of sweat rolling down his temple as he tried to keep a lid on his terror. He grabbed the headset and connected to the nearest tower. She saw they were gaining height as the plane swayed and wobbled. 'You know how to fly?'

Greg nodded. 'I never told you. Like so much else in my life, I never told you.'

'You mean you can land this plane?' A manic giggle erupted from deep inside Nicky's belly as Greg hurriedly reported Lawrence's actions to the tower. She had been staring down into the darkest abyss, and suddenly and inexplicably she had been released. 'What happened in Le Touquet, Greg? What happened to Cathy?'

Greg didn't look at her. 'I met Cathy learning to fly. I was twenty. I had dreams of becoming a pilot, going off to Africa and ferrying important people around – the stupid dreams you have when you're young. But I fell in love with her and used to come down and see her when he was away working in London. Hayersleigh was our playground. We wanted to celebrate when I got my pilot's licence. She left the baby with Connie and we took Lawrence's plane. I flew us to Le Touquet.' He sobbed. 'It was cloudless.' The plane swung violently as if in protest at the present conditions 'We—'

An alarm sounded and cut through the roar of the wind in the cabin. Greg swore. Nicky looked out of the windscreen and at that moment her heart learned the real definition of agony. The propeller wasn't moving.

Greg let out a strangled noise. He thumped the control panel and vainly began trying to restart the engine.

'What's happening?' she cried.

'There's no fuel.' The useless sound of the engine not engaging carried through to her. 'He's cut the fuel line!' The plane was slowing down, gliding not flying, drifting inexorably towards the ground. The French coast came closer as they drifted earthwards. 'Not again!' screamed Greg. 'We never got to Le Touquet. My first flight as a qualified pilot and I didn't do the proper safety checks. We ran out of fuel. We were coming down and I didn't think we'd make land. There was only one parachute—'

The parachute! Nicky cast about wildly for the parachute that Lawrence had taken off before he jumped, and saw it at her feet. She picked it up and gripped it tightly. 'We have to jump together.'

'No! The one not in the chute would be ripped away when it opened.' Greg shook his head. 'Lawrence wants me to choose. He's a cunning old bastard!' The plane wobbled again in the wind. 'You're staying here with me, Nicky. You're not going out there! You see, I made Cathy put the parachute on. She wanted to stay with me, but I didn't think we were going to make it. I forced her to jump because I thought it would be safer. I crash-landed on the beach and . . .' He paused, fighting for breath. 'I walked away without a scratch. They were running across the sand towards me, so many people, and I was screaming Cathy's name, shouting at them to find her.' He stopped talking as they passed over the beach into France.

'It took them twelve hours to find her. Her parachute never opened, or maybe she never tried to get it open. I basically pushed her out to her death. I was called the miracle man, the luckiest man in Dorset. And the woman I loved had free-fallen thousands of feet to her death. If she had stayed in the plane with me, like she begged to do . . . she would have lived.' Greg gave a sob and held his head in his hands. 'And so would the others!'

'Greg, this is not your fault.'

'But it is, Nicky! Don't you see? It's entirely my fault! She died because of decisions I took.'

'It was an accident! You are not to blame for the others!'

'I haven't been in a cockpit since that day. Like so much other shit in my life, it all started then! I walked away from that life, the people I knew. I walked off into the sunset, but it followed me, it stalked me every day that came after! He took everyone I loved from me! Every single one . . .'

Nicky reached out and put her hand on Greg's arm. 'But he didn't take me.'

Greg glanced at her and looked away. 'Lawrence murdered Francesca and Grace because those were the people I was closest to. He knew their loss would hurt me the most. Nicky, what were you doing with Adam?' The plane was dropping lower and lower, rooftops and cattle visible through the rain, the grey strip of the runway at Le Touquet tantalizingly far away. 'I can't do it!' He was starting to panic again.

'Yes, you can, Greg! Francesca and Grace were snatched from you – I am still here, I am still here. I am not perfect. I did so many things wrong; I am as flawed as you are and I'm sorry. Lawrence wanted your one mistake to colour your life for ever but he's gone. And he was wrong. It's over. It's finally over. For their memories and for Cathy's, land this plane!'

'I'm too low!'

Nicky sat rigid as the plane coasted closer to the runway. They just missed the top of a low outbuilding and somehow, with the help of a gust of wind, rose over a chain-link fence. Greg tried to ease them down to earth but they didn't have the force to carry them to tarmac and they hit the rough grassy ground before the runway. The wheels bumped down and the plane sheared sideways, forcing it airborne for a few seconds before it slammed down on its opposite wing.

Nicky heard the drawn-out crunch of metal warping as Greg rammed down on the brake and began a skid towards the runway, the grey blur of tarmac sliding past inches from her husband's shoulder through the open door. She could hear Greg shouting incoherently as the wing disintegrated, shrapnel cartwheeling away across the runway. They were spun around and thrown about as the plane bumped along the unyielding concrete, buckling and distorting with every smack, the force of which slammed up her spine and made her teeth chatter. They slid to a halt at a forty-five-degree angle in a heap of burning rubber, friction sparks and a disintegrated wing.

'Get out, get out!' Nicky hollered, trying to beat back visions of fire engulfing them. She heard the distant squeal of the emergency services racing towards them. She tried to push at the door next to her and get it open but it had buckled with the force of the impact and wouldn't open. She jabbed at her seatbelt to get free, the frantic motion her reaction to finally coming to a stop. It was then she realized that Greg wasn't moving. He lay slumped over the crumpled flight controls, his head cradled in his arms. Nicky reached out a tentative hand for the back of his head and placed her palm upon it. There was no reaction. The sirens got louder but she simply lay her head on his neck and waited.

55

Two Weeks Later

'Circulation have told me that last week's sales were the biggest jump in two years, so a big slap on the back for you all!' The new editor certainly had enthusiasm, Nicky thought. Well, he should have, she reasoned; he was younger than she was. His round John Lennon glasses caught the strip lights in the conference room and made it difficult to see his eyes. His hair was already receding. 'The Lord Chief Justice is making a statement about Lawrence Thornton today. We'll run that on the front page, and do we have that first-person piece about the tragedy of fathers who commit suicide?' He looked at the features editor, who slurped coffee and nodded. 'Let's run that big –' he glanced at Nicky – 'if Nicky doesn't mind.'

'I've just heard that Hayersleigh House is on the market,' said the homes editor excitedly. 'We could tie in a feature on country houses with grisly histories, for Thursday.' She paused. 'If Nicky doesn't mind.'

'Yes, good,' said the editor. He turned to Bruton. 'What's happening on that woman who was shot at through her window at the carnival? Has she given us an interview yet?'

There was silence while they all waited for Bruton to open his mouth. 'I've got the story,' Bruton growled. He turned to Nicky and raised one eyebrow sarcastically. 'Nicky, you mind?'

'Oh for God's sake!' scoffed Maria, slapping some papers down on the desk. 'Of course she bloody minds!'

Nicky put her head in her hands. It was too early to be back at work. She should have taken more time off. They were only doing their jobs, but talking about what she had just lived through as though it was nothing more than copy to fill column inches was making her head spin. 'I'll just be a minute,' she said and left the room. Maria came out behind her. 'I'm sorry, Maria, I shouldn't be here.'

'No, you shouldn't.'

'I thought I could cope—'

'You know, you can take all the time you need. Go and put your feet up. You look pale.'

'Walk with me.'

They took the lift to the ground floor and paused in the lobby. 'Things will be difficult for a while, but it will get better.' Maria put her hand on Nicky's arm. 'You've already been through so much.'

Nicky shook her head. 'I didn't believe Greg, I—'

'Don't be hard on yourself. I'm the one who feels guilty and ashamed. I didn't believe *you*, remember? And I'm sorry.' Maria hugged her. 'Now you go home and get some rest.' Nicky looked at the revolving doors at the entrance. She had met Adam here, back on one of those hot days in the summer. How long ago it seemed now. 'Nicky . . .' She turned to Maria, her thoughts elsewhere. 'You are going home, aren't you? Nicky?'

There was another reason she couldn't be at work today. There was somewhere she had to go.

The hospital receptionist had large hooped earrings and clacked the keyboard with long fake nails as she typed in the name and directed Nicky along a series of low-ceilinged white corridors to the room she needed. She came to a nurses' station and stopped.

'I'm here to see Connie Thornton. She's been asking for me.'

The nurse pursed her lips. 'She gets tired easily. Let me just check if she's awake.' She walked over to a door and looked through the viewing window, and at that moment round the corner of the ward walked Adam.

He had changed a lot in just two weeks. His face was thinner and he looked tired, a baggy jumper swamping his shoulders. He stumbled when he saw her and looked about as if for help from somewhere. They stood staring at each other as he recovered and came towards her. 'I didn't think you'd come.' The last time she had seen him he was clinging to the bonnet of Struan's car, shouting that her life had been in danger. She had accelerated away, throwing him to the dirt as she escaped. She had ignored his warnings and followed her own course. 'Were you expecting to see me?'

'I hoped I would.' The words were out before she could stop herself.

His brown eyes were searching her face, trying to read what she was thinking. 'I'm sorry for what I did. Please believe me.'

He seemed to lose energy in his legs at that, and slumped on the row of hard plastic chairs along the wall by the nurses' station. She sat down next to him and felt tiredness overwhelm her. The contrast between the two of them now, bent and sunken under the hospital lights, and their last battle at Hayersleigh was plain to see. But neither of them had known the truth then. They had not been weighed down by it.

'Why didn't you tell me what was going on when we were at the house?'

He made a small scoffing noise. 'You'd have thought I was nuts.' He shifted on his seat and let his hands hang between his knees. 'I'd found your photo in his darkroom. You, hidden amongst all those trees. Connie knew your name; she said you needed to be saved – that you were going to die.' He looked embarrassed. 'I have a lot of free time and I like crazy stories, challenges.'

'And you set out to meet me on that plane?'

'I planned to meet you in London but your workmate was so nice and chatty, explaining all about your trip to Spain. The rest was easy . . .' He tailed off. 'I hadn't expected you to make such an impression on me.' He ran a hand through his hair and continued. 'And then you told me Grace had been murdered, that you'd both had the same husband, and I sensed things running out of control. Connie also said you were a threat to all of us. Remember that my mother's death had already driven a stake through the heart of my family – maybe I was trying to be a hero, acting to save what was left.'

Nicky put her hand on his shoulder in silent recognition of all that he had now lost.

'Connie kept saying there was something incriminating at the house. I didn't expect to read what I did.' He paused and shook his head. 'We were similar, you and I. You never knew your own mother, Nicky, just like me. Hearing what she really felt, reading about who she was, was . . .' He groped for the right word. 'Powerful. It was the closest I had ever been to her.' After I fought Struan I became desperate to uncover the truth, I was mad to get to the truth. I couldn't accept that my own father could be involved. He was so respected. If anything I was the wayward one. I needed to find the answers myself, at almost any cost.'

Nicky plucked at some lint on her black skirt. When truth shines a light into the darkest corners of family life, it can be blinding. Adam had done the wrong things for the right reasons. She could see that now.

'Connie's awake now, you can go in,' the nurse said.

They both stood. 'I was expecting to go to jail for what I'd done, but then you retracted. I took a lot of hope from that, hope that maybe you did believe me, that you didn't simply think I was a psycho.' He broke off and stared at her. 'I'm glad I saved your life. I'm sorry that I couldn't save the others.'

Nicky stopped him talking by grabbing his elbows. She looked into his big brown eyes, gathered him to her and gave him a hug. 'I forgive you,' she whispered in his ear, and they held each other for a long moment in the corridor, swaying gently this way and that. When he pulled away she saw him wipe away a tear.

'Shall we go in?' he asked. She nodded and he pushed open the door of Connie's room.

Connie was propped up in a semi-sitting position, her eyes closed. She looked tiny in the huge bed, her bony fingers clutching the bed sheets. From the centre of her neck a tracheotomy tube snaked away to a machine by the side of her bed, allowing her to breathe without using her mouth or nose. Connie's breath made a rasping rattle in her throat in the quiet room. A cannula connected the back of her hand to the IV drip by the head of the bed.

'Her latest stroke affected her breathing,' Adam said, moving round to the far side of the bed and pulling up a chair.

The nurse dragged another chair from by the door towards the head of the bed, for Nicky to sit on. She stayed standing. This was not a conversation to sit down for. 'She has difficulty talking so you'll need to be quite close,' the nurse said. Her voice made Connie open her eyes. 'If you have any problems, just ring the bell.' She pointed to the emergency button hanging from the bedframe and left the room.

The two women stared at each other in silence.

'What did you want to see me about?'

'I want to talk to you.' Her voice rattled in her throat.

Nicky snorted. 'I can't absolve you of your sins.' Connie tried to lift her head off the pillow but she had lost the strength to do it; the tendons stood proud in her neck as she strained. 'Greg said something when we were in that plane.' Connie tried to gulp, her hand fluttering to her throat, the IV tube swaying. 'He was screaming at Lawrence that a woman had phoned the hit man for him.' Connie began to jerk in her bed, her shoulders heaving in discomfort. Nicky folded her arms. 'It was you, wasn't it, Connie? *You* gave the order for me to be killed.'

A fat tear brimmed and fell down a rivulet in Connie's cheek. Adam sat down on the chair by the bed and leaned over his aunt. 'Why, Connie? Why did you do that?'

Her voice when it came was a distorted and scratchy whisper. 'I loved my brother. You and he were the only family I had. I would have done anything for him.'

Nicky felt the anger blooming inside. 'I don't believe you. One moment you're telling Adam to save me while the next moment you're trying to get me killed.'

A sound came from Connie that might have been a sob. The machine made a beeping noise and then her rattling breath came back. 'Contradictions make a life.' Her voice faded away and she had to use more effort to make it audible. 'Lawrence was shattered when Cathy died; revenge for her death became his driving passion. It was what he lived for. It gave his life meaning.'

'I don't have to listen to this justification,' Nicky snapped. 'You dragged me all the way out here to this hospital to tell me this? I'd worked it out on my own. What's really going on?'

'I wanted him to have a reason to live, so I helped him, even though I knew it was wrong . . . At the end of your life, you look back, you start to see how well you've lived it. Well, my life has been a lie—'

'I read Cathy's diary. I found what was under the lawn.' Adam's head jerked up towards her. Connie's breath was shallow and panicky, her eyes full of fear.

'What's under the lawn?' Adam was staring at Nicky while his aunt moaned beneath them.

Nicky stared down at Connie. 'It's a photo of Greg. Let's hear it from you, Connie: why is Greg a secret worth digging up a generation later?'

Connie's chestnut hair twisted and tangled round itself as she thrashed her head to and fro on the pillow. She gulped and gasped for air through the tube in her throat. When she could talk again her voice was a whisper and they both had to lean close to hear her. 'She shoved her affair in Lawrence's face, mooning around Hayersleigh with a man half her age, shaming my brother, causing him pain.'

Nicky shook her head. 'No, Connie! You want confessions, you want to be released from your suffering? You're talking about Lawrence but I'm asking about *you*. Tell me what you *really* felt! You hated Cathy, didn't you? Had she stolen your lover? Is that it?'

A line of tears was flowing out of Connie's damaged eye now, draining away into the pillow. 'No . . . no.' Connie plucked at the bed sheets with her ineffectual hands, her back arching off the mattress as some spasm gripped her.

'You're pathetic. You want to unburden yourself before you die, and you're lying even now!'

Connie went rigid for a moment and her mouth contorted into a grimace.

'I'm getting the doctor,' Adam said but Connie managed

to hold up her hand and collapsed down, a sagging mess in the sheets.

'You loathed Cathy, didn't you? She had a husband and baby and a young lover, and you had nothing, was that it? You did this because you were jealous?'

Connie turned her head to stare at Nicky and her hard, unyielding eyes made Nicky lean back. She could see the rage pulsing beneath the papery skin on her face. 'You – women like you—'

'Women like me?'

Connie's anger had given her the energy to rally. 'You think you know about passion, can understand rejection, but you have no idea.' The endless rasp in, rattle out of every breath clung to the room. 'Yes, I hated Cathy. I was jealous of all the things she so effortlessly had that I had never found. I craved her ability to be loved. I was forty. I'd squandered my beauty and my chances—'

'That's not true,' Adam said.

But Connie, with great effort, carried on. 'I was brittle and ageing and had nobody, doing a job which was about watching people connect and have fun, and deep down I was alone. You think you know about loneliness, Nicky? Try it for decades and see how it fits. Feel that crushing weight on your soul. Cathy rubbed it in and it made me so mad. These feelings of jealousy and hate are all-consuming at the time. I had to punish her . . .' Connie tailed off as exhaustion overwhelmed her.

Cathy's searing words on the page from a generation ago came back to Nicky. *The depths of what I've got that you'll never have . . .*

Connie started to moan again. The anger was spent now, fear contorting her features instead. Her voice was a whisper. 'They were going to fly to France, so I damaged the fuel line. I never imagined that Greg would survive and she would die. I had destroyed the life of the brother I loved. I couldn't tell Lawrence what I had done. It was my burden to carry that secret alone.' Her tears were back now, flowing silently into the cotton beneath her. 'His thirst for revenge gave him a kind of peace, and my guilt meant I went along with it to ease his suffering.'

Nicky stared in disbelief at the pathetic bundle of bones in the hospital bed. 'Your brother lived his last twenty years carrying out a revenge on the wrong person?' Connie's breath was becoming shallower; she grabbed the tracheotomy tube and pushed it tighter to her throat, willing it to give her the air she needed. 'And you nurtured that lie, allowed it to flourish, to save yourself?' Connie stretched her neck, strained to get it higher, as if she was drowning in a rising ride. Her eyes were wide with terror.

Adam stood up so suddenly the chair banged back on the floor. 'I lost my parents because of you!'

Connie was trying to say something, clawing at the tube in her neck, her skinny legs thrashing under the bedcovers. The veins in her neck stood proud, bulging and straining for oxygen and life. They were a horrid tableau: the two of them staring open-mouthed at the struggling figure in front of them. Connie's eyes were white circles of fear in her face as she stared at Nicky, her dry mouth working but incapable of speech. Nicky looked down at her. She saw a woman stricken by terror and remorse, a woman whose passions from long ago had unleashed a sequence of events that had cast Nicky into a hell on earth.

'You're asking for my forgiveness but it's not mine to give. It's the others, whose lives you've taken, that you must ask forgiveness from.'

Connie's thrashing intensified as every sinew in her body strained to cling onto life for a few more seconds.

'Only God can judge you, Connie. Good luck with that.' Nicky turned her back and headed for the door.

Adam cried out in agony as Connie went into cardiac arrest. He grabbed the emergency call button and the buzz of the alarm exploded in the room as the door sucked itself closed behind her. She walked away down the corridor while an untidy line of nurses and doctors ran past her to force Connie back to life.

56

Nicky bent down in front of the grave and arranged the flowers in the pot. A weak sun shone through the bare branches of the large trees that dotted the cemetery, crunchy autumn leaves swirled in the light eddies. It was so peaceful here. It was a good place to end up, she thought, all things considered. She was trying to be positive, but it wasn't really working. It had all been too soon, so desperately early in the course of a life. She leaned forward and brushed some dust from the grooves of the letter F. 'For ever in our hearts' it said. She stood back but she didn't cry. Not this time.

'Revenge is cleansing,' Lawrence had said before he'd thrown himself out, but Lawrence had been wrong. Resolution was what had helped; getting answers was the salve to the nightmare that had started all those years ago on a hot night in Tangiers, that had carried on through that evening she wrestled with Grace's body in the lake, to her capture at Hayersleigh and the plane ride to hell.

It was cool up here on the hill. Nicky leaned over and caressed the top edge of the gravestone: Grace Peterson, 1976–2006.

She felt a hand close over her own and squeeze. 'You ready?' Greg asked.

She nodded. He handed her a trowel. His leg was still in plaster – he had broken it when landing the plane – and he had difficulty moving, so she bent over and dug a hole in the soft grass. He handed her Grace's wedding ring and she held it in her palm for a minute, watching the light bounce off its smooth edges, before she buried it in the soil. She stood as Greg gently trod on the dirt to fix it all together again. She reached out for his hand and felt his warmth radiate back to her.

Greg turned to her and gave her a weak smile. He had a scar on his forehead now, still purple but beginning to fade. In some ways he had aged terribly in the last two months, but in others the weight had lifted from him and even with his injuries and his crutches he seemed years younger than she had ever known him. He was going to counselling and the nightmares had stopped. His sleep was free of the terrors that had dogged him most of his adult life.

Nicky stood still and looked at him for a moment. He was not perfect; he had made mistakes. But she understood that she too had made bad choices and stupid decisions, and that he was perfect for her. They turned away and walked slowly up the hill towards the cemetery gates, Greg's crutches tapping out a plaintive note on the concrete path. The road curved away in front of them. Nicky didn't know where it led, but she was happy to be on the journey with him.

Acknowledgements

I would like to thank the great team at Hodder for all their help on this book and for their enthusiasm, insight and guidance: Carolyn Mays, my editor, Francesca Best, Jaime Frost and Clare Parkinson. A big thank you also to my agent, Peter Straus, and to my family.

Read on for an extract from Ali Knight's first
psychological thriller

Wink Murder

Kate Forman has an enviable life: a loving family and a
perfect husband, Paul. But late one night Paul comes
home drunk and covered in blood, mumbling about having
killed something – or someone.

When an attractive young woman who works for Paul is
found murdered, Kate's suspicions about what he has
really done send her on an increasingly desperate search
for the truth that threatens to smash her carefully
constructed life.

Doing the right thing should seem obvious, but as the lies
multiply, the truth is not as straightforward as it seems.
How well do you know the person you're married to?

Out now in paperback

HODDER

I

I snap my eyes open in the dark, sensing something is not right. The room is instantly familiar, coming into focus with the help of the city light that sneaks past the roman blinds. Tasteful prints hang on the wall, armchairs guard the fireplace opposite, one has Paul's clothes piled on it in a disordered mountain, the other cradles my dressing gown, neatly folded. I'm in our bedroom, a place of safety, a haven from life. The other side of the king-size is empty, the pillow fluffed. Paul is not home. I hold my breath because there is the noise again, a shuffly scraping that's coming from everywhere and nowhere. My heart pounds in my ears. The clock clicks to 3.32 a.m. as I hear a crash downstairs. It might wake the children and this thought alone forces me out from under the comforting warmth of the duvet. I am a mother; point one on the job description is to protect them, at all costs. My movements are slow and deliberate as I try to steel myself for what I'm about to do. I pick up my mobile and turn the handle on the bedroom door hard to ensure it opens without a sound. Someone is groaning in the hallway and it doesn't sound like Paul.

I have mentally rehearsed what happens next quite often because Paul is away for work a lot at the moment and I think it's important to know how I would fight for the only thing that really matters to me – my family. I like to be prepared. So, as if I'm a fire warden at work, I'm putting it all into action. I take a deep breath, punch 999 into the keypad but don't press the green button, turn on the light and run for the stairs, shouting as loudly as I can into the night silence 'Get out of my house!', phone aloft like a burning spear.

I thump loudly down the stairs and use my gathering momentum to swing round the swirly circle at the bottom of the banister as a shape heaves itself across the kitchen at the end of the hall. 'Get out, get out! The police are outside!' I flood my world with light at the flick of a switch as the dark bundle clatters to the floor with a chair. I pull a cricket bat from the coat stand and feel its comforting weight in my palm and am in the kitchen in a second, the weapon close to my chest. 'Get out of my house!' He has his face on my kitchen tiles but as I raise the bat the shape turns to me and I see my husband, staring up at me from the floor.

It is my husband, but not as I have ever seen him before. He is crying, taking great gulps of air, snot running down to his mouth. I toss the phone on the table and drop the bat to the floor. 'Paul, what on earth's the matter?'

He doesn't answer, because he can't. He looks up at me and my former fear for myself is replaced by a more acute worry for him. I try to pull him upright but he is like a dead weight in my arms; he's folded over and crushed, his demeanour transformed. That was why I didn't recognise him from behind, he is not the man he used to be. 'What's happened?'

Paul smashes his fist into the side of his head and groans again. 'Kate, Kate—'

'Oh my God, what's going on?'

He gets to his knees, shaking, leaving the car key on the floor. Paul is a big man; he's tall, with wide palms, and shoulders you can fall asleep on, it was one of the many things about him that I fell in love with all those years ago. He made me feel protected. 'Kate, oh help me—'

His hands are caked with blood.

'You're bleeding!'

He looks down at them in disgust. He staggers to his feet and I pull limply at his coat, he must be cut somewhere under the thick wool, 'Are you hurt?'

'I . . . I, oh God, it's come to this.'

'What?' He closes his eyes and sniffs, swaying. 'What has happened?' He shakes his head and drags himself into the downstairs toilet and starts washing his hands, flakes of blood and brown water swirling away down the plughole. 'Paul!'

He wipes his face on his shoulder and nods his head. 'I killed her . . .'

He shakes the water off his hands and I slap him, hard. 'Tell me what is going on!'

My husband looks at me, his arresting brown eyes blood-shot from his tears. 'What a mess, what a stupid load of . . .' He sighs from deep within. 'Oh fuck, Kate, I love you so much.' And with that he falls right past me on to the hallway floor in a faint no manner of prods, shoves and screams will wake him from.

Something at least becomes clear to me: Paul is pissed. He must be completely rat-arsed. There are probably many things I should do at this moment but first I must pee. I sit on the toilet and stare at the long body of my husband passed out on the floor, his feet turned inwards, his palms up as if he's indulging in a spot of yoga. I am shivering with anger that he could get in a car and drive home in such a state. I shake his shoulders but he doesn't move. I am not a spontaneous person, I need to plan things, to think; I have never imag-ined a situation like this before and I am at a loss, paralysed in the face of so much that needs to be discovered. After a lot of pushing and heaving I manage to turn Paul over on to his back and pull his coat apart checking everywhere for a wound. When I find nothing I am pathetically thankful – blood makes me faint. I sit back on my heels and stare. The hard planes of his handsome face have dissolved into a puffy mess, his strong jaw has receded into his neck. Paul is snoring, his chest rising and falling. The house is silent, my children slumber on unaware. The kitchen clock accompanies him with its staccato beat. The fridge hums and a window rattles. The house settles back into its night-time rhythm. At 3.50 a.m. I get to my feet, tiredness moving over me in waves. I can think of nothing better to do than go to bed. He'll wake up in the end.

2

What seems like a second later a small hand pokes me in the stomach. 'Ava! Stop that!' My daughter is squirming over me in bed.

'Mummy, let me get in,' she pleads, letting blasts of cold air into the warm fug under the covers. Normally my four-year-old wriggling in for an early-morning cuddle is one of my greatest pleasures, her soft, flawless skin so close, cold little feet pressing into my back, but it's 7.10 a.m., my head is pounding, my eyes scratchy. Paul is not here and the flashing memory of last night pulls me sharply upright, my heart banging in my chest. 'Mummy, I'm cold, Mummy . . .' I cannot believe I slept, that I could leave my husband in such a state on the floor. Horrible images of his dead body being casually stepped over by Josh on his way to turn on the cartoons hurry me out of bed. '. . . Daddy's on the sofa hiding under a blanky.'

I stumble from bed, pulling on my dressing gown. Ava scratches her blonde head. 'Mummy, can Phoebe come and play?' I ignore her as I busy towards the bedroom door. It's time to get the truth about last night.

Paul isn't in the front room. I find him in the kitchen leaning against the counter, a cup of tea in one hand and a slice of toast in the other. He is dressed and shaved and talking at Josh, who's bent over a cereal bowl. My husband looks completely normal. 'Here, I made you one.' He holds up a steaming cup and smiles. I don't smile back but cross my arms in a "try me" gesture. He puts the tea down, packs his grin away.

'What happened last—?'

'Nothing.'

'That was *nothing*?'

'I got drunk and maudlin, that's all.' He shrugs as if trying to make light of it.

My eyes narrow in sceptical disbelief. 'But you were saying you . . .' We both look at Josh's head to see if it's moved. I don't need to use the word. I'm not even sure I can say 'killed', it seems so bizarre and melodramatic with the sun shining in the window and talk of congestion on the M25 coming over the radio.

'Don't be daft.'

'So what happened?'

'Nothing!'

'Who were you talking about?' Josh begins to sense something different from the normal morning pattern and like a tortoise emerging from a long hibernation lifts his head from his bowl, blinking at his parents.

Paul glares at me. 'No one.' I hold up my hands and wave them at him sarcastically. He knows I'm referring to the blood.

'I ran over a dog.'

'What's "ran over"?' Ava skips into the kitchen in a policeman's hat.

'I can't believe you drove in that state!'

'Kate, please! I'm contrite enough, I've got an awful hangover.' We lock eyes.

'Shreddies or toast, Ava?' I ask crisply, moving to the cupboard.

'Krispies. I want Krispies.' I reach for a bowl and spoon.

'A dog?'

'Yeah. I felt I had to move it and I got covered in . . . you know.'

Blood. Your hands had blood on them, Paul, is what I want to say, but I hold back. 'What kind of dog?'

'What?'

'What kind of dog was it?'

'Labrador cross, I think.' He looks at his feet. 'I had to drag it, I got upset.'

I stare at my husband as he stands in the kitchen, the beating heart of our home, his progeny around him. I know him better than he knows himself. He often tells me that. And I know that when he looks at his feet he's lying.

'You know what breed, but you don't know what sex.' Paul looks blank. 'Last night this dog was a "she". This morning it's an "it".'

He shrugs, his face revealing nothing. 'It all seemed more real last night, I suppose. Dogs can seem like people when they're hurt.' He drains the last of his tea and brushes crumbs off his suit. 'I've got to go.' He moves towards me and gives me a long, tight hug, rocking me slowly from side to side and planting an affectionate kiss in the middle of my forehead. 'Oh, Eggy, you're always looking out for my welfare.'

I have a high forehead, which I've always hated. Almost as soon as I started hanging out with Paul and his crowd, lovesick and in awe of him, to my severe mortification he made his friends laugh by calling me Egghead. But as the months went on and I started to dream that he was falling for me, I became Eggy, and of all his endearments it's the one I love the most. He smiles weakly at me as we walk arm in arm to the front door. I help him into his coat as he hunts around for his scarf and work bag.

'Mum, Ava's spilled milk on my comic!' There are screams and shouts from the kitchen.

'You'd better go,' Paul says, opening the door.

'Are you OK?' I cling on to him for a bit longer, trying

to massage away the dissatisfaction from my unresolved questioning. He nods, pulling my arms away. 'Are you sure?'

'Never better,' he says, but he looks sad as he walks down the path.

'Mum!' I wander into the living room, Ava's scream rising through the octaves. I see a screwed-up blanket under which he spent the night, the indentations of his body are still visible in the cushions. He must have been up early to wash away the effects of last night. When we talked there was something I couldn't bear to ask him, the lid on a box of emotions I was too scared to lift. What could have made him weep on our kitchen floor like that? Five years ago Paul's father died of a sudden stroke. I never thought any man could show such grief as he had then – until last night.

3

My name is Kate Forman and I am very lucky. I have been told this often enough by friends and family and I truly believe it. My successes are many: I have been married for eight years to the most wonderful man on the planet, we have two beautiful, healthy children and a house far bigger and grander than I ever imagined I would live in. I'm thirty-seven years old, I don't have to dye my hair and I can still wear the clothes I bought before Ava was born (though not Josh; motherhood takes it's toll on us all, however much we pretend otherwise). Accident, design, hard work or chance, I don't really care; I am happy and so is Paul, and that is all that counts.

I know that Paul is happy, because he admitted to me recently that he thought he loved me more than our children. He asked me if I thought that was wrong, and I laughed and shook my head. I sometimes think I don't deserve Paul. His family is much grander than mine, he went to a top public school, his mum lives in a manor house in a nice bit of countryside, he grew up with a tennis court, lots of brothers and sisters, first editions on the shelves and paintings that may or may not be valuable, nobody seems to know or care. It's all much more impressive and romantic than my mum and stepdad's sterile box on a suburban estate, photos of mine and my sister Lynda's graduation hung proudly on the lounge wall.

I met Paul on my first day at university. I was Katy Brown

then. In fact, he was the very first person I met after I'd left home. I arrived at the station with my bike; Mum was bringing my stuff up in the car and was meeting me on campus. Paul was the third-year student driving the van ferrying strays and cyclists to our accommodation. I was the only one he picked up on that run and I fell in love with him instantly. He was deeply tanned and ridiculously fit after a long summer break somewhere in Europe. He drove one-handed with his elbow jutting out of the rolled-down window, the late-summer heat bringing a pleasing other-worldliness to our journey. As we careered round huge roundabouts and sped down the dual carriageways of a big and unknown city, I felt an unadulterated joy at what life held, sensed excitements that have been hard to recapture since. He was two years older than me and teased me not unkindly for being a fresher. He was flirting and I lapped it up. He had big brown eyes and dark hair that sat up in tufts, which he would rub distractedly. He still has all his hair today. As he lifted my bike out of the back of the van I couldn't believe that university would be so full of such gorgeous, exciting men. Needless to say, it wasn't. In the next few weeks I scanned the campus but caught only brief glimpses of him. He waved at me a couple of times through the crowd that surrounded him, and that's as far as it went. I made new friends, threw myself into first-year university life, got distracted by other relationships. I came to London after graduation giving him barely a thought. Five years later my friend Jessie started dating Pug, and besides having a ridiculous name Pug hung out with Paul.

Paul was married to Eloide then. At first I thought Paul must have said Eloise, but no, even her name had to be different – and difficult. She was a natural blonde. I'm not proud of what happened a year later, but they had no children, thank God, which made things cleaner. We just had a connection that couldn't be denied. The first night we spent together was one of the most supreme moments of my life. It goes without saying that the sex we had was . . . I have no words to properly describe the intensity, the honesty of it. I got pregnant two months after his divorce came through.

Our story doesn't end there, it just gets better and better. Paul proposed on a weekend in Paris when I was seven months gone, we were married when Josh was one. Our baby looked so cute on our wedding, wriggling in his little white sailor suit with blue trim. My mum jiggled him all through the service in the pretty rural church. Afterwards she cried and told me I'd done very well.

We've moved house three times since we've been together; from the flat to a pretty Victorian terrace to our imposing three-storey near the park. Paul runs a TV production company and has been very successful. We've traded up. If things stay as they are, who knows what we might acquire or how soon Paul can retire. I don't work full-time any more. Before I met Paul I worked in market research analysing consumer behaviour – 'poking our noses in and getting paid for it' we used to say over the water cooler – but after I had Josh my interests dovetailed with Paul's and I got my break as a TV researcher, which I've been doing ever since. I now work on *Crime Time*, a tabloid-style weekly show that relies heavily on CCTV footage and viewers' mobile phone videos to catch criminals, from petty thieves to murderers. Even though I work three days a week, Paul still says that I'm 'dabbling'. While sometimes that annoys me, it's also fair to say that my sphere is the home, Paul's is work, and we unite in the middle, like a neat Venn diagram.

This morning should be like any other, fiddling with packed lunches before hustling Josh and Ava off to school. Normally I can take almost anything in my stride but today the children's bickering shoots right to my irritation vein. There is milk all over the kitchen table and chair, Josh is flicking a sodden magazine so splatters hit the paintwork. My children are spoiled, and guilt steals over me at how I overindulge them, overcompensate for what was lacking in my own childhood. Paul doesn't mind though, he's very forgiving.

I step through the kitchen chaos and pick up Paul's cricket bat, untouched and ignored by his unsporty son, and return it to its place in the hall. I'm suddenly struck by how close I came to really battering him with it, and he doesn't even know. Roll on 12.30 and lunch with Jessie. Today I'm drinking wine.

In the best books, the ending often comes as a shock.
Not just because of that one last twist in the tale,
but because you have been so absorbed in their world,
that coming back to the harsh light of reality is a jolt.

If that describes you now, then perhaps you should track down
some new leads, and find new suspense in other worlds.

Join us at www.hodder.co.uk, or follow us on
Twitter @hodderbooks, and you can tap in to a
community of fellow thrill-seekers.

Whether you want to find out more about this book,
or a particular author, watch trailers and interviews, have
the chance to win early limited editions, or simply browse
our expert readers' selection of the very best books,
we think you'll find what you're looking for.

And if you don't, that's the place to tell us what's missing.

We love what we do, and we'd love you to be part of it.

www.hodder.co.uk

@hodderbooks

HodderBooks

HodderBooks